ARTEMIS FOWL

THE OPAL DECEPTION

THE GRAPHIC NOVEL

Adapted by

EOIN COLFER
&
ANDREW DONKIN

Art by GIOVANNI RIGANO

Color by PAOLO LAMANNA

Color Separation by STUDIO BLINQ

Lettering by CHRIS DICKEY

DISNEp • HYPERION BOOKS

Los Angeles   New York

Adapted from the novel *Artemis Fowl: The Opal Deception*
Text copyright © 2014 by Eoin Colfer
Illustrations copyright © 2014 by Giovanni Rigano

Printed in the United States of America
First Edition
10 9 8 7 6 5 4 3 2 1
V381-8386-5-14105

Library of Congress Cataloging-in-Publication Data
Colfer, Eoin.
  Artemis Fowl. The opal deception : the graphic novel / adapted by Eoin Colfer and Andrew Donkin ; art by Giovanni Rigano ; color by Paolo Lamanna ; lettering by Chris Dickey.
—First edition.
     pages cm — (Artemis Fowl ; 4)
  "Adapted from the novel Artemis Fowl: The Opal Deception."
  Summary: After his last run-in with the fairies, Artemis Fowl's mind was wiped of memories of the world belowground and any goodness grudgingly learned is now gone with the young genius reverting to his criminal lifestyle.
  ISBN 978-1-4231-4528-8 (hardcover) — ISBN 978-1-4231-4549-3 (paperback)
  1. Graphic novels. [1. Graphic novels. 2. Adventure and adventurers—Fiction. 3. Pixies—Fiction. 4. Fairies—Fiction. 5. Magic—Fiction. 6. Computers—Fiction. 7. England—Fiction.]
  I. Donkin, Andrew. II. Rigano, Giovanni, illustrator. III. Title. IV. Title: Opal deception.
  PZ7.7.C645Aso 2014
  741.5'9415—dc23   2014004121

Visit www.DisneyBooks.com and www.artemisfowl.com

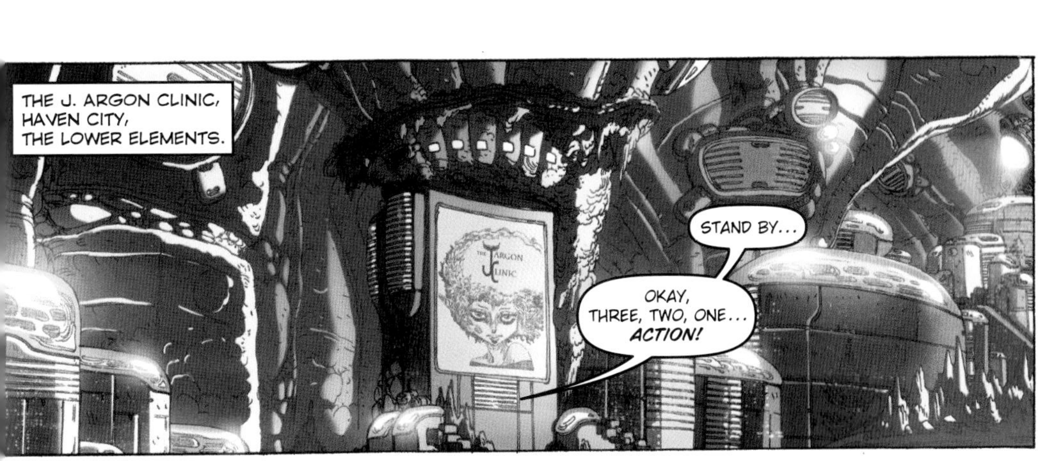
THE J. ARGON CLINIC, HAVEN CITY, THE LOWER ELEMENTS.
STAND BY...
OKAY, THREE, TWO, ONE... *ACTION!*

CHAPTER 1: TOTALLY OBSESSED

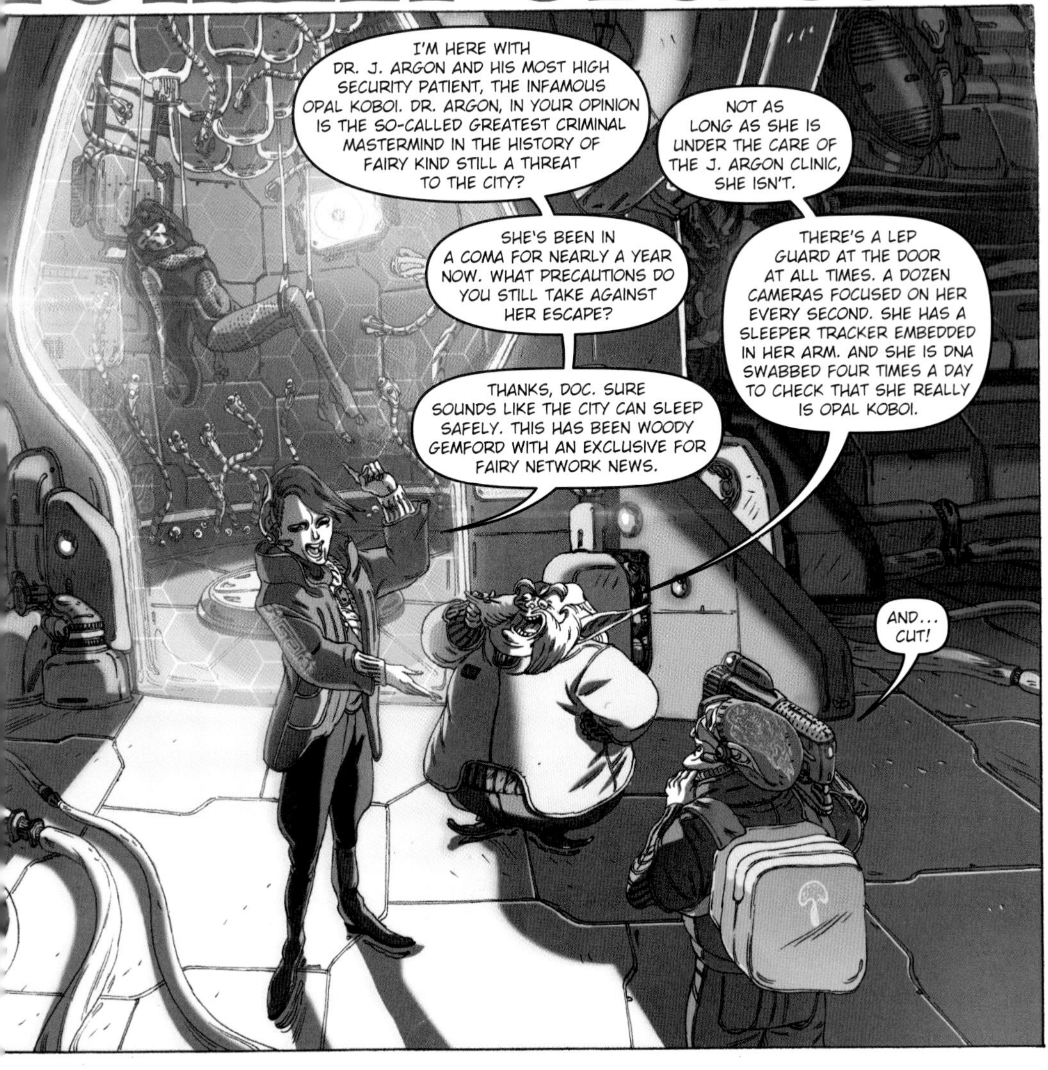
I'M HERE WITH DR. J. ARGON AND HIS MOST HIGH SECURITY PATIENT, THE INFAMOUS OPAL KOBOI. DR. ARGON, IN YOUR OPINION IS THE SO-CALLED GREATEST CRIMINAL MASTERMIND IN THE HISTORY OF FAIRY KIND STILL A THREAT TO THE CITY?
NOT AS LONG AS SHE IS UNDER THE CARE OF THE J. ARGON CLINIC, SHE ISN'T.
SHE'S BEEN IN A COMA FOR NEARLY A YEAR NOW. WHAT PRECAUTIONS DO YOU STILL TAKE AGAINST HER ESCAPE?
THERE'S A LEP GUARD AT THE DOOR AT ALL TIMES. A DOZEN CAMERAS FOCUSED ON HER EVERY SECOND. SHE HAS A SLEEPER TRACKER EMBEDDED IN HER ARM. AND SHE IS DNA SWABBED FOUR TIMES A DAY TO CHECK THAT SHE REALLY IS OPAL KOBOI.
THANKS, DOC. SURE SOUNDS LIKE THE CITY CAN SLEEP SAFELY. THIS HAS BEEN WOODY GEMFORD WITH AN EXCLUSIVE FOR FAIRY NETWORK NEWS.
AND... CUT!

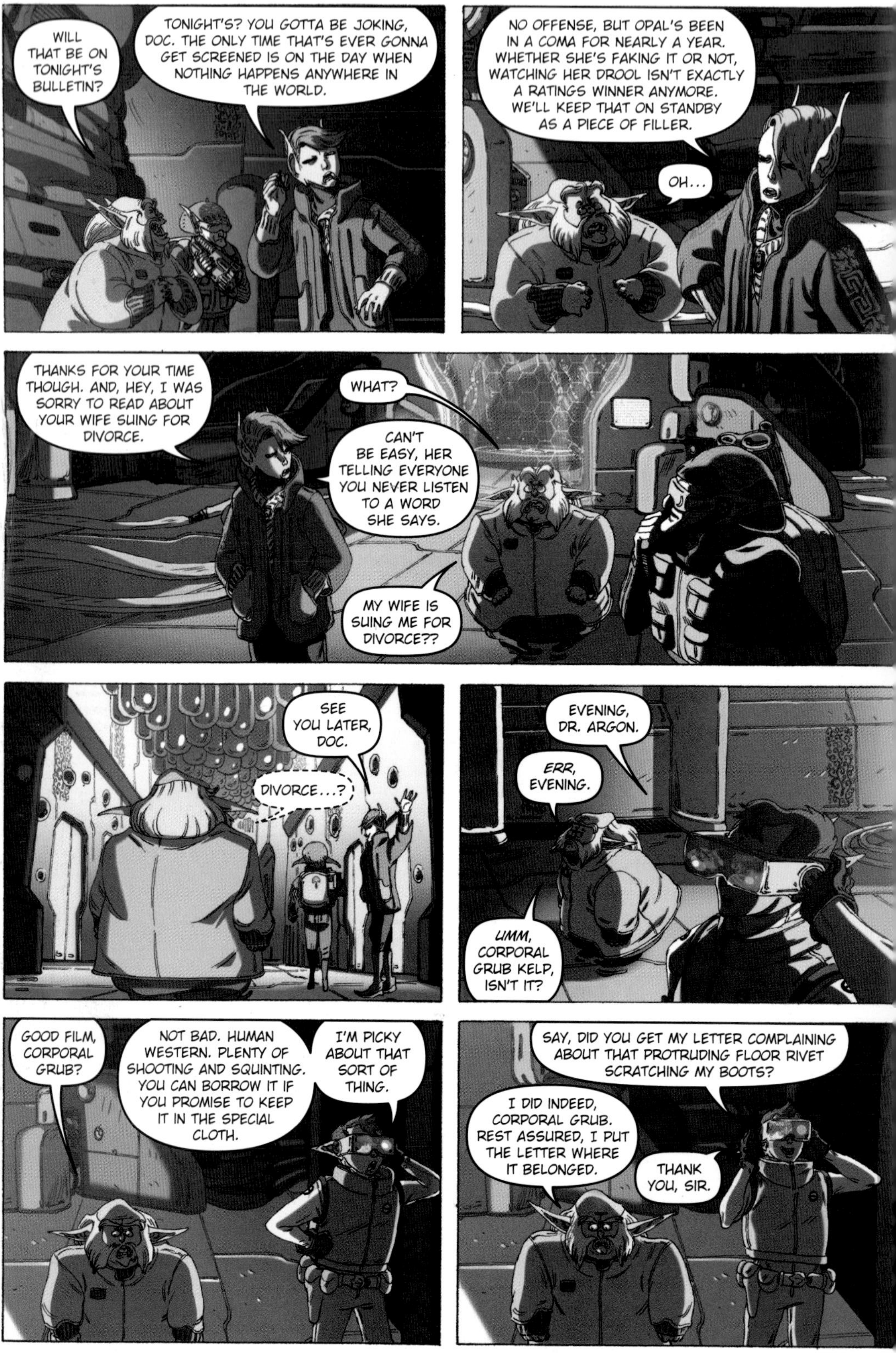
WILL THAT BE ON TONIGHT'S BULLETIN?
TONIGHT'S? YOU GOTTA BE JOKING, DOC. THE ONLY TIME THAT'S EVER GONNA GET SCREENED IS ON THE DAY WHEN NOTHING HAPPENS ANYWHERE IN THE WORLD.
NO OFFENSE, BUT OPAL'S BEEN IN A COMA FOR NEARLY A YEAR. WHETHER SHE'S FAKING IT OR NOT, WATCHING HER DROOL ISN'T EXACTLY A RATINGS WINNER ANYMORE. WE'LL KEEP THAT ON STANDBY AS A PIECE OF FILLER.
OH...
THANKS FOR YOUR TIME THOUGH. AND, HEY, I WAS SORRY TO READ ABOUT YOUR WIFE SUING FOR DIVORCE.
WHAT?
CAN'T BE EASY, HER TELLING EVERYONE YOU NEVER LISTEN TO A WORD SHE SAYS.
MY WIFE IS SUING ME FOR DIVORCE??
SEE YOU LATER, DOC.
DIVORCE...?
EVENING, DR. ARGON.
ERR, EVENING.
UMM, CORPORAL GRUB KELP, ISN'T IT?
GOOD FILM, CORPORAL GRUB?
NOT BAD. HUMAN WESTERN. PLENTY OF SHOOTING AND SQUINTING. YOU CAN BORROW IT IF YOU PROMISE TO KEEP IT IN THE SPECIAL CLOTH.
I'M PICKY ABOUT THAT SORT OF THING.
SAY, DID YOU GET MY LETTER COMPLAINING ABOUT THAT PROTRUDING FLOOR RIVET SCRATCHING MY BOOTS?
I DID INDEED, CORPORAL GRUB. REST ASSURED, I PUT THE LETTER WHERE IT BELONGED.
THANK YOU, SIR.

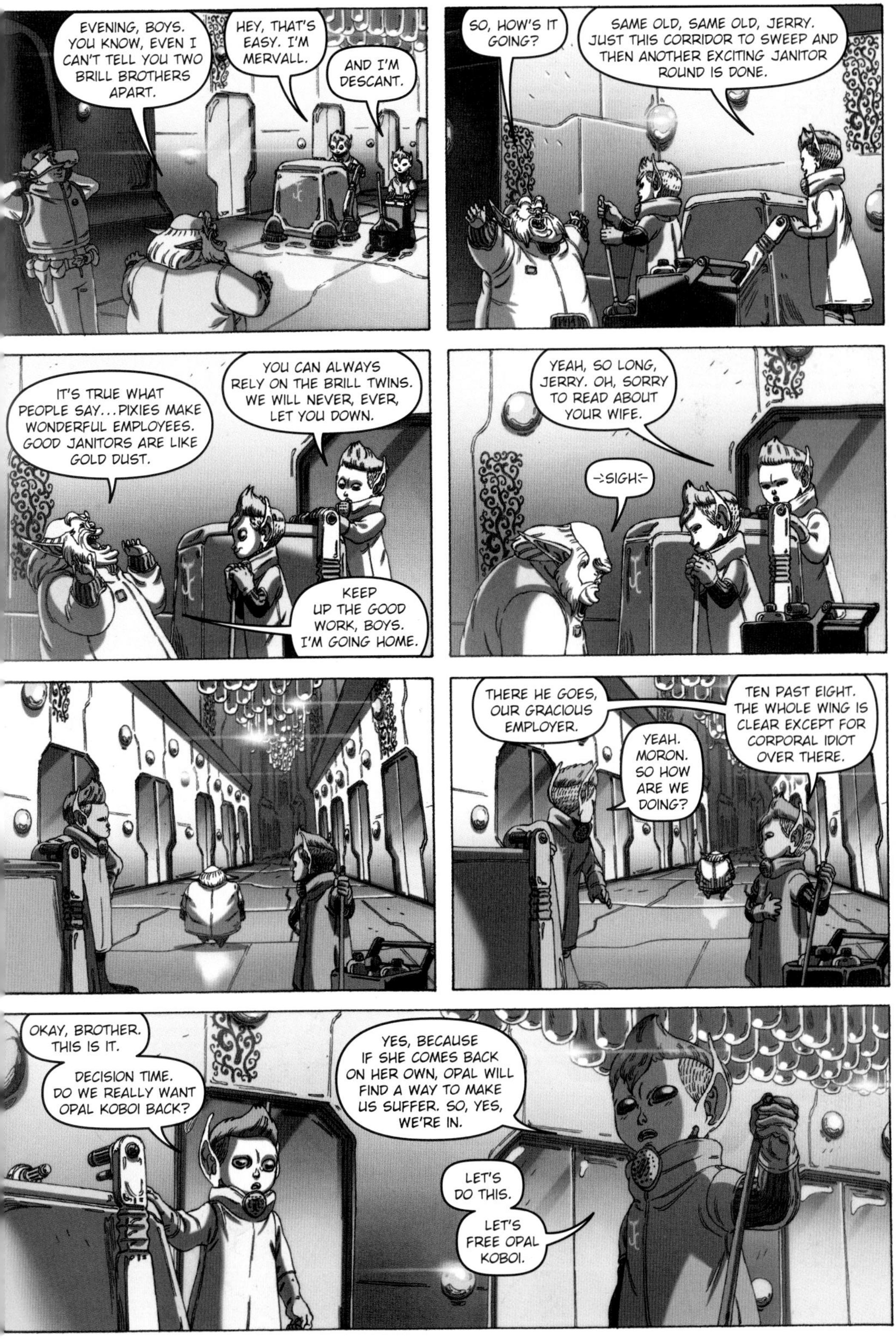
EVENING, BOYS. YOU KNOW, EVEN I CAN'T TELL YOU TWO BRILL BROTHERS APART.
HEY, THAT'S EASY. I'M MERVALL.
AND I'M DESCANT.
SO, HOW'S IT GOING?
SAME OLD, SAME OLD, JERRY. JUST THIS CORRIDOR TO SWEEP AND THEN ANOTHER EXCITING JANITOR ROUND IS DONE.
IT'S TRUE WHAT PEOPLE SAY...PIXIES MAKE WONDERFUL EMPLOYEES. GOOD JANITORS ARE LIKE GOLD DUST.
YOU CAN ALWAYS RELY ON THE BRILL TWINS. WE WILL NEVER, EVER, LET YOU DOWN.
KEEP UP THE GOOD WORK, BOYS. I'M GOING HOME.
YEAH, SO LONG, JERRY. OH, SORRY TO READ ABOUT YOUR WIFE.
SIGH
THERE HE GOES, OUR GRACIOUS EMPLOYER.
YEAH. MORON. SO HOW ARE WE DOING?
TEN PAST EIGHT. THE WHOLE WING IS CLEAR EXCEPT FOR CORPORAL IDIOT OVER THERE.
OKAY, BROTHER. THIS IS IT.
DECISION TIME. DO WE REALLY WANT OPAL KOBOI BACK?
YES, BECAUSE IF SHE COMES BACK ON HER OWN, OPAL WILL FIND A WAY TO MAKE US SUFFER. SO, YES, WE'RE IN.
LET'S DO THIS.
LET'S FREE OPAL KOBOI.

HOW TO RELEASE A DANGEROUS PSYCHOPATH IN TEN EASY STEPS:

STEP 1: ACTIVATE SONIX REMOTE CONTROL.

OKAY, HERE WE GO.

CLICK!

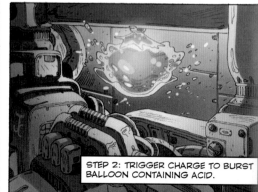

STEP 2: TRIGGER CHARGE TO BURST BALLOON CONTAINING ACID.

STEP 3: MELT THE CLINIC'S POWER CUBES AND THE BACKUP UNIT.

STEP 4: ENSURE LIGHTS AND ALL SECURITY SYSTEMS ARE OFF-LINE FOR TWO MINUTES.

HEY!

STEP 5: SLIP SEDATIVE PATCH ONTO UNWITTING GUARD.

WHAT'S GOING ON? I'M GONNA...

STEP 6: USE DOOR CODE STOLEN FROM DR. ARGON.

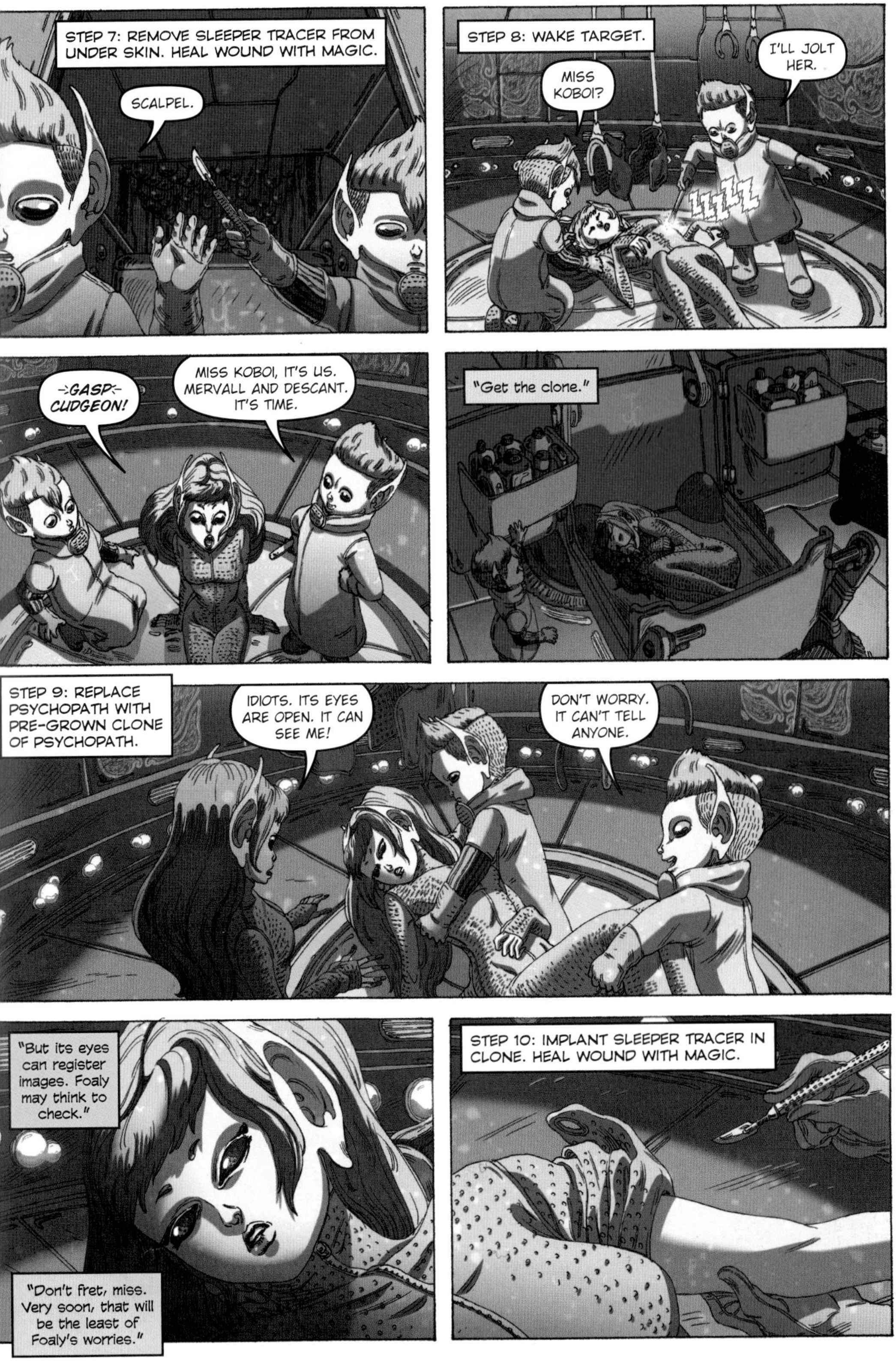
STEP 7: REMOVE SLEEPER TRACER FROM UNDER SKIN. HEAL WOUND WITH MAGIC.
SCALPEL.
STEP 8: WAKE TARGET.
MISS KOBOI?
I'LL JOLT HER.
ZZZZ
-GASP- CUDGEON!
MISS KOBOI, IT'S US. MERVALL AND DESCANT. IT'S TIME.
"Get the clone."
STEP 9: REPLACE PSYCHOPATH WITH PRE-GROWN CLONE OF PSYCHOPATH.
IDIOTS. ITS EYES ARE OPEN. IT CAN SEE ME!
DON'T WORRY. IT CAN'T TELL ANYONE.
"But its eyes can register images. Foaly may think to check."
"Don't fret, miss. Very soon, that will be the least of Foaly's worries."
STEP 10: IMPLANT SLEEPER TRACER IN CLONE. HEAL WOUND WITH MAGIC.

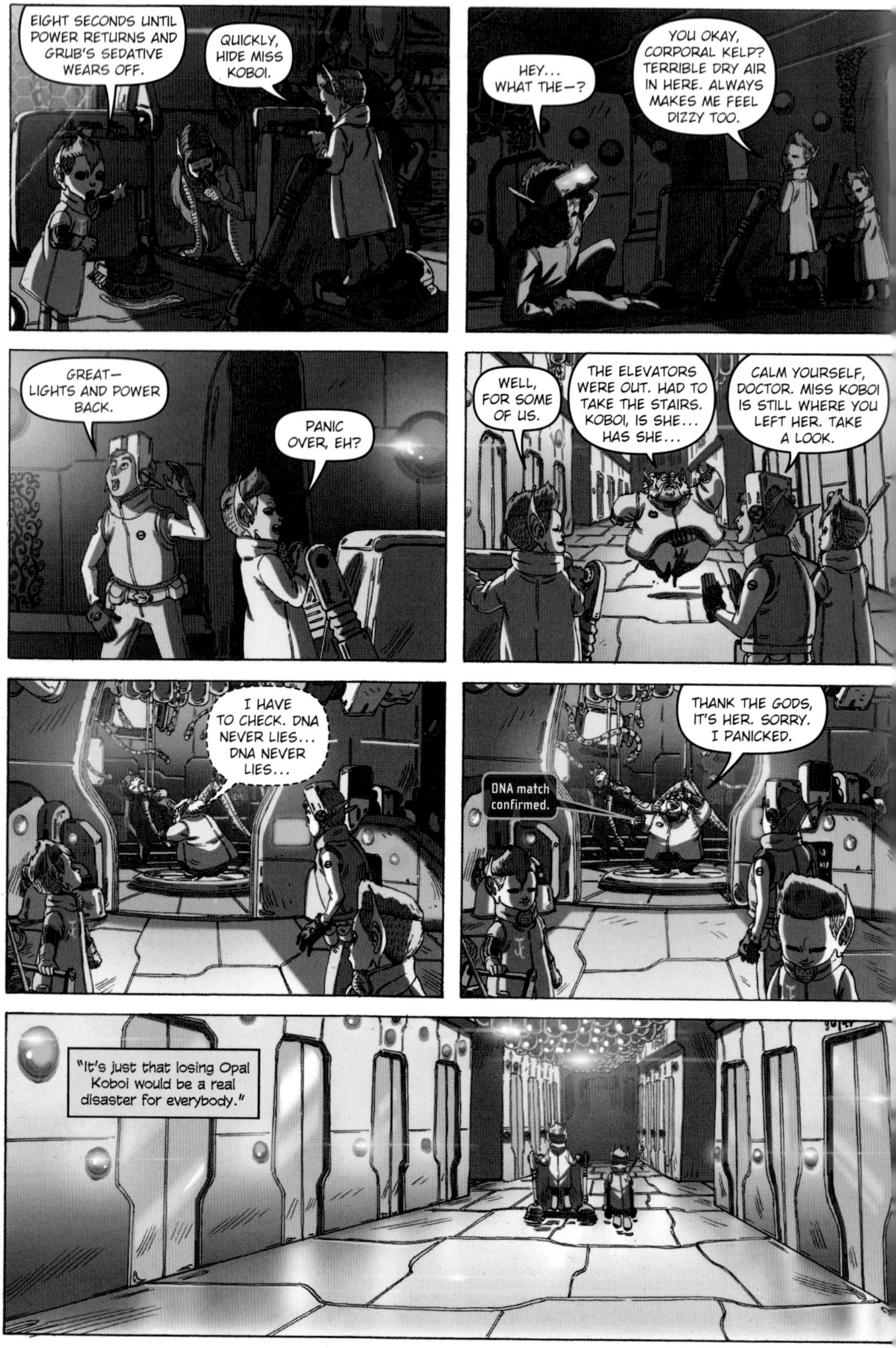
EIGHT SECONDS UNTIL POWER RETURNS AND GRUB'S SEDATIVE WEARS OFF.
QUICKLY, HIDE MISS KOBOI.
HEY... WHAT THE—?
YOU OKAY, CORPORAL KELP? TERRIBLE DRY AIR IN HERE. ALWAYS MAKES ME FEEL DIZZY TOO.
GREAT— LIGHTS AND POWER BACK.
PANIC OVER, EH?
WELL, FOR SOME OF US.
THE ELEVATORS WERE OUT. HAD TO TAKE THE STAIRS. KOBOI, IS SHE... HAS SHE...
CALM YOURSELF, DOCTOR. MISS KOBOI IS STILL WHERE YOU LEFT HER. TAKE A LOOK.
I HAVE TO CHECK. DNA NEVER LIES... DNA NEVER LIES...
DNA match confirmed.
THANK THE GODS, IT'S HER. SORRY. I PANICKED.
"It's just that losing Opal Koboi would be a real disaster for everybody."

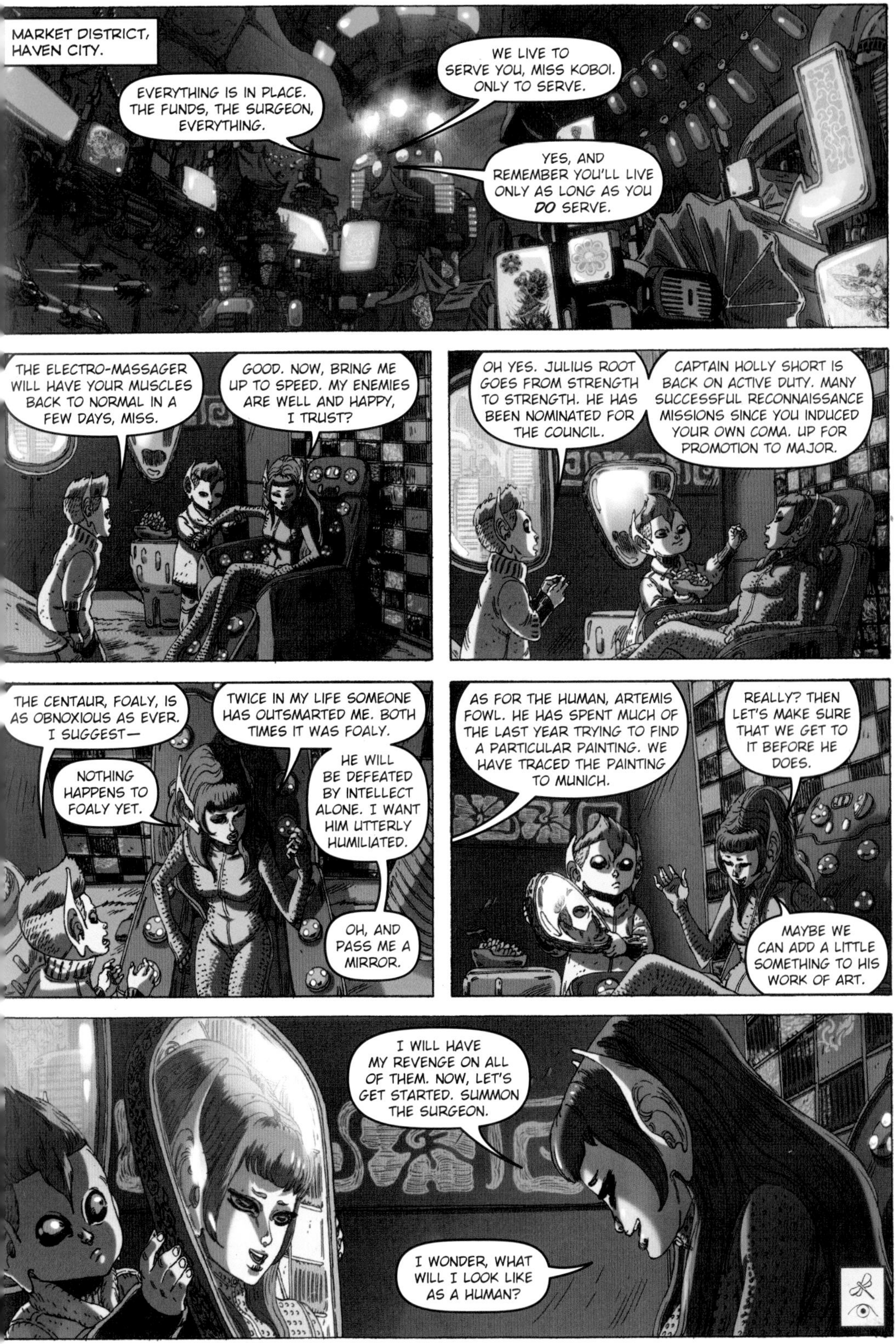
MARKET DISTRICT, HAVEN CITY.
EVERYTHING IS IN PLACE. THE FUNDS, THE SURGEON, EVERYTHING.
WE LIVE TO SERVE YOU, MISS KOBOI. ONLY TO SERVE.
YES, AND REMEMBER YOU'LL LIVE ONLY AS LONG AS YOU DO SERVE.
THE ELECTRO-MASSAGER WILL HAVE YOUR MUSCLES BACK TO NORMAL IN A FEW DAYS, MISS.
GOOD. NOW, BRING ME UP TO SPEED. MY ENEMIES ARE WELL AND HAPPY, I TRUST?
OH YES. JULIUS ROOT GOES FROM STRENGTH TO STRENGTH. HE HAS BEEN NOMINATED FOR THE COUNCIL.
CAPTAIN HOLLY SHORT IS BACK ON ACTIVE DUTY. MANY SUCCESSFUL RECONNAISSANCE MISSIONS SINCE YOU INDUCED YOUR OWN COMA. UP FOR PROMOTION TO MAJOR.
THE CENTAUR, FOALY, IS AS OBNOXIOUS AS EVER. I SUGGEST—
NOTHING HAPPENS TO FOALY YET.
TWICE IN MY LIFE SOMEONE HAS OUTSMARTED ME. BOTH TIMES IT WAS FOALY.
HE WILL BE DEFEATED BY INTELLECT ALONE. I WANT HIM UTTERLY HUMILIATED.
OH, AND PASS ME A MIRROR.
AS FOR THE HUMAN, ARTEMIS FOWL. HE HAS SPENT MUCH OF THE LAST YEAR TRYING TO FIND A PARTICULAR PAINTING. WE HAVE TRACED THE PAINTING TO MUNICH.
REALLY? THEN LET'S MAKE SURE THAT WE GET TO IT BEFORE HE DOES.
MAYBE WE CAN ADD A LITTLE SOMETHING TO HIS WORK OF ART.
I WILL HAVE MY REVENGE ON ALL OF THEM. NOW, LET'S GET STARTED. SUMMON THE SURGEON.
I WONDER, WHAT WILL I LOOK LIKE AS A HUMAN?

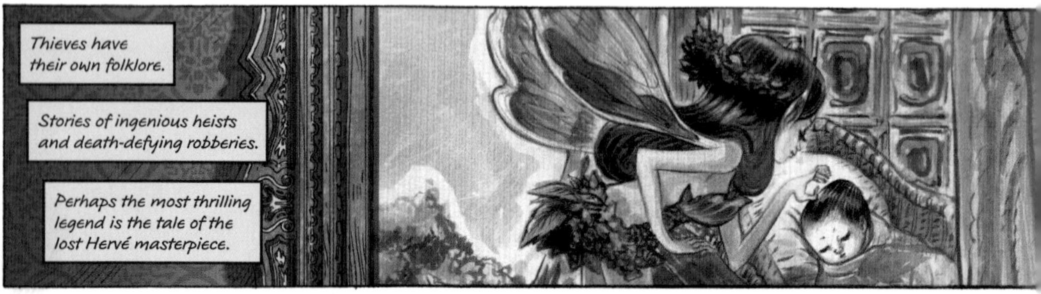
Thieves have their own folklore.
Stories of ingenious heists and death-defying robberies.
Perhaps the most thrilling legend is the tale of the lost Hervé masterpiece.

CHAPTER 2: THE FAIRY THIEF

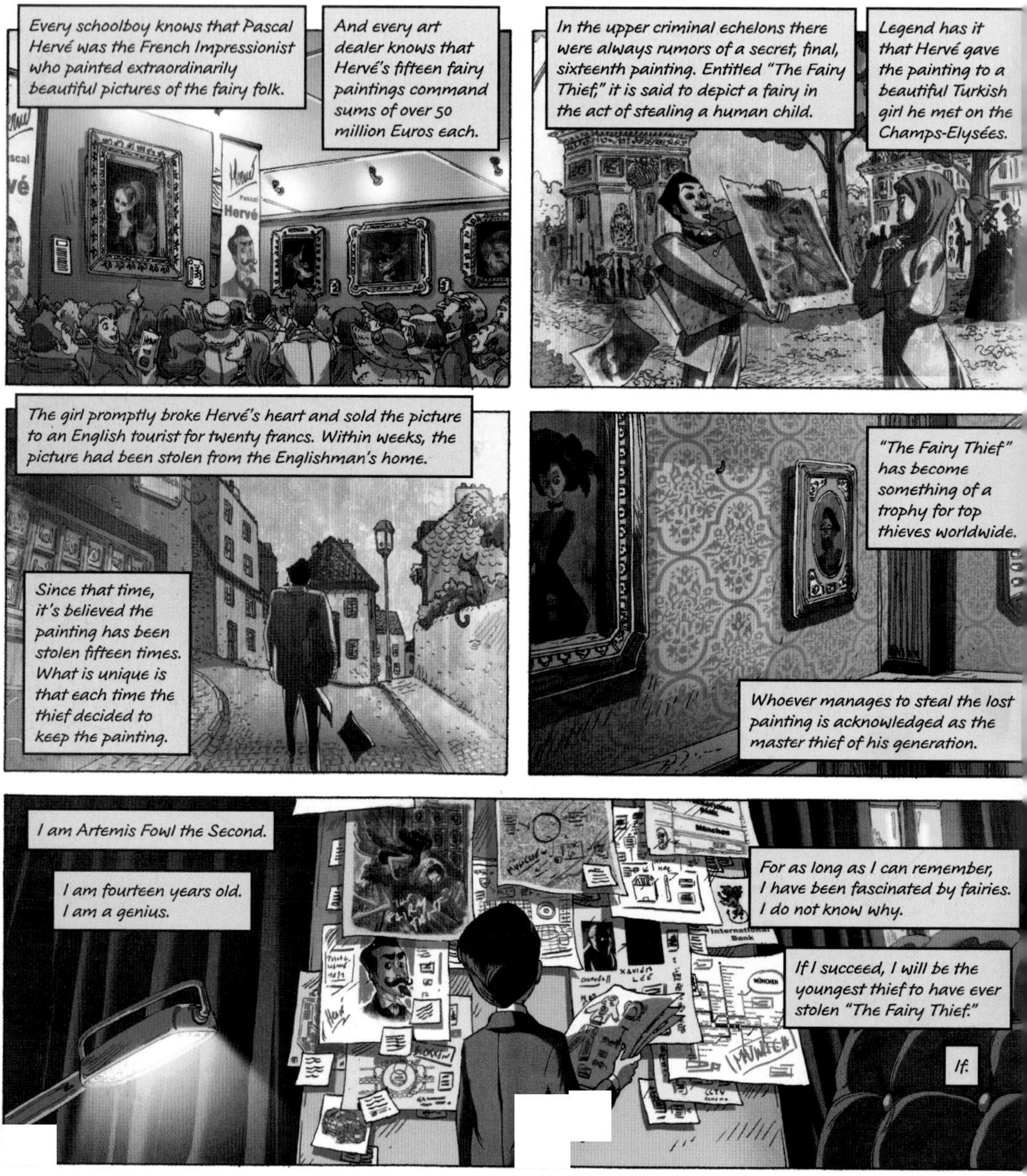
Every schoolboy knows that Pascal Hervé was the French Impressionist who painted extraordinarily beautiful pictures of the fairy folk.
And every art dealer knows that Hervé's fifteen fairy paintings command sums of over 50 million Euros each.
In the upper criminal echelons there were always rumors of a secret, final, sixteenth painting. Entitled "The Fairy Thief," it is said to depict a fairy in the act of stealing a human child.
Legend has it that Hervé gave the painting to a beautiful Turkish girl he met on the Champs-Elysées.
The girl promptly broke Hervé's heart and sold the picture to an English tourist for twenty francs. Within weeks, the picture had been stolen from the Englishman's home.
Since that time, it's believed the painting has been stolen fifteen times. What is unique is that each time the thief decided to keep the painting.
"The Fairy Thief" has become something of a trophy for top thieves worldwide.
Whoever manages to steal the lost painting is acknowledged as the master thief of his generation.
I am Artemis Fowl the Second.
I am fourteen years old. I am a genius.
For as long as I can remember, I have been fascinated by fairies. I do not know why.
If I succeed, I will be the youngest thief to have ever stolen "The Fairy Thief."
If.

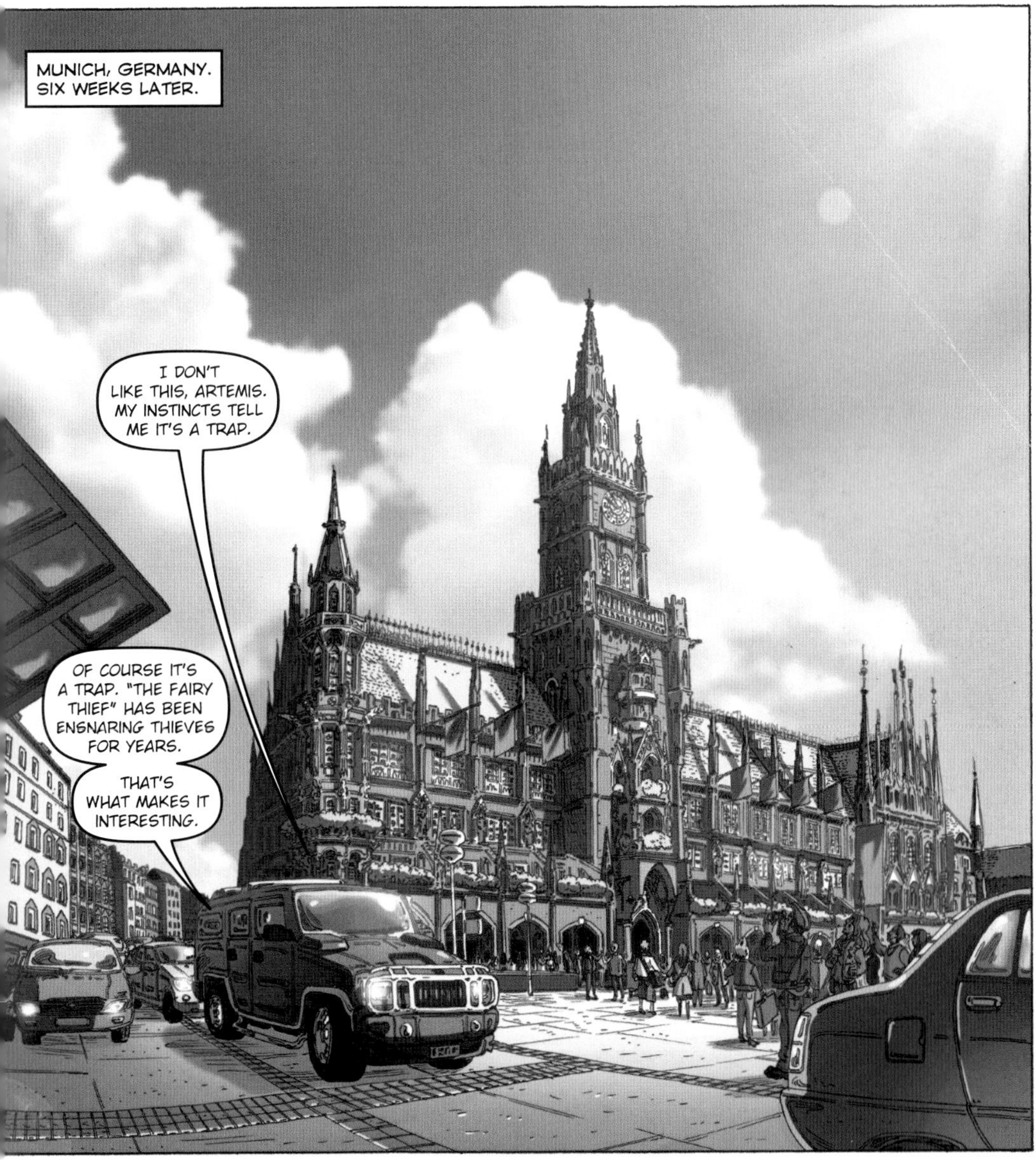
MUNICH, GERMANY. SIX WEEKS LATER.
I DON'T LIKE THIS, ARTEMIS. MY INSTINCTS TELL ME IT'S A TRAP.
OF COURSE IT'S A TRAP. "THE FAIRY THIEF" HAS BEEN ENSNARING THIEVES FOR YEARS.
THAT'S WHAT MAKES IT INTERESTING.

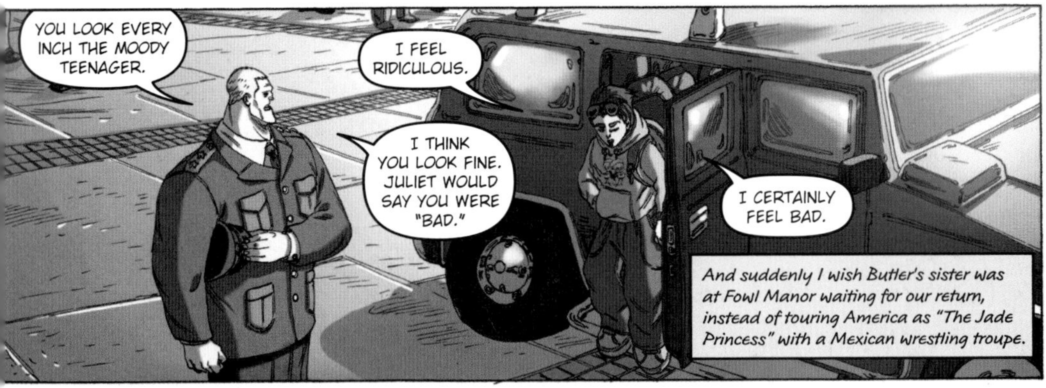
YOU LOOK EVERY INCH THE MOODY TEENAGER.
I FEEL RIDICULOUS.
I THINK YOU LOOK FINE. JULIET WOULD SAY YOU WERE "BAD."
I CERTAINLY FEEL BAD.
And suddenly I wish Butler's sister was at Fowl Manor waiting for our return, instead of touring America as "The Jade Princess" with a Mexican wrestling troupe.

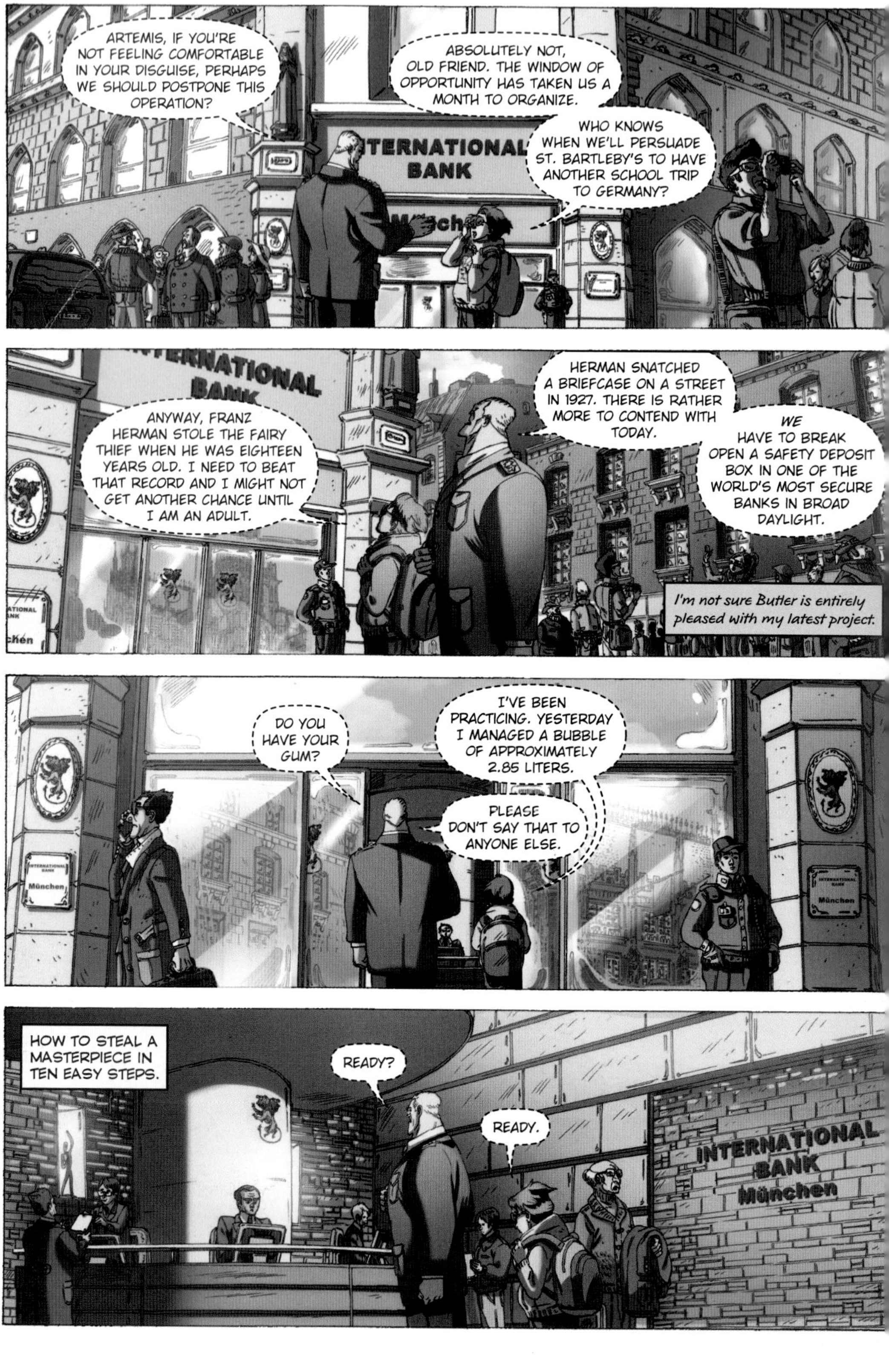
ARTEMIS, IF YOU'RE NOT FEELING COMFORTABLE IN YOUR DISGUISE, PERHAPS WE SHOULD POSTPONE THIS OPERATION?
ABSOLUTELY NOT, OLD FRIEND. THE WINDOW OF OPPORTUNITY HAS TAKEN US A MONTH TO ORGANIZE.
WHO KNOWS WHEN WE'LL PERSUADE ST. BARTLEBY'S TO HAVE ANOTHER SCHOOL TRIP TO GERMANY?
INTERNATIONAL BANK
ANYWAY, FRANZ HERMAN STOLE THE FAIRY THIEF WHEN HE WAS EIGHTEEN YEARS OLD. I NEED TO BEAT THAT RECORD AND I MIGHT NOT GET ANOTHER CHANCE UNTIL I AM AN ADULT.
HERMAN SNATCHED A BRIEFCASE ON A STREET IN 1927. THERE IS RATHER MORE TO CONTEND WITH TODAY.
WE HAVE TO BREAK OPEN A SAFETY DEPOSIT BOX IN ONE OF THE WORLD'S MOST SECURE BANKS IN BROAD DAYLIGHT.
I'm not sure Butler is entirely pleased with my latest project.
DO YOU HAVE YOUR GUM?
I'VE BEEN PRACTICING. YESTERDAY I MANAGED A BUBBLE OF APPROXIMATELY 2.85 LITERS.
PLEASE DON'T SAY THAT TO ANYONE ELSE.
HOW TO STEAL A MASTERPIECE IN TEN EASY STEPS.
READY?
READY.
INTERNATIONAL BANK München

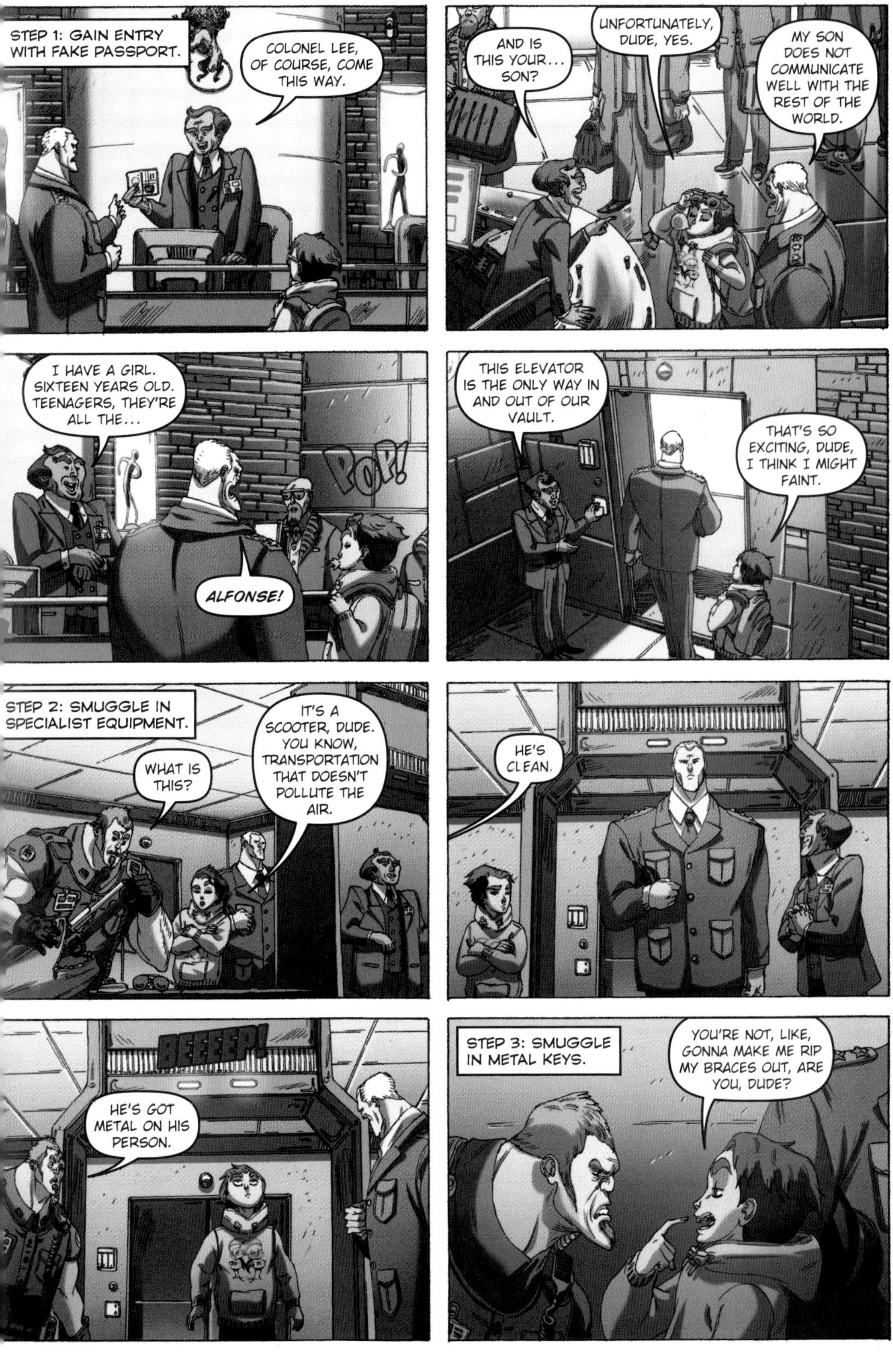
STEP 1: GAIN ENTRY WITH FAKE PASSPORT.
COLONEL LEE, OF COURSE, COME THIS WAY.
AND IS THIS YOUR... SON?
UNFORTUNATELY, DUDE, YES.
MY SON DOES NOT COMMUNICATE WELL WITH THE REST OF THE WORLD.
I HAVE A GIRL. SIXTEEN YEARS OLD. TEENAGERS, THEY'RE ALL THE...
POP!
ALFONSE!
THIS ELEVATOR IS THE ONLY WAY IN AND OUT OF OUR VAULT.
THAT'S SO EXCITING, DUDE, I THINK I MIGHT FAINT.
STEP 2: SMUGGLE IN SPECIALIST EQUIPMENT.
WHAT IS THIS?
IT'S A SCOOTER, DUDE. YOU KNOW, TRANSPORTATION THAT DOESN'T POLLUTE THE AIR.
HE'S CLEAN.
BEEEEP!
HE'S GOT METAL ON HIS PERSON.
STEP 3: SMUGGLE IN METAL KEYS.
YOU'RE NOT, LIKE, GONNA MAKE ME RIP MY BRACES OUT, ARE YOU, DUDE?

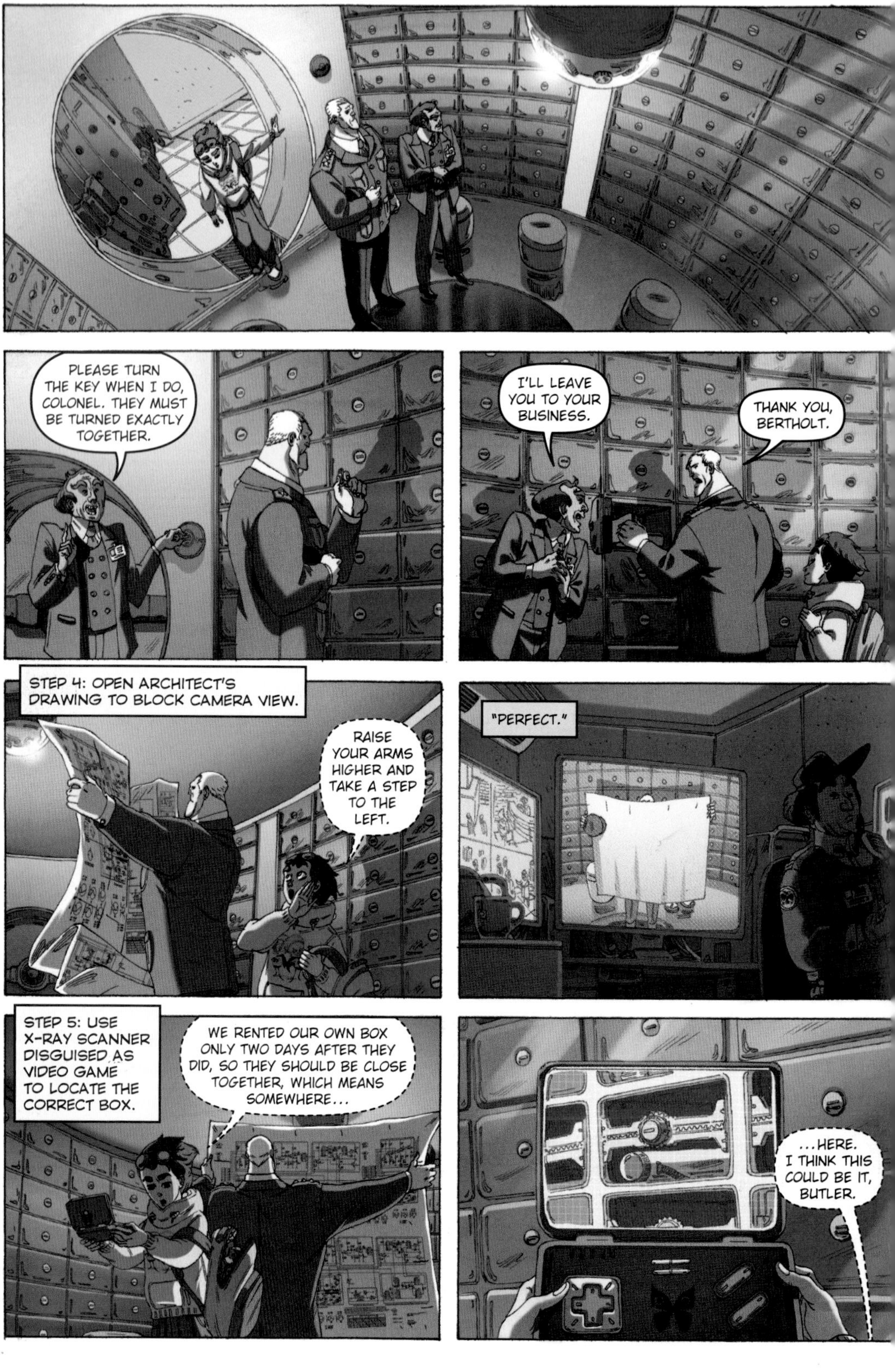
PLEASE TURN THE KEY WHEN I DO, COLONEL. THEY MUST BE TURNED EXACTLY TOGETHER.
I'LL LEAVE YOU TO YOUR BUSINESS.
THANK YOU, BERTHOLT.
STEP 4: OPEN ARCHITECT'S DRAWING TO BLOCK CAMERA VIEW.
RAISE YOUR ARMS HIGHER AND TAKE A STEP TO THE LEFT.
"PERFECT."
STEP 5: USE X-RAY SCANNER DISGUISED AS VIDEO GAME TO LOCATE THE CORRECT BOX.
WE RENTED OUR OWN BOX ONLY TWO DAYS AFTER THEY DID, SO THEY SHOULD BE CLOSE TOGETHER, WHICH MEANS SOMEWHERE...
...HERE. I THINK THIS COULD BE IT, BUTLER.

STEP 6: LOCATE THE LOCKSMITH'S SIGNATURE.

STEP 7: RETRIEVE MASTER KEYS ALLOWED THROUGH METAL DETECTOR.

STEP 8: USE SPECIALLY ADAPTED SCOOTER COLUMN TO TURN TWO KEYS AT SAME TIME.

HERE WE GO...

CLICK

YES!

CLICK

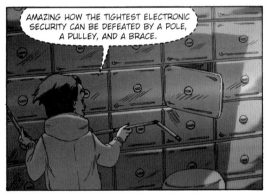

AMAZING HOW THE TIGHTEST ELECTRONIC SECURITY CAN BE DEFEATED BY A POLE, A PULLEY, AND A BRACE.

STEP 9: CHECK DEPOSIT BOX FOR BOOBY TRAPS.

HA—A CIRCUIT BREAKER ATTACHED TO A PORTABLE KLAXON.

HOW EMBARRASSING FOR ANY THIEF TO GET CAUGHT LIKE THAT. SOMEONE HAS A SENSE OF HUMOR.

STEP 10: DISCONNECT BOOBY TRAP.

ARE WE DONE, ARTEMIS? MY ARMS ARE GETTING RATHER TIRED.

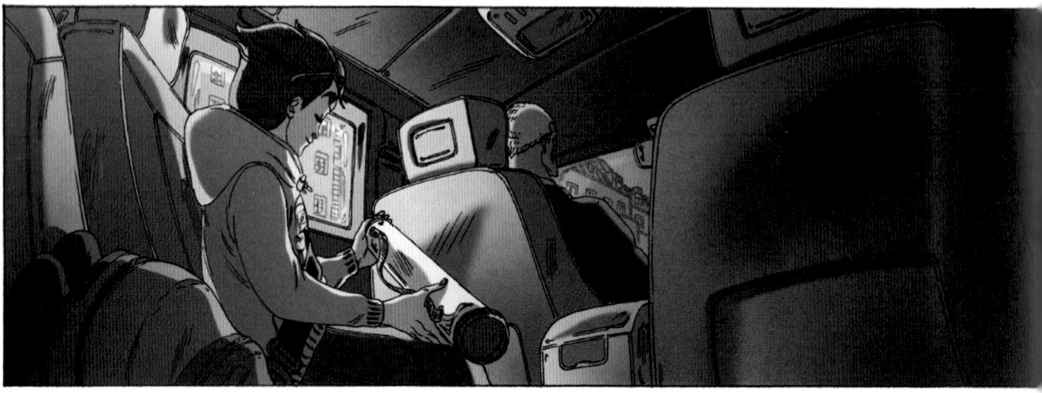

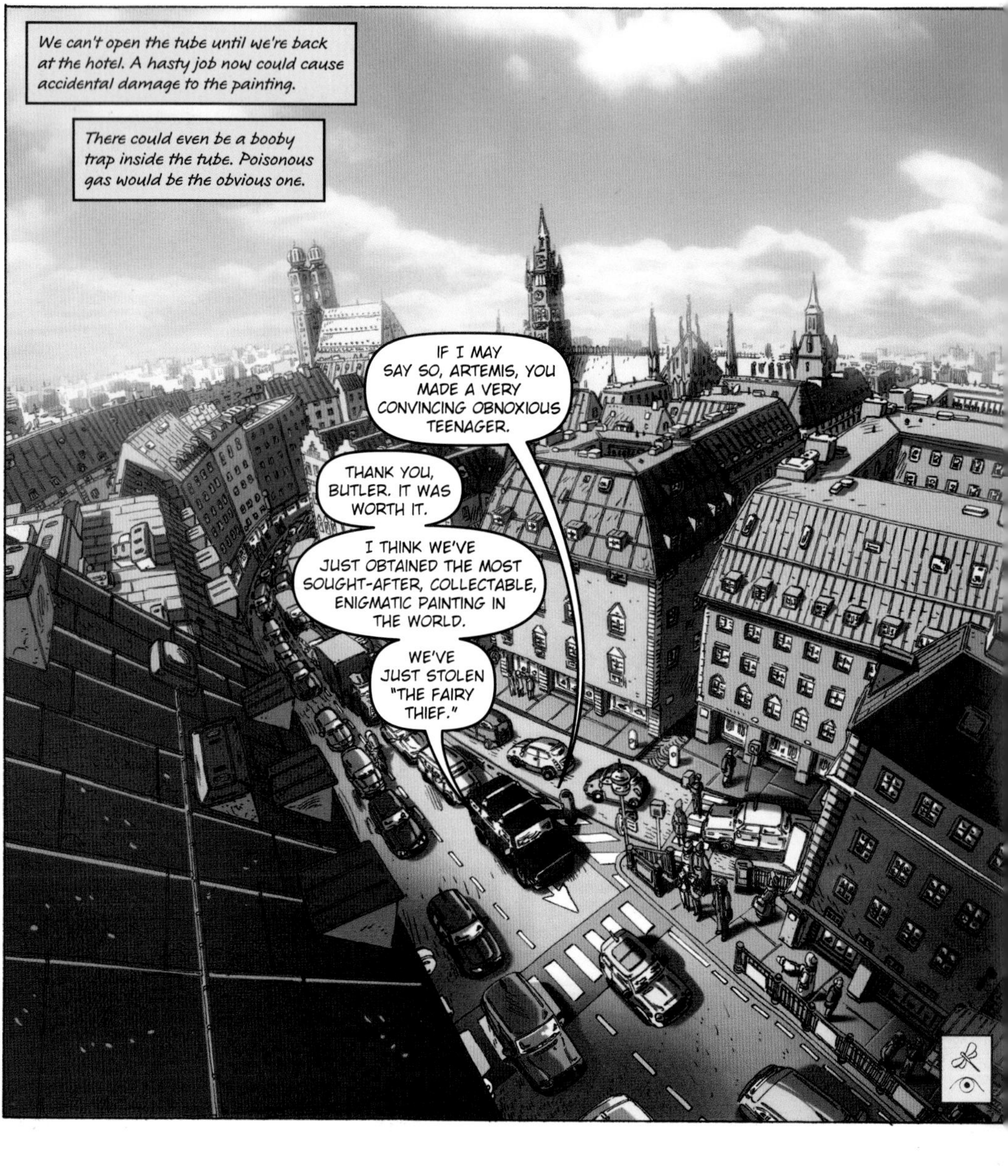

We can't open the tube until we're back at the hotel. A hasty job now could cause accidental damage to the painting.
There could even be a booby trap inside the tube. Poisonous gas would be the obvious one.
IF I MAY SAY SO, ARTEMIS, YOU MADE A VERY CONVINCING OBNOXIOUS TEENAGER.
THANK YOU, BUTLER. IT WAS WORTH IT.
I THINK WE'VE JUST OBTAINED THE MOST SOUGHT-AFTER, COLLECTABLE, ENIGMATIC PAINTING IN THE WORLD.
WE'VE JUST STOLEN "THE FAIRY THIEF."

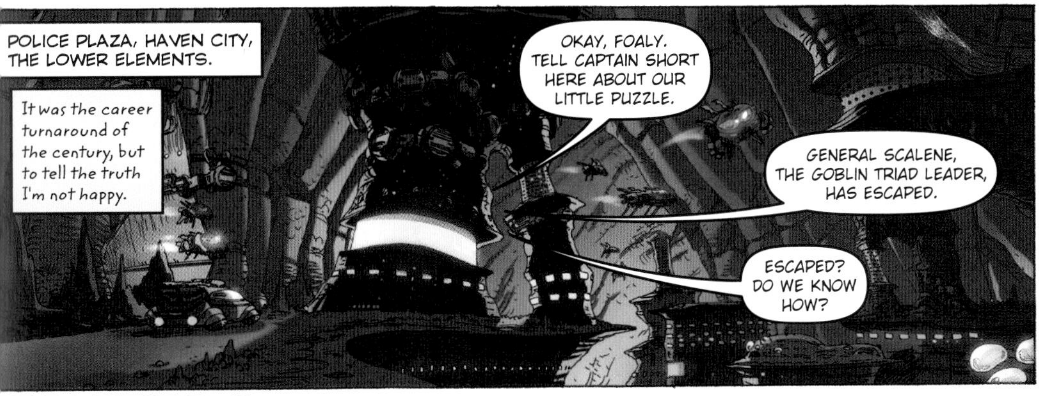
POLICE PLAZA, HAVEN CITY, THE LOWER ELEMENTS.
It was the career turnaround of the century, but to tell the truth I'm not happy.
OKAY, FOALY. TELL CAPTAIN SHORT HERE ABOUT OUR LITTLE PUZZLE.
GENERAL SCALENE, THE GOBLIN TRIAD LEADER, HAS ESCAPED.
ESCAPED? DO WE KNOW HOW?

CHAPTER 3: NEARLY DEPARTED

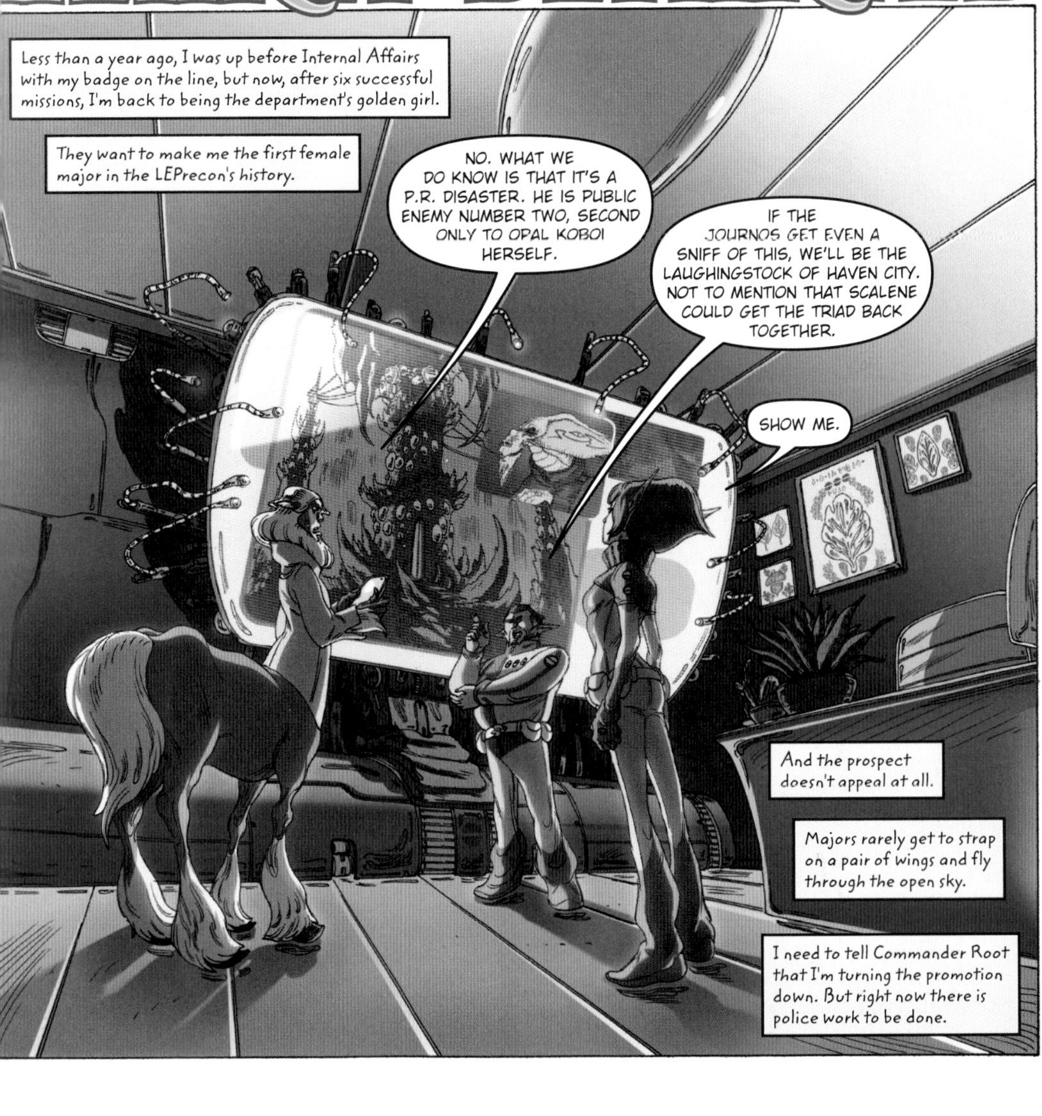
Less than a year ago, I was up before Internal Affairs with my badge on the line, but now, after six successful missions, I'm back to being the department's golden girl.
They want to make me the first female major in the LEPrecon's history.
NO. WHAT WE DO KNOW IS THAT IT'S A P.R. DISASTER. HE IS PUBLIC ENEMY NUMBER TWO, SECOND ONLY TO OPAL KOBOI HERSELF.
IF THE JOURNOS GET EVEN A SNIFF OF THIS, WE'LL BE THE LAUGHINGSTOCK OF HAVEN CITY. NOT TO MENTION THAT SCALENE COULD GET THE TRIAD BACK TOGETHER.
SHOW ME.
And the prospect doesn't appeal at all.
Majors rarely get to strap on a pair of wings and fly through the open sky.
I need to tell Commander Root that I'm turning the promotion down. But right now there is police work to be done.

HOWLER'S PEAK, GOBLIN CORRECTIONAL FACILITY. CAMERA EIGHTY-SIX. THE VISITING ROOM. SCALENE WENT IN, BUT HE NEVER CAME OUT.

SO ACTIVATE THE SEEKER-SLEEPER. THAT'LL KNOCK HIM OUT WHEREVER HE IS.

THE SEEKER-SLEEPER IS NOT BROADCASTING. OR IF IT IS, WE'RE NOT PICKING UP THE SIGNAL.

OKAY, THAT IS A PROBLEM.

SO WHO WAS VISITING GENERAL SCALENE?

ONE OF HIS THOUSAND NEPHEWS, A GOBLIN CALLED BOOHN. HERE'S THE VIDEO OF BOOHN CHECKING IN.

THE VISITOR'S LIST HAS BOOHN ARRIVING AT SEVEN FIFTY. AND THEN CHECKING OUT AT EIGHT FIFTEEN.

HE PASSES THE INTERNAL SECURITY CAMERAS AND THEN HEADS FOR HIS CAR.

08:15 am

SO IF BOOHN CHECKED OUT AT EIGHT FIFTEEN, THEN HOW DID HE MANAGE TO CHECK OUT AGAIN AT EIGHT TWENTY?

I SAW THAT. IT'S A GLITCH. MUST BE.

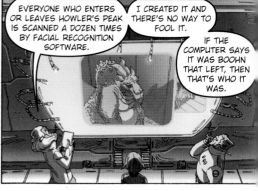

EVERYONE WHO ENTERS OR LEAVES HOWLER'S PEAK IS SCANNED A DOZEN TIMES BY FACIAL RECOGNITION SOFTWARE.

I CREATED IT AND THERE'S NO WAY TO FOOL IT.

IF THE COMPUTER SAYS IT WAS BOOHN THAT LEFT, THEN THAT'S WHO IT WAS.

FOALY, CAN YOU ENLARGE HIS HEAD? SHARPEN THE IMAGE? SHOW ME BOOHN GOING IN AND THE OTHER SHOT OF HIM COMING OUT.

WHAT ARE YOU LOOKING FOR, CAPTAIN?

I DON'T KNOW. SOMETHING. ANYTHING.

My intuition is buzzing like a swarm of bees.

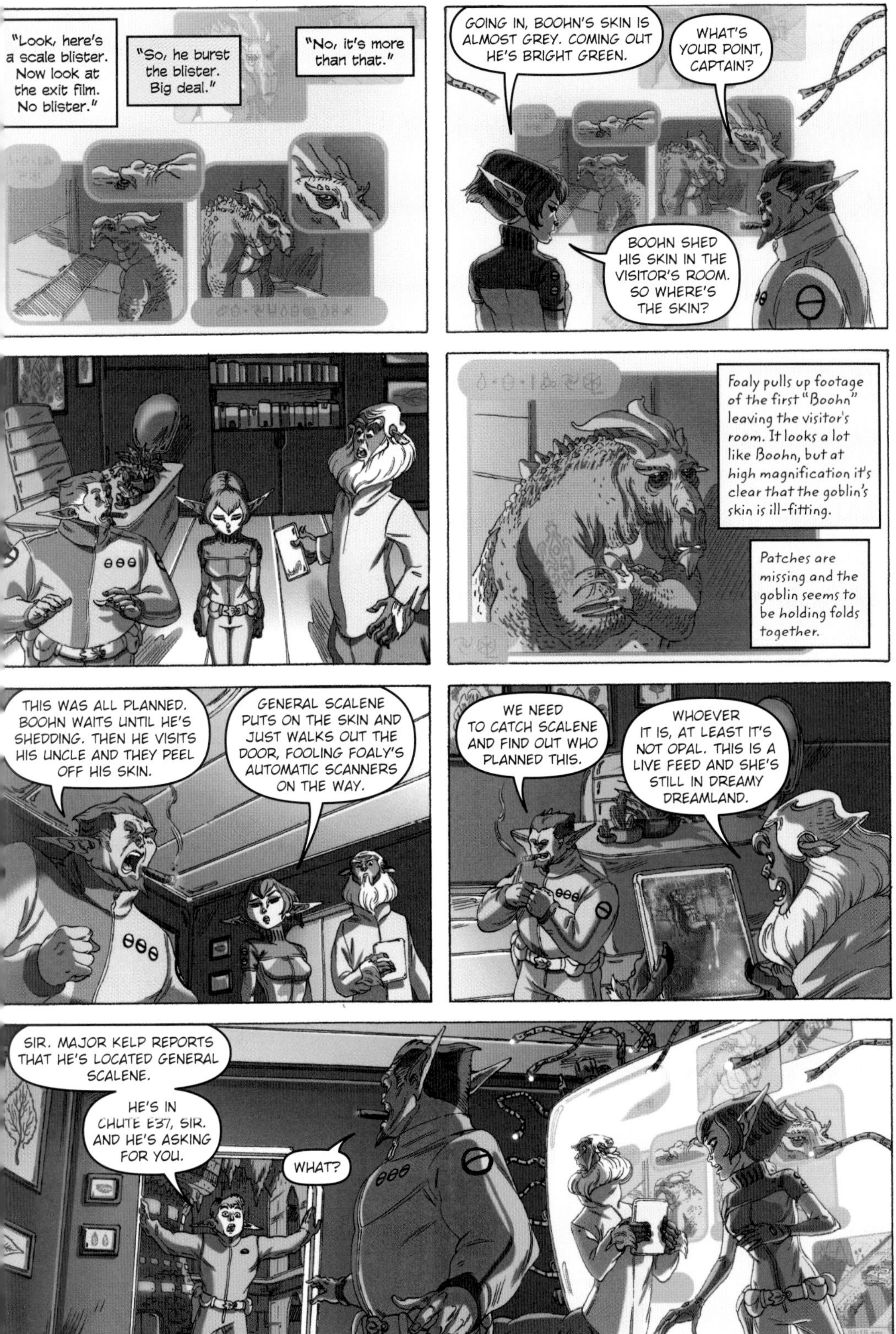
"Look, here's a scale blister. Now look at the exit film. No blister."
"So, he burst the blister. Big deal."
"No, it's more than that."
GOING IN, BOOHN'S SKIN IS ALMOST GREY. COMING OUT HE'S BRIGHT GREEN.
WHAT'S YOUR POINT, CAPTAIN?
BOOHN SHED HIS SKIN IN THE VISITOR'S ROOM. SO WHERE'S THE SKIN?
Foaly pulls up footage of the first "Boohn" leaving the visitor's room. It looks a lot like Boohn, but at high magnification it's clear that the goblin's skin is ill-fitting.
Patches are missing and the goblin seems to be holding folds together.
THIS WAS ALL PLANNED. BOOHN WAITS UNTIL HE'S SHEDDING. THEN HE VISITS HIS UNCLE AND THEY PEEL OFF HIS SKIN.
GENERAL SCALENE PUTS ON THE SKIN AND JUST WALKS OUT THE DOOR, FOOLING FOALY'S AUTOMATIC SCANNERS ON THE WAY.
WE NEED TO CATCH SCALENE AND FIND OUT WHO PLANNED THIS.
WHOEVER IT IS, AT LEAST IT'S NOT OPAL. THIS IS A LIVE FEED AND SHE'S STILL IN DREAMY DREAMLAND.
SIR. MAJOR KELP REPORTS THAT HE'S LOCATED GENERAL SCALENE.
HE'S IN CHUTE E37, SIR. AND HE'S ASKING FOR YOU.
WHAT?

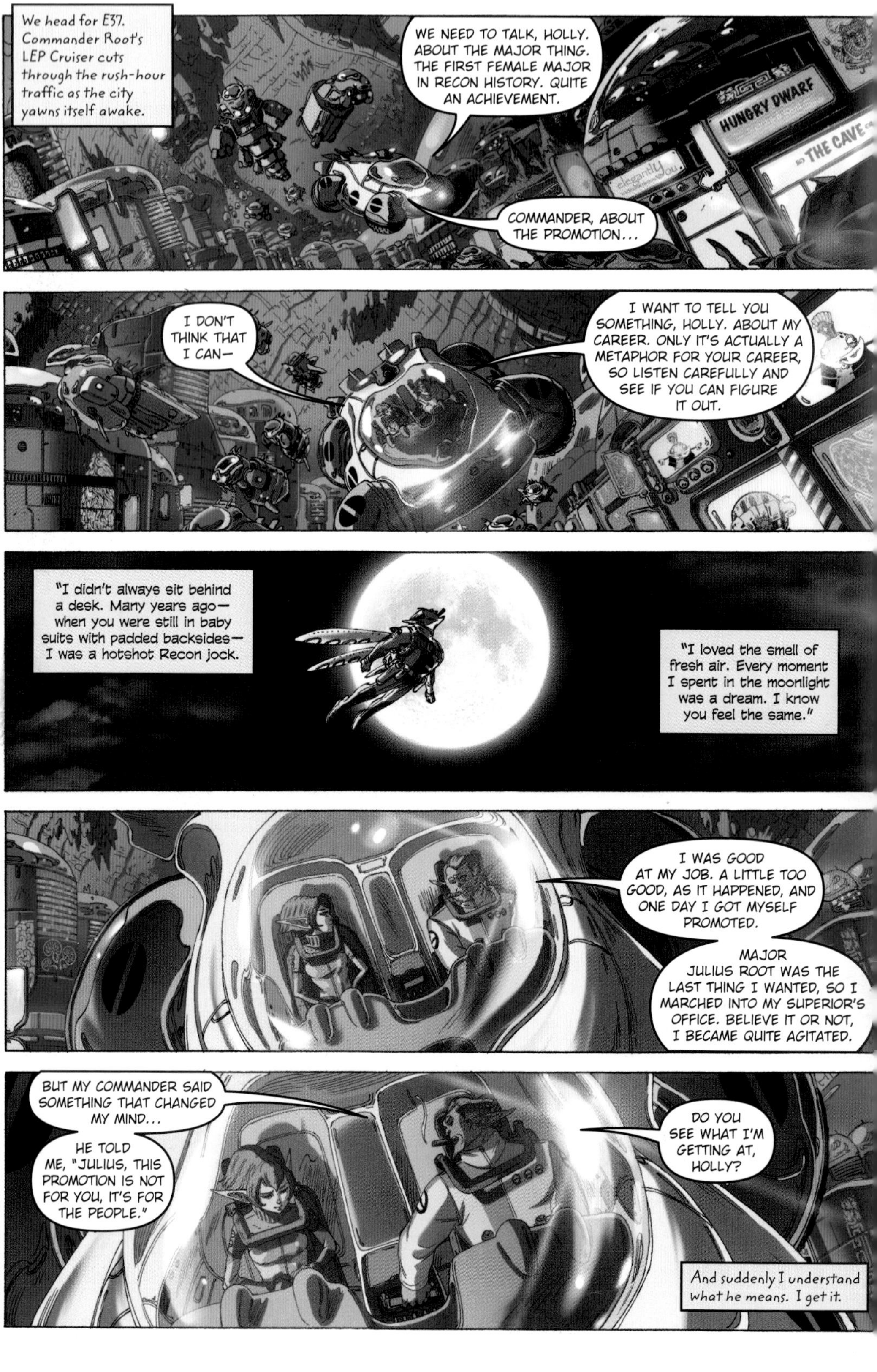

We head for E37. Commander Root's LEP Cruiser cuts through the rush-hour traffic as the city yawns itself awake.
WE NEED TO TALK, HOLLY. ABOUT THE MAJOR THING. THE FIRST FEMALE MAJOR IN RECON HISTORY. QUITE AN ACHIEVEMENT.
HUNGRY DWARF
THE CAVE
COMMANDER, ABOUT THE PROMOTION...
I DON'T THINK THAT I CAN—
I WANT TO TELL YOU SOMETHING, HOLLY. ABOUT MY CAREER. ONLY IT'S ACTUALLY A METAPHOR FOR YOUR CAREER, SO LISTEN CAREFULLY AND SEE IF YOU CAN FIGURE IT OUT.
"I didn't always sit behind a desk. Many years ago—when you were still in baby suits with padded backsides—I was a hotshot Recon jock.
"I loved the smell of fresh air. Every moment I spent in the moonlight was a dream. I know you feel the same."
I WAS GOOD AT MY JOB. A LITTLE TOO GOOD, AS IT HAPPENED, AND ONE DAY I GOT MYSELF PROMOTED.
MAJOR JULIUS ROOT WAS THE LAST THING I WANTED, SO I MARCHED INTO MY SUPERIOR'S OFFICE. BELIEVE IT OR NOT, I BECAME QUITE AGITATED.
BUT MY COMMANDER SAID SOMETHING THAT CHANGED MY MIND...
HE TOLD ME, "JULIUS, THIS PROMOTION IS NOT FOR YOU, IT'S FOR THE PEOPLE."
DO YOU SEE WHAT I'M GETTING AT, HOLLY?
And suddenly I understand what he means. I get it.

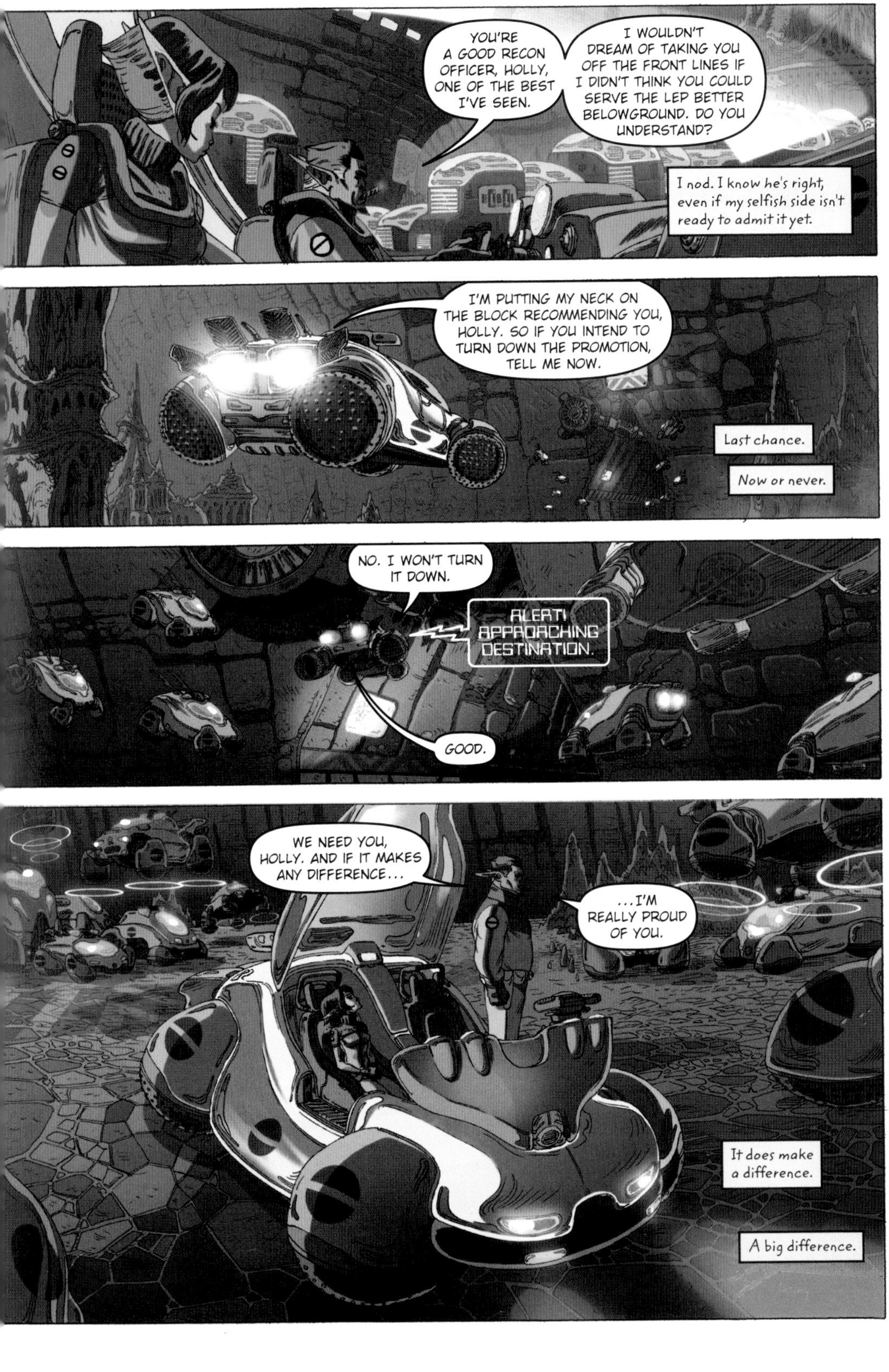
YOU'RE A GOOD RECON OFFICER, HOLLY, ONE OF THE BEST I'VE SEEN.
I WOULDN'T DREAM OF TAKING YOU OFF THE FRONT LINES IF I DIDN'T THINK YOU COULD SERVE THE LEP BETTER BELOWGROUND. DO YOU UNDERSTAND?
I nod. I know he's right, even if my selfish side isn't ready to admit it yet.
I'M PUTTING MY NECK ON THE BLOCK RECOMMENDING YOU, HOLLY. SO IF YOU INTEND TO TURN DOWN THE PROMOTION, TELL ME NOW.
Last chance.
Now or never.
NO. I WON'T TURN IT DOWN.
ALERT! APPROACHING DESTINATION.
GOOD.
WE NEED YOU, HOLLY. AND IF IT MAKES ANY DIFFERENCE...
...I'M REALLY PROUD OF YOU.
It does make a difference.
A big difference.

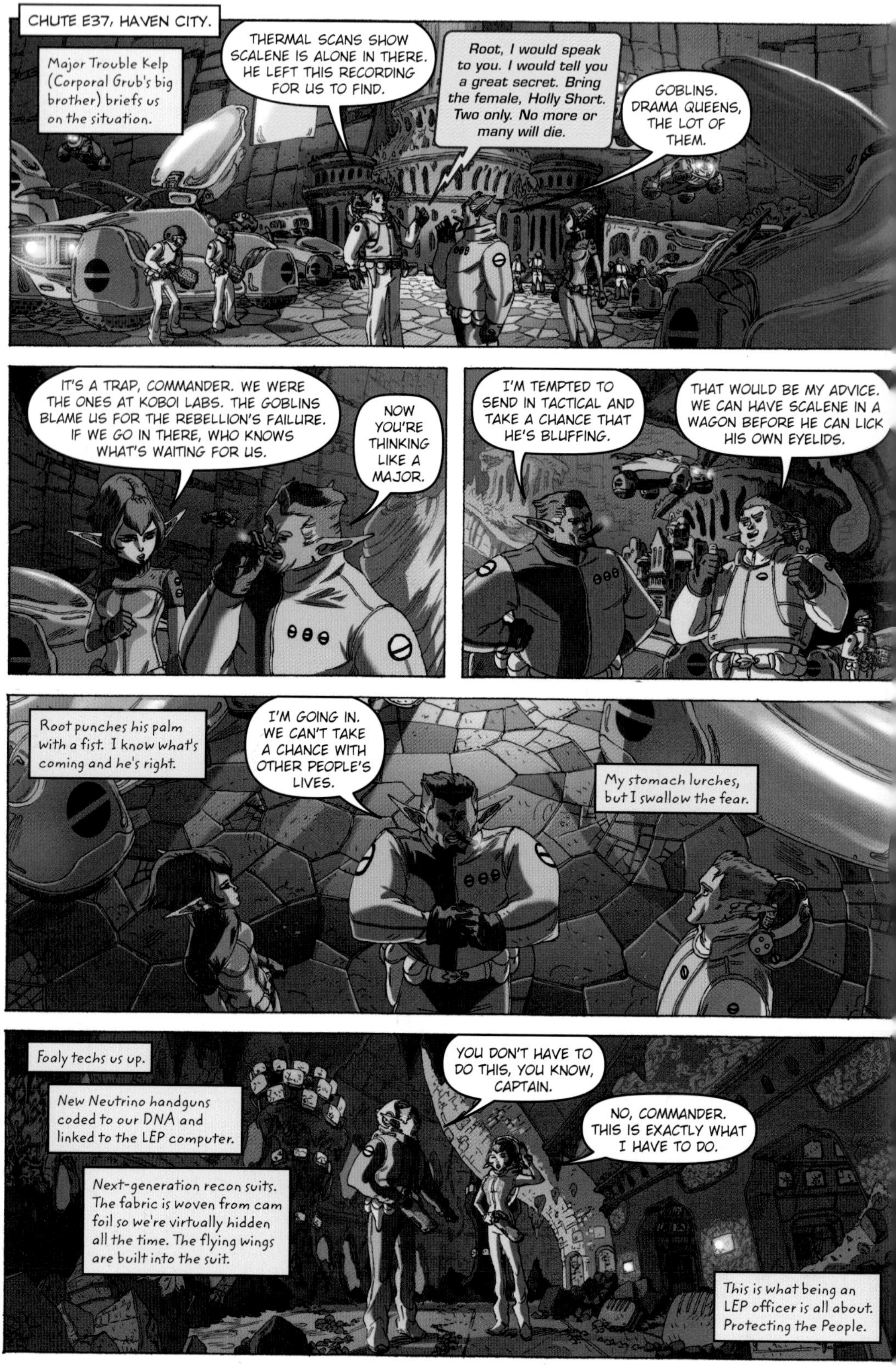
CHUTE E37, HAVEN CITY.
Major Trouble Kelp (Corporal Grub's big brother) briefs us on the situation.
THERMAL SCANS SHOW SCALENE IS ALONE IN THERE. HE LEFT THIS RECORDING FOR US TO FIND.
Root, I would speak to you. I would tell you a great secret. Bring the female, Holly Short. Two only. No more or many will die.
GOBLINS. DRAMA QUEENS, THE LOT OF THEM.
IT'S A TRAP, COMMANDER. WE WERE THE ONES AT KOBOI LABS. THE GOBLINS BLAME US FOR THE REBELLION'S FAILURE. IF WE GO IN THERE, WHO KNOWS WHAT'S WAITING FOR US.
NOW YOU'RE THINKING LIKE A MAJOR.
I'M TEMPTED TO SEND IN TACTICAL AND TAKE A CHANCE THAT HE'S BLUFFING.
THAT WOULD BE MY ADVICE. WE CAN HAVE SCALENE IN A WAGON BEFORE HE CAN LICK HIS OWN EYELIDS.
Root punches his palm with a fist. I know what's coming and he's right.
I'M GOING IN. WE CAN'T TAKE A CHANCE WITH OTHER PEOPLE'S LIVES.
My stomach lurches, but I swallow the fear.
Foaly techs us up.
New Neutrino handguns coded to our DNA and linked to the LEP computer.
Next-generation recon suits. The fabric is woven from cam foil so we're virtually hidden all the time. The flying wings are built into the suit.
YOU DON'T HAVE TO DO THIS, YOU KNOW, CAPTAIN.
NO, COMMANDER. THIS IS EXACTLY WHAT I HAVE TO DO.
This is what being an LEP officer is all about. Protecting the People.

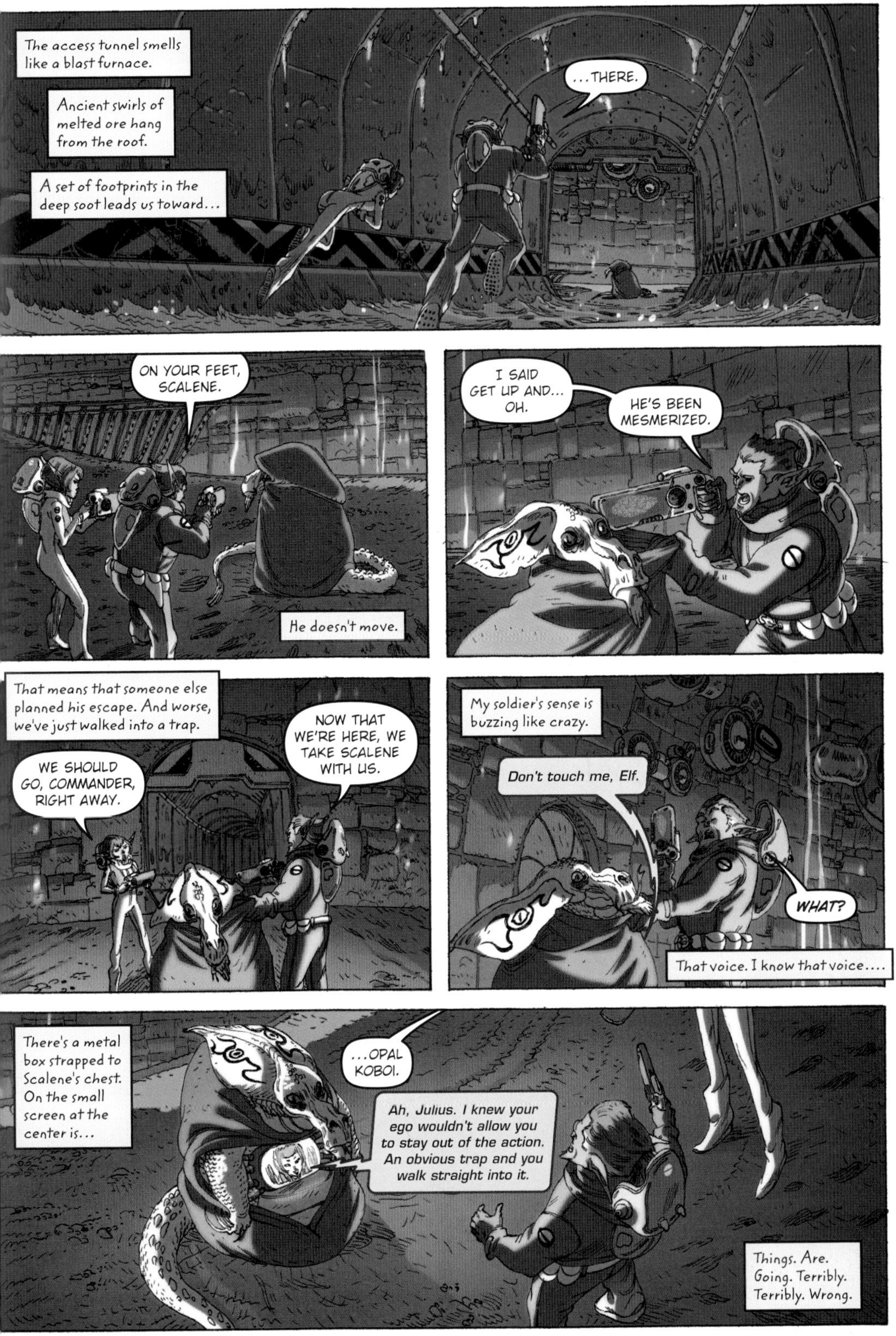

The access tunnel smells like a blast furnace.
Ancient swirls of melted ore hang from the roof.
A set of footprints in the deep soot leads us toward...
...THERE.
ON YOUR FEET, SCALENE.
He doesn't move.
I SAID GET UP AND... OH.
HE'S BEEN MESMERIZED.
That means that someone else planned his escape. And worse, we've just walked into a trap.
WE SHOULD GO, COMMANDER, RIGHT AWAY.
NOW THAT WE'RE HERE, WE TAKE SCALENE WITH US.
My soldier's sense is buzzing like crazy.
Don't touch me, Elf.
WHAT?
That voice. I know that voice....
There's a metal box strapped to Scalene's chest. On the small screen at the center is...
...OPAL KOBOI.
Ah, Julius. I knew your ego wouldn't allow you to stay out of the action. An obvious trap and you walk straight into it.
Things. Are. Going. Terribly. Terribly. Wrong.

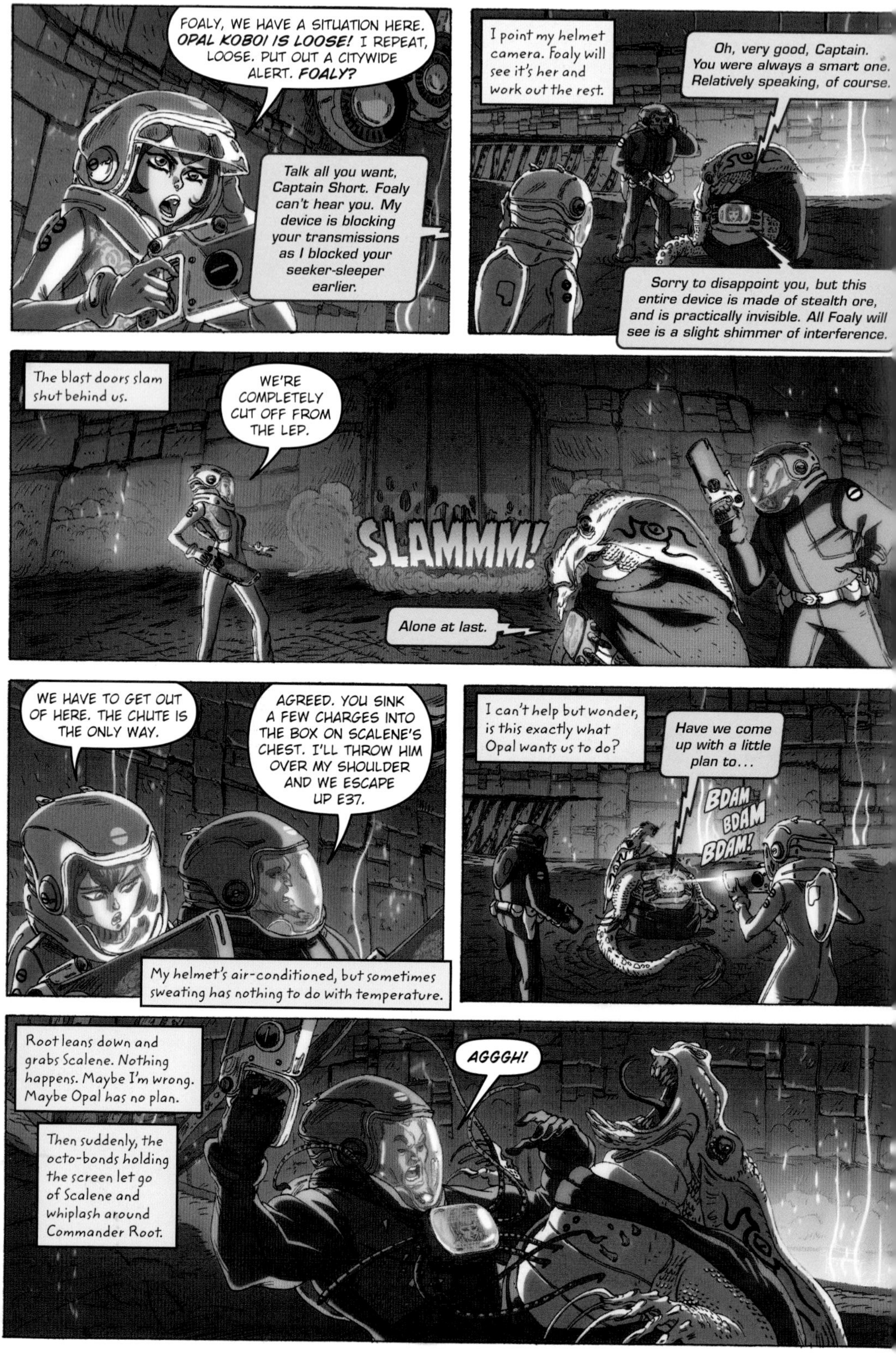

FOALY, WE HAVE A SITUATION HERE. OPAL KOBOI IS LOOSE! I REPEAT, LOOSE. PUT OUT A CITYWIDE ALERT. FOALY?
Talk all you want, Captain Short. Foaly can't hear you. My device is blocking your transmissions as I blocked your seeker-sleeper earlier.
I point my helmet camera. Foaly will see it's her and work out the rest.
Oh, very good, Captain. You were always a smart one. Relatively speaking, of course.
Sorry to disappoint you, but this entire device is made of stealth ore, and is practically invisible. All Foaly will see is a slight shimmer of interference.
The blast doors slam shut behind us.
WE'RE COMPLETELY CUT OFF FROM THE LEP.
SLAMMM!
Alone at last.
WE HAVE TO GET OUT OF HERE. THE CHUTE IS THE ONLY WAY.
AGREED. YOU SINK A FEW CHARGES INTO THE BOX ON SCALENE'S CHEST. I'LL THROW HIM OVER MY SHOULDER AND WE ESCAPE UP E37.
My helmet's air-conditioned, but sometimes sweating has nothing to do with temperature.
I can't help but wonder, is this exactly what Opal wants us to do?
Have we come up with a little plan to...
BDAM
BDAM
BDAM!
Root leans down and grabs Scalene. Nothing happens. Maybe I'm wrong. Maybe Opal has no plan.
Then suddenly, the octo-bonds holding the screen let go of Scalene and whiplash around Commander Root.
AGGGH!

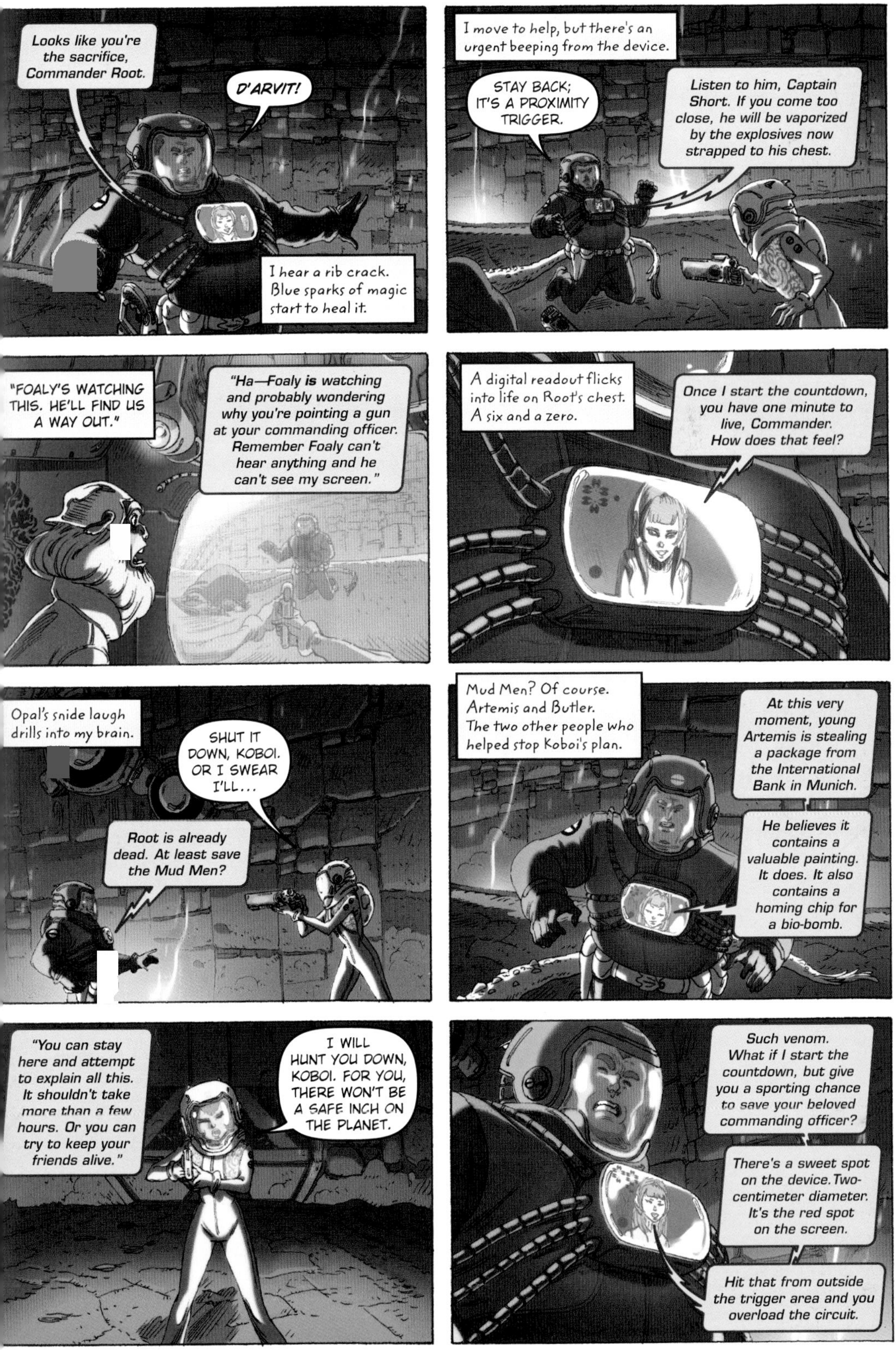

Looks like you're the sacrifice, Commander Root.
D'ARVIT!
I hear a rib crack. Blue sparks of magic start to heal it.
I move to help, but there's an urgent beeping from the device.
STAY BACK; IT'S A PROXIMITY TRIGGER.
Listen to him, Captain Short. If you come too close, he will be vaporized by the explosives now strapped to his chest.
"FOALY'S WATCHING THIS. HE'LL FIND US A WAY OUT."
"Ha—Foaly is watching and probably wondering why you're pointing a gun at your commanding officer. Remember Foaly can't hear anything and he can't see my screen."
A digital readout flicks into life on Root's chest. A six and a zero.
Once I start the countdown, you have one minute to live, Commander. How does that feel?
Opal's snide laugh drills into my brain.
SHUT IT DOWN, KOBOI. OR I SWEAR I'LL...
Root is already dead. At least save the Mud Men?
Mud Men? Of course. Artemis and Butler. The two other people who helped stop Koboi's plan.
At this very moment, young Artemis is stealing a package from the International Bank in Munich.
He believes it contains a valuable painting. It does. It also contains a homing chip for a bio-bomb.
"You can stay here and attempt to explain all this. It shouldn't take more than a few hours. Or you can try to keep your friends alive."
I WILL HUNT YOU DOWN, KOBOI. FOR YOU, THERE WON'T BE A SAFE INCH ON THE PLANET.
Such venom. What if I start the countdown, but give you a sporting chance to save your beloved commanding officer?
There's a sweet spot on the device. Two-centimeter diameter. It's the red spot on the screen.
Hit that from outside the trigger area and you overload the circuit.

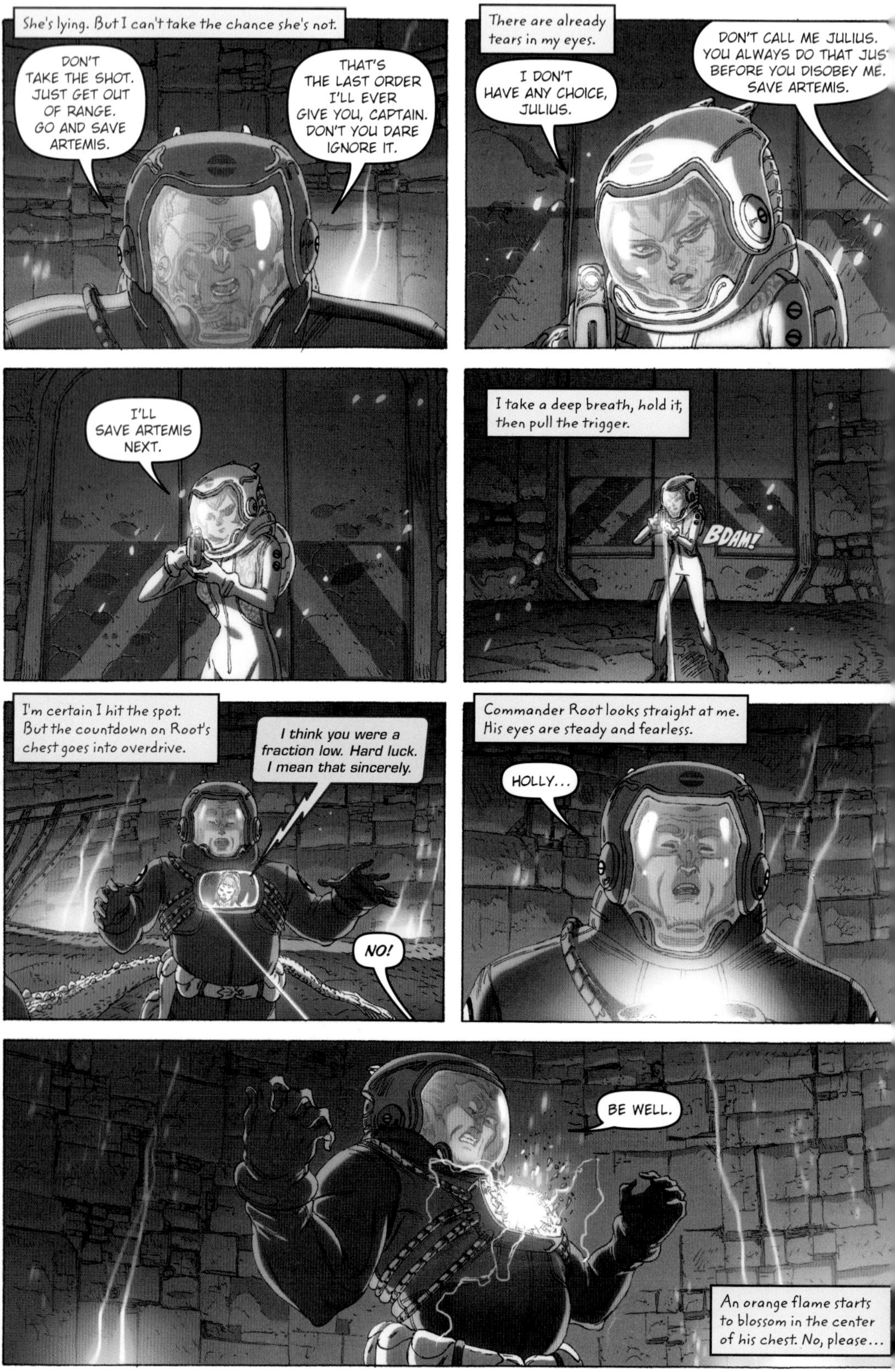
She's lying. But I can't take the chance she's not.
DON'T TAKE THE SHOT. JUST GET OUT OF RANGE. GO AND SAVE ARTEMIS.
THAT'S THE LAST ORDER I'LL EVER GIVE YOU, CAPTAIN. DON'T YOU DARE IGNORE IT.
There are already tears in my eyes.
I DON'T HAVE ANY CHOICE, JULIUS.
DON'T CALL ME JULIUS. YOU ALWAYS DO THAT JUST BEFORE YOU DISOBEY ME. SAVE ARTEMIS.
I'LL SAVE ARTEMIS NEXT.
I take a deep breath, hold it, then pull the trigger.
BDAM!
I'm certain I hit the spot. But the countdown on Root's chest goes into overdrive.
I think you were a fraction low. Hard luck. I mean that sincerely.
NO!
Commander Root looks straight at me. His eyes are steady and fearless.
HOLLY...
BE WELL.
An orange flame starts to blossom in the center of his chest. No, please...

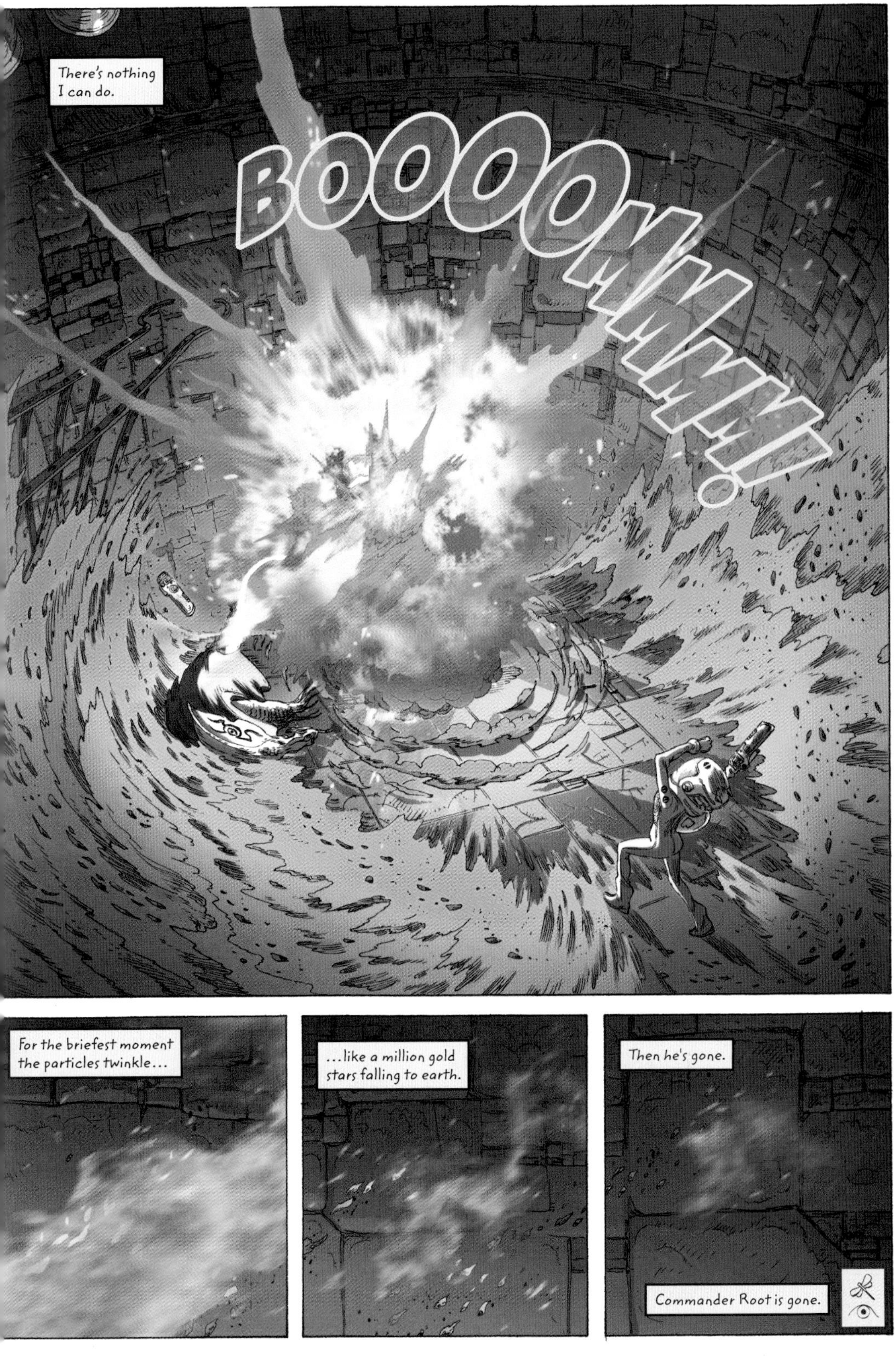
There's nothing I can do.
BOOOOMMMM!
For the briefest moment the particles twinkle...
...like a million gold stars falling to earth.
Then he's gone.
Commander Root is gone.

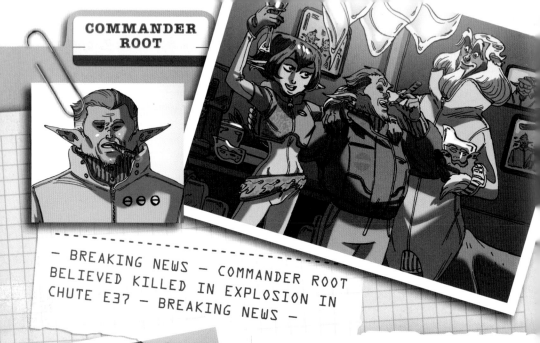

COMMANDER ROOT

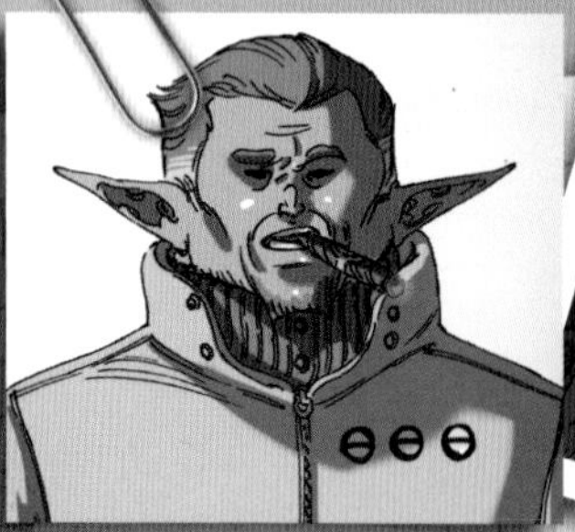

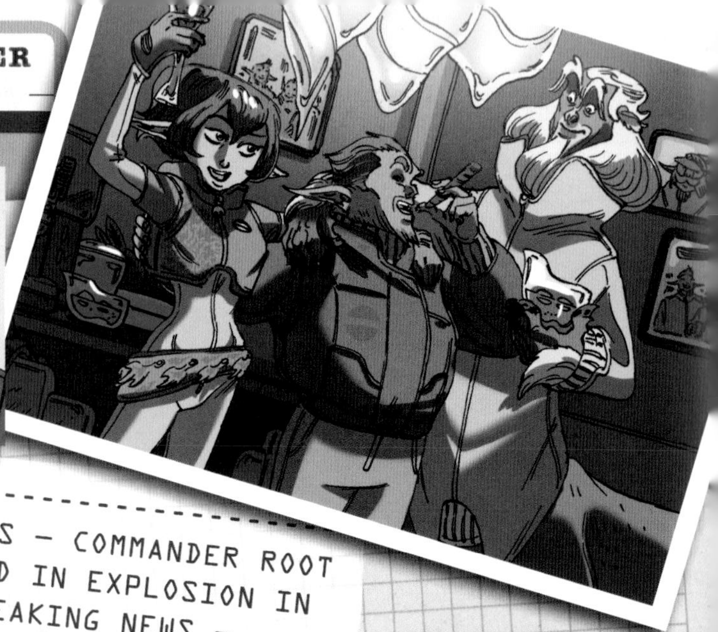

– BREAKING NEWS – COMMANDER ROOT BELIEVED KILLED IN EXPLOSION IN CHUTE E37 – BREAKING NEWS –

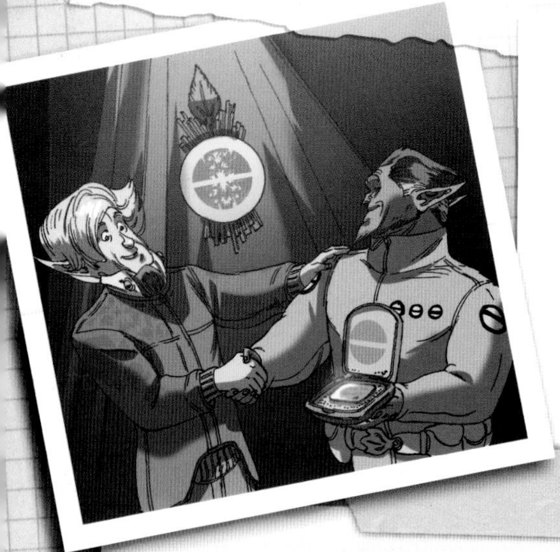

—MEMO—

FROM: EDITOR IN CHIEF
TO: NEWSROOM STAFF

If this terrible news is true then we're going to need wall-to-wall coverage of this tragic (and potentially ratings-increasing) event.

TO-DO LIST

1. *Get a camera crew over to chute E37 and another to Police Plaza.*
2. *Pull all archive files on Commander Root and his decades in charge of the LEP recon unit.*
3. *Find out who sold him those noxious fungus cigars and interview them—adds character.*
4. *Avoid all mention of his brother, Turnball Root. Best not to drag that low-life criminal into this story. Keep it heroic.*
5. *Why are you still reading this? Get out there and get me this story!*
6. *Err . . . And find out how he died!?*

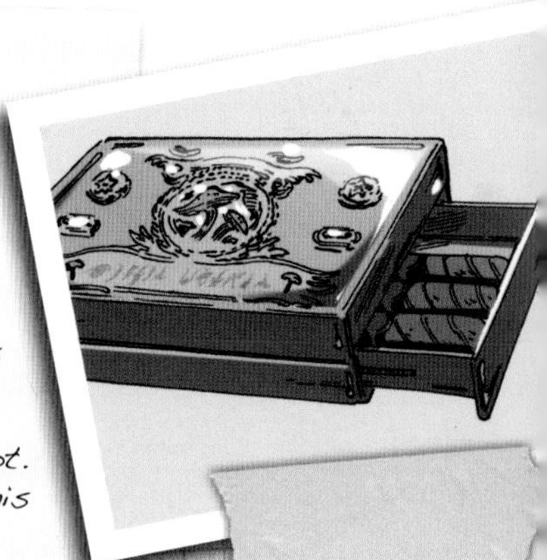

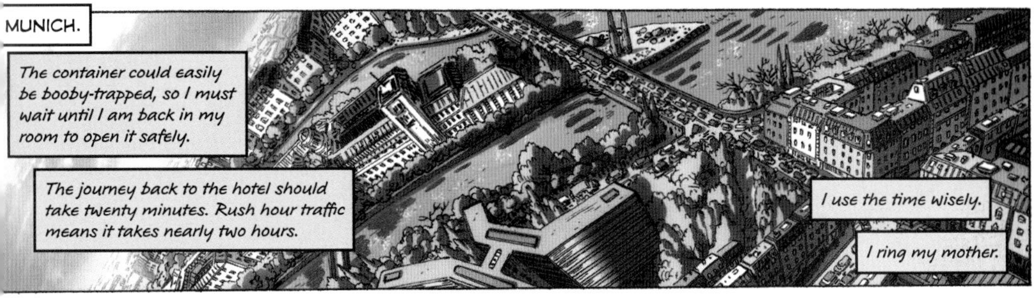
MUNICH.
The container could easily be booby-trapped, so I must wait until I am back in my room to open it safely.
The journey back to the hotel should take twenty minutes. Rush hour traffic means it takes nearly two hours.
I use the time wisely.
I ring my mother.

CHAPTER 4: NARROW ESCAPES

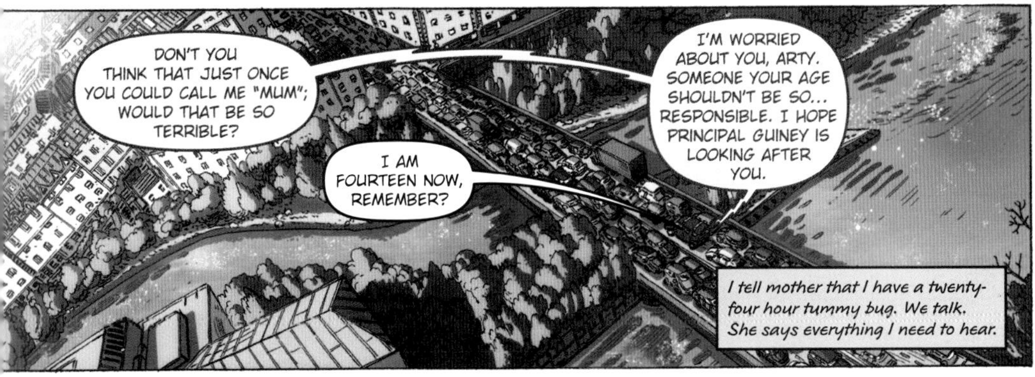
DON'T YOU THINK THAT JUST ONCE YOU COULD CALL ME "MUM"; WOULD THAT BE SO TERRIBLE?
I AM FOURTEEN NOW, REMEMBER?
I'M WORRIED ABOUT YOU, ARTY. SOMEONE YOUR AGE SHOULDN'T BE SO... RESPONSIBLE. I HOPE PRINCIPAL GUINEY IS LOOKING AFTER YOU.
I tell mother that I have a twenty-four hour tummy bug. We talk. She says everything I need to hear.

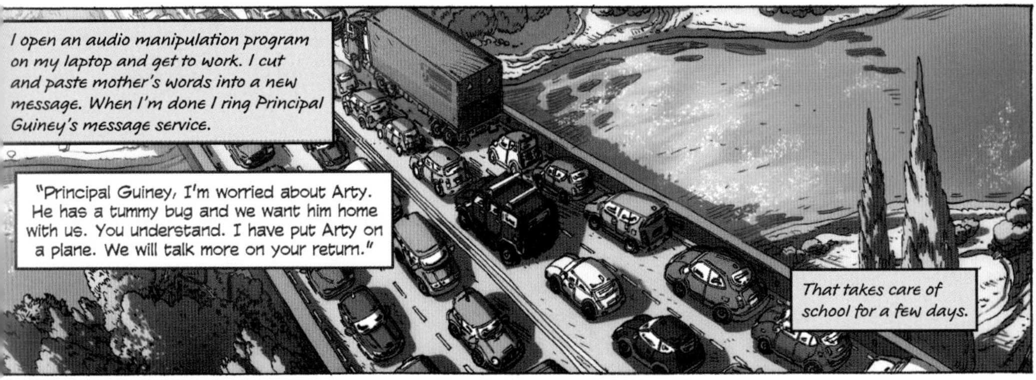
I open an audio manipulation program on my laptop and get to work. I cut and paste mother's words into a new message. When I'm done I ring Principal Guiney's message service.
"Principal Guiney, I'm worried about Arty. He has a tummy bug and we want him home with us. You understand. I have put Arty on a plane. We will talk more on your return."
That takes care of school for a few days.

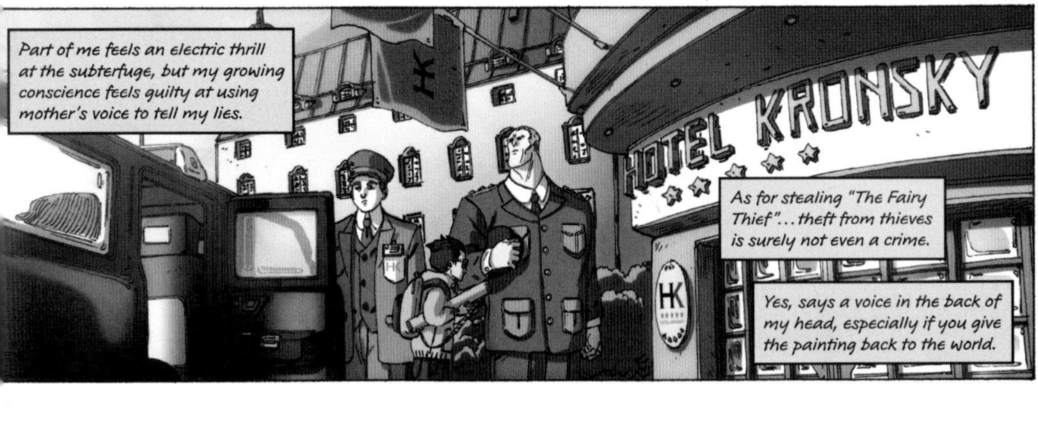
Part of me feels an electric thrill at the subterfuge, but my growing conscience feels guilty at using mother's voice to tell my lies.
HOTEL KRONSKY
As for stealing "The Fairy Thief"... theft from thieves is surely not even a crime.
Yes, says a voice in the back of my head, especially if you give the painting back to the world.

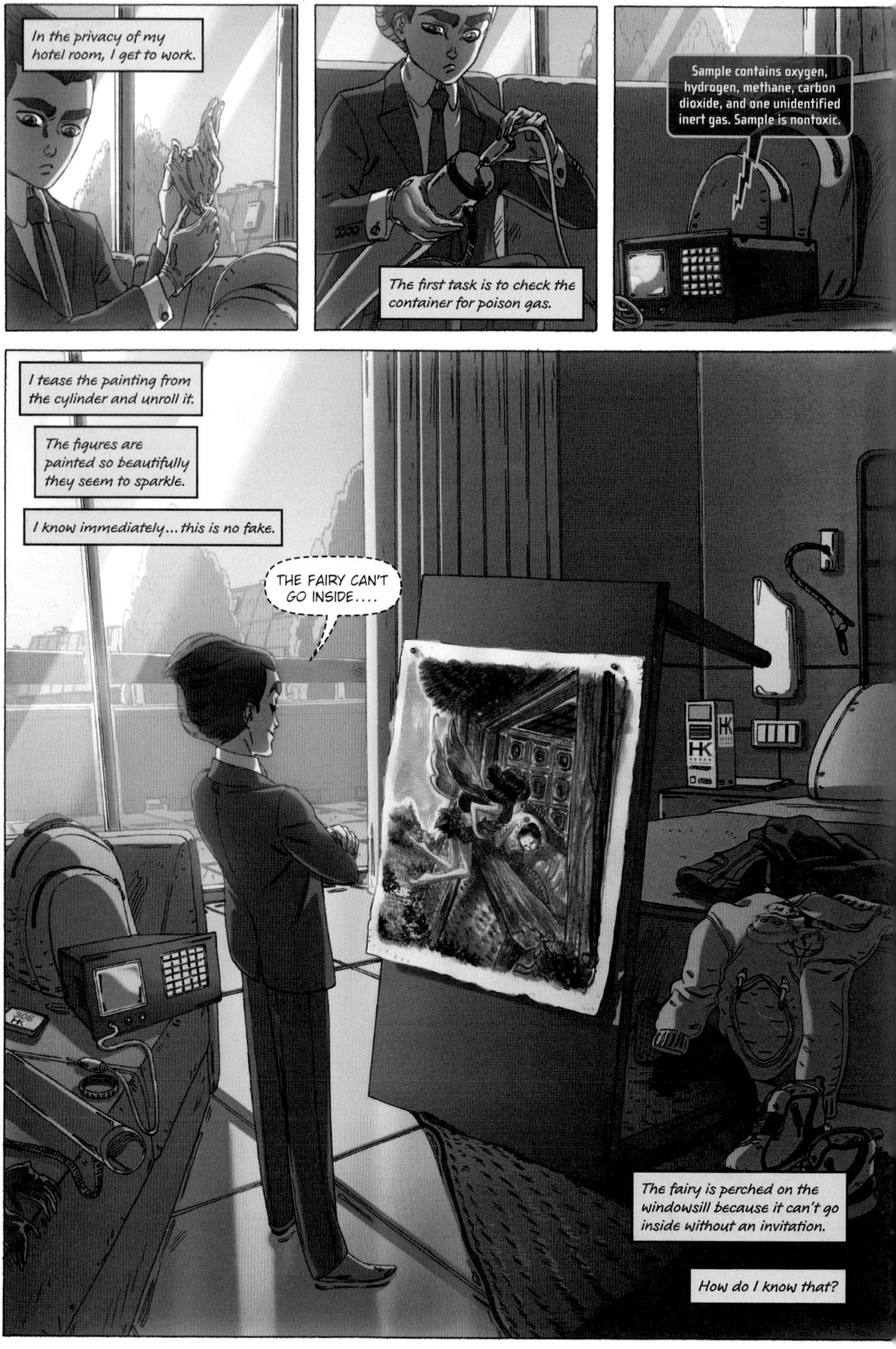
In the privacy of my hotel room, I get to work.
The first task is to check the container for poison gas.
Sample contains oxygen, hydrogen, methane, carbon dioxide, and one unidentified inert gas. Sample is nontoxic.
I tease the painting from the cylinder and unroll it.
The figures are painted so beautifully they seem to sparkle.
I know immediately... this is no fake.
THE FAIRY CAN'T GO INSIDE....
The fairy is perched on the windowsill because it can't go inside without an invitation.
How do I know that?

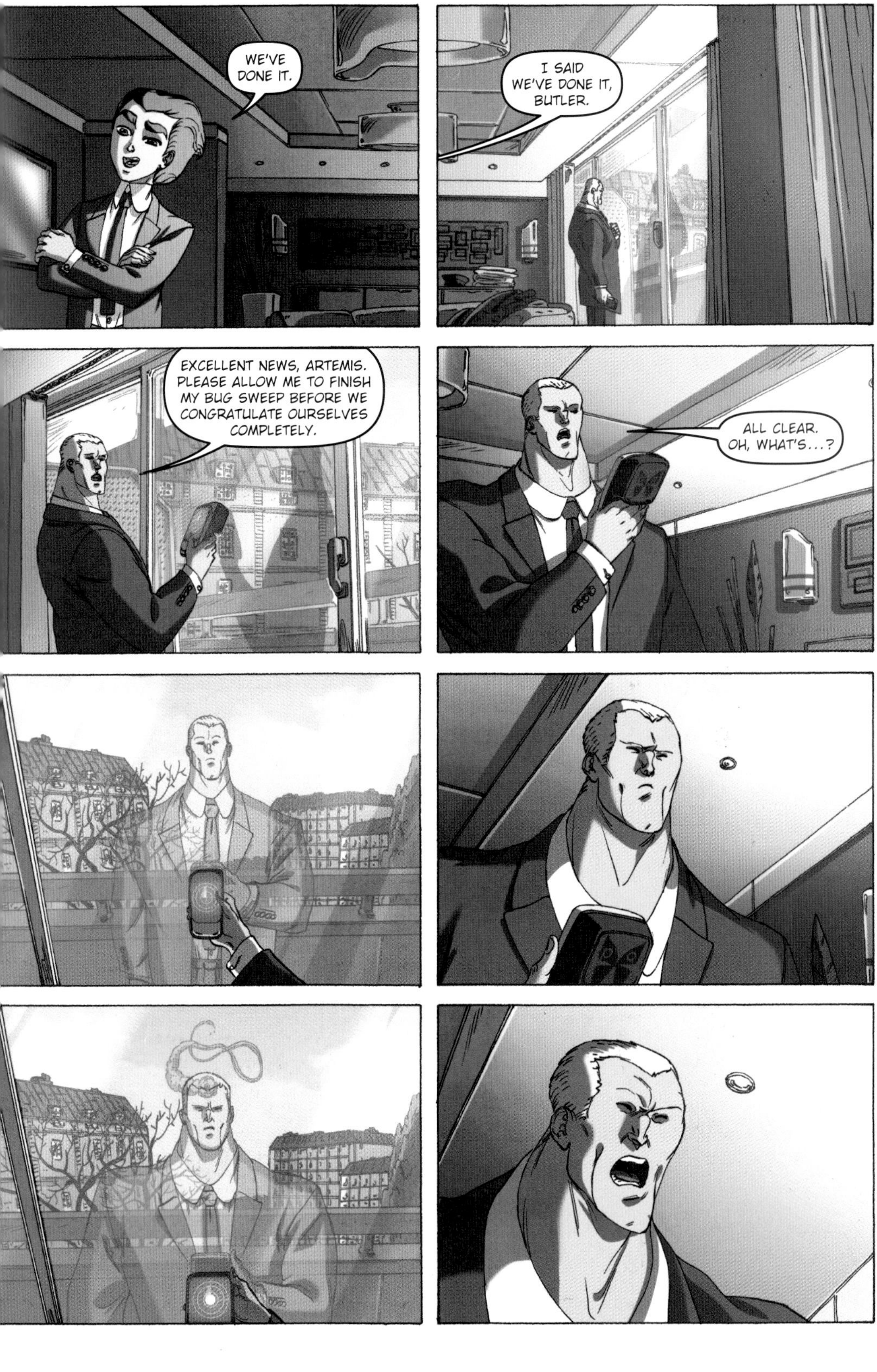
WE'VE DONE IT.
I SAID WE'VE DONE IT, BUTLER.
EXCELLENT NEWS, ARTEMIS. PLEASE ALLOW ME TO FINISH MY BUG SWEEP BEFORE WE CONGRATULATE OURSELVES COMPLETELY.
ALL CLEAR. OH, WHAT'S...?

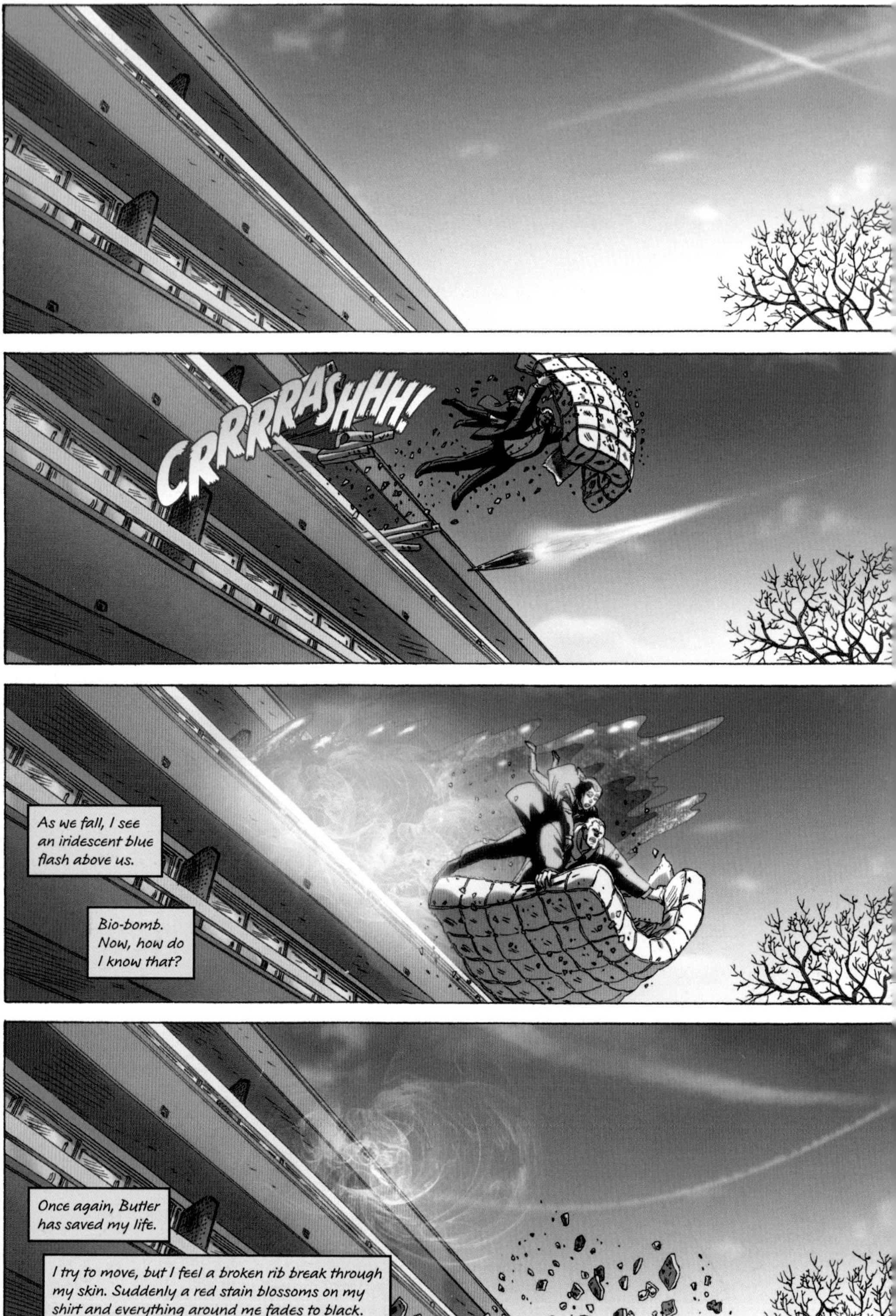
CRRRRASHHH!
As we fall, I see an iridescent blue flash above us.
Bio-bomb. Now, how do I know that?
Once again, Butler has saved my life.
I try to move, but I feel a broken rib break through my skin. Suddenly a red stain blossoms on my shirt and everything around me fades to black.

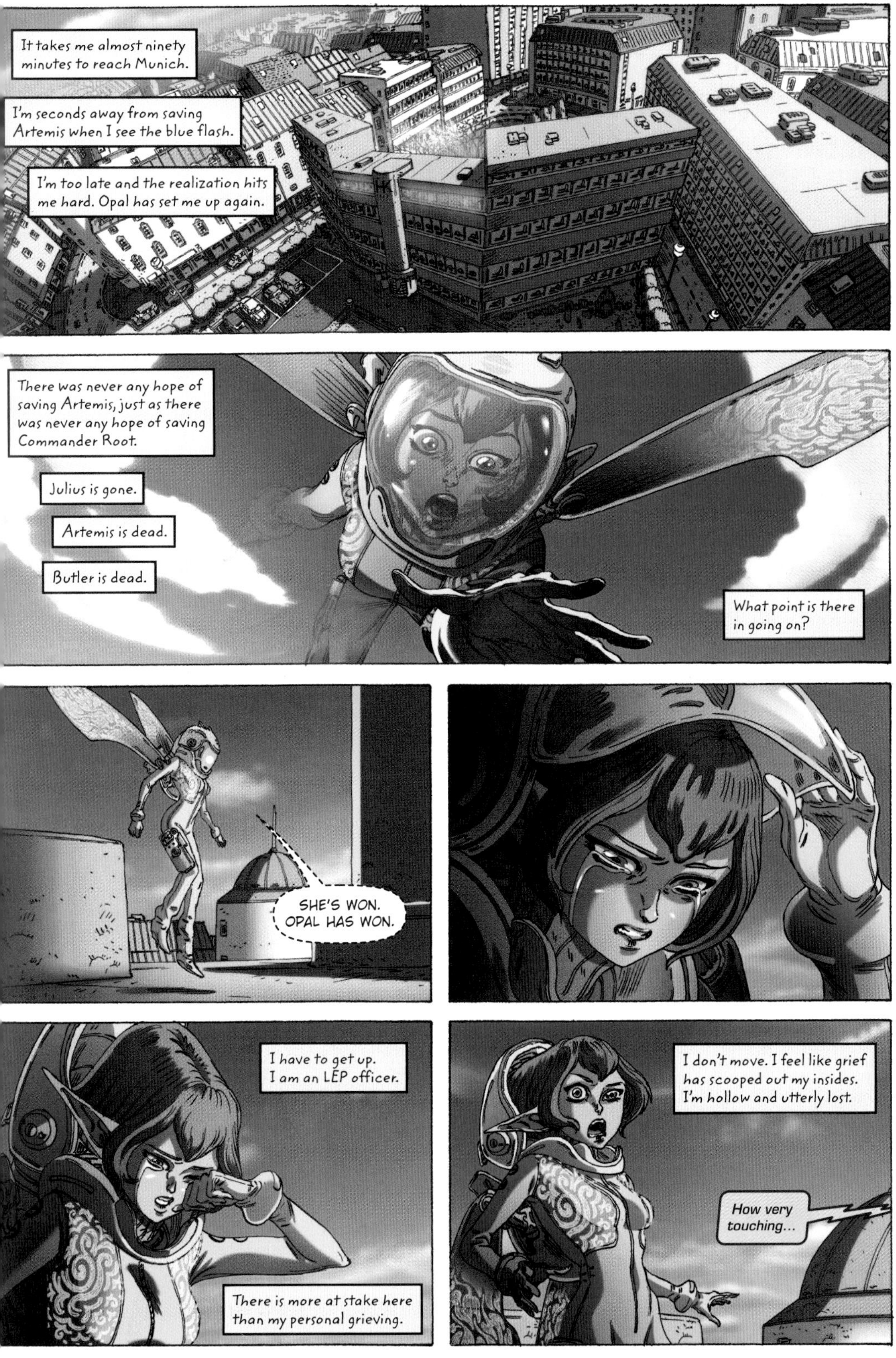
It takes me almost ninety minutes to reach Munich.
I'm seconds away from saving Artemis when I see the blue flash.
I'm too late and the realization hits me hard. Opal has set me up again.
There was never any hope of saving Artemis, just as there was never any hope of saving Commander Root.
Julius is gone.
Artemis is dead.
Butler is dead.
What point is there in going on?
SHE'S WON. OPAL HAS WON.
I have to get up. I am an LEP officer.
There is more at stake here than my personal grieving.
I don't move. I feel like grief has scooped out my insides. I'm hollow and utterly lost.
How very touching...

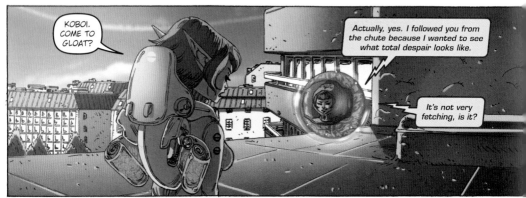

KOBOI. COME TO GLOAT?

Actually, yes. I followed you from the chute because I wanted to see what total despair looks like.

It's not very fetching, is it?

DETONATE AND GET IT OVER WITH.

Oh, I will. But it's what happens after that's important.

DON'T TELL ME, KOBOI: WORLD DOMINATION.

World domination? You make it sound so unattainable. The first step is simplicity itself. All I have to do is put humans in contact with the People.

The LEP studied me like an animal in a cage. Now let's see how they like it.

ALL THIS FOR A CHILDISH PIXIE'S REVENGE?

Oh I'm not a pixie anymore. Look...no pointy ears. I intend to be on the winning side once that probe goes down.

WHAT PROBE?

Enough explaining. You cost me a year of my life, Short. A year.

On the screen I see the hatred in Opal's eyes. Then she holds up a small remote and presses the button.

I have seconds before the bio-bomb explodes.

The killing agent in a bio-bomb is solinium, and LEP helmets are supposed to be able to deflect solinium flares.

Let's see if they can.

I hook my helmet over the bomb and point it away from me.

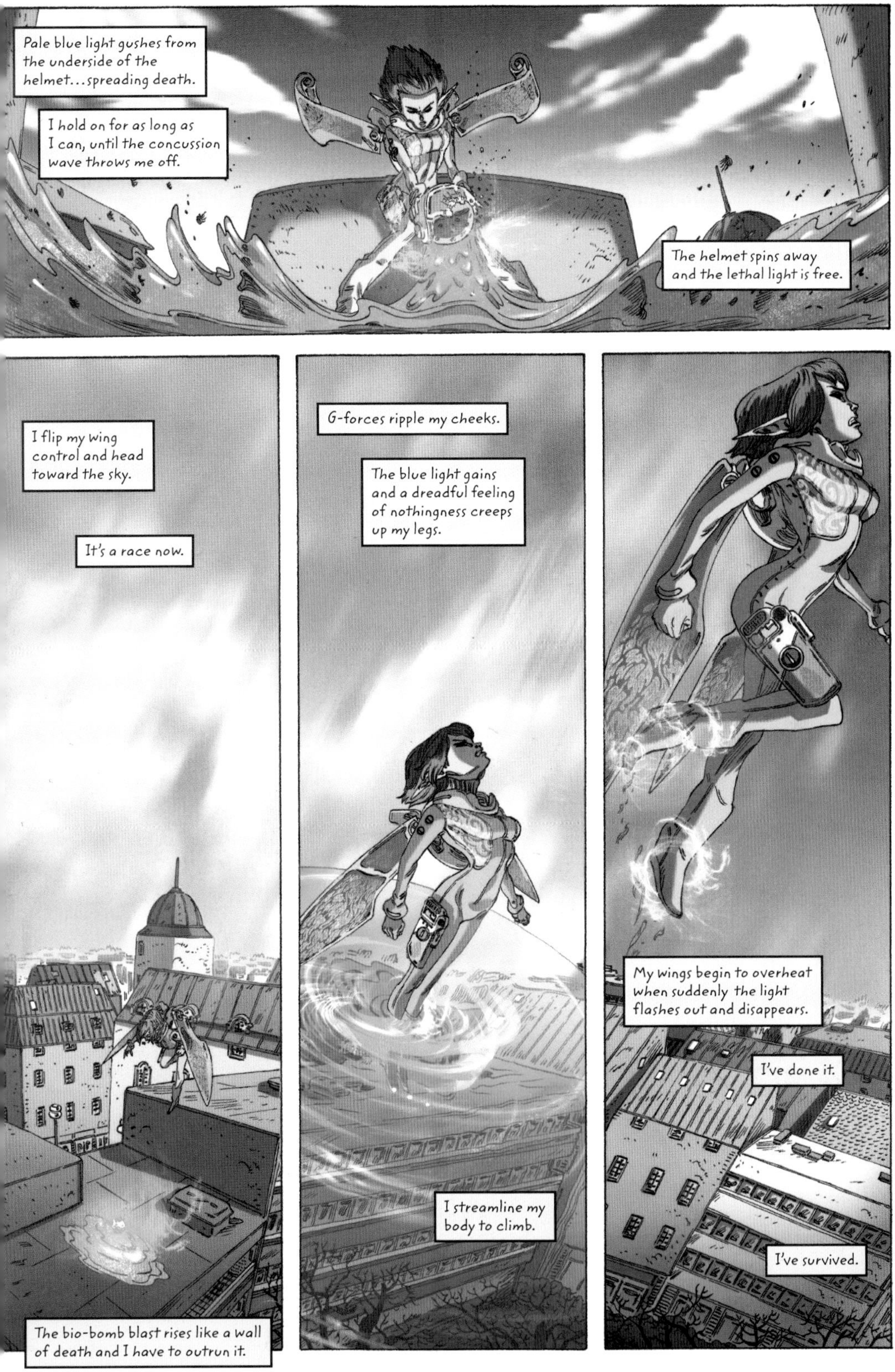
Pale blue light gushes from the underside of the helmet...spreading death.
I hold on for as long as I can, until the concussion wave throws me off.
The helmet spins away and the lethal light is free.
I flip my wing control and head toward the sky.
It's a race now.
The bio-bomb blast rises like a wall of death and I have to outrun it.
G-forces ripple my cheeks.
The blue light gains and a dreadful feeling of nothingness creeps up my legs.
I streamline my body to climb.
My wings begin to overheat when suddenly the light flashes out and disappears.
I've done it.
I've survived.

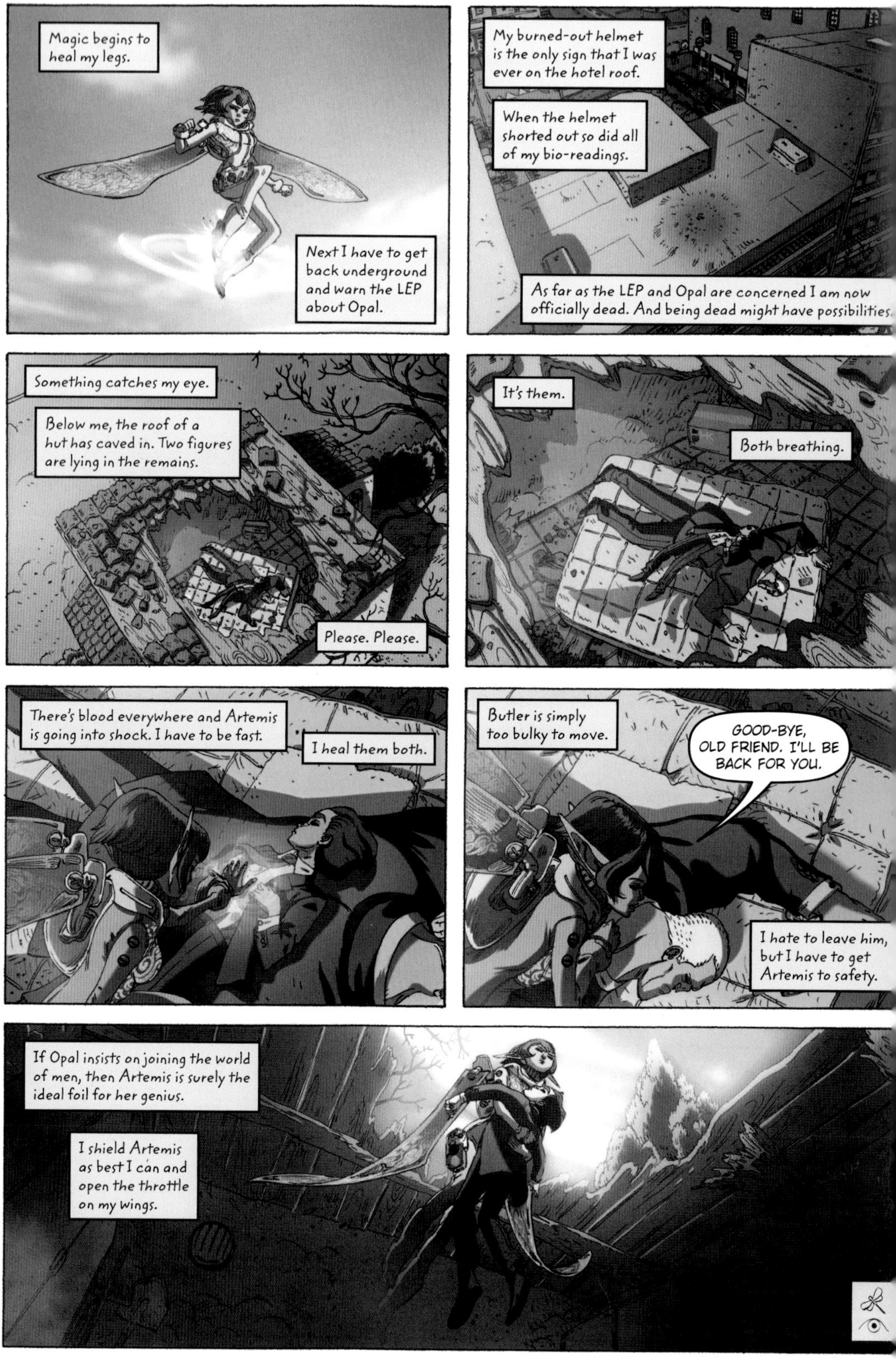

Magic begins to heal my legs.
Next I have to get back underground and warn the LEP about Opal.
My burned-out helmet is the only sign that I was ever on the hotel roof.
When the helmet shorted out so did all of my bio-readings.
As far as the LEP and Opal are concerned I am now officially dead. And being dead might have possibilities.
Something catches my eye.
Below me, the roof of a hut has caved in. Two figures are lying in the remains.
Please. Please.
It's them.
Both breathing.
There's blood everywhere and Artemis is going into shock. I have to be fast.
I heal them both.
Butler is simply too bulky to move.
GOOD-BYE, OLD FRIEND. I'LL BE BACK FOR YOU.
I hate to leave him, but I have to get Artemis to safety.
If Opal insists on joining the world of men, then Artemis is surely the ideal foil for her genius.
I shield Artemis as best I can and open the throttle on my wings.

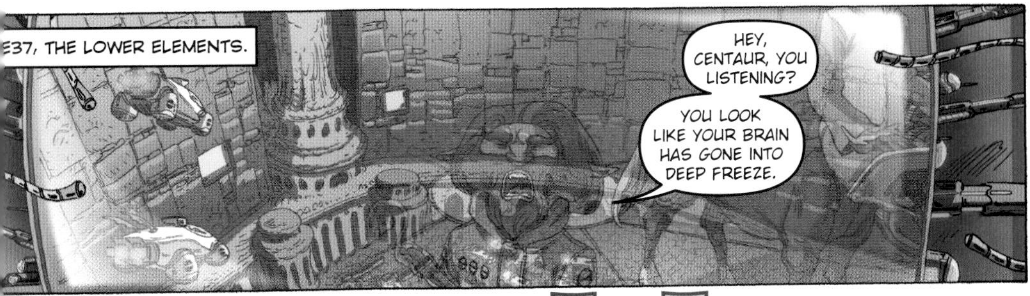
E37, THE LOWER ELEMENTS.
HEY, CENTAUR, YOU LISTENING?
YOU LOOK LIKE YOUR BRAIN HAS GONE INTO DEEP FREEZE.

CHAPTER 5: MEET THE NEIGHBORS

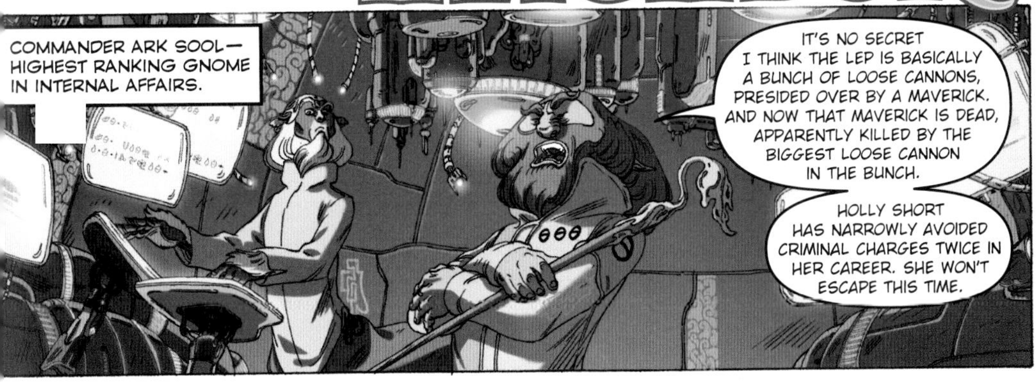
COMMANDER ARK SOOL— HIGHEST RANKING GNOME IN INTERNAL AFFAIRS.
IT'S NO SECRET I THINK THE LEP IS BASICALLY A BUNCH OF LOOSE CANNONS, PRESIDED OVER BY A MAVERICK. AND NOW THAT MAVERICK IS DEAD, APPARENTLY KILLED BY THE BIGGEST LOOSE CANNON IN THE BUNCH.
HOLLY SHORT HAS NARROWLY AVOIDED CRIMINAL CHARGES TWICE IN HER CAREER. SHE WON'T ESCAPE THIS TIME.

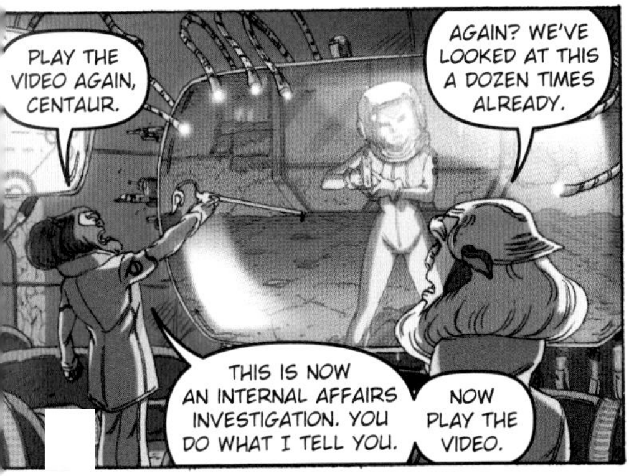
PLAY THE VIDEO AGAIN, CENTAUR.
AGAIN? WE'VE LOOKED AT THIS A DOZEN TIMES ALREADY.
THIS IS NOW AN INTERNAL AFFAIRS INVESTIGATION. YOU DO WHAT I TELL YOU.
NOW PLAY THE VIDEO.

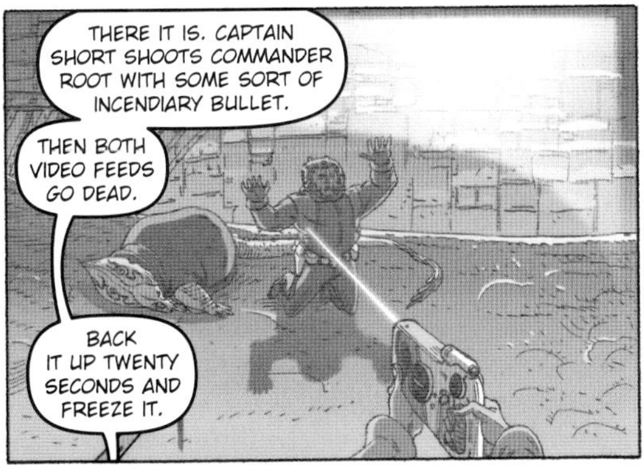
THERE IT IS. CAPTAIN SHORT SHOOTS COMMANDER ROOT WITH SOME SORT OF INCENDIARY BULLET.
THEN BOTH VIDEO FEEDS GO DEAD.
BACK IT UP TWENTY SECONDS AND FREEZE IT.

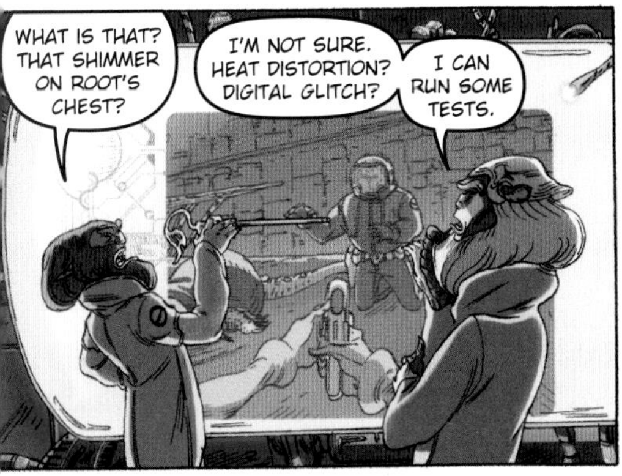
WHAT IS THAT? THAT SHIMMER ON ROOT'S CHEST?
I'M NOT SURE. HEAT DISTORTION? DIGITAL GLITCH?
I CAN RUN SOME TESTS.

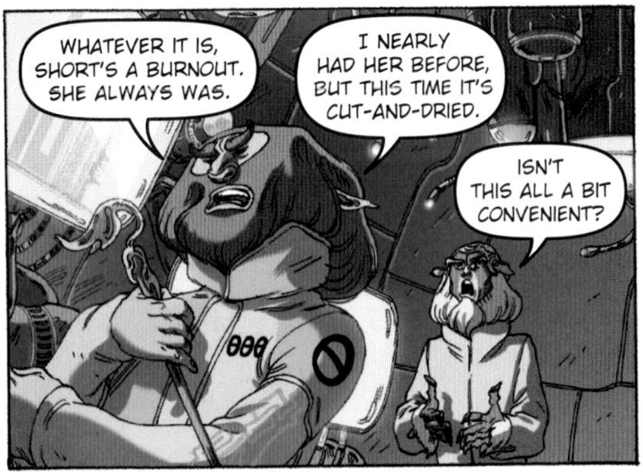
WHATEVER IT IS, SHORT'S A BURNOUT. SHE ALWAYS WAS.
I NEARLY HAD HER BEFORE, BUT THIS TIME IT'S CUT-AND-DRIED.
ISN'T THIS ALL A BIT CONVENIENT?

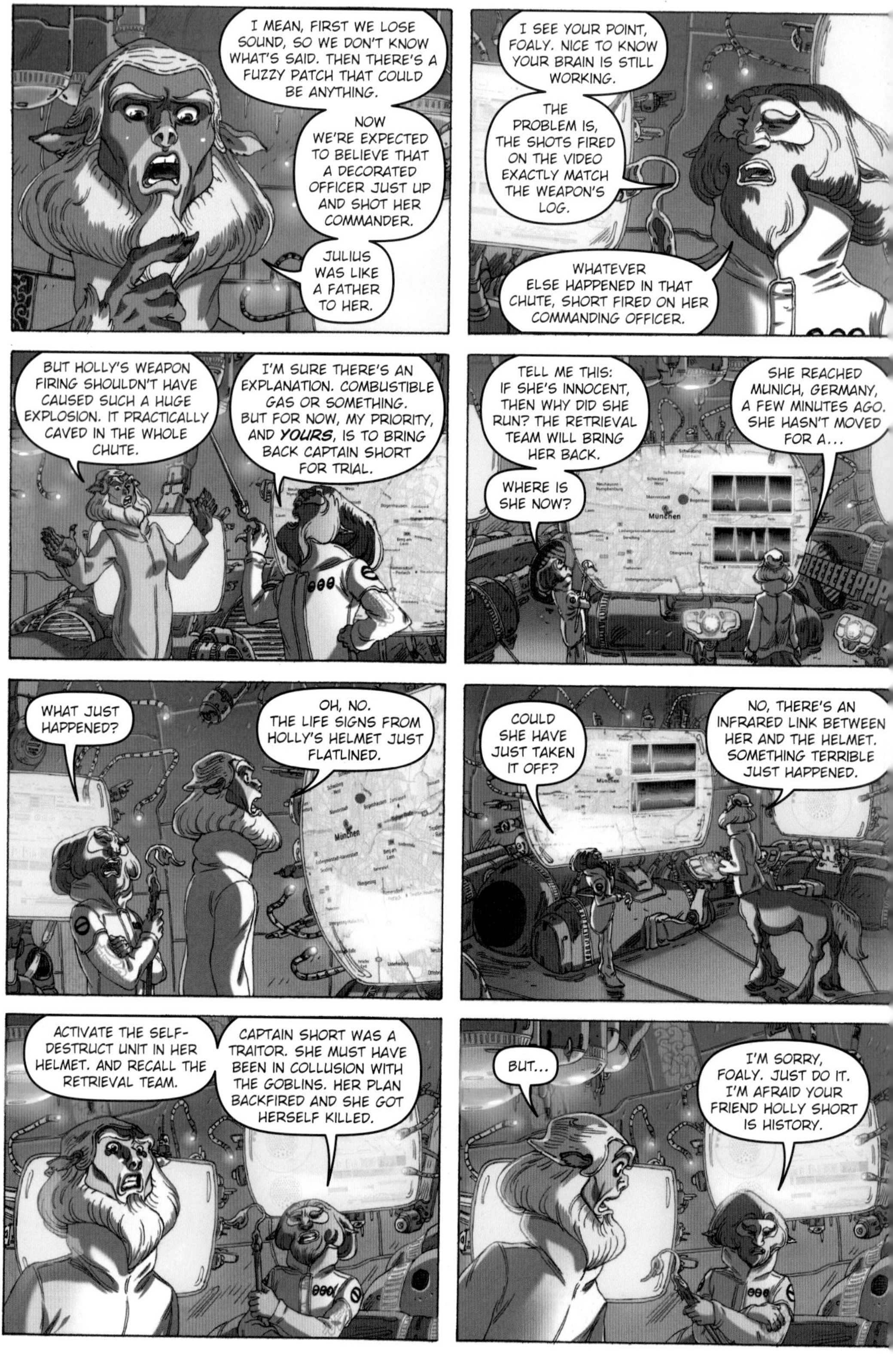
I MEAN, FIRST WE LOSE SOUND, SO WE DON'T KNOW WHAT'S SAID. THEN THERE'S A FUZZY PATCH THAT COULD BE ANYTHING.
NOW WE'RE EXPECTED TO BELIEVE THAT A DECORATED OFFICER JUST UP AND SHOT HER COMMANDER.
JULIUS WAS LIKE A FATHER TO HER.
I SEE YOUR POINT, FOALY. NICE TO KNOW YOUR BRAIN IS STILL WORKING.
THE PROBLEM IS, THE SHOTS FIRED ON THE VIDEO EXACTLY MATCH THE WEAPON'S LOG.
WHATEVER ELSE HAPPENED IN THAT CHUTE, SHORT FIRED ON HER COMMANDING OFFICER.
BUT HOLLY'S WEAPON FIRING SHOULDN'T HAVE CAUSED SUCH A HUGE EXPLOSION. IT PRACTICALLY CAVED IN THE WHOLE CHUTE.
I'M SURE THERE'S AN EXPLANATION. COMBUSTIBLE GAS OR SOMETHING. BUT FOR NOW, MY PRIORITY, AND ***YOURS***, IS TO BRING BACK CAPTAIN SHORT FOR TRIAL.
TELL ME THIS: IF SHE'S INNOCENT, THEN WHY DID SHE RUN? THE RETRIEVAL TEAM WILL BRING HER BACK.
WHERE IS SHE NOW?
SHE REACHED MUNICH, GERMANY, A FEW MINUTES AGO. SHE HASN'T MOVED FOR A...
BEEEEEEEPPP
WHAT JUST HAPPENED?
OH, NO. THE LIFE SIGNS FROM HOLLY'S HELMET JUST FLATLINED.
COULD SHE HAVE JUST TAKEN IT OFF?
NO, THERE'S AN INFRARED LINK BETWEEN HER AND THE HELMET. SOMETHING TERRIBLE JUST HAPPENED.
ACTIVATE THE SELF-DESTRUCT UNIT IN HER HELMET. AND RECALL THE RETRIEVAL TEAM.
CAPTAIN SHORT WAS A TRAITOR. SHE MUST HAVE BEEN IN COLLUSION WITH THE GOBLINS. HER PLAN BACKFIRED AND SHE GOT HERSELF KILLED.
BUT...
I'M SORRY, FOALY. JUST DO IT. I'M AFRAID YOUR FRIEND HOLLY SHORT IS HISTORY.

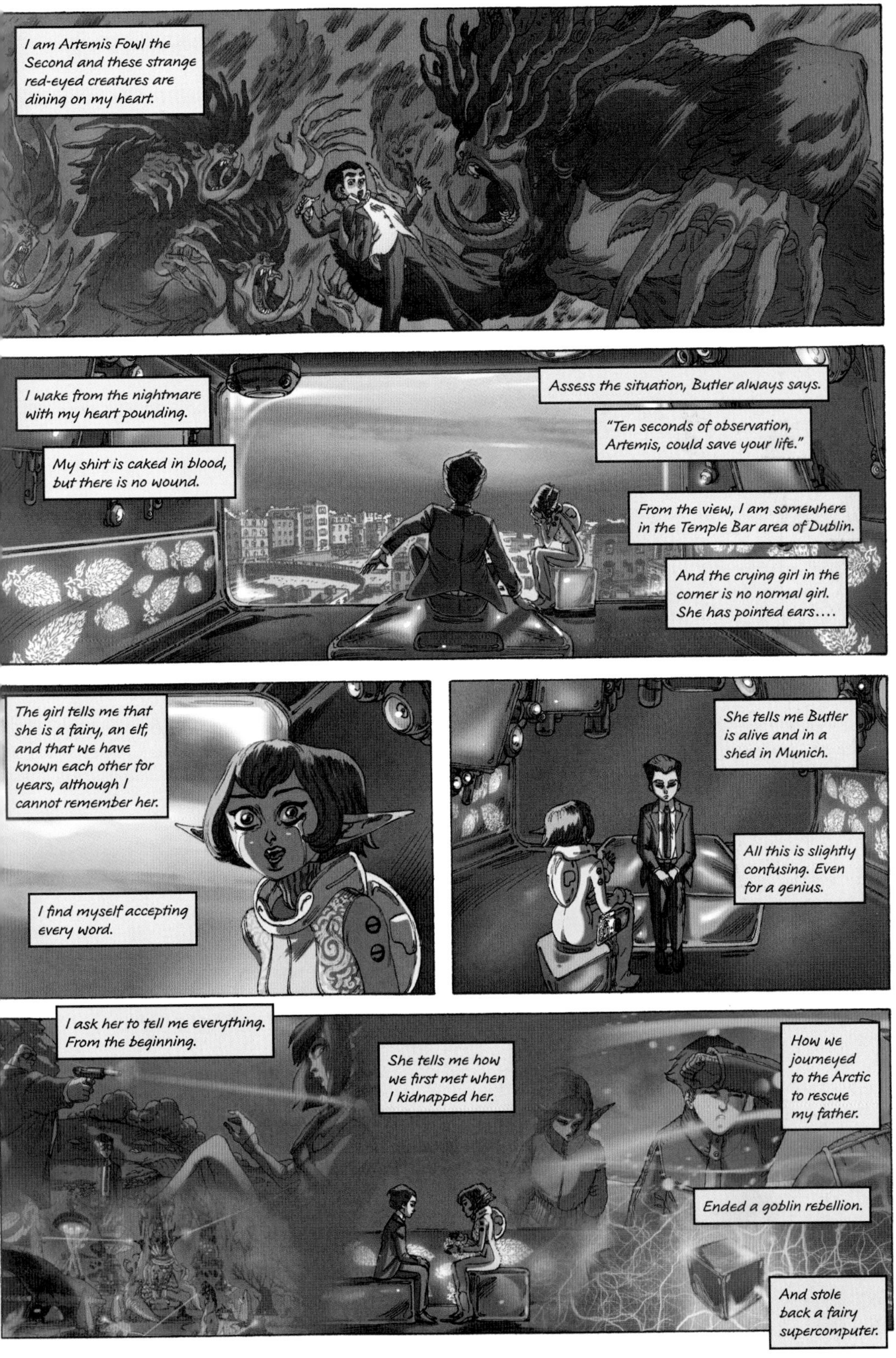
I am Artemis Fowl the Second and these strange red-eyed creatures are dining on my heart.
I wake from the nightmare with my heart pounding.
My shirt is caked in blood, but there is no wound.
Assess the situation, Butler always says.
"Ten seconds of observation, Artemis, could save your life."
From the view, I am somewhere in the Temple Bar area of Dublin.
And the crying girl in the corner is no normal girl. She has pointed ears....
The girl tells me that she is a fairy, an elf, and that we have known each other for years, although I cannot remember her.
I find myself accepting every word.
She tells me Butler is alive and in a shed in Munich.
All this is slightly confusing. Even for a genius.
I ask her to tell me everything. From the beginning.
She tells me how we first met when I kidnapped her.
How we journeyed to the Arctic to rescue my father.
Ended a goblin rebellion.
And stole back a fairy supercomputer.

VERY WELL. I DON'T REMEMBER ANY OF THIS, BUT I DO BELIEVE YOU. I ACCEPT THAT WE HUMANS HAVE FAIRY NEIGHBORS BELOW THE PLANET'S SURFACE.

JUST LIKE THAT?

HARDLY. BUT I HAVE TAKEN YOUR STORY AND CROSS-REFERENCED IT WITH THE FACTS AS I KNOW THEM.

YOUR STORY FITS, RIGHT DOWN TO SOMETHING THAT YOU COULD NOT POSSIBLY KNOW ABOUT, CAPTAIN SHORT.

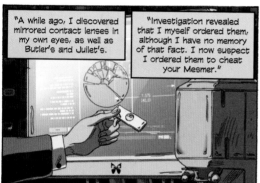

"A while ago, I discovered mirrored contact lenses in my own eyes, as well as Butler's and Juliet's.

"Investigation revealed that I myself ordered them, although I have no memory of that fact. I now suspect I ordered them to cheat your Mesmer."

I MUST HAVE PLANTED A TRIGGER SOMEWHERE. SOMETHING THAT WOULD MAKE ME REMEMBER. BUT WHAT?

I HAVE NO IDEA. I WAS HOPING THAT JUST SEEING ME WOULD TRIGGER A RECALL.

THE ONLY WAY MY MEMORIES WILL BE RETURNED TO ME IS IF THE ONE PERSON I TRUST COMPLETELY AND UTTERLY PRESENTED ME WITH IRREFUTABLE EVIDENCE.

I feel myself growing annoyed. I am reminded that Artemis can get under my skin like nobody else.

AND WHO IS THIS ONE PERSON WHOM YOU COMPLETELY AND UTTERLY TRUST?

WHY, MYSELF, OF COURSE.

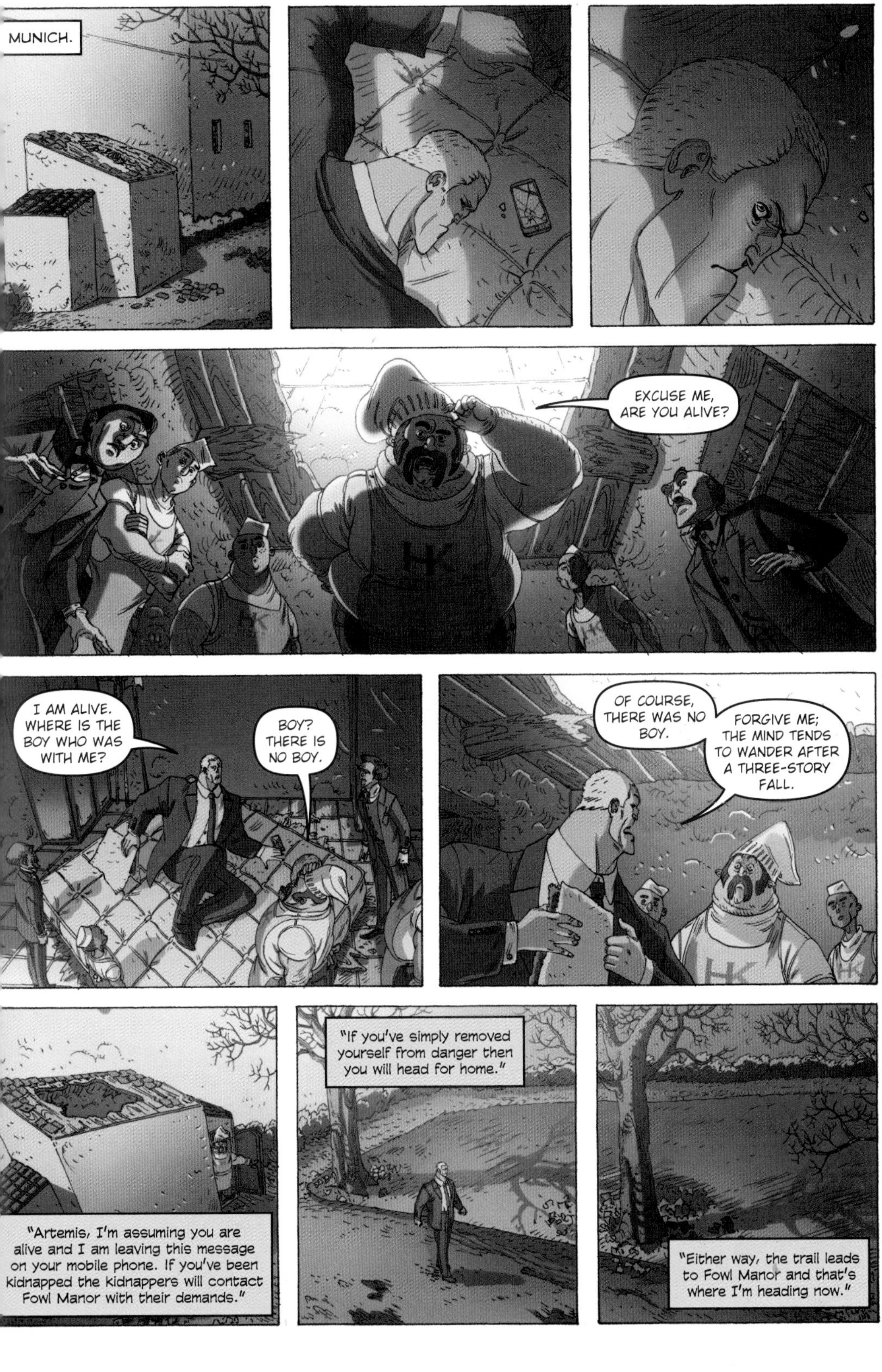
MUNICH.
EXCUSE ME, ARE YOU ALIVE?
I AM ALIVE. WHERE IS THE BOY WHO WAS WITH ME?
BOY? THERE IS NO BOY.
OF COURSE, THERE WAS NO BOY.
FORGIVE ME; THE MIND TENDS TO WANDER AFTER A THREE-STORY FALL.
"Artemis, I'm assuming you are alive and I am leaving this message on your mobile phone. If you've been kidnapped the kidnappers will contact Fowl Manor with their demands."
"If you've simply removed yourself from danger then you will head for home."
"Either way, the trail leads to Fowl Manor and that's where I'm heading now."

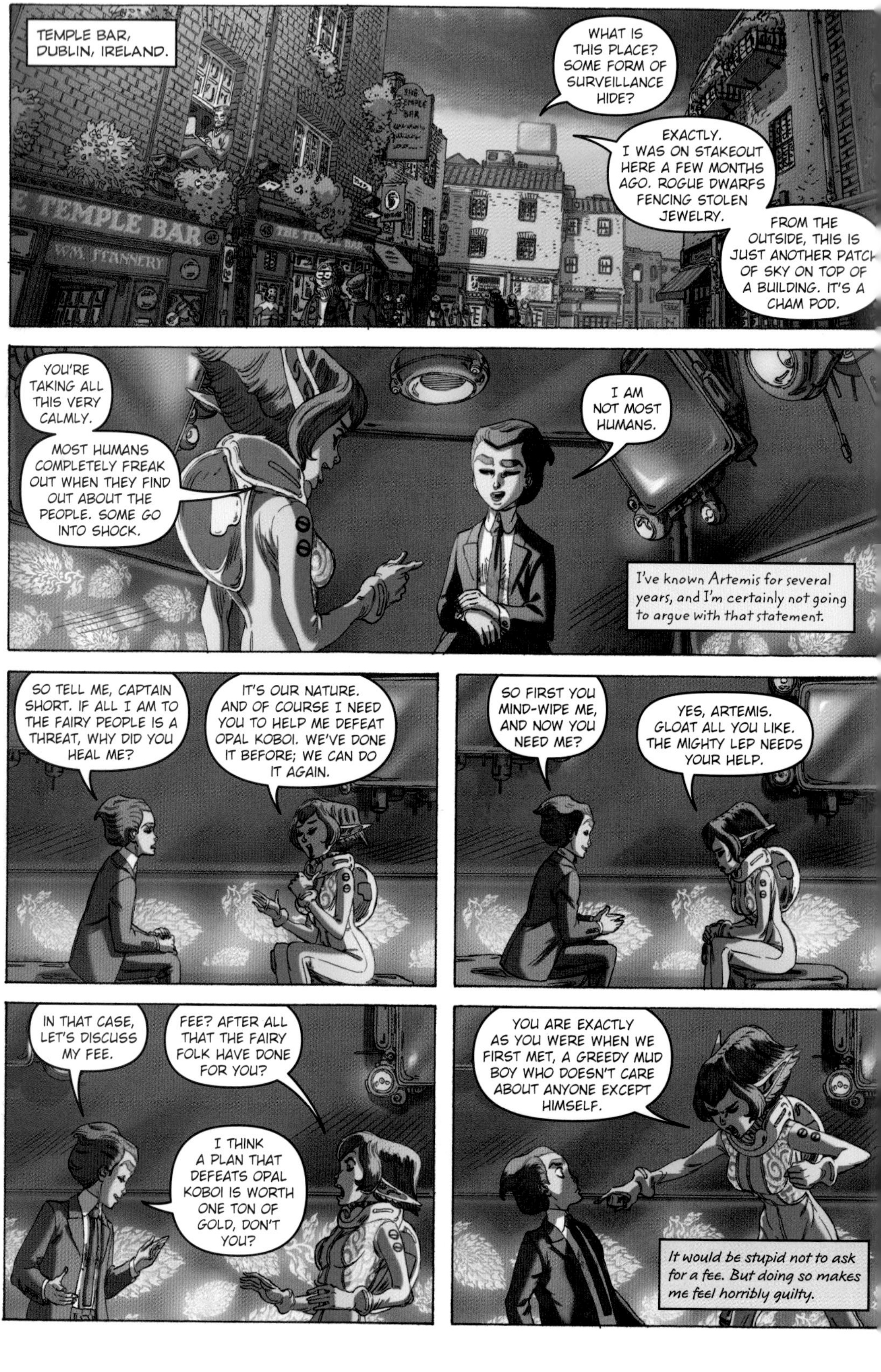
TEMPLE BAR, DUBLIN, IRELAND.
THE TEMPLE BAR
WHAT IS THIS PLACE? SOME FORM OF SURVEILLANCE HIDE?
EXACTLY. I WAS ON STAKEOUT HERE A FEW MONTHS AGO. ROGUE DWARFS FENCING STOLEN JEWELRY.
FROM THE OUTSIDE, THIS IS JUST ANOTHER PATCH OF SKY ON TOP OF A BUILDING. IT'S A CHAM POD.
YOU'RE TAKING ALL THIS VERY CALMLY.
MOST HUMANS COMPLETELY FREAK OUT WHEN THEY FIND OUT ABOUT THE PEOPLE. SOME GO INTO SHOCK.
I AM NOT MOST HUMANS.
I've known Artemis for several years, and I'm certainly not going to argue with that statement.
SO TELL ME, CAPTAIN SHORT. IF ALL I AM TO THE FAIRY PEOPLE IS A THREAT, WHY DID YOU HEAL ME?
IT'S OUR NATURE. AND OF COURSE I NEED YOU TO HELP ME DEFEAT OPAL KOBOI. WE'VE DONE IT BEFORE; WE CAN DO IT AGAIN.
SO FIRST YOU MIND-WIPE ME, AND NOW YOU NEED ME?
YES, ARTEMIS. GLOAT ALL YOU LIKE. THE MIGHTY LEP NEEDS YOUR HELP.
IN THAT CASE, LET'S DISCUSS MY FEE.
FEE? AFTER ALL THAT THE FAIRY FOLK HAVE DONE FOR YOU?
I THINK A PLAN THAT DEFEATS OPAL KOBOI IS WORTH ONE TON OF GOLD, DON'T YOU?
YOU ARE EXACTLY AS YOU WERE WHEN WE FIRST MET, A GREEDY MUD BOY WHO DOESN'T CARE ABOUT ANYONE EXCEPT HIMSELF.
It would be stupid not to ask for a fee. But doing so makes me feel horribly guilty.

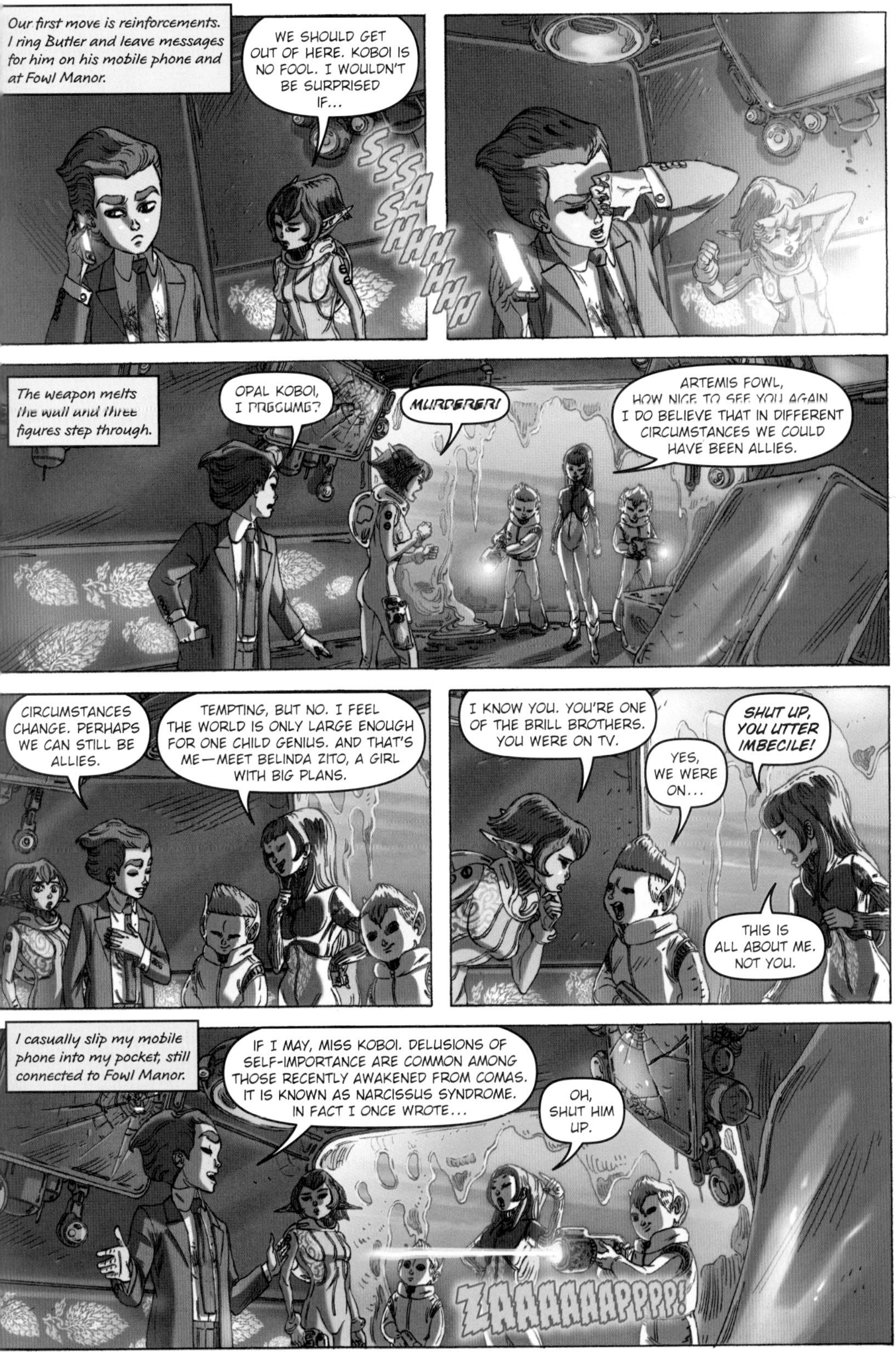

Our first move is reinforcements. I ring Butler and leave messages for him on his mobile phone and at Fowl Manor.
WE SHOULD GET OUT OF HERE. KOBOI IS NO FOOL. I WOULDN'T BE SURPRISED IF...
SSSSAAHHHHHHH
The weapon melts the wall and three figures step through.
OPAL KOBOI, I PRESUME?
MURDERER!
ARTEMIS FOWL, HOW NICE TO SEE YOU AGAIN. I DO BELIEVE THAT IN DIFFERENT CIRCUMSTANCES WE COULD HAVE BEEN ALLIES.
CIRCUMSTANCES CHANGE. PERHAPS WE CAN STILL BE ALLIES.
TEMPTING, BUT NO. I FEEL THE WORLD IS ONLY LARGE ENOUGH FOR ONE CHILD GENIUS. AND THAT'S ME—MEET BELINDA ZITO, A GIRL WITH BIG PLANS.
I KNOW YOU. YOU'RE ONE OF THE BRILL BROTHERS. YOU WERE ON TV.
YES, WE WERE ON...
SHUT UP, YOU UTTER IMBECILE!
THIS IS ALL ABOUT ME. NOT YOU.
I casually slip my mobile phone into my pocket, still connected to Fowl Manor.
IF I MAY, MISS KOBOI. DELUSIONS OF SELF-IMPORTANCE ARE COMMON AMONG THOSE RECENTLY AWAKENED FROM COMAS. IT IS KNOWN AS NARCISSUS SYNDROME. IN FACT I ONCE WROTE...
OH, SHUT HIM UP.
ZAAAAAAPPPP!

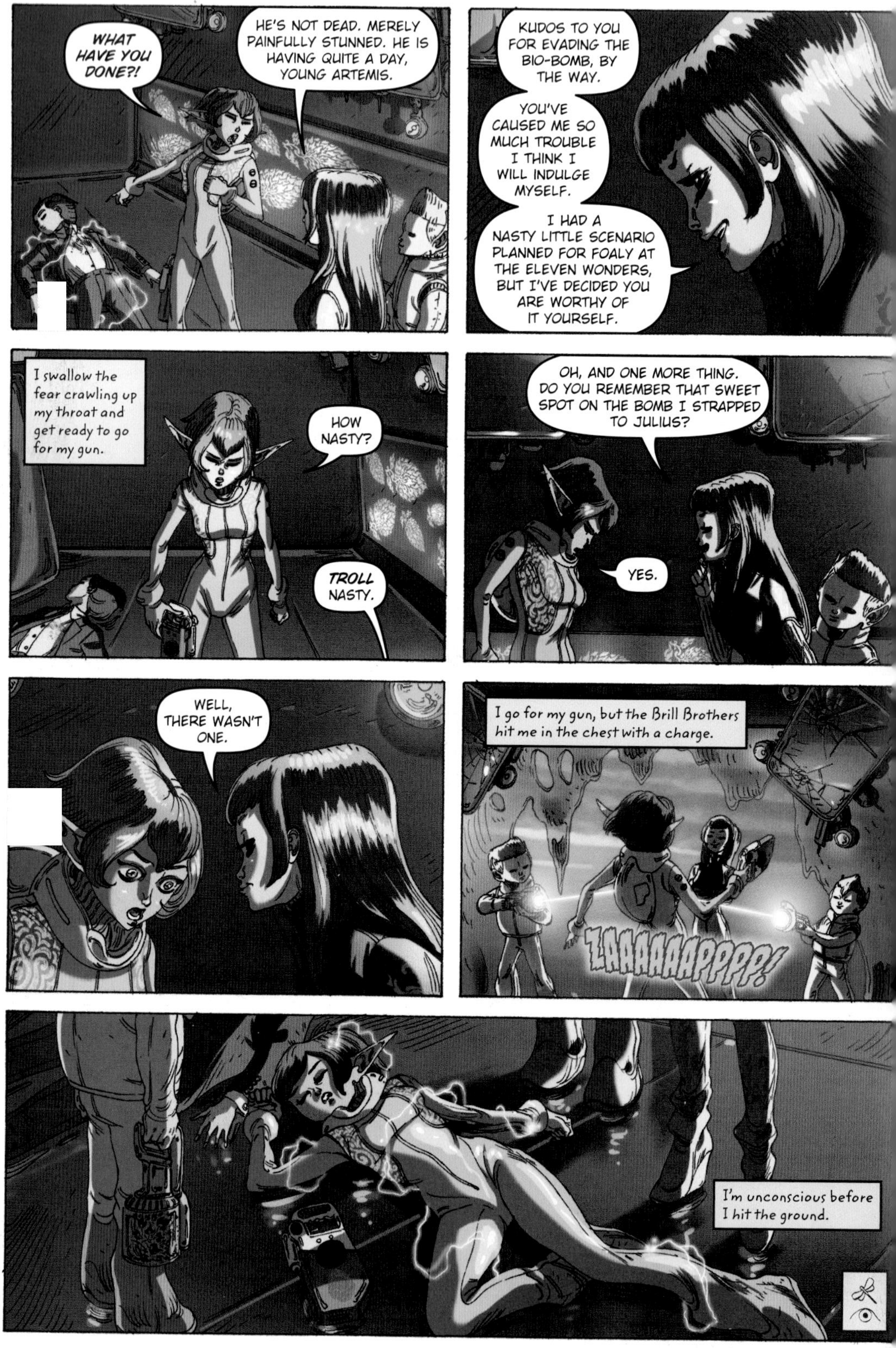
WHAT HAVE YOU DONE?!
HE'S NOT DEAD. MERELY PAINFULLY STUNNED. HE IS HAVING QUITE A DAY, YOUNG ARTEMIS.
KUDOS TO YOU FOR EVADING THE BIO-BOMB, BY THE WAY.
YOU'VE CAUSED ME SO MUCH TROUBLE I THINK I WILL INDULGE MYSELF.
I HAD A NASTY LITTLE SCENARIO PLANNED FOR FOALY AT THE ELEVEN WONDERS, BUT I'VE DECIDED YOU ARE WORTHY OF IT YOURSELF.
I swallow the fear crawling up my throat and get ready to go for my gun.
HOW NASTY?
TROLL NASTY.
OH, AND ONE MORE THING. DO YOU REMEMBER THAT SWEET SPOT ON THE BOMB I STRAPPED TO JULIUS?
YES.
WELL, THERE WASN'T ONE.
I go for my gun, but the Brill Brothers hit me in the chest with a charge.
ZAAAAAAPPPP!
I'm unconscious before I hit the ground.

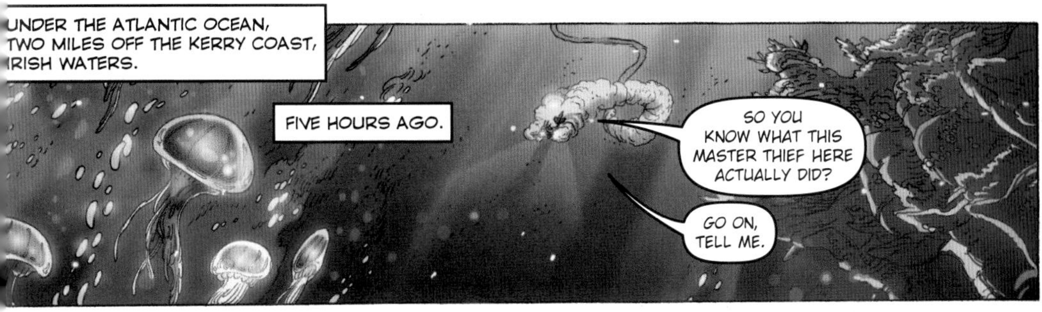
UNDER THE ATLANTIC OCEAN, TWO MILES OFF THE KERRY COAST, IRISH WATERS.
FIVE HOURS AGO.
SO YOU KNOW WHAT THIS MASTER THIEF HERE ACTUALLY DID?
GO ON, TELL ME.

CHAPTER 6: TROLL NASTY

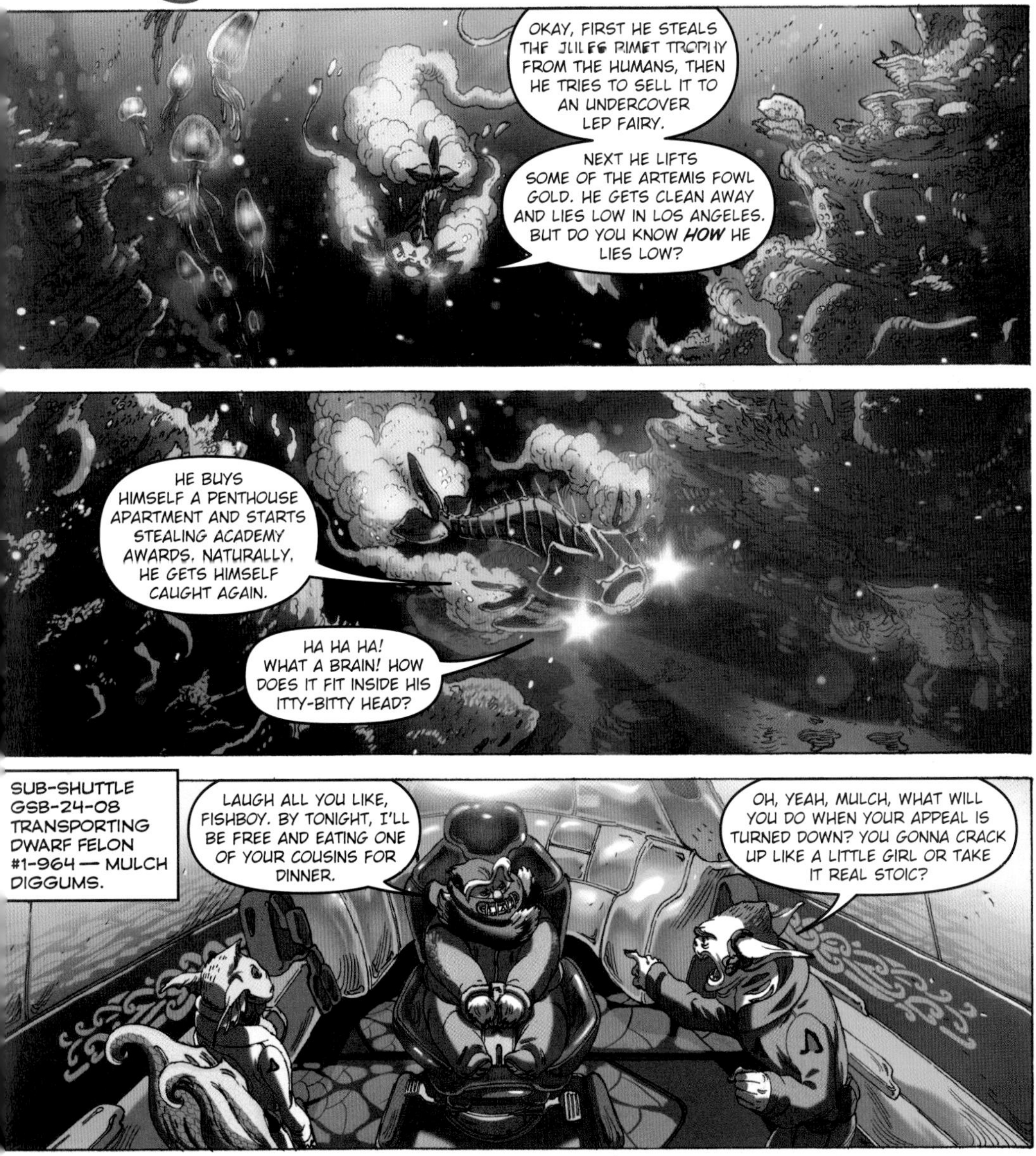
OKAY, FIRST HE STEALS THE JULES RIMET TROPHY FROM THE HUMANS, THEN HE TRIES TO SELL IT TO AN UNDERCOVER LEP FAIRY.
NEXT HE LIFTS SOME OF THE ARTEMIS FOWL GOLD. HE GETS CLEAN AWAY AND LIES LOW IN LOS ANGELES. BUT DO YOU KNOW *HOW* HE LIES LOW?
HE BUYS HIMSELF A PENTHOUSE APARTMENT AND STARTS STEALING ACADEMY AWARDS. NATURALLY, HE GETS HIMSELF CAUGHT AGAIN.
HA HA HA! WHAT A BRAIN! HOW DOES IT FIT INSIDE HIS ITTY-BITTY HEAD?
SUB-SHUTTLE GSB-24-08 TRANSPORTING DWARF FELON #1-964 — MULCH DIGGUMS.
LAUGH ALL YOU LIKE, FISHBOY. BY TONIGHT, I'LL BE FREE AND EATING ONE OF YOUR COUSINS FOR DINNER.
OH, YEAH, MULCH, WHAT WILL YOU DO WHEN YOUR APPEAL IS TURNED DOWN? YOU GONNA CRACK UP LIKE A LITTLE GIRL OR TAKE IT REAL STOIC?

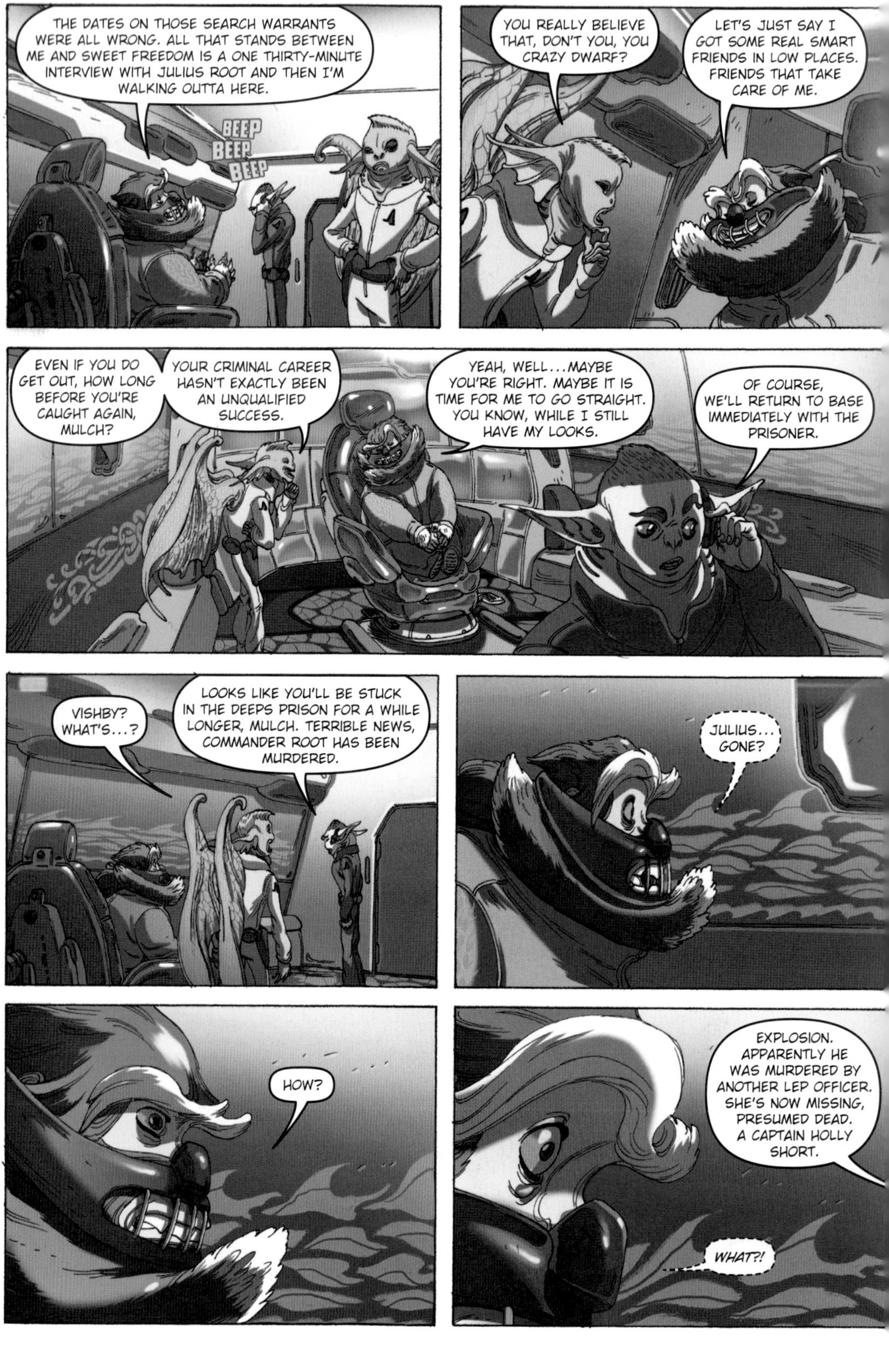

THE DATES ON THOSE SEARCH WARRANTS WERE ALL WRONG. ALL THAT STANDS BETWEEN ME AND SWEET FREEDOM IS A ONE THIRTY-MINUTE INTERVIEW WITH JULIUS ROOT AND THEN I'M WALKING OUTTA HERE.
BEEP
BEEP
BEEP
YOU REALLY BELIEVE THAT, DON'T YOU, YOU CRAZY DWARF?
LET'S JUST SAY I GOT SOME REAL SMART FRIENDS IN LOW PLACES. FRIENDS THAT TAKE CARE OF ME.
EVEN IF YOU DO GET OUT, HOW LONG BEFORE YOU'RE CAUGHT AGAIN, MULCH?
YOUR CRIMINAL CAREER HASN'T EXACTLY BEEN AN UNQUALIFIED SUCCESS.
YEAH, WELL...MAYBE YOU'RE RIGHT. MAYBE IT IS TIME FOR ME TO GO STRAIGHT. YOU KNOW, WHILE I STILL HAVE MY LOOKS.
OF COURSE, WE'LL RETURN TO BASE IMMEDIATELY WITH THE PRISONER.
VISHBY? WHAT'S...?
LOOKS LIKE YOU'LL BE STUCK IN THE DEEPS PRISON FOR A WHILE LONGER, MULCH. TERRIBLE NEWS, COMMANDER ROOT HAS BEEN MURDERED.
JULIUS... GONE?
HOW?
EXPLOSION. APPARENTLY HE WAS MURDERED BY ANOTHER LEP OFFICER. SHE'S NOW MISSING, PRESUMED DEAD. A CAPTAIN HOLLY SHORT.
WHAT?!

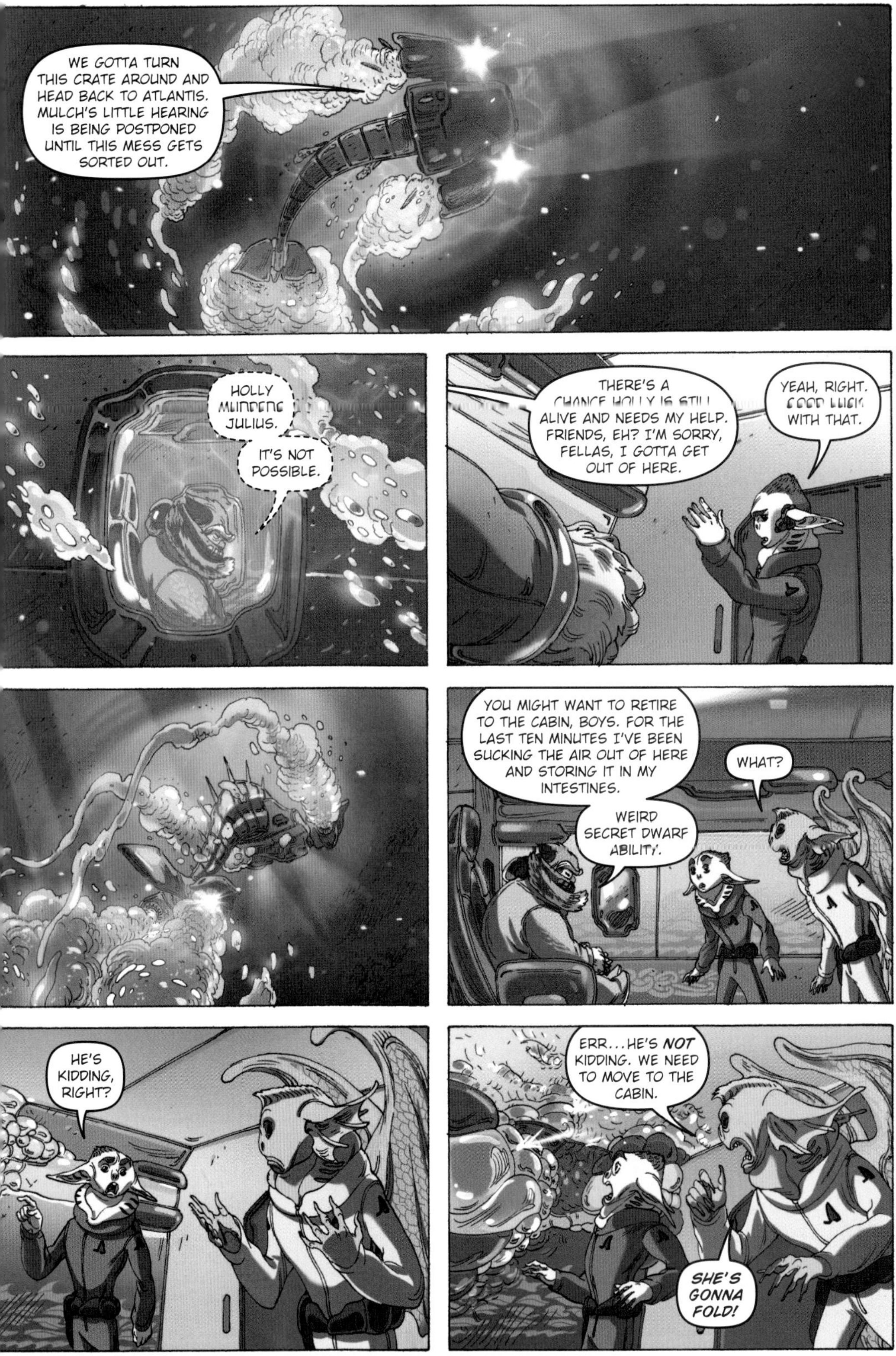
WE GOTTA TURN THIS CRATE AROUND AND HEAD BACK TO ATLANTIS. MULCH'S LITTLE HEARING IS BEING POSTPONED UNTIL THIS MESS GETS SORTED OUT.
HOLLY MURDERED JULIUS.
IT'S NOT POSSIBLE.
THERE'S A CHANCE HOLLY IS STILL ALIVE AND NEEDS MY HELP. FRIENDS, EH? I'M SORRY, FELLAS, I GOTTA GET OUT OF HERE.
YEAH, RIGHT. GOOD LUCK WITH THAT.
YOU MIGHT WANT TO RETIRE TO THE CABIN, BOYS. FOR THE LAST TEN MINUTES I'VE BEEN SUCKING THE AIR OUT OF HERE AND STORING IT IN MY INTESTINES.
WEIRD SECRET DWARF ABILITY.
WHAT?
HE'S KIDDING, RIGHT?
ERR...HE'S NOT KIDDING. WE NEED TO MOVE TO THE CABIN.
SHE'S GONNA FOLD!

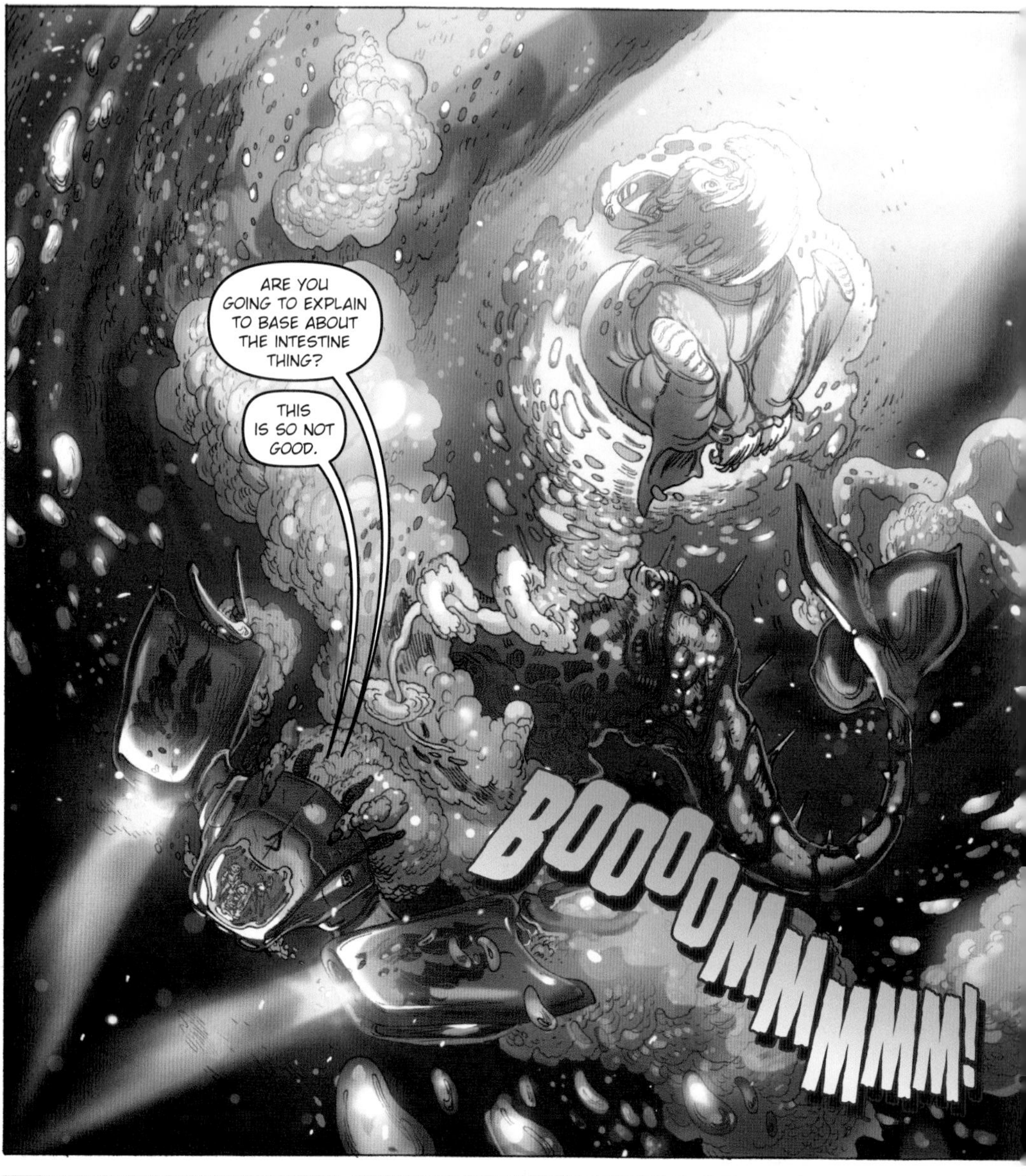
ARE YOU GOING TO EXPLAIN TO BASE ABOUT THE INTESTINE THING?
THIS IS SO NOT GOOD.
BOOOOMMMMMM!
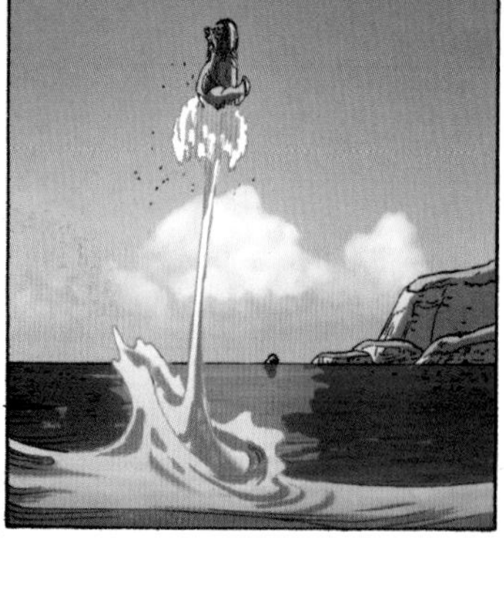
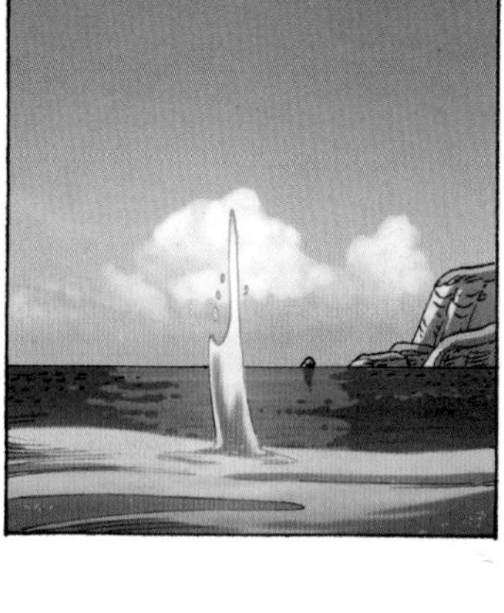
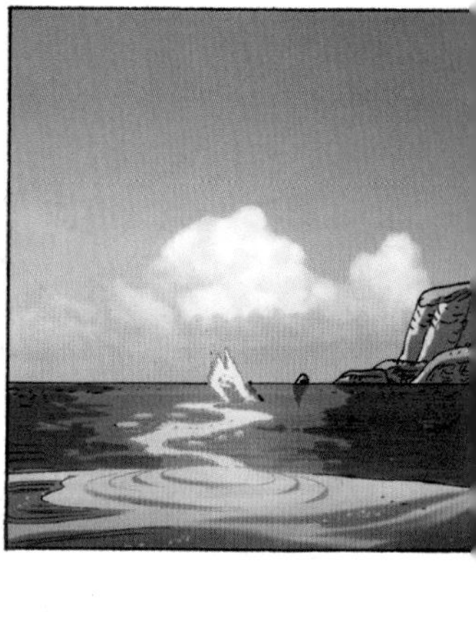

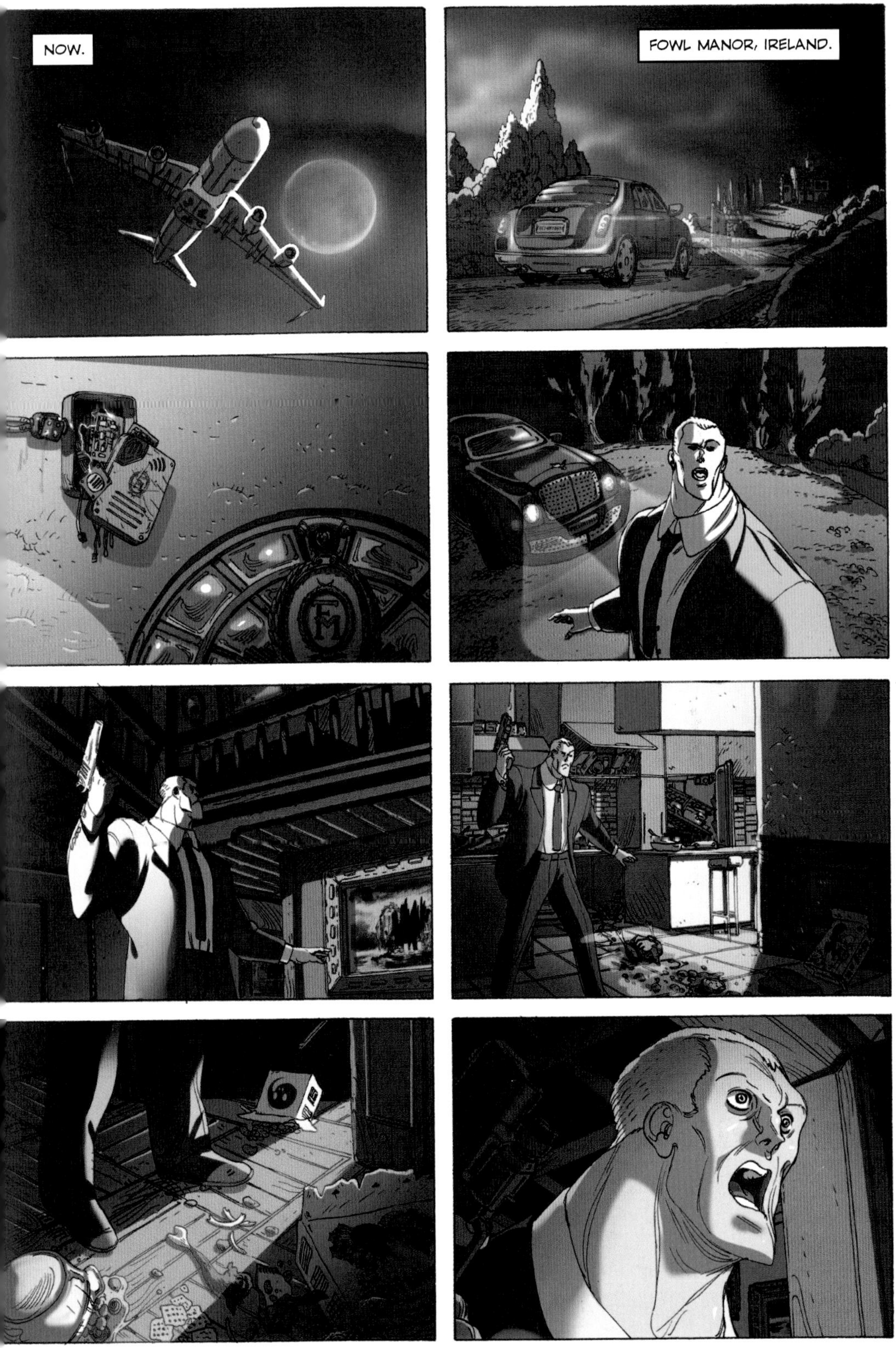
NOW.
FOWL MANOR, IRELAND.

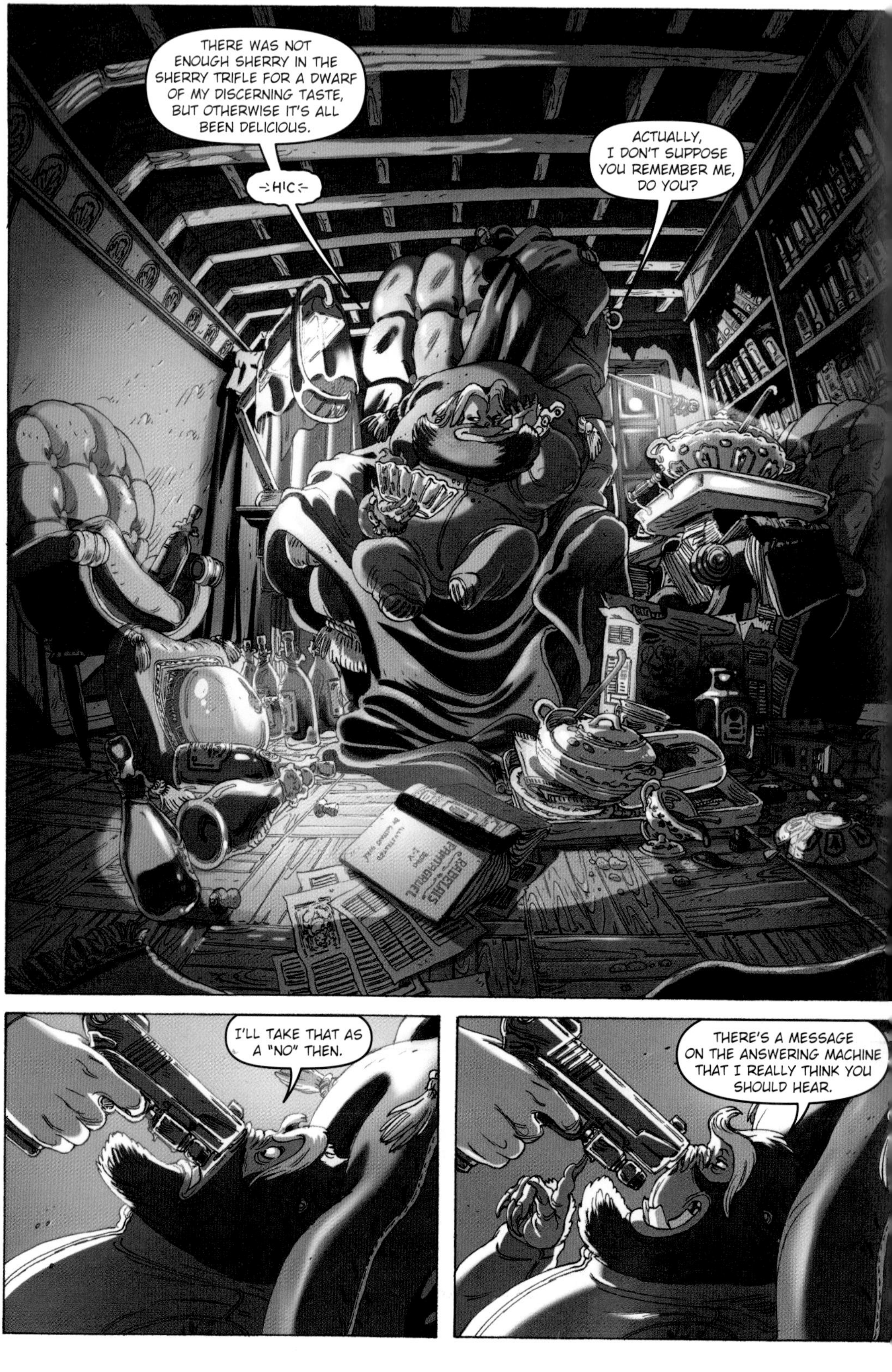
THERE WAS NOT ENOUGH SHERRY IN THE SHERRY TRIFLE FOR A DWARF OF MY DISCERNING TASTE, BUT OTHERWISE IT'S ALL BEEN DELICIOUS.
HIC
ACTUALLY, I DON'T SUPPOSE YOU REMEMBER ME, DO YOU?
I'LL TAKE THAT AS A "NO" THEN.
THERE'S A MESSAGE ON THE ANSWERING MACHINE THAT I REALLY THINK YOU SHOULD HEAR.

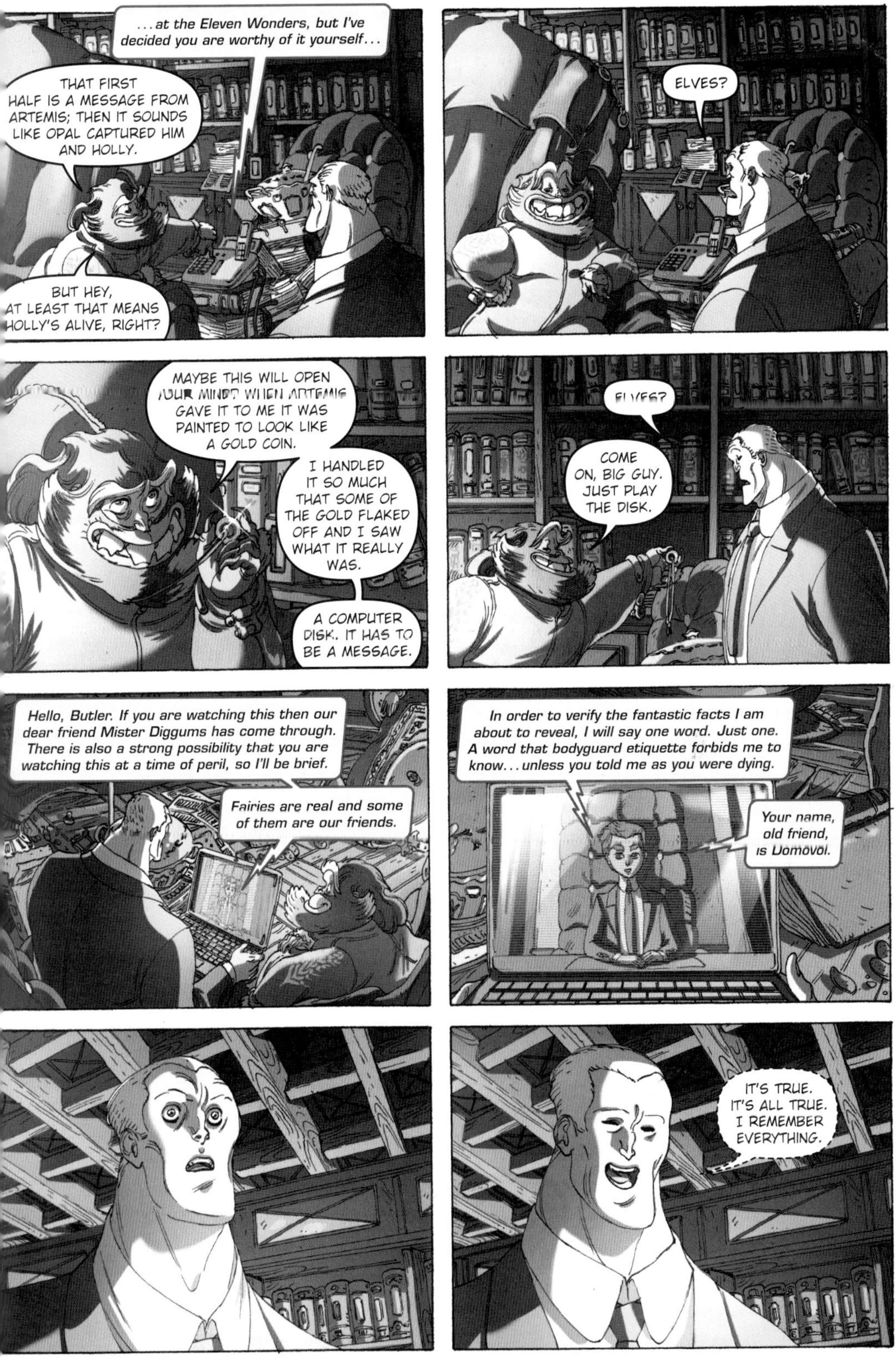
...at the Eleven Wonders, but I've decided you are worthy of it yourself...
THAT FIRST HALF IS A MESSAGE FROM ARTEMIS; THEN IT SOUNDS LIKE OPAL CAPTURED HIM AND HOLLY.
BUT HEY, AT LEAST THAT MEANS HOLLY'S ALIVE, RIGHT?
ELVES?
MAYBE THIS WILL OPEN YOUR MIND? WHEN ARTEMIS GAVE IT TO ME IT WAS PAINTED TO LOOK LIKE A GOLD COIN.
I HANDLED IT SO MUCH THAT SOME OF THE GOLD FLAKED OFF AND I SAW WHAT IT REALLY WAS.
A COMPUTER DISK. IT HAS TO BE A MESSAGE.
ELVES?
COME ON, BIG GUY. JUST PLAY THE DISK.
Hello, Butler. If you are watching this then our dear friend Mister Diggums has come through. There is also a strong possibility that you are watching this at a time of peril, so I'll be brief.
Fairies are real and some of them are our friends.
In order to verify the fantastic facts I am about to reveal, I will say one word. Just one. A word that bodyguard etiquette forbids me to know... unless you told me as you were dying.
Your name, old friend, is Domovoi.
IT'S TRUE. IT'S ALL TRUE. I REMEMBER EVERYTHING.

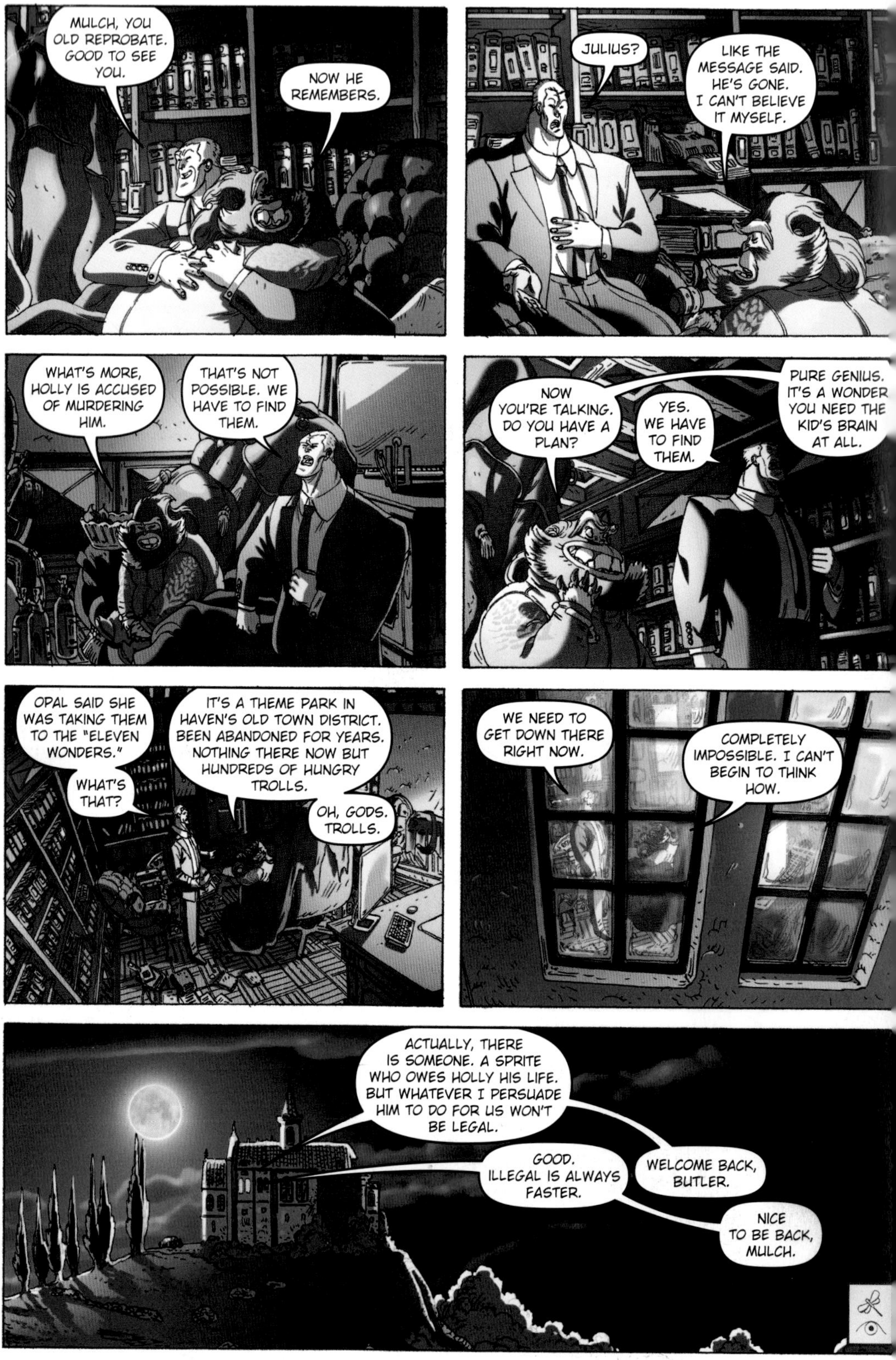
MULCH, YOU OLD REPROBATE. GOOD TO SEE YOU.
NOW HE REMEMBERS.
JULIUS?
LIKE THE MESSAGE SAID. HE'S GONE. I CAN'T BELIEVE IT MYSELF.
WHAT'S MORE, HOLLY IS ACCUSED OF MURDERING HIM.
THAT'S NOT POSSIBLE. WE HAVE TO FIND THEM.
NOW YOU'RE TALKING. DO YOU HAVE A PLAN?
YES. WE HAVE TO FIND THEM.
PURE GENIUS. IT'S A WONDER YOU NEED THE KID'S BRAIN AT ALL.
OPAL SAID SHE WAS TAKING THEM TO THE "ELEVEN WONDERS."
WHAT'S THAT?
IT'S A THEME PARK IN HAVEN'S OLD TOWN DISTRICT. BEEN ABANDONED FOR YEARS. NOTHING THERE NOW BUT HUNDREDS OF HUNGRY TROLLS.
OH, GODS. TROLLS.
WE NEED TO GET DOWN THERE RIGHT NOW.
COMPLETELY IMPOSSIBLE. I CAN'T BEGIN TO THINK HOW.
ACTUALLY, THERE IS SOMEONE. A SPRITE WHO OWES HOLLY HIS LIFE. BUT WHATEVER I PERSUADE HIM TO DO FOR US WON'T BE LEGAL.
GOOD. ILLEGAL IS ALWAYS FASTER.
WELCOME BACK, BUTLER.
NICE TO BE BACK, MULCH.

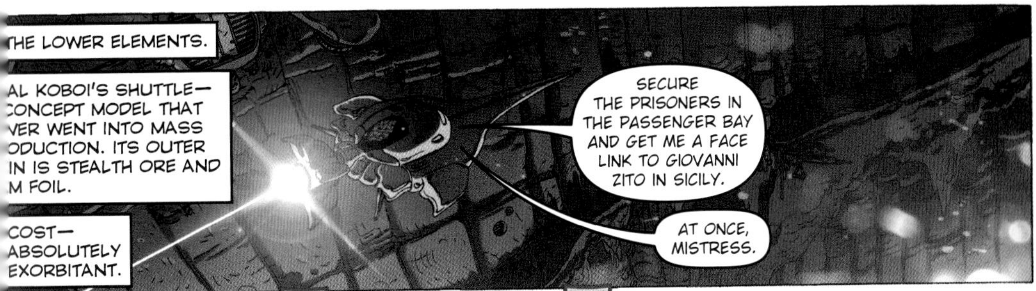
HE LOWER ELEMENTS.
AL KOBOI'S SHUTTLE—
CONCEPT MODEL THAT
VER WENT INTO MASS
ODUCTION. ITS OUTER
IN IS STEALTH ORE AND
M FOIL.
SECURE THE PRISONERS IN THE PASSENGER BAY AND GET ME A FACE LINK TO GIOVANNI ZITO IN SICILY.
COST—ABSOLUTELY EXORBITANT.
AT ONCE, MISTRESS.

HAPTER 7: THE TEMPLE OF ARTEMIS

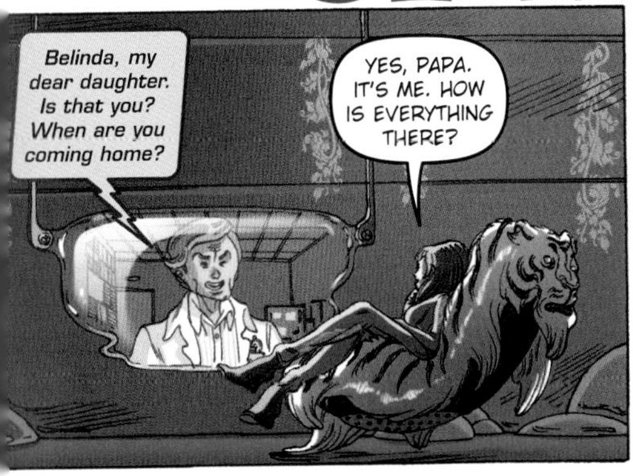
Belinda, my dear daughter. Is that you? When are you coming home?
YES, PAPA. IT'S ME. HOW IS EVERYTHING THERE?

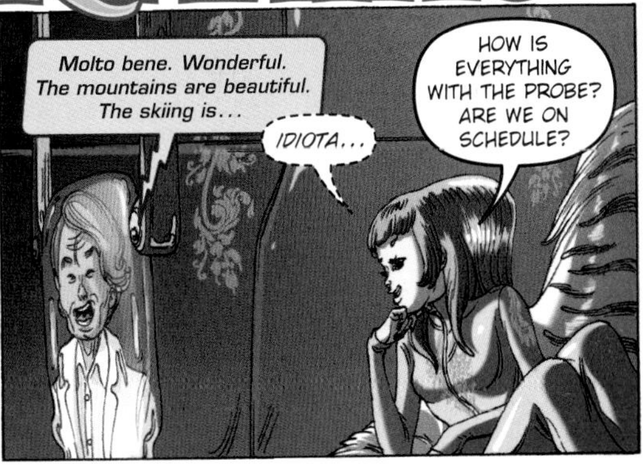
Molto bene. Wonderful. The mountains are beautiful. The skiing is...
IDIOTA...
HOW IS EVERYTHING WITH THE PROBE? ARE WE ON SCHEDULE?

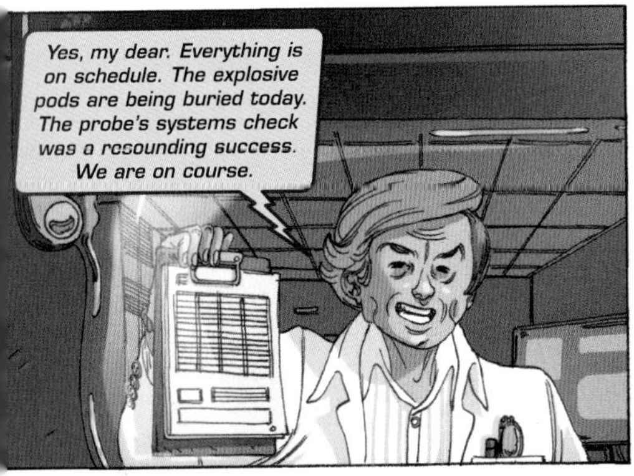
Yes, my dear. Everything is on schedule. The explosive pods are being buried today. The probe's systems check was a resounding success. We are on course.

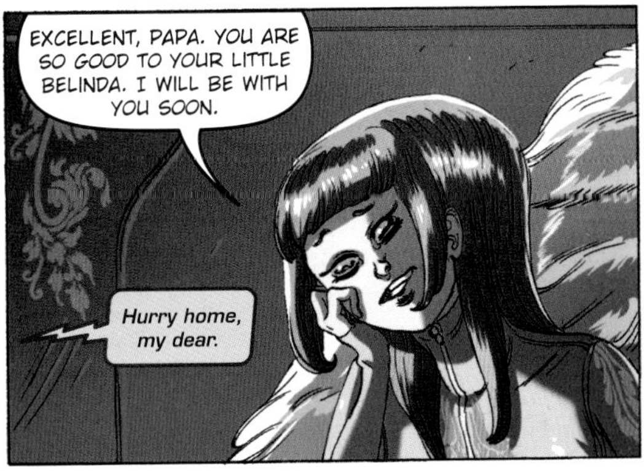
EXCELLENT, PAPA. YOU ARE SO GOOD TO YOUR LITTLE BELINDA. I WILL BE WITH YOU SOON.
Hurry home, my dear.

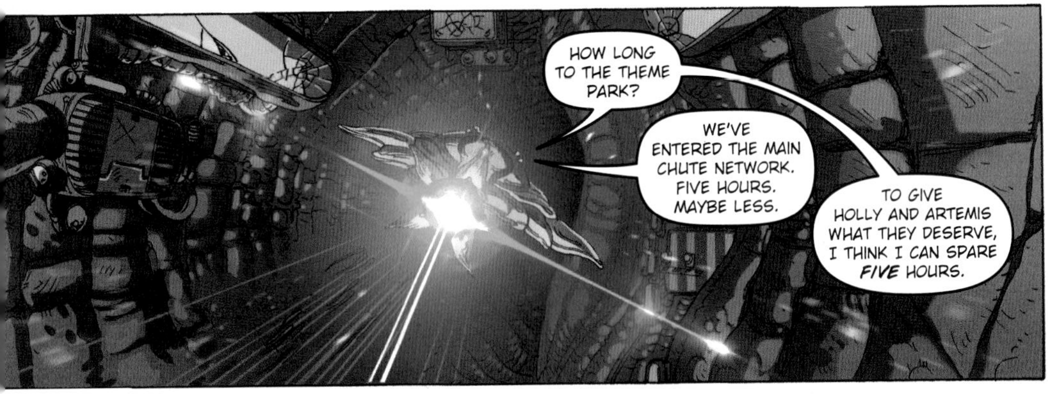
HOW LONG TO THE THEME PARK?
WE'VE ENTERED THE MAIN CHUTE NETWORK. FIVE HOURS. MAYBE LESS.
TO GIVE HOLLY AND ARTEMIS WHAT THEY DESERVE, I THINK I CAN SPARE FIVE HOURS.

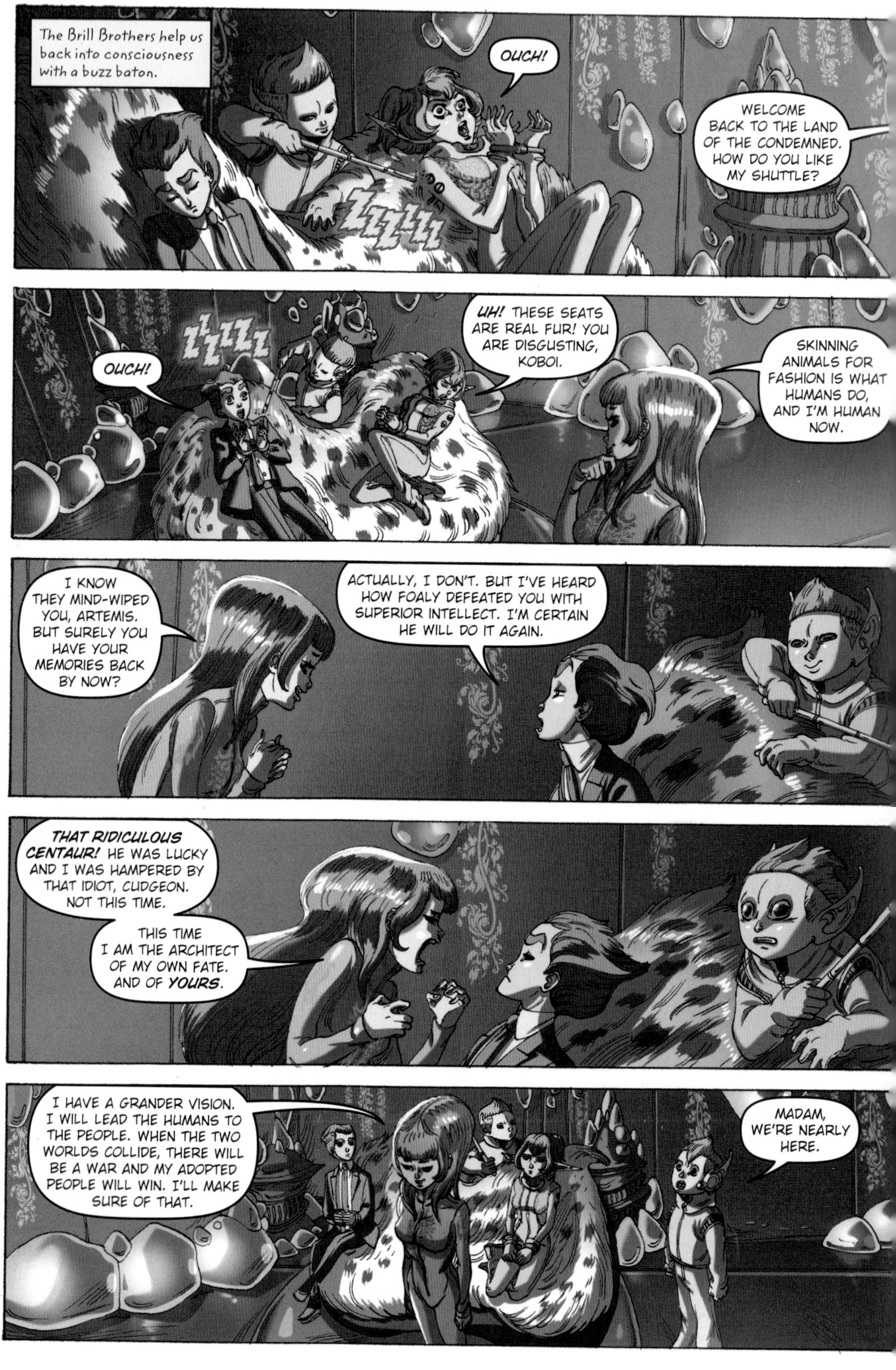
The Brill Brothers help us back into consciousness with a buzz baton.
OUCH!
WELCOME BACK TO THE LAND OF THE CONDEMNED. HOW DO YOU LIKE MY SHUTTLE?
ZZZZZZ
ZZZZZ
OUCH!
UH! THESE SEATS ARE REAL FUR! YOU ARE DISGUSTING, KOBOI.
SKINNING ANIMALS FOR FASHION IS WHAT HUMANS DO, AND I'M HUMAN NOW.
I KNOW THEY MIND-WIPED YOU, ARTEMIS. BUT SURELY YOU HAVE YOUR MEMORIES BACK BY NOW?
ACTUALLY, I DON'T. BUT I'VE HEARD HOW FOALY DEFEATED YOU WITH SUPERIOR INTELLECT. I'M CERTAIN HE WILL DO IT AGAIN.
THAT RIDICULOUS CENTAUR! HE WAS LUCKY AND I WAS HAMPERED BY THAT IDIOT, CUDGEON. NOT THIS TIME.
THIS TIME I AM THE ARCHITECT OF MY OWN FATE. AND OF YOURS.
I HAVE A GRANDER VISION. I WILL LEAD THE HUMANS TO THE PEOPLE. WHEN THE TWO WORLDS COLLIDE, THERE WILL BE A WAR AND MY ADOPTED PEOPLE WILL WIN. I'LL MAKE SURE OF THAT.
MADAM, WE'RE NEARLY HERE.

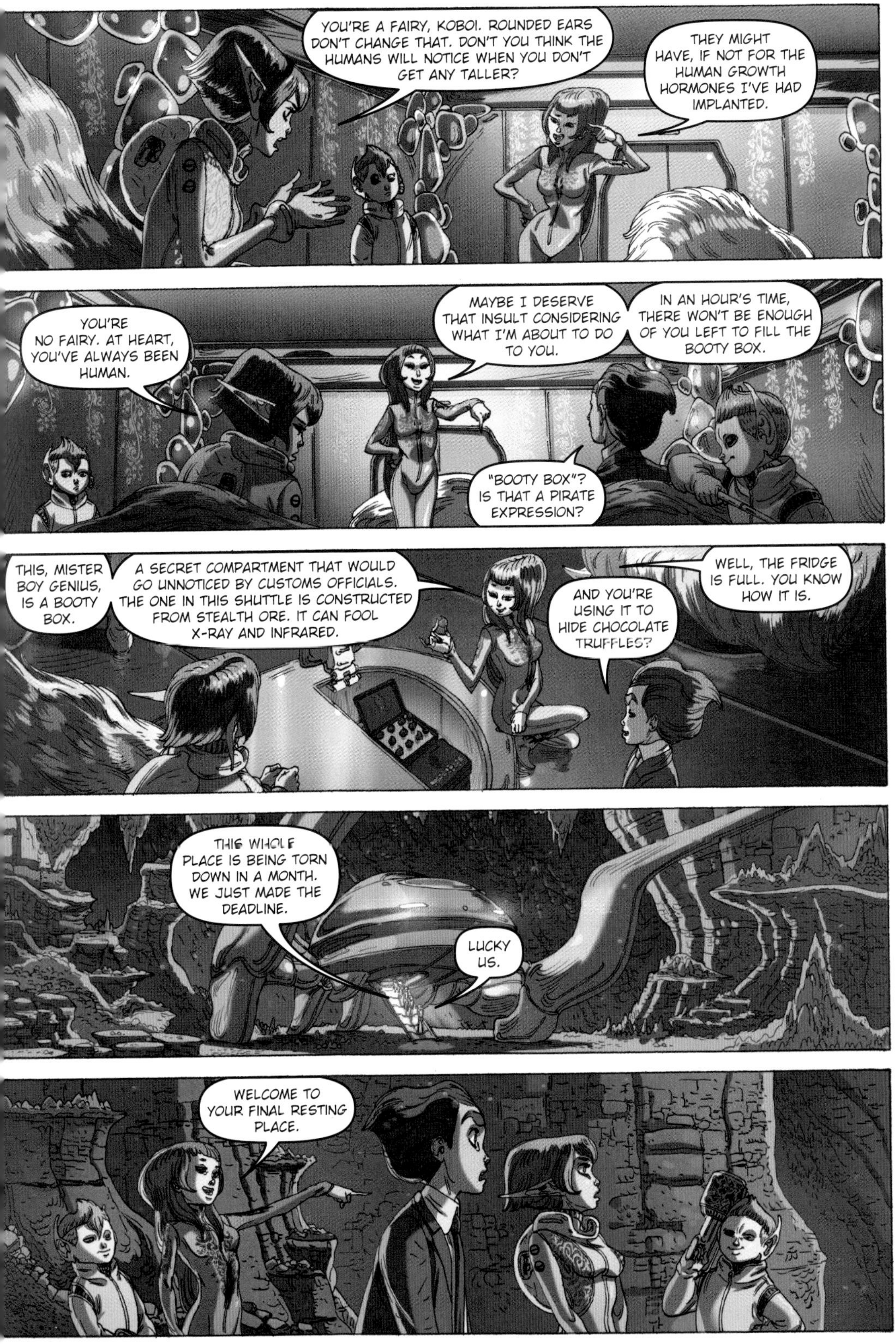

YOU'RE A FAIRY, KOBOI. ROUNDED EARS DON'T CHANGE THAT. DON'T YOU THINK THE HUMANS WILL NOTICE WHEN YOU DON'T GET ANY TALLER?
THEY MIGHT HAVE, IF NOT FOR THE HUMAN GROWTH HORMONES I'VE HAD IMPLANTED.
YOU'RE NO FAIRY. AT HEART, YOU'VE ALWAYS BEEN HUMAN.
MAYBE I DESERVE THAT INSULT CONSIDERING WHAT I'M ABOUT TO DO TO YOU.
IN AN HOUR'S TIME, THERE WON'T BE ENOUGH OF YOU LEFT TO FILL THE BOOTY BOX.
"BOOTY BOX"? IS THAT A PIRATE EXPRESSION?
THIS, MISTER BOY GENIUS, IS A BOOTY BOX.
A SECRET COMPARTMENT THAT WOULD GO UNNOTICED BY CUSTOMS OFFICIALS. THE ONE IN THIS SHUTTLE IS CONSTRUCTED FROM STEALTH ORE. IT CAN FOOL X-RAY AND INFRARED.
AND YOU'RE USING IT TO HIDE CHOCOLATE TRUFFLES?
WELL, THE FRIDGE IS FULL. YOU KNOW HOW IT IS.
THIS WHOLE PLACE IS BEING TORN DOWN IN A MONTH. WE JUST MADE THE DEADLINE.
LUCKY US.
WELCOME TO YOUR FINAL RESTING PLACE.

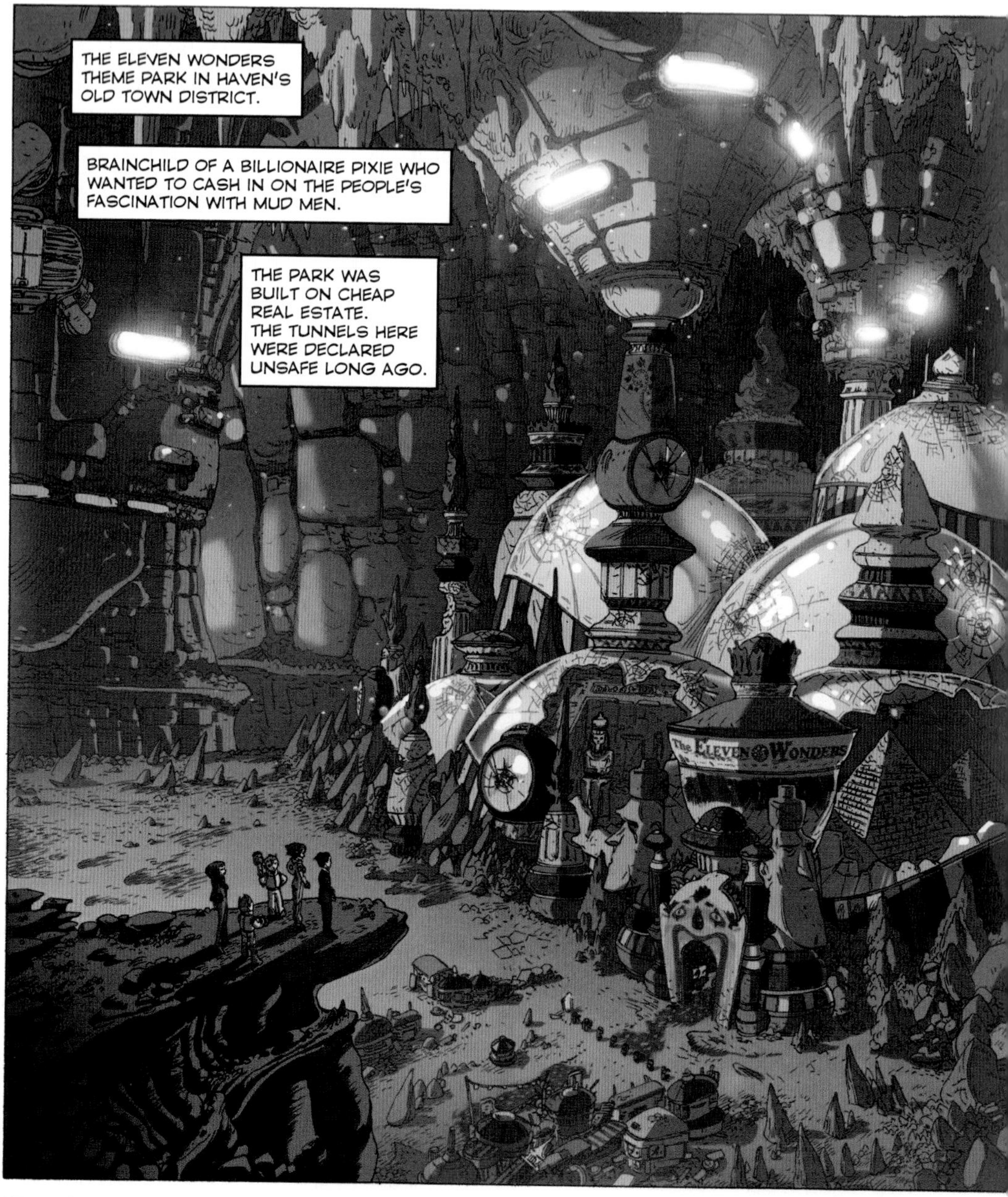
THE ELEVEN WONDERS THEME PARK IN HAVEN'S OLD TOWN DISTRICT.
BRAINCHILD OF A BILLIONAIRE PIXIE WHO WANTED TO CASH IN ON THE PEOPLE'S FASCINATION WITH MUD MEN.
THE PARK WAS BUILT ON CHEAP REAL ESTATE. THE TUNNELS HERE WERE DECLARED UNSAFE LONG AGO.
The ELEVEN WONDERS

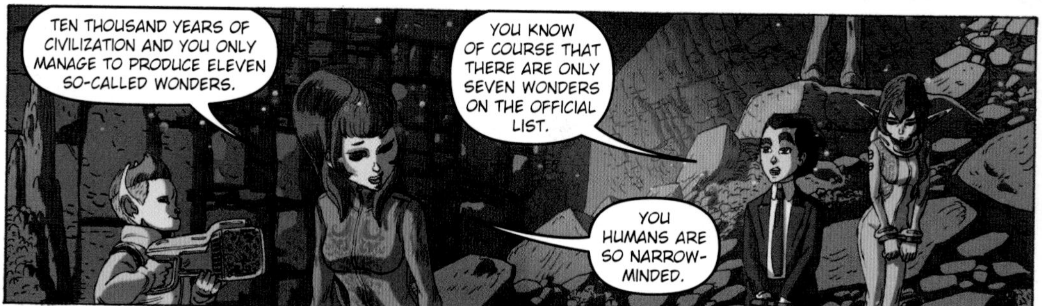
TEN THOUSAND YEARS OF CIVILIZATION AND YOU ONLY MANAGE TO PRODUCE ELEVEN SO-CALLED WONDERS.
YOU KNOW OF COURSE THAT THERE ARE ONLY SEVEN WONDERS ON THE OFFICIAL LIST.
YOU HUMANS ARE SO NARROW-MINDED.

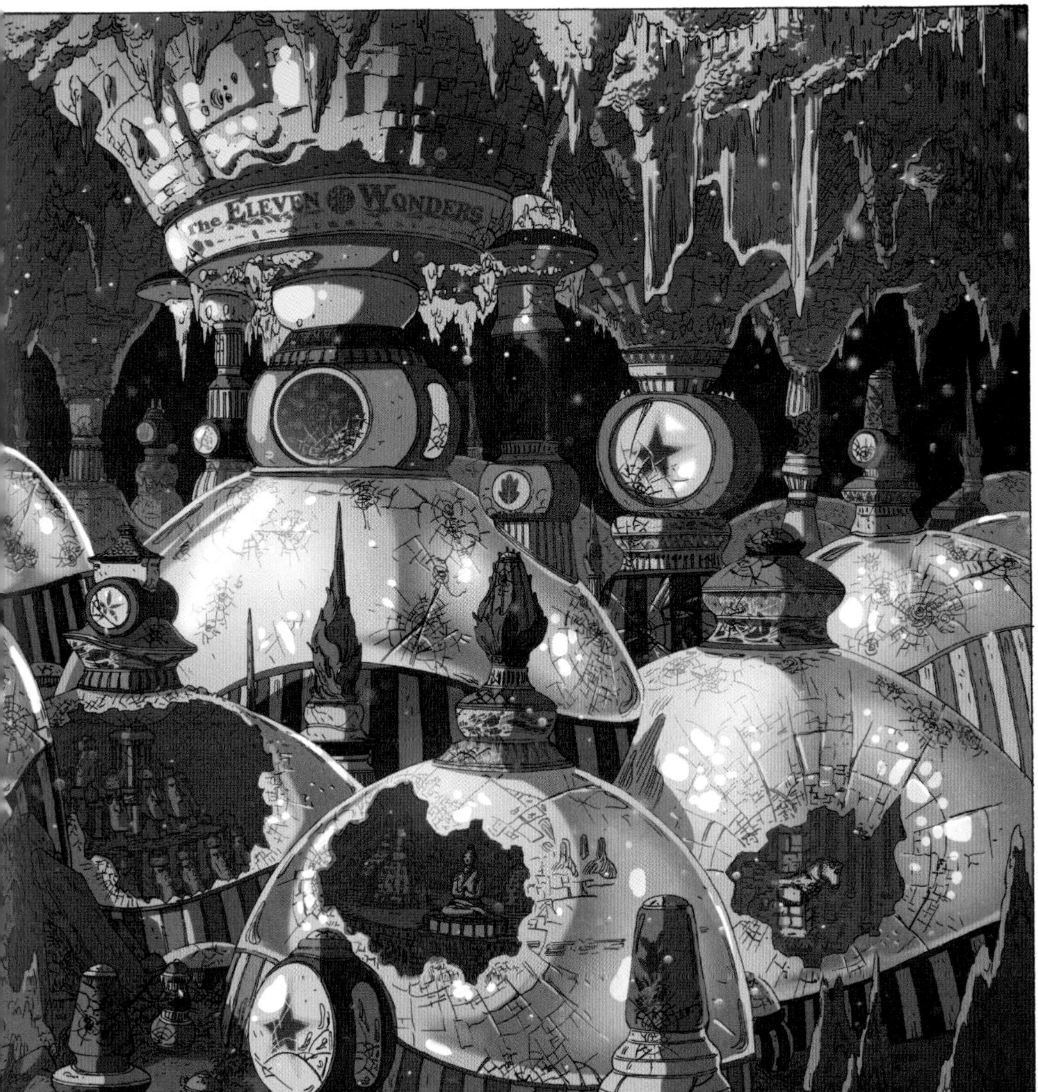
the ELEVEN WONDERS

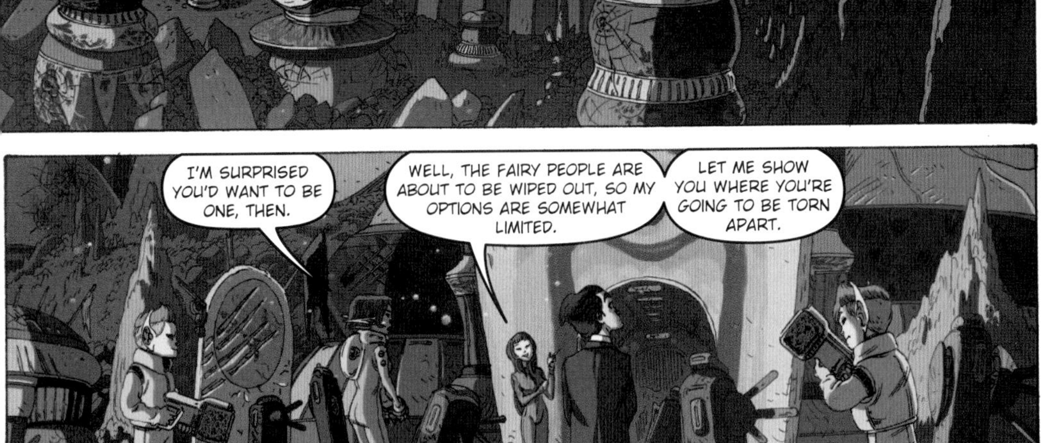
I'M SURPRISED YOU'D WANT TO BE ONE, THEN.
WELL, THE FAIRY PEOPLE ARE ABOUT TO BE WIPED OUT, SO MY OPTIONS ARE SOMEWHAT LIMITED.
LET ME SHOW YOU WHERE YOU'RE GOING TO BE TORN APART.

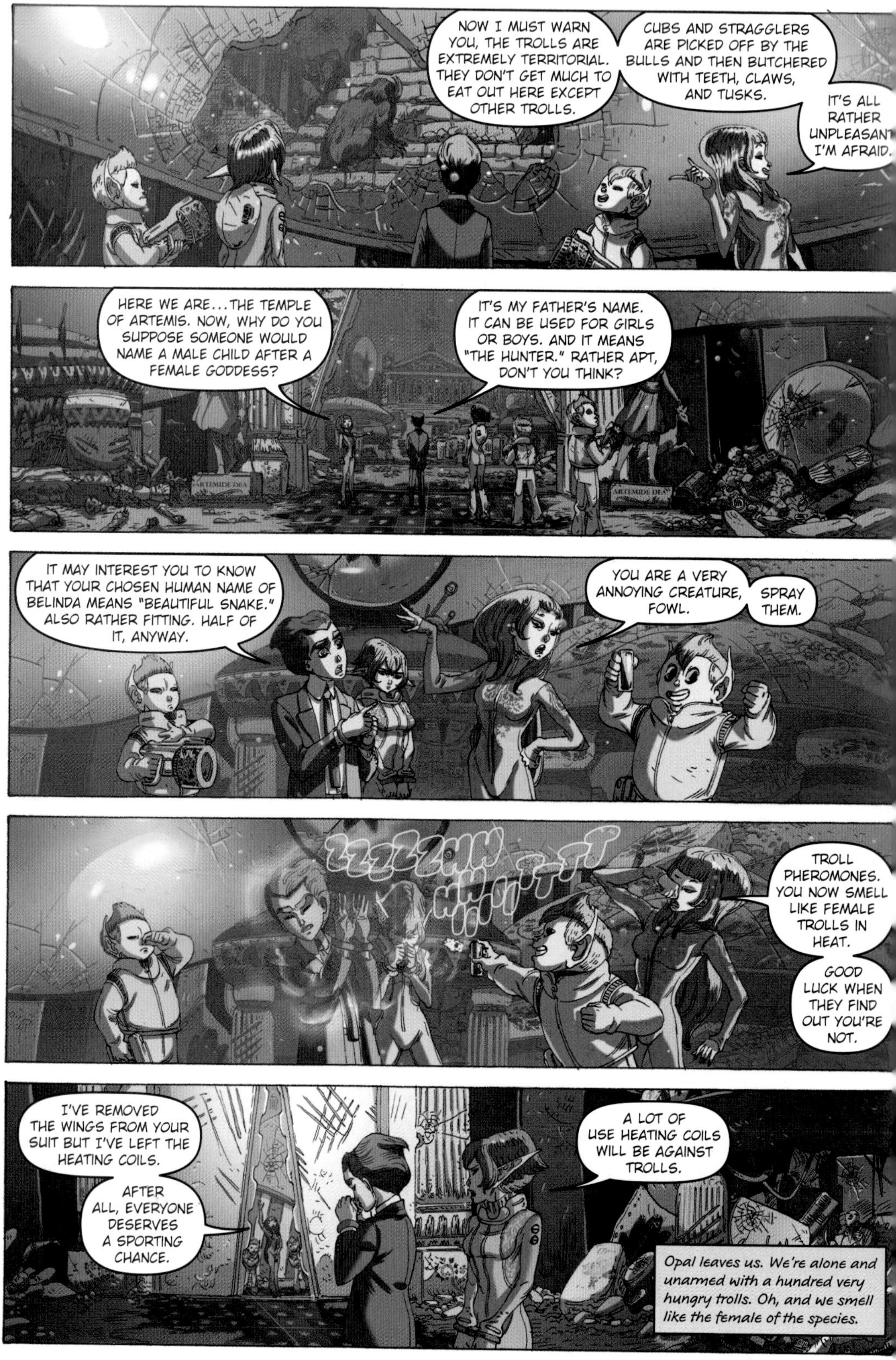

NOW I MUST WARN YOU, THE TROLLS ARE EXTREMELY TERRITORIAL. THEY DON'T GET MUCH TO EAT OUT HERE EXCEPT OTHER TROLLS.
CUBS AND STRAGGLERS ARE PICKED OFF BY THE BULLS AND THEN BUTCHERED WITH TEETH, CLAWS, AND TUSKS.
IT'S ALL RATHER UNPLEASANT I'M AFRAID.
HERE WE ARE... THE TEMPLE OF ARTEMIS. NOW, WHY DO YOU SUPPOSE SOMEONE WOULD NAME A MALE CHILD AFTER A FEMALE GODDESS?
IT'S MY FATHER'S NAME. IT CAN BE USED FOR GIRLS OR BOYS. AND IT MEANS "THE HUNTER." RATHER APT, DON'T YOU THINK?
ARTEMIDE DEA
ARTEMIDE DEA
IT MAY INTEREST YOU TO KNOW THAT YOUR CHOSEN HUMAN NAME OF BELINDA MEANS "BEAUTIFUL SNAKE." ALSO RATHER FITTING. HALF OF IT, ANYWAY.
YOU ARE A VERY ANNOYING CREATURE, FOWL.
SPRAY THEM.
ZZZZZHHHHHHHTTTT
TROLL PHEROMONES. YOU NOW SMELL LIKE FEMALE TROLLS IN HEAT.
GOOD LUCK WHEN THEY FIND OUT YOU'RE NOT.
I'VE REMOVED THE WINGS FROM YOUR SUIT BUT I'VE LEFT THE HEATING COILS.
AFTER ALL, EVERYONE DESERVES A SPORTING CHANCE.
A LOT OF USE HEATING COILS WILL BE AGAINST TROLLS.
Opal leaves us. We're alone and unarmed with a hundred very hungry trolls. Oh, and we smell like the female of the species.

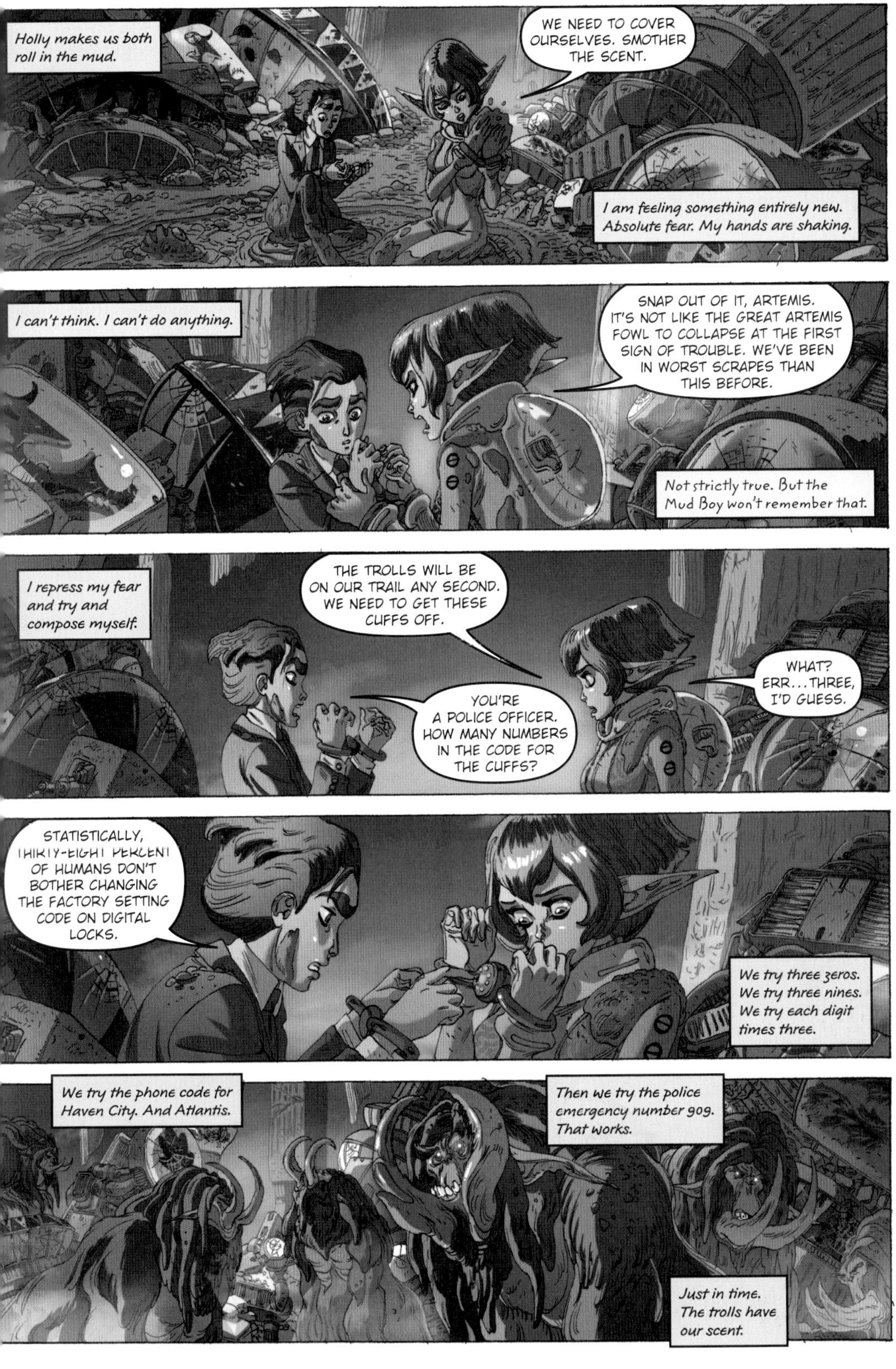
Holly makes us both roll in the mud.
WE NEED TO COVER OURSELVES. SMOTHER THE SCENT.
I am feeling something entirely new. Absolute fear. My hands are shaking.
I can't think. I can't do anything.
SNAP OUT OF IT, ARTEMIS. IT'S NOT LIKE THE GREAT ARTEMIS FOWL TO COLLAPSE AT THE FIRST SIGN OF TROUBLE. WE'VE BEEN IN WORST SCRAPES THAN THIS BEFORE.
Not strictly true. But the Mud Boy won't remember that.
I repress my fear and try and compose myself.
THE TROLLS WILL BE ON OUR TRAIL ANY SECOND. WE NEED TO GET THESE CUFFS OFF.
YOU'RE A POLICE OFFICER. HOW MANY NUMBERS IN THE CODE FOR THE CUFFS?
WHAT? ERR... THREE, I'D GUESS.
STATISTICALLY, THIRTY-EIGHT PERCENT OF HUMANS DON'T BOTHER CHANGING THE FACTORY SETTING CODE ON DIGITAL LOCKS.
We try three zeros. We try three nines. We try each digit times three.
We try the phone code for Haven City. And Atlantis.
Then we try the police emergency number 909. That works.
Just in time. The trolls have our scent.

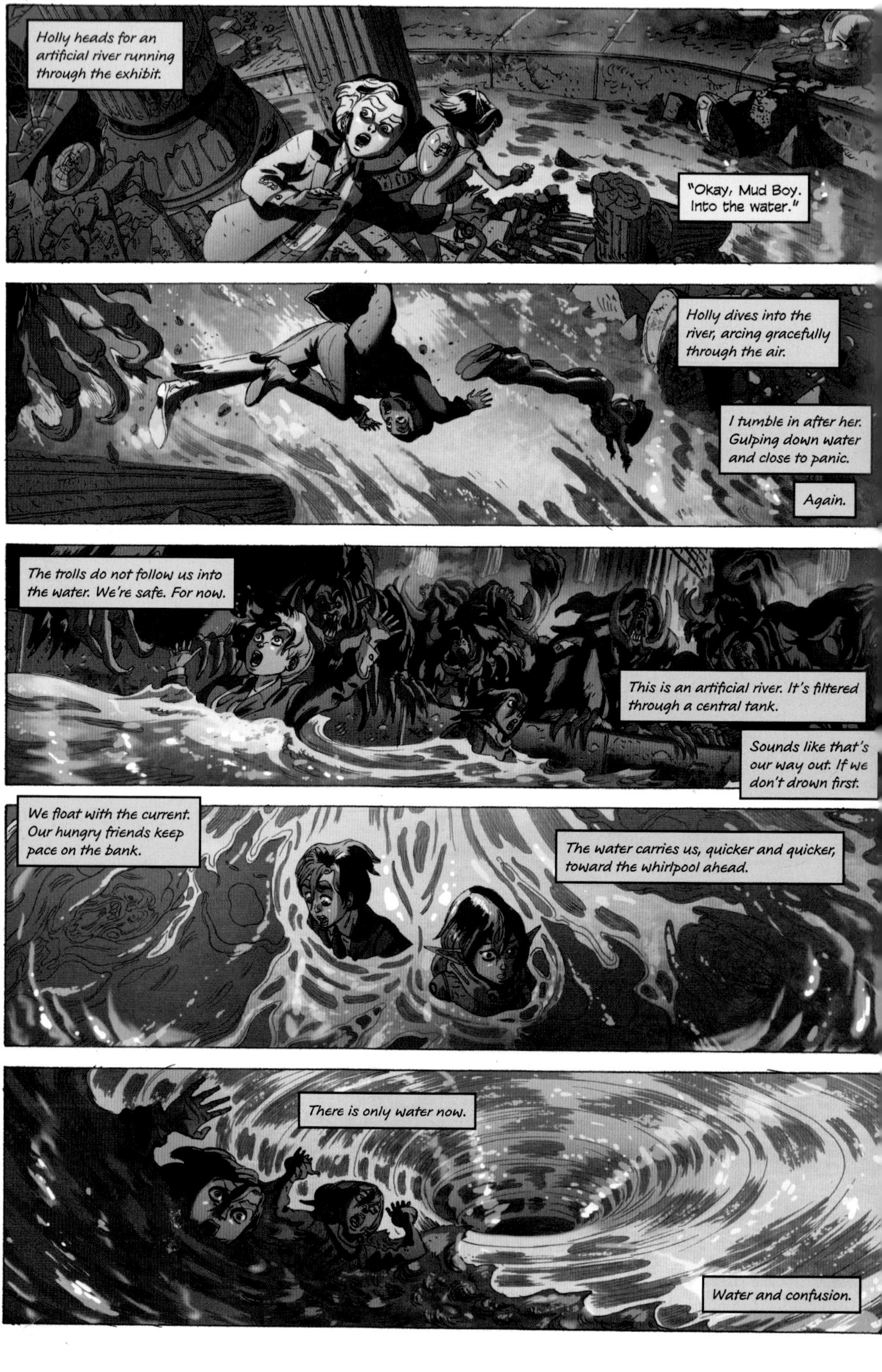
Holly heads for an artificial river running through the exhibit.
"Okay, Mud Boy. Into the water."
Holly dives into the river, arcing gracefully through the air.
I tumble in after her. Gulping down water and close to panic.
Again.
The trolls do not follow us into the water. We're safe. For now.
This is an artificial river. It's filtered through a central tank.
Sounds like that's our way out. If we don't drown first.
We float with the current. Our hungry friends keep pace on the bank.
The water carries us, quicker and quicker, toward the whirlpool ahead.
There is only water now.
Water and confusion.

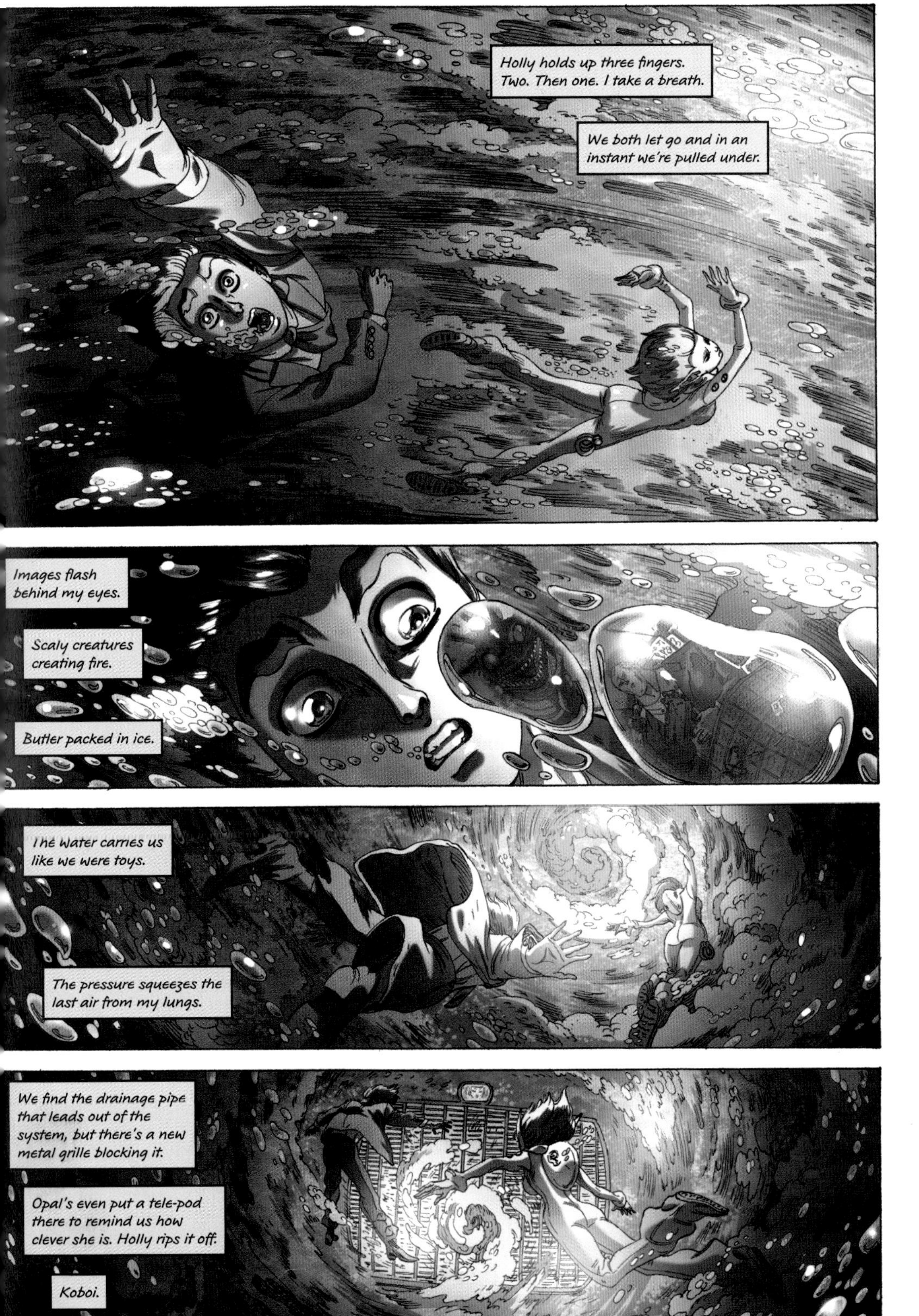
Holly holds up three fingers. Two. Then one. I take a breath.
We both let go and in an instant we're pulled under.
Images flash behind my eyes.
Scaly creatures creating fire.
Butler packed in ice.
The water carries us like we were toys.
The pressure squeezes the last air from my lungs.
We find the drainage pipe that leads out of the system, but there's a new metal grille blocking it.
Opal's even put a tele-pod there to remind us how clever she is. Holly rips it off.
Koboi.

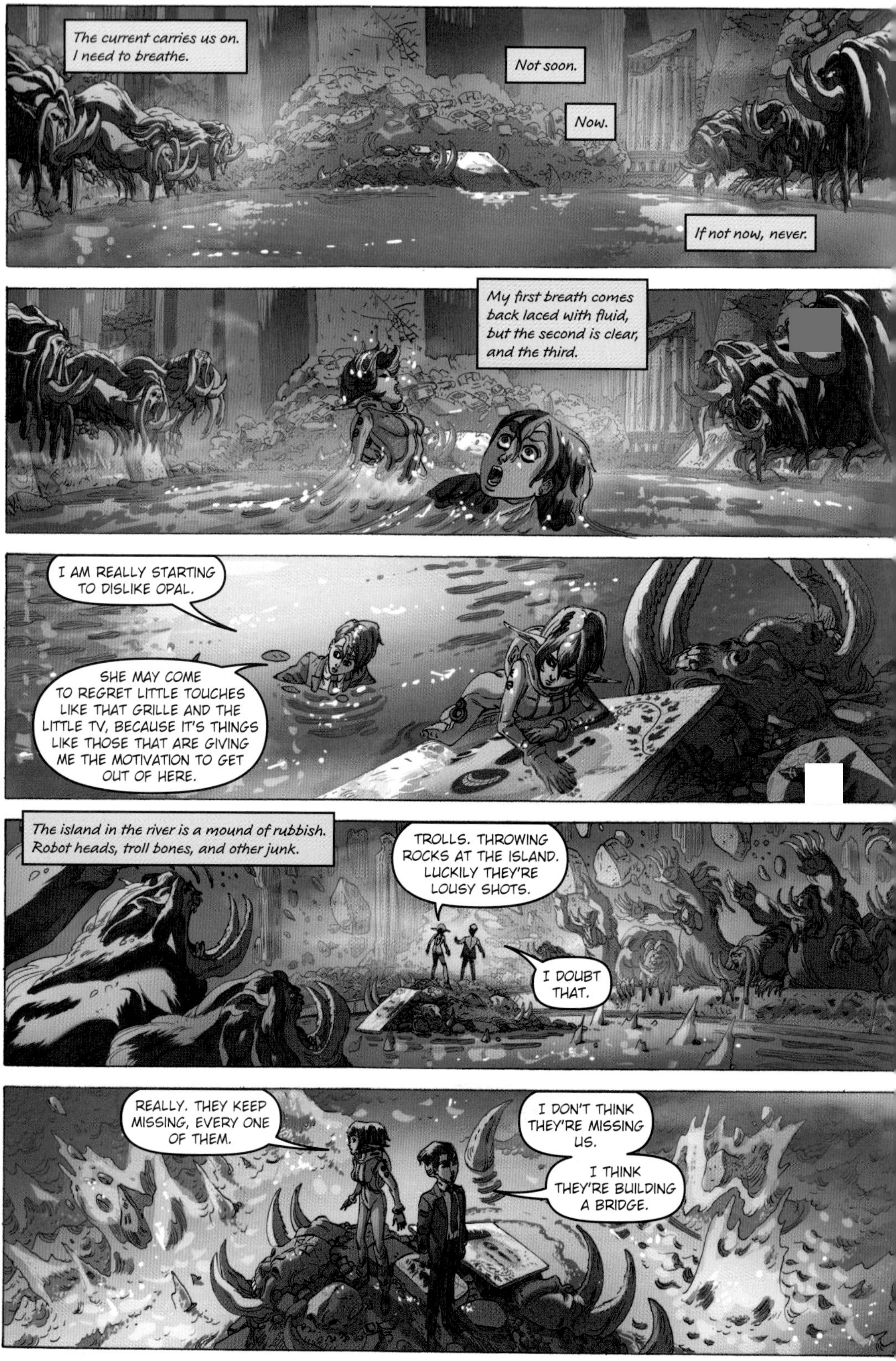
The current carries us on.
I need to breathe.
Not soon.
Now.
If not now, never.
My first breath comes back laced with fluid, but the second is clear, and the third.
I AM REALLY STARTING TO DISLIKE OPAL.
SHE MAY COME TO REGRET LITTLE TOUCHES LIKE THAT GRILLE AND THE LITTLE TV, BECAUSE IT'S THINGS LIKE THOSE THAT ARE GIVING ME THE MOTIVATION TO GET OUT OF HERE.
The island in the river is a mound of rubbish. Robot heads, troll bones, and other junk.
TROLLS. THROWING ROCKS AT THE ISLAND. LUCKILY THEY'RE LOUSY SHOTS.
I DOUBT THAT.
REALLY. THEY KEEP MISSING, EVERY ONE OF THEM.
I DON'T THINK THEY'RE MISSING US.
I THINK THEY'RE BUILDING A BRIDGE.

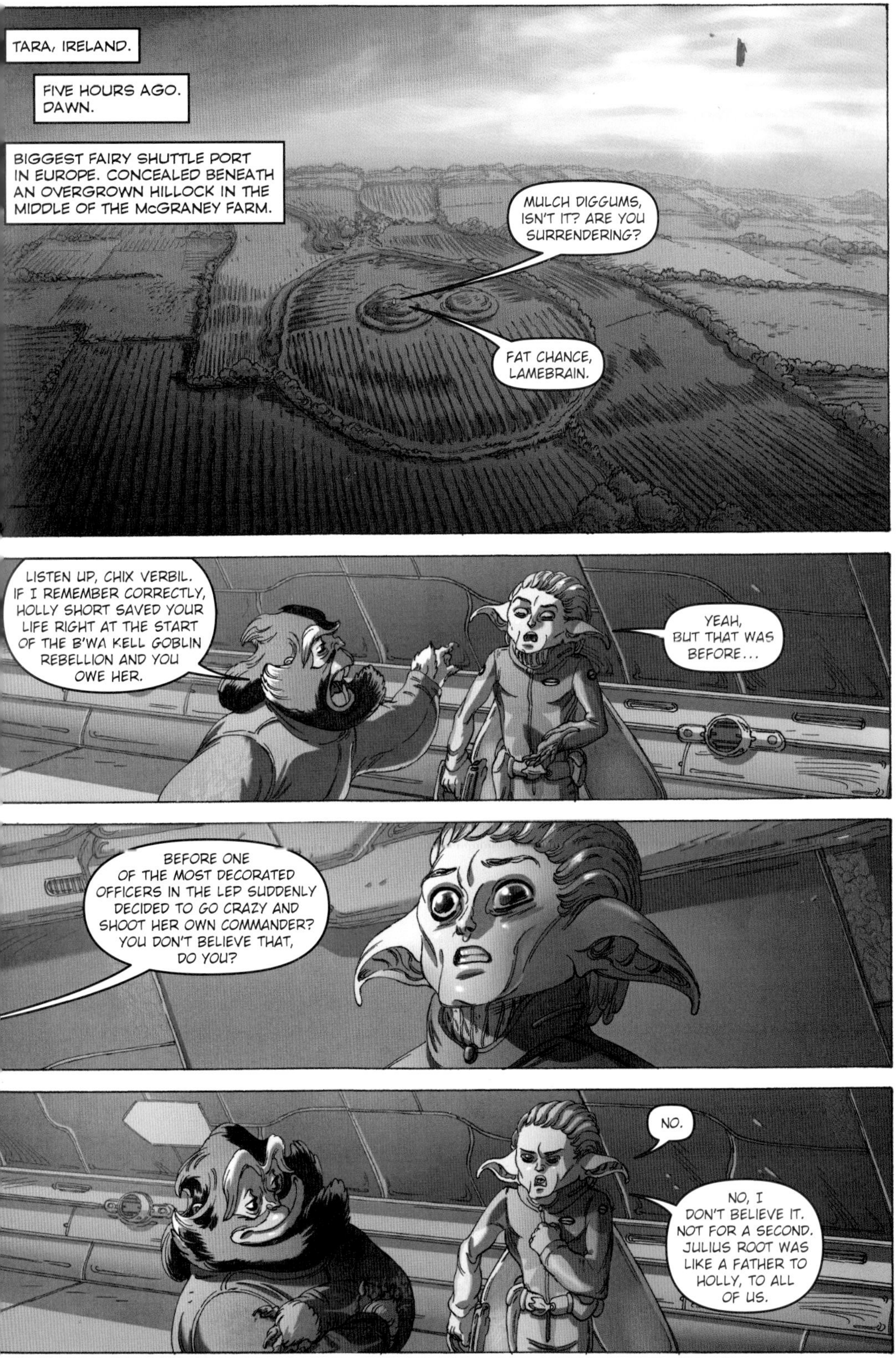
TARA, IRELAND.
FIVE HOURS AGO. DAWN.
BIGGEST FAIRY SHUTTLE PORT IN EUROPE. CONCEALED BENEATH AN OVERGROWN HILLOCK IN THE MIDDLE OF THE McGRANEY FARM.
MULCH DIGGUMS, ISN'T IT? ARE YOU SURRENDERING?
FAT CHANCE, LAMEBRAIN.
LISTEN UP, CHIX VERBIL. IF I REMEMBER CORRECTLY, HOLLY SHORT SAVED YOUR LIFE RIGHT AT THE START OF THE B'WA KELL GOBLIN REBELLION AND YOU OWE HER.
YEAH, BUT THAT WAS BEFORE...
BEFORE ONE OF THE MOST DECORATED OFFICERS IN THE LEP SUDDENLY DECIDED TO GO CRAZY AND SHOOT HER OWN COMMANDER? YOU DON'T BELIEVE THAT, DO YOU?
NO.
NO, I DON'T BELIEVE IT. NOT FOR A SECOND. JULIUS ROOT WAS LIKE A FATHER TO HOLLY, TO ALL OF US.

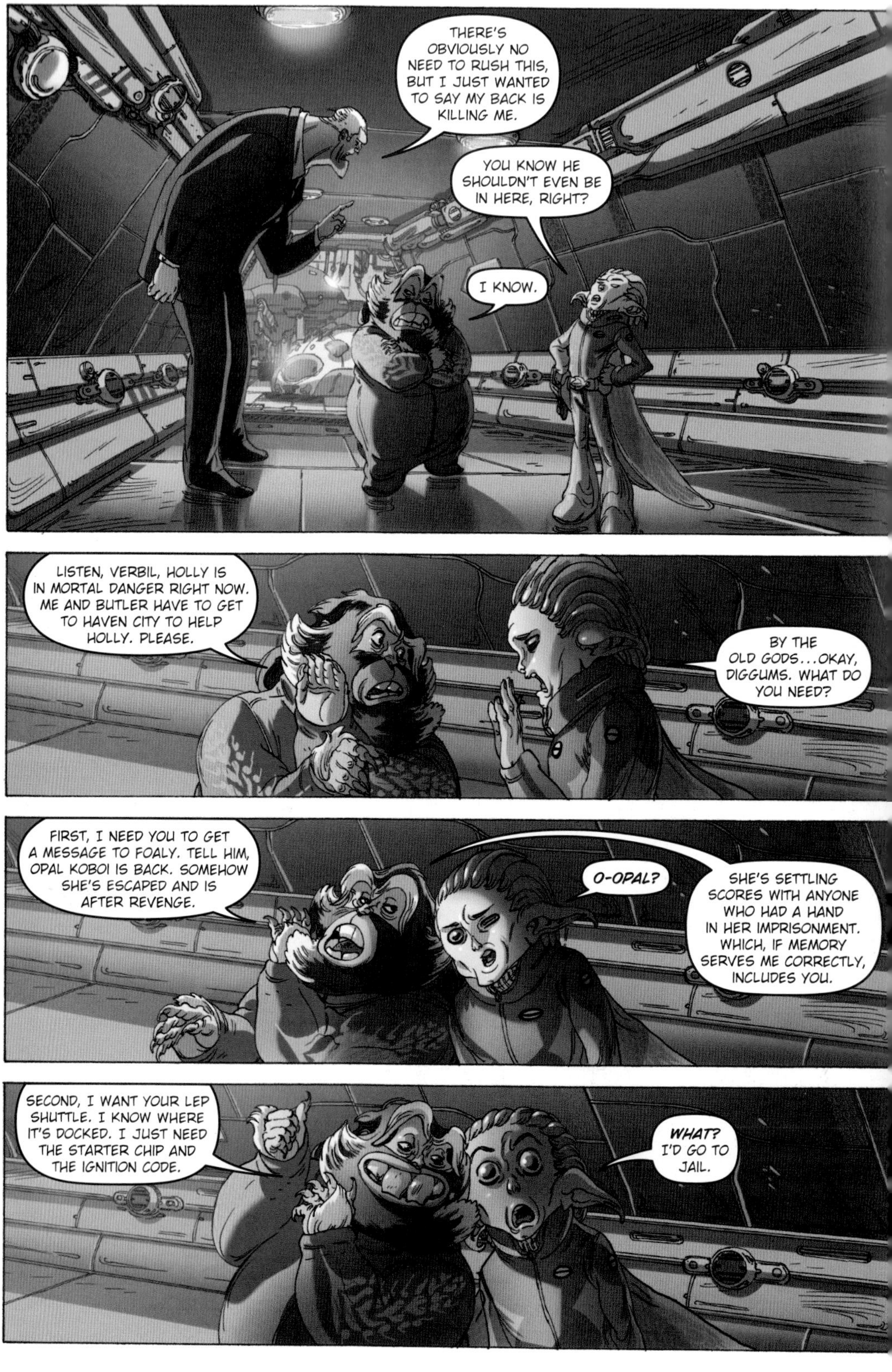
THERE'S OBVIOUSLY NO NEED TO RUSH THIS, BUT I JUST WANTED TO SAY MY BACK IS KILLING ME.
YOU KNOW HE SHOULDN'T EVEN BE IN HERE, RIGHT?
I KNOW.
LISTEN, VERBIL, HOLLY IS IN MORTAL DANGER RIGHT NOW. ME AND BUTLER HAVE TO GET TO HAVEN CITY TO HELP HOLLY. PLEASE.
BY THE OLD GODS...OKAY, DIGGUMS. WHAT DO YOU NEED?
FIRST, I NEED YOU TO GET A MESSAGE TO FOALY. TELL HIM, OPAL KOBOI IS BACK. SOMEHOW SHE'S ESCAPED AND IS AFTER REVENGE.
O-OPAL?
SHE'S SETTLING SCORES WITH ANYONE WHO HAD A HAND IN HER IMPRISONMENT. WHICH, IF MEMORY SERVES ME CORRECTLY, INCLUDES YOU.
SECOND, I WANT YOUR LEP SHUTTLE. I KNOW WHERE IT'S DOCKED. I JUST NEED THE STARTER CHIP AND THE IGNITION CODE.
WHAT? I'D GO TO JAIL.

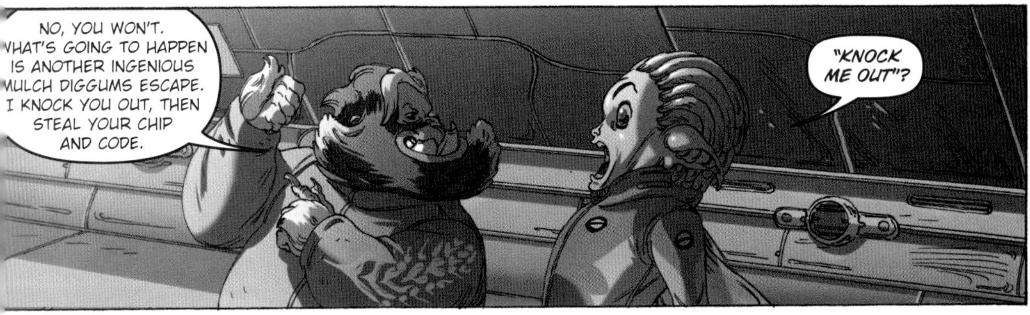
NO, YOU WON'T. WHAT'S GOING TO HAPPEN IS ANOTHER INGENIOUS MULCH DIGGUMS ESCAPE. I KNOCK YOU OUT, THEN STEAL YOUR CHIP AND CODE.
"KNOCK ME OUT"?

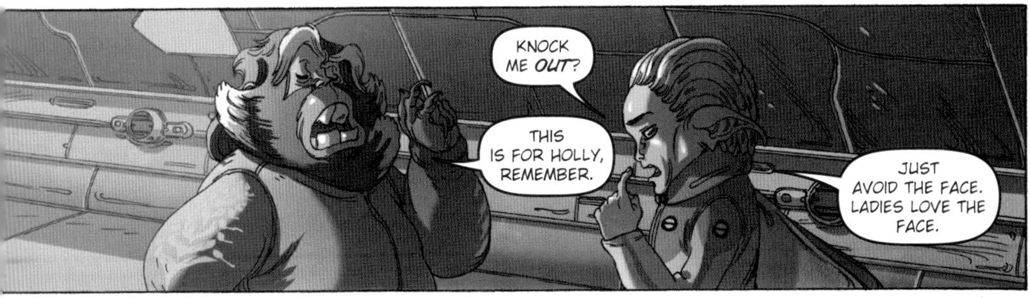
KNOCK ME OUT?
THIS IS FOR HOLLY, REMEMBER.
JUST AVOID THE FACE. LADIES LOVE THE FACE.

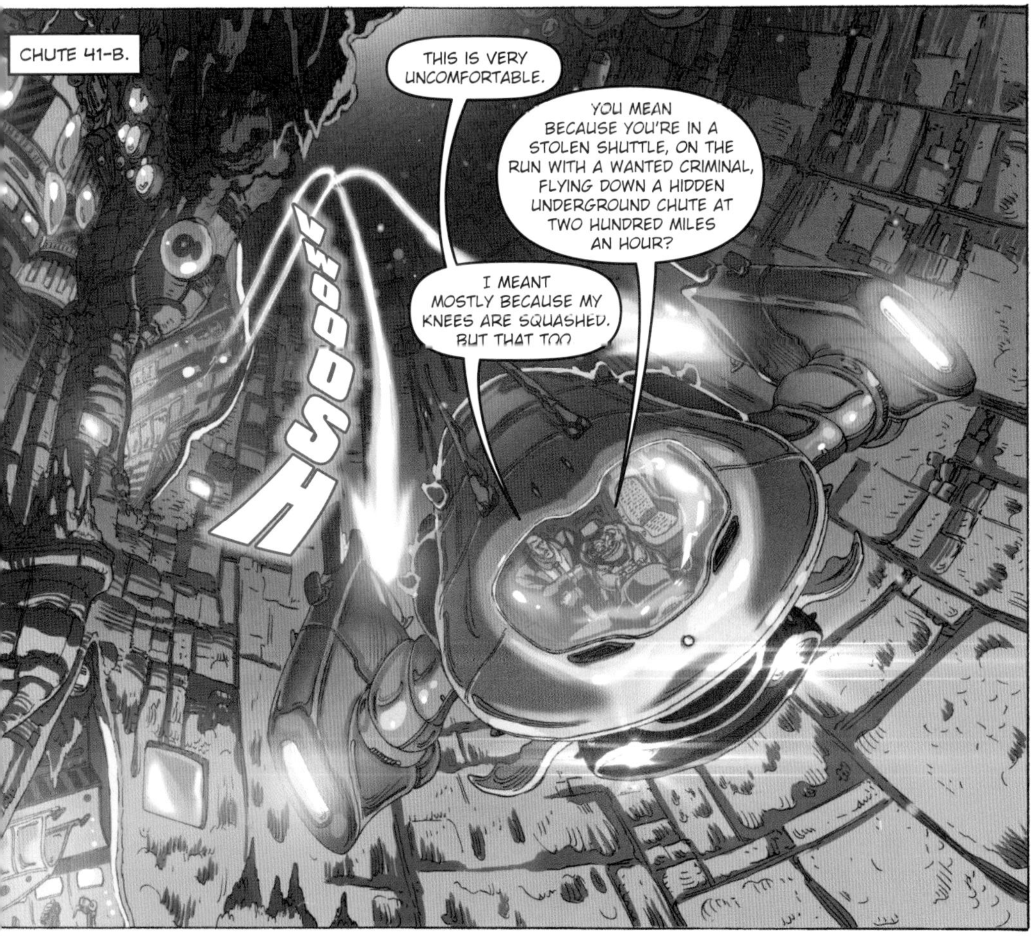
CHUTE 41-B.
THIS IS VERY UNCOMFORTABLE.
YOU MEAN BECAUSE YOU'RE IN A STOLEN SHUTTLE, ON THE RUN WITH A WANTED CRIMINAL, FLYING DOWN A HIDDEN UNDERGROUND CHUTE AT TWO HUNDRED MILES AN HOUR?
I MEANT MOSTLY BECAUSE MY KNEES ARE SQUASHED. BUT THAT TOO.
WHOOOOSH

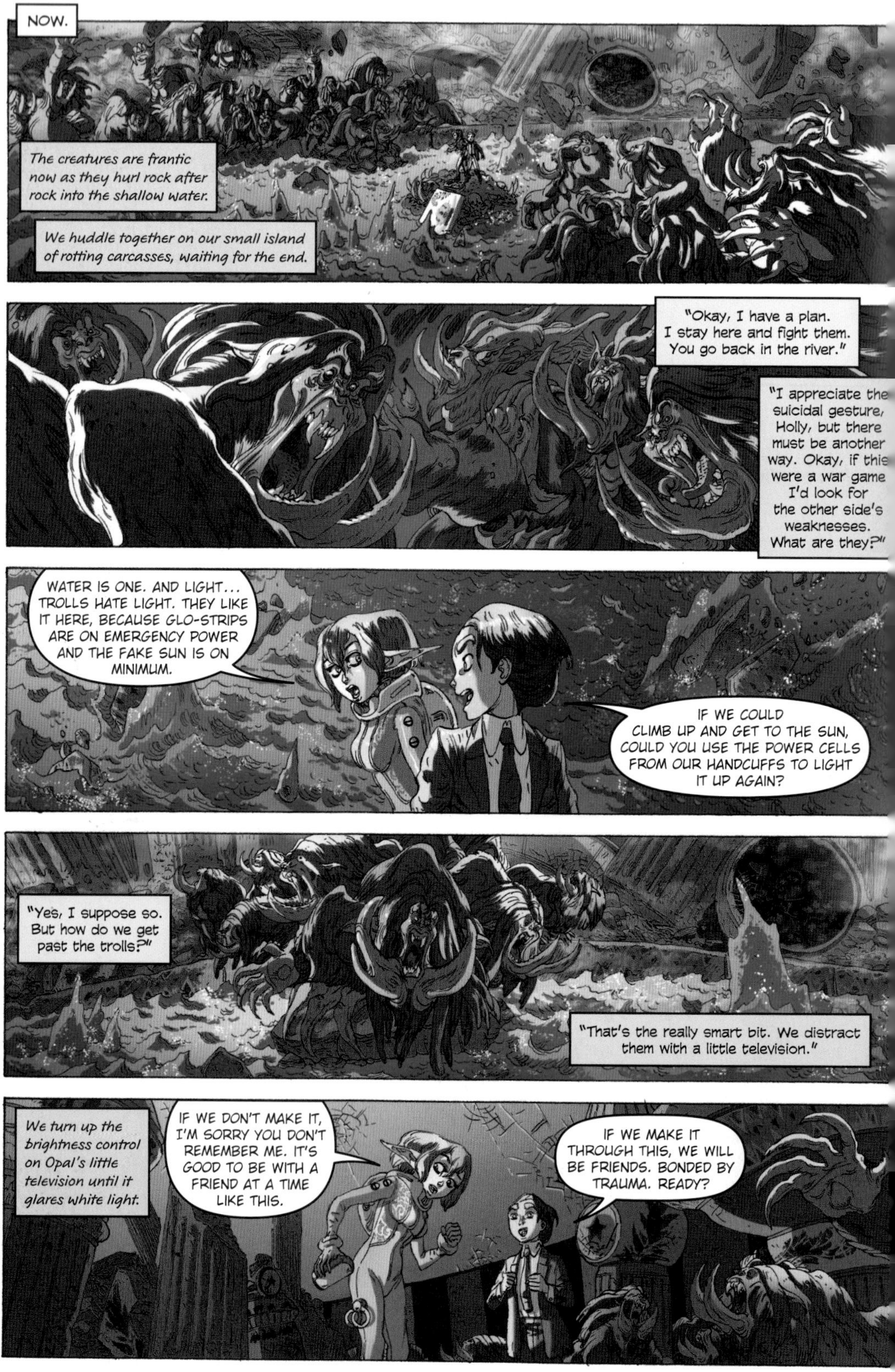
NOW.
The creatures are frantic now as they hurl rock after rock into the shallow water.
We huddle together on our small island of rotting carcasses, waiting for the end.
"Okay, I have a plan. I stay here and fight them. You go back in the river."
"I appreciate the suicidal gesture, Holly, but there must be another way. Okay, if this were a war game I'd look for the other side's weaknesses. What are they?"
WATER IS ONE. AND LIGHT... TROLLS HATE LIGHT. THEY LIKE IT HERE, BECAUSE GLO-STRIPS ARE ON EMERGENCY POWER AND THE FAKE SUN IS ON MINIMUM.
IF WE COULD CLIMB UP AND GET TO THE SUN, COULD YOU USE THE POWER CELLS FROM OUR HANDCUFFS TO LIGHT IT UP AGAIN?
"Yes, I suppose so. But how do we get past the trolls?"
"That's the really smart bit. We distract them with a little television."
We turn up the brightness control on Opal's little television until it glares white light.
IF WE DON'T MAKE IT, I'M SORRY YOU DON'T REMEMBER ME. IT'S GOOD TO BE WITH A FRIEND AT A TIME LIKE THIS.
IF WE MAKE IT THROUGH THIS, WE WILL BE FRIENDS. BONDED BY TRAUMA. READY?

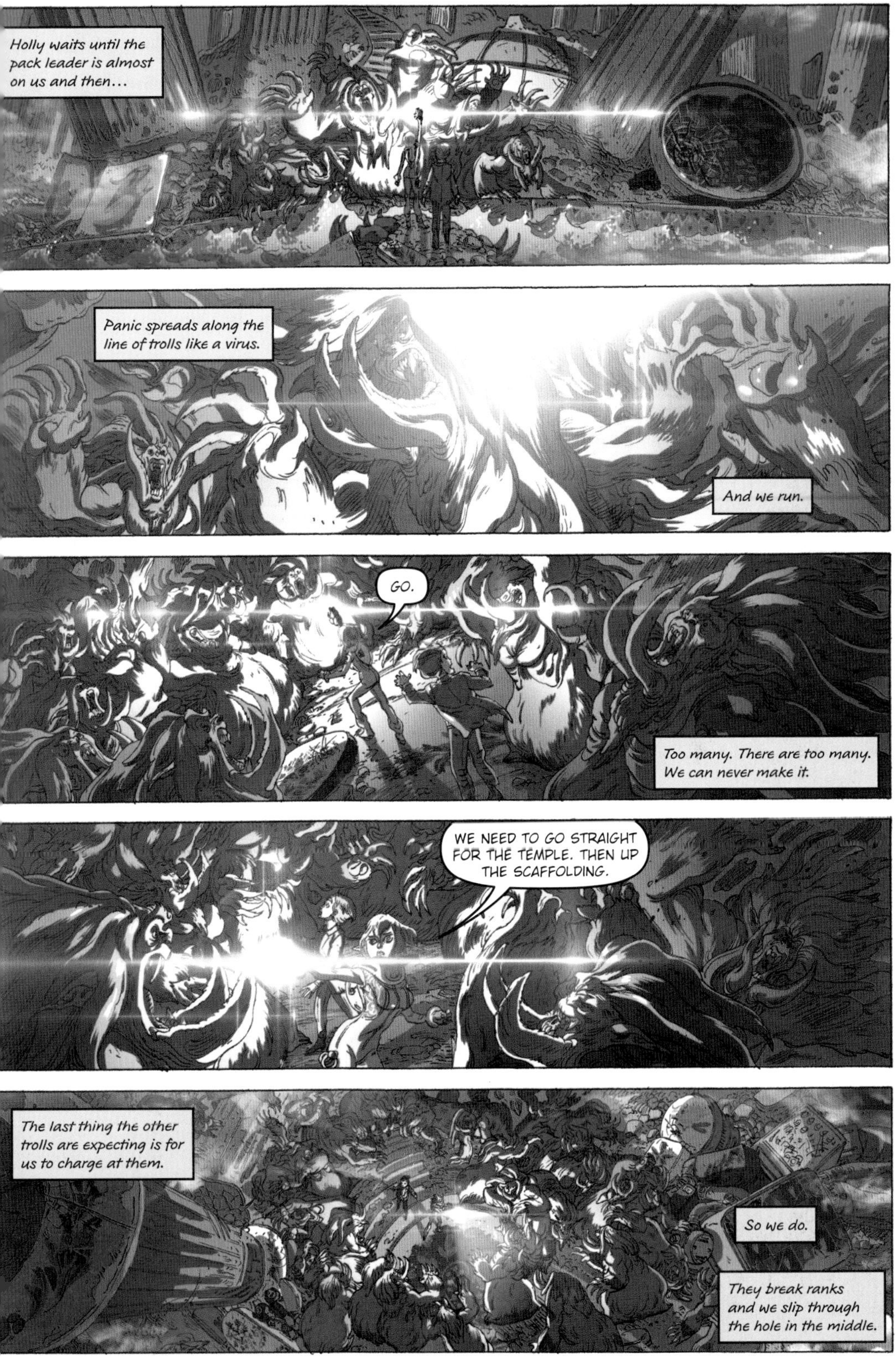
Holly waits until the pack leader is almost on us and then...
Panic spreads along the line of trolls like a virus.
And we run.
GO.
Too many. There are too many. We can never make it.
WE NEED TO GO STRAIGHT FOR THE TEMPLE. THEN UP THE SCAFFOLDING.
The last thing the other trolls are expecting is for us to charge at them.
So we do.
They break ranks and we slip through the hole in the middle.

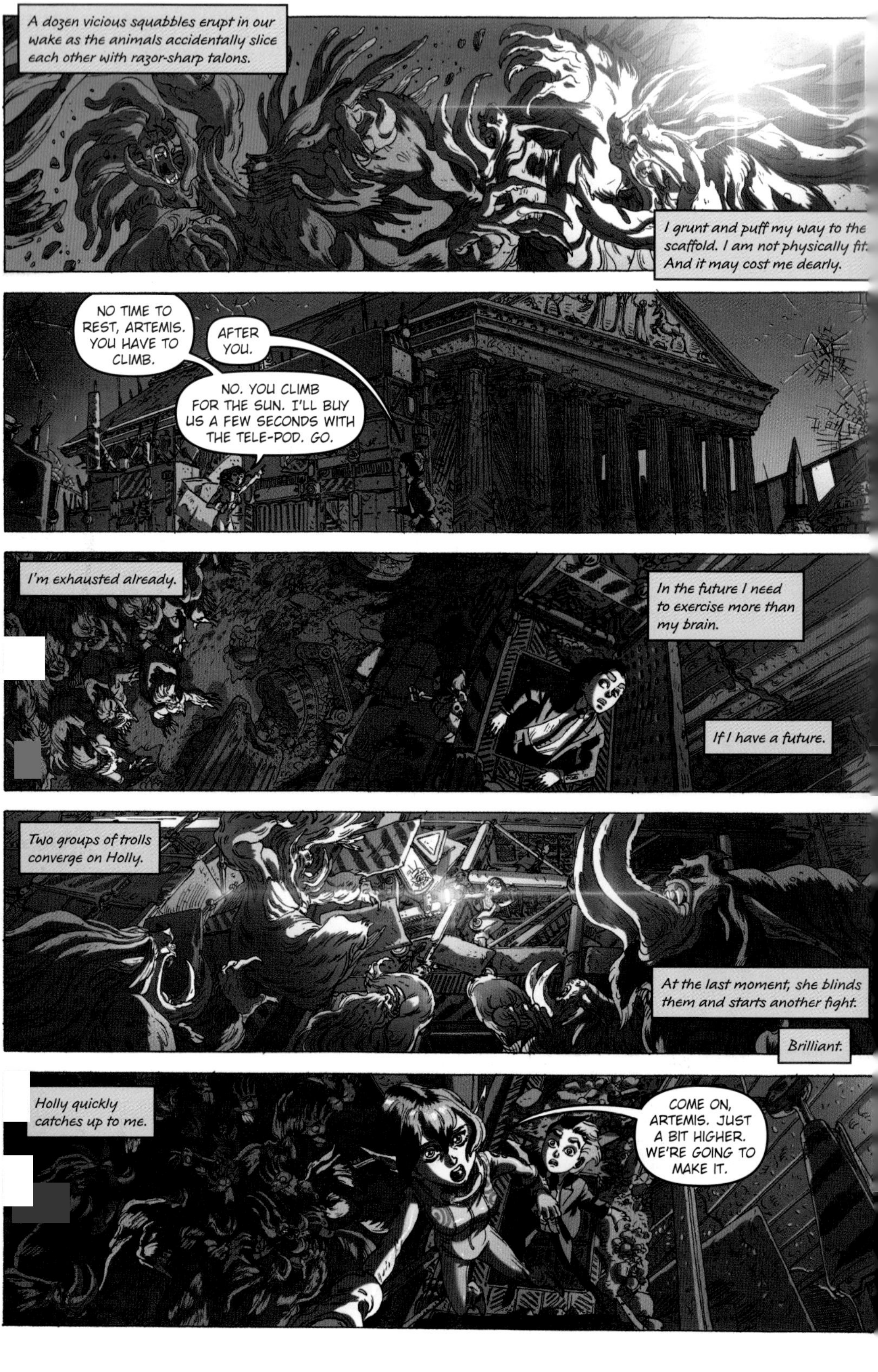
A dozen vicious squabbles erupt in our wake as the animals accidentally slice each other with razor-sharp talons.
I grunt and puff my way to the scaffold. I am not physically fit. And it may cost me dearly.
NO TIME TO REST, ARTEMIS. YOU HAVE TO CLIMB.
AFTER YOU.
NO. YOU CLIMB FOR THE SUN. I'LL BUY US A FEW SECONDS WITH THE TELE-POD. GO.
I'm exhausted already.
In the future I need to exercise more than my brain.
If I have a future.
Two groups of trolls converge on Holly.
At the last moment, she blinds them and starts another fight.
Brilliant.
Holly quickly catches up to me.
COME ON, ARTEMIS. JUST A BIT HIGHER. WE'RE GOING TO MAKE IT.

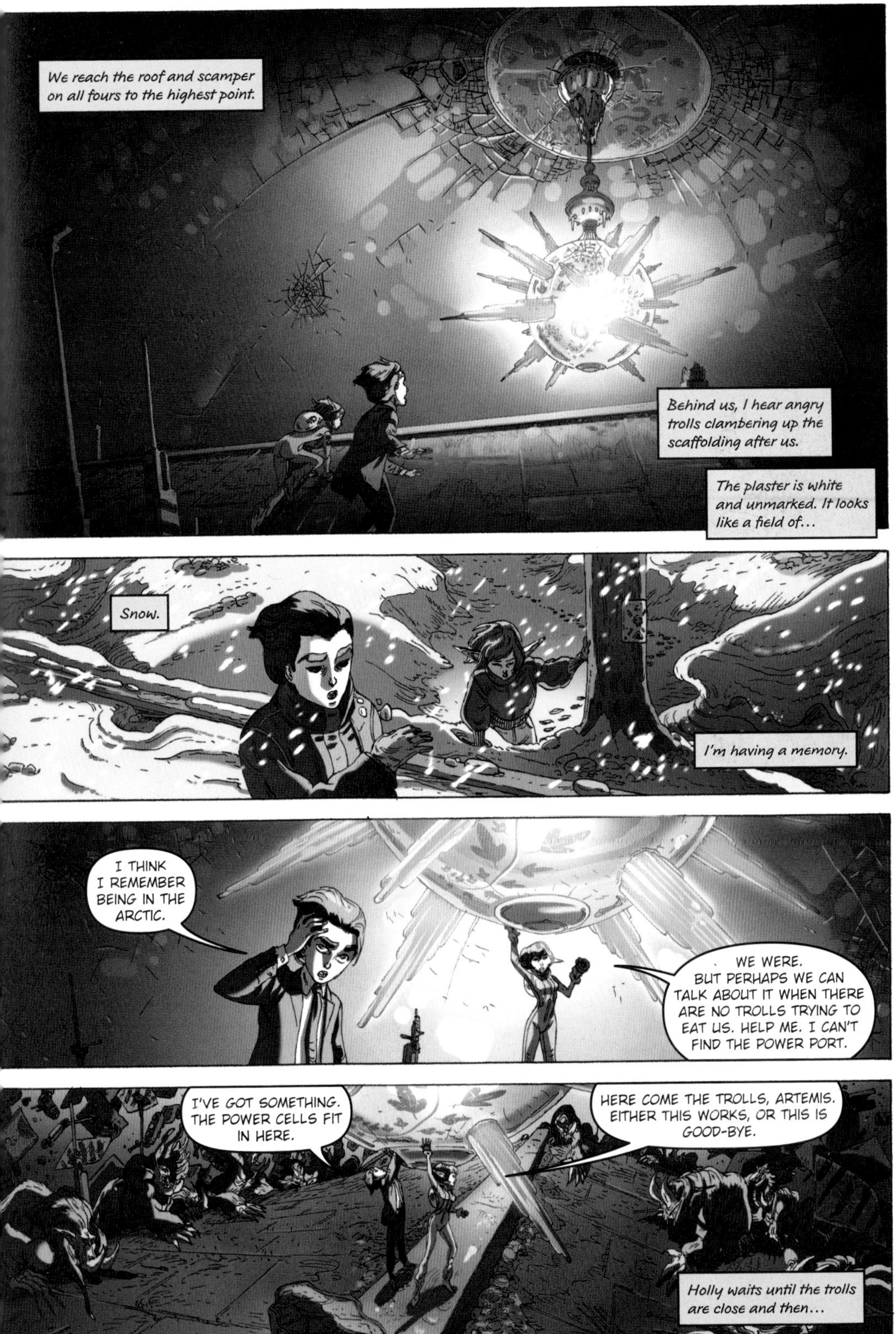
We reach the roof and scamper on all fours to the highest point.
Behind us, I hear angry trolls clambering up the scaffolding after us.
The plaster is white and unmarked. It looks like a field of...
Snow.
I'm having a memory.
I THINK I REMEMBER BEING IN THE ARCTIC.
WE WERE. BUT PERHAPS WE CAN TALK ABOUT IT WHEN THERE ARE NO TROLLS TRYING TO EAT US. HELP ME. I CAN'T FIND THE POWER PORT.
I'VE GOT SOMETHING. THE POWER CELLS FIT IN HERE.
HERE COME THE TROLLS, ARTEMIS. EITHER THIS WORKS, OR THIS IS GOOD-BYE.
Holly waits until the trolls are close and then...

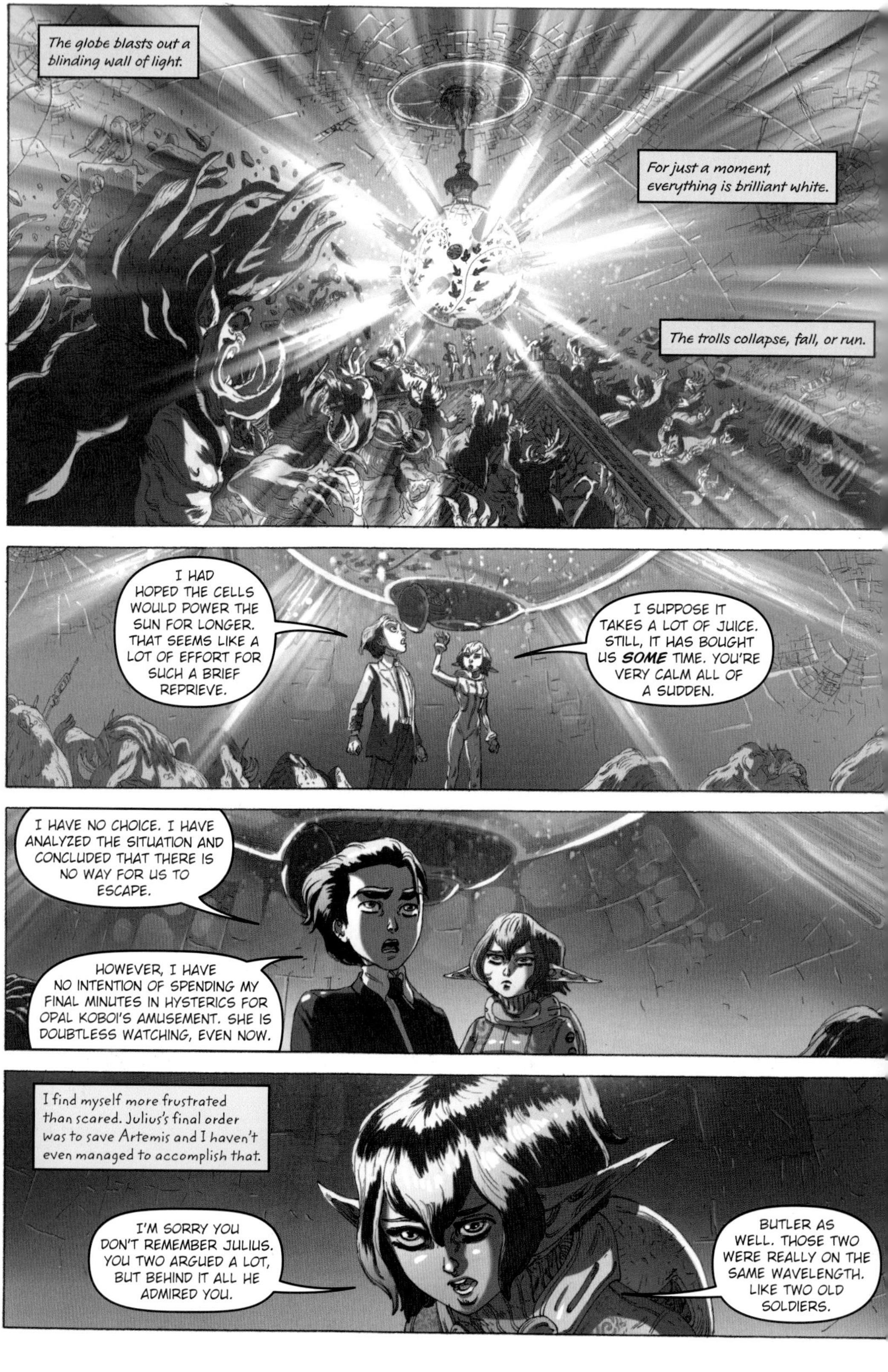
The globe blasts out a blinding wall of light.
For just a moment, everything is brilliant white.
The trolls collapse, fall, or run.
I HAD HOPED THE CELLS WOULD POWER THE SUN FOR LONGER. THAT SEEMS LIKE A LOT OF EFFORT FOR SUCH A BRIEF REPRIEVE.
I SUPPOSE IT TAKES A LOT OF JUICE. STILL, IT HAS BOUGHT US SOME TIME. YOU'RE VERY CALM ALL OF A SUDDEN.
I HAVE NO CHOICE. I HAVE ANALYZED THE SITUATION AND CONCLUDED THAT THERE IS NO WAY FOR US TO ESCAPE.
HOWEVER, I HAVE NO INTENTION OF SPENDING MY FINAL MINUTES IN HYSTERICS FOR OPAL KOBOI'S AMUSEMENT. SHE IS DOUBTLESS WATCHING, EVEN NOW.
I find myself more frustrated than scared. Julius's final order was to save Artemis and I haven't even managed to accomplish that.
I'M SORRY YOU DON'T REMEMBER JULIUS. YOU TWO ARGUED A LOT, BUT BEHIND IT ALL HE ADMIRED YOU.
BUTLER AS WELL. THOSE TWO WERE REALLY ON THE SAME WAVELENGTH. LIKE TWO OLD SOLDIERS.

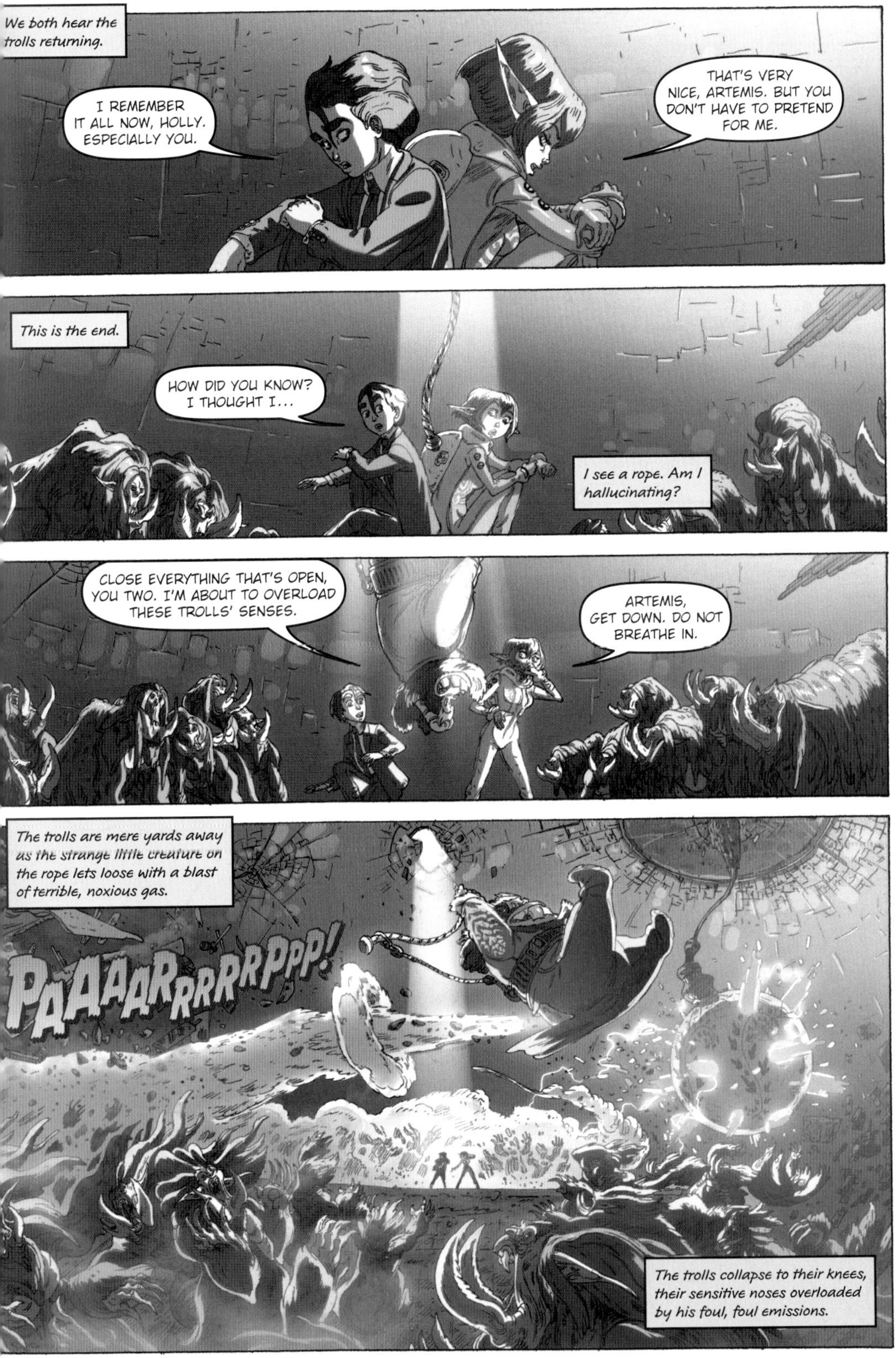

We both hear the trolls returning.
I REMEMBER IT ALL NOW, HOLLY. ESPECIALLY YOU.
THAT'S VERY NICE, ARTEMIS. BUT YOU DON'T HAVE TO PRETEND FOR ME.
This is the end.
HOW DID YOU KNOW? I THOUGHT I...
I see a rope. Am I hallucinating?
CLOSE EVERYTHING THAT'S OPEN, YOU TWO. I'M ABOUT TO OVERLOAD THESE TROLLS' SENSES.
ARTEMIS, GET DOWN. DO NOT BREATHE IN.
The trolls are mere yards away as the strange little creature on the rope lets loose with a blast of terrible, noxious gas.
PAAAARRRRRPPP!
The trolls collapse to their knees, their sensitive noses overloaded by his foul, foul emissions.

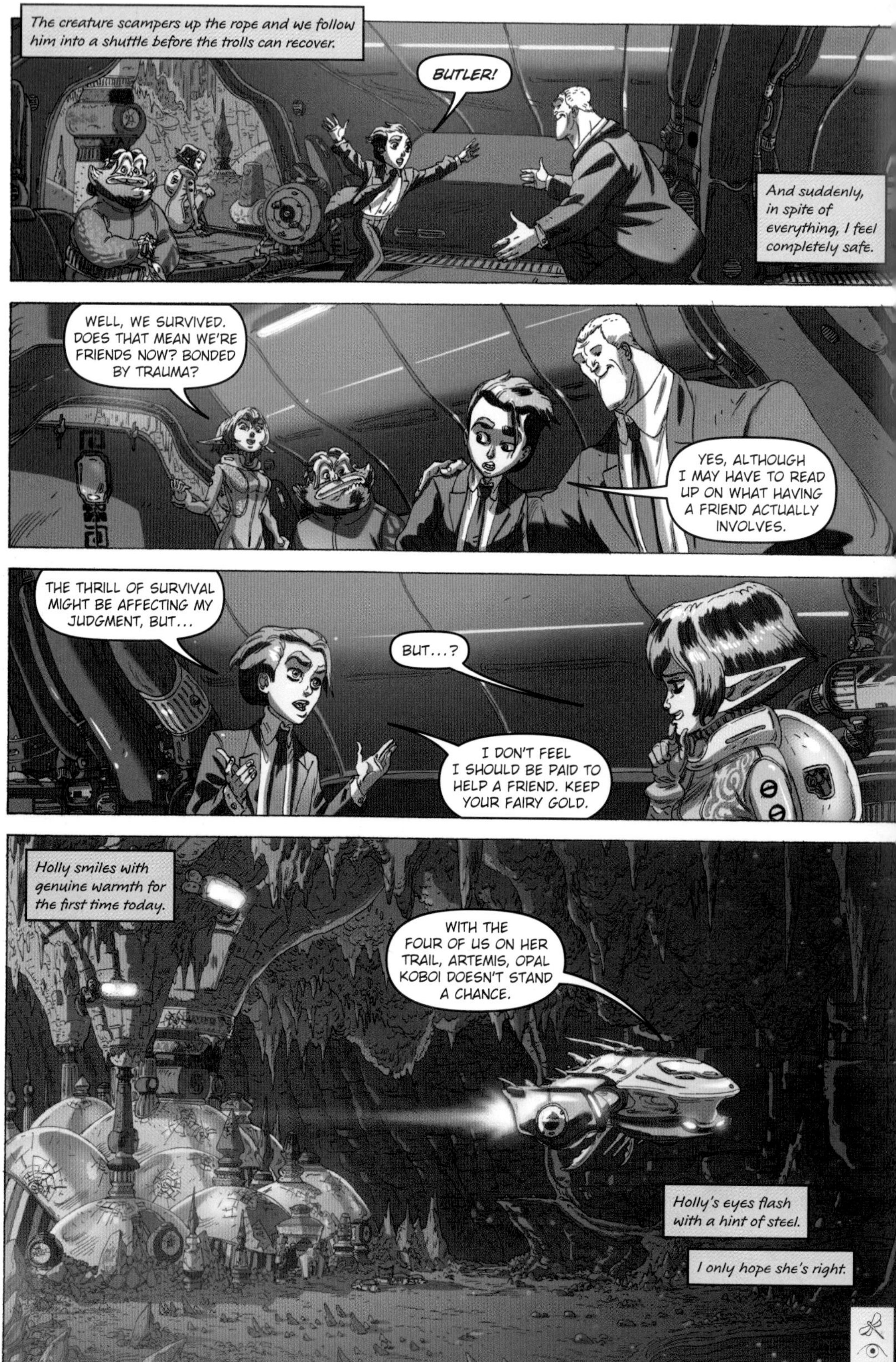
The creature scampers up the rope and we follow him into a shuttle before the trolls can recover.
BUTLER!
And suddenly, in spite of everything, I feel completely safe.
WELL, WE SURVIVED. DOES THAT MEAN WE'RE FRIENDS NOW? BONDED BY TRAUMA?
YES, ALTHOUGH I MAY HAVE TO READ UP ON WHAT HAVING A FRIEND ACTUALLY INVOLVES.
THE THRILL OF SURVIVAL MIGHT BE AFFECTING MY JUDGMENT, BUT...
BUT...?
I DON'T FEEL I SHOULD BE PAID TO HELP A FRIEND. KEEP YOUR FAIRY GOLD.
Holly smiles with genuine warmth for the first time today.
WITH THE FOUR OF US ON HER TRAIL, ARTEMIS, OPAL KOBOI DOESN'T STAND A CHANCE.
Holly's eyes flash with a hint of steel.
I only hope she's right.

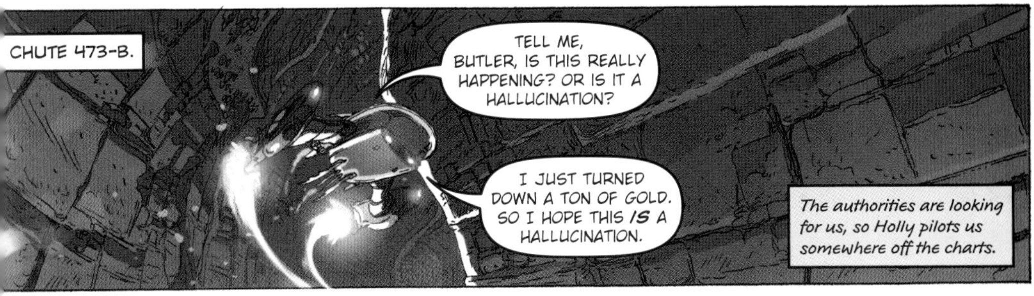
CHUTE 473-B.
TELL ME, BUTLER, IS THIS REALLY HAPPENING? OR IS IT A HALLUCINATION?
I JUST TURNED DOWN A TON OF GOLD. SO I HOPE THIS *IS* A HALLUCINATION.
The authorities are looking for us, so Holly pilots us somewhere off the charts.

CHAPTER 8: SOME INTELLIGENT CONVERSATION

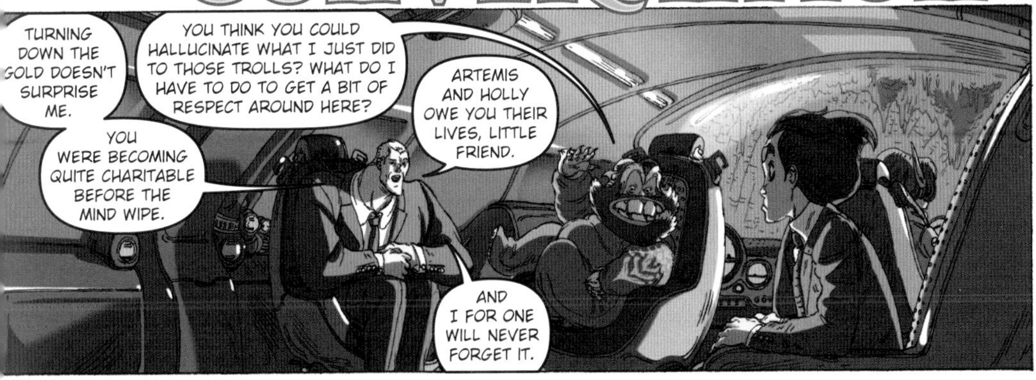
TURNING DOWN THE GOLD DOESN'T SURPRISE ME.
YOU WERE BECOMING QUITE CHARITABLE BEFORE THE MIND WIPE.
YOU THINK YOU COULD HALLUCINATE WHAT I JUST DID TO THOSE TROLLS? WHAT DO I HAVE TO DO TO GET A BIT OF RESPECT AROUND HERE?
ARTEMIS AND HOLLY OWE YOU THEIR LIVES, LITTLE FRIEND.
AND I FOR ONE WILL NEVER FORGET IT.

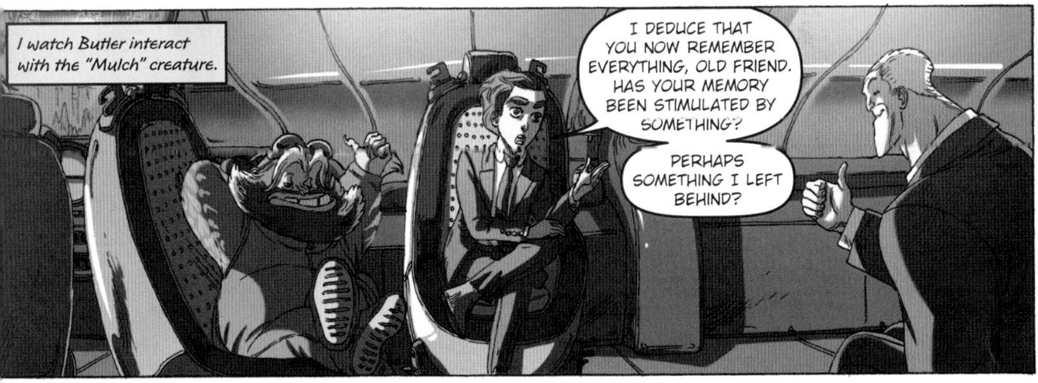
I watch Butler interact with the "Mulch" creature.
I DEDUCE THAT YOU NOW REMEMBER EVERYTHING, OLD FRIEND. HAS YOUR MEMORY BEEN STIMULATED BY SOMETHING?
PERHAPS SOMETHING I LEFT BEHIND?

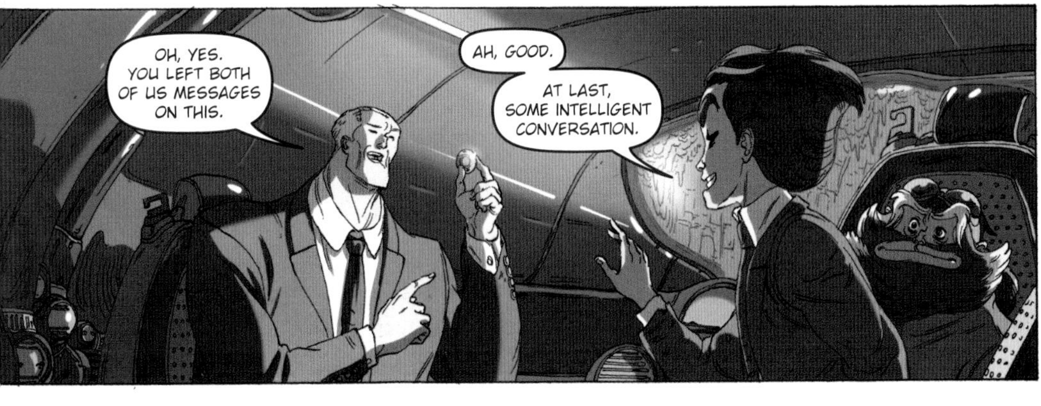
OH, YES. YOU LEFT BOTH OF US MESSAGES ON THIS.
AH, GOOD.
AT LAST, SOME INTELLIGENT CONVERSATION.

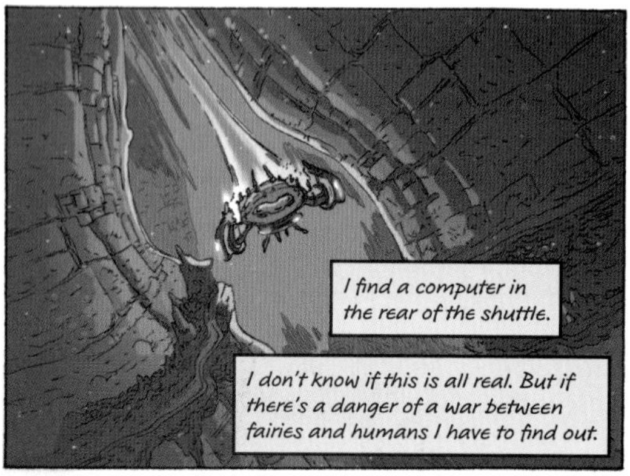
I find a computer in the rear of the shuttle.
I don't know if this is all real. But if there's a danger of a war between fairies and humans I have to find out.

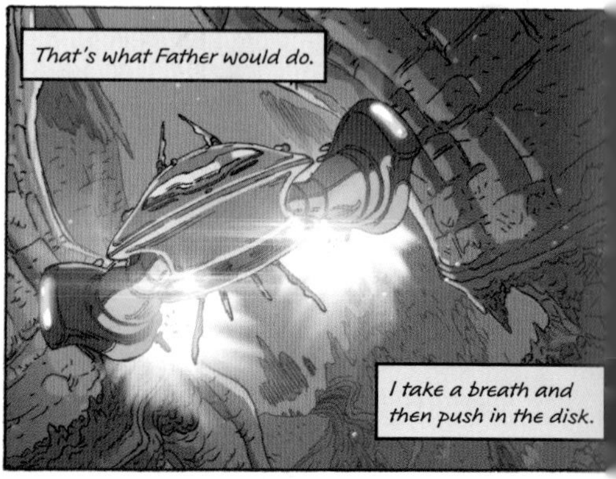
That's what Father would do.
I take a breath and then push in the disk.

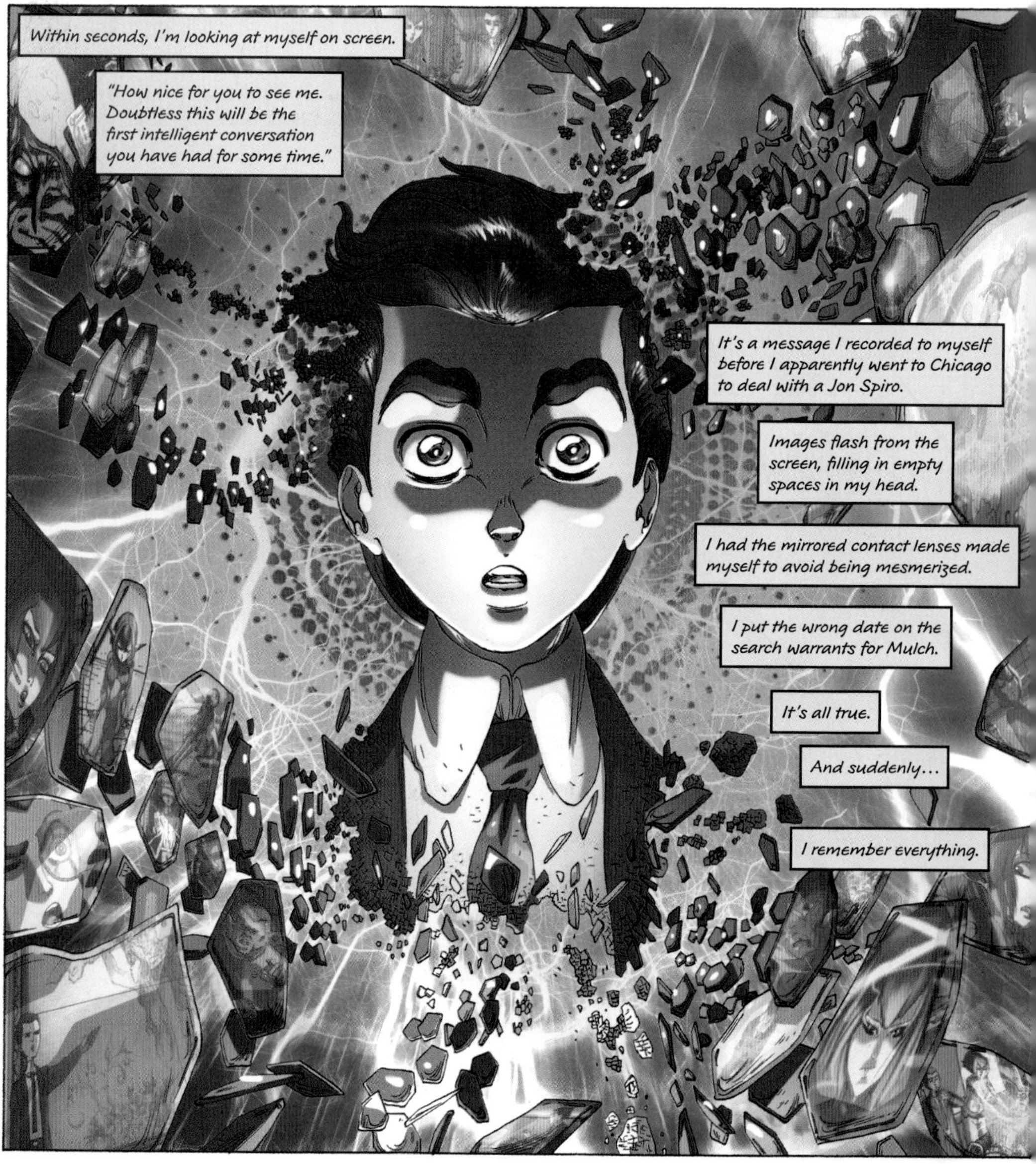
Within seconds, I'm looking at myself on screen.
"How nice for you to see me. Doubtless this will be the first intelligent conversation you have had for some time."
It's a message I recorded to myself before I apparently went to Chicago to deal with a Jon Spiro.
Images flash from the screen, filling in empty spaces in my head.
I had the mirrored contact lenses made myself to avoid being mesmerized.
I put the wrong date on the search warrants for Mulch.
It's all true.
And suddenly...
I remember everything.

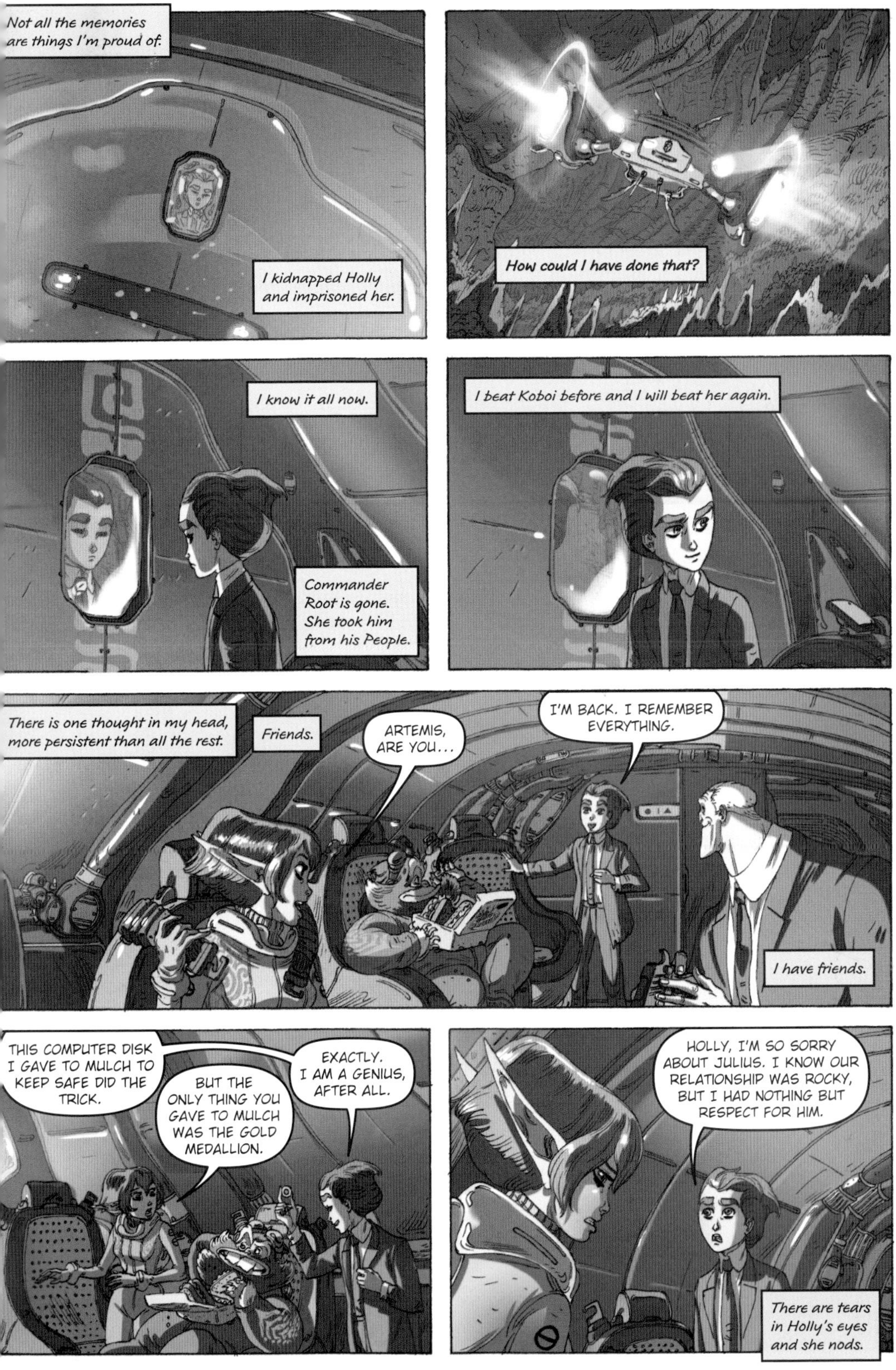
Not all the memories are things I'm proud of.
I kidnapped Holly and imprisoned her.
How could I have done that?
I know it all now.
Commander Root is gone. She took him from his People.
I beat Koboi before and I will beat her again.
There is one thought in my head, more persistent than all the rest.
Friends.
ARTEMIS, ARE YOU...
I'M BACK. I REMEMBER EVERYTHING.
I have friends.
THIS COMPUTER DISK I GAVE TO MULCH TO KEEP SAFE DID THE TRICK.
BUT THE ONLY THING YOU GAVE TO MULCH WAS THE GOLD MEDALLION.
EXACTLY. I AM A GENIUS, AFTER ALL.
HOLLY, I'M SO SORRY ABOUT JULIUS. I KNOW OUR RELATIONSHIP WAS ROCKY, BUT I HAD NOTHING BUT RESPECT FOR HIM.
There are tears in Holly's eyes and she nods.

NOW WE'RE ALL REACQUAINTED, WE NEED TO LOCATE OPAL KOBOI. SHE COULD BE ANYWHERE.

NO NEED. I KNOW EXACTLY WHERE OUR WOULD-BE WAR STARTER IS. LIKE ALL MEGALOMANIACS, SHE HAS A TENDENCY TO SHOW OFF.

OPAL REVEALED MORE OF HER PLANS THAN SHE KNEW WHEN SHE SAID HER HUMAN NAME WAS BELINDA ZITO.

IF YOU WISHED TO SOMEHOW LEAD THE HUMANS TO THE FAIRY PEOPLE, WHO BETTER TO ADOPT YOU THAN BILLIONAIRE ENVIRONMENTALIST GIOVANNI ZITO?

THERE'S BEEN A MUD MAN NAMED ZITO ALL OVER THE HUMAN NEWS CHANNELS TODAY. DO YOU THINK IT'S THE SAME ONE?

I REALLY HOPE NOT, BUT I'D BET MY LIFE IT IS.

Of course, it is.

We have sent craft into space, and yet we have no idea what is at the center of our own planet. Today we will make history and find out.

Today, for the first time ever, we will send a probe all the way down into the outer core.

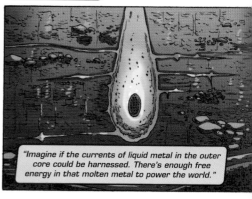

"Imagine if the currents of liquid metal in the outer core could be harnessed. There's enough free energy in that molten metal to power the world."

SO TODAY WE ARE SENDING AN UNMANNED PROBE, BRISTLING WITH SENSORS. WHATEVER IS DOWN THERE, WE WILL FIND IT.

SEVERAL LARGE CHARGES WILL BE DETONATED UNDERGROUND. THEY WILL CREATE A MILLION TONS OF MOLTEN IRON TO ALLOW THE PROBE TO DESCEND.

AND WHEN IS THIS HAPPENING, MR. ZITO?

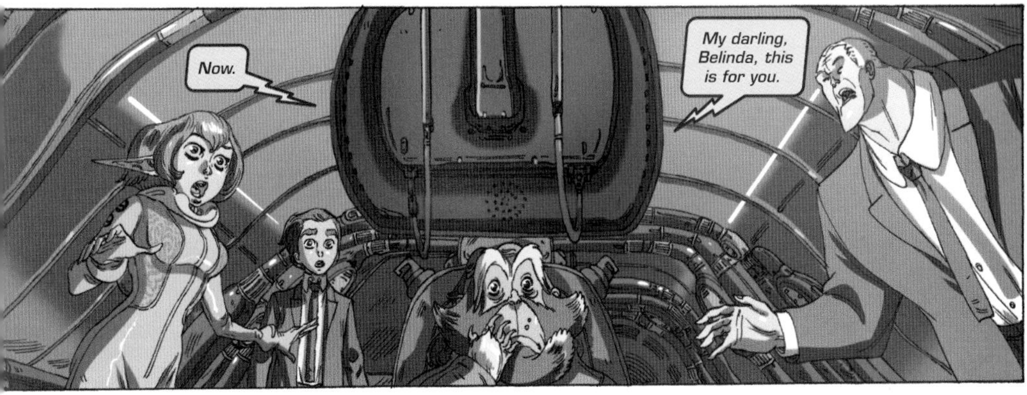
Now.
My darling, Belinda, this is for you.

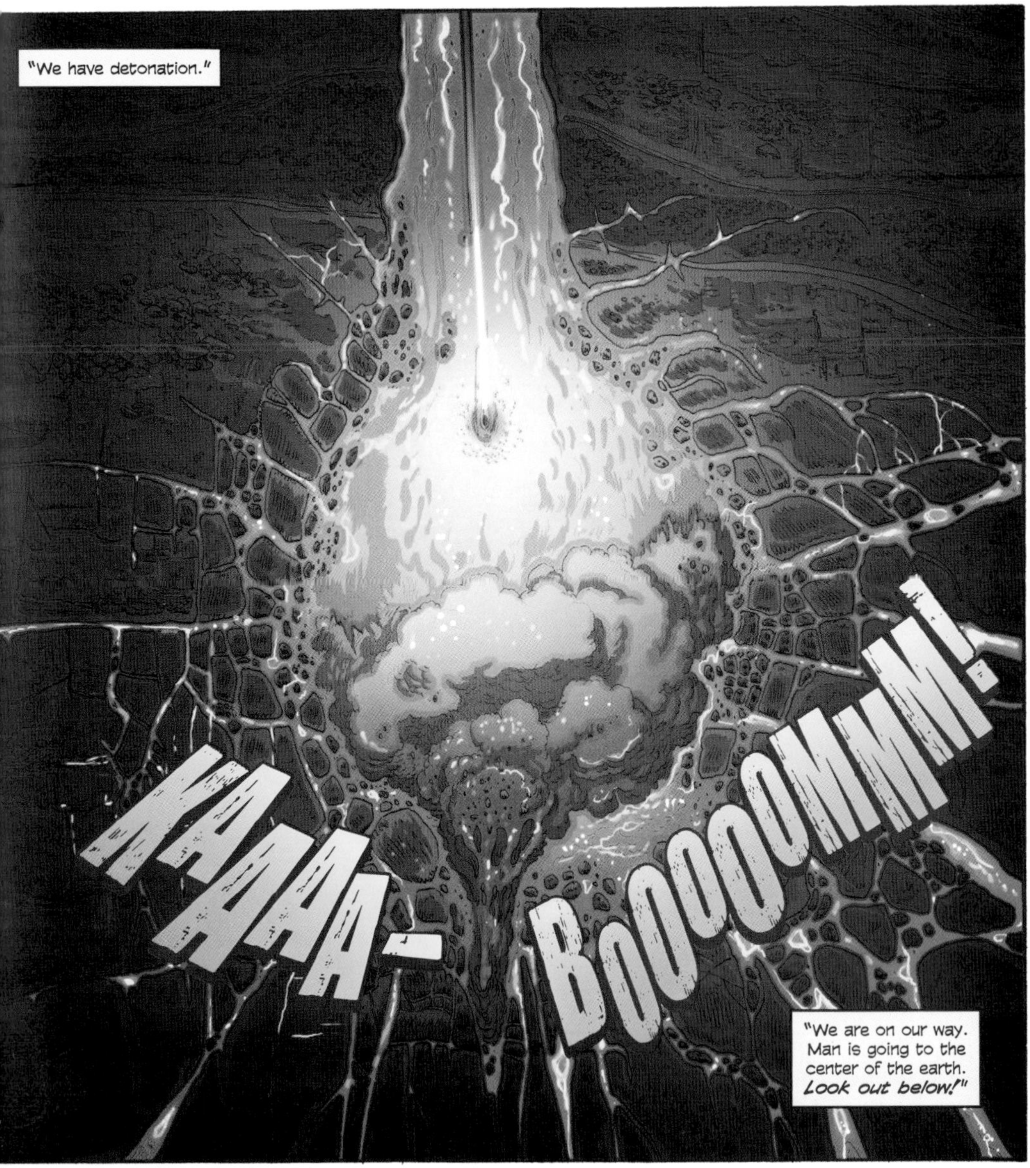
"We have detonation."
KAAAA-BOOOOOMMM!
"We are on our way. Man is going to the center of the earth. *Look out below!*"

The moods in our shuttle range from glum to desolate. Our communications are down and we have no way to warn Foaly.

I HAVE NO DOUBT HE ALREADY KNOWS, HOLLY. THAT CENTAUR MONITORS ALL THE HUMAN NEWS.

I'M SURE HE DOES. BUT HE'S PLANNING FOR A CRACKPOT HUMAN SCHEME. NOT ONE BACKED UP BY OPAL'S ADVANCED FAIRY KNOWLEDGE.

I HAVE TO TURN MYSELF IN, EVEN IF I AM A MURDER SUSPECT.

YOU DO THAT AND THEY'LL LOCK YOU UP AND WE'LL NEVER STOP THAT PROBE.

ARTEMIS IS RIGHT, HOLLY.

ASK YOURSELF: WHAT WOULD COMMANDER ROOT DO?

JULIUS WOULD TAKE CARE OF OPAL KOBOI HIMSELF. YOU KNOW HE WOULD.

AND THAT'S EXACTLY WHAT WE'RE GOING TO DO.

EXCELLENT.

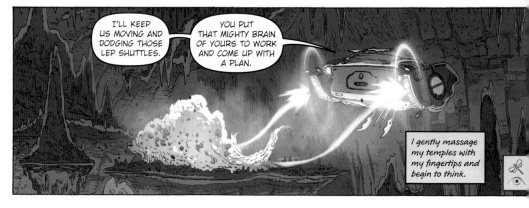

I'LL KEEP US MOVING AND DODGING THOSE LEP SHUTTLES.

YOU PUT THAT MIGHTY BRAIN OF YOURS TO WORK AND COME UP WITH A PLAN.

I gently massage my temples with my fingertips and begin to think.

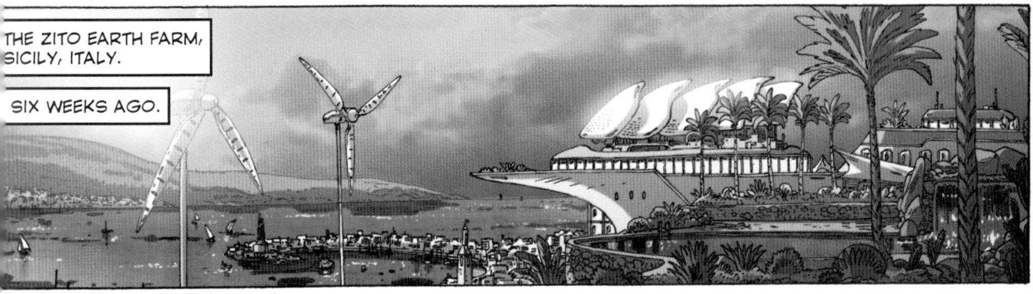
THE ZITO EARTH FARM, SICILY, ITALY.
SIX WEEKS AGO.

CHAPTER 9: DADDY'S GIRL

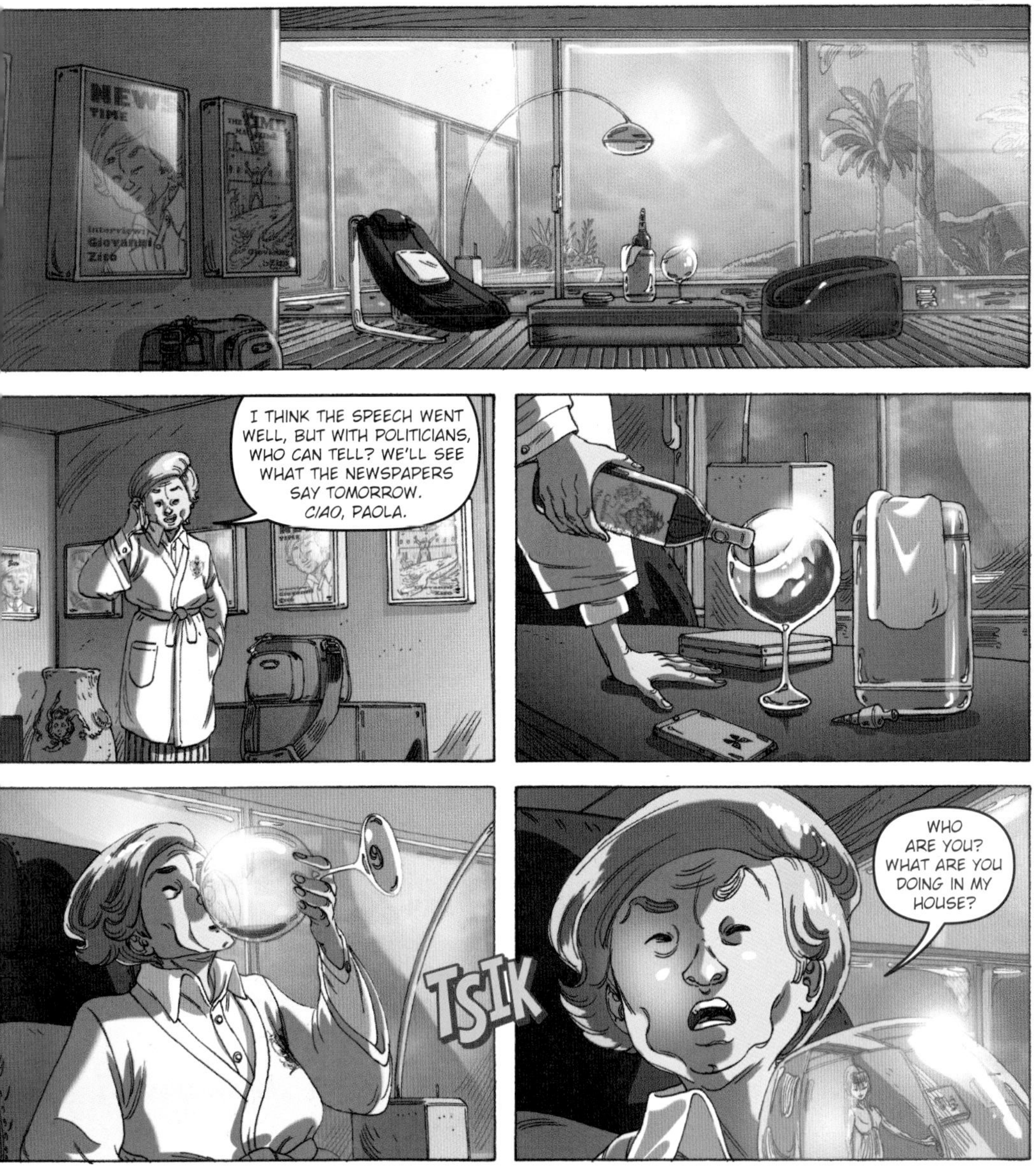
I THINK THE SPEECH WENT WELL, BUT WITH POLITICIANS, WHO CAN TELL? WE'LL SEE WHAT THE NEWSPAPERS SAY TOMORROW. *CIAO*, PAOLA.
TSIK
WHO ARE YOU? WHAT ARE YOU DOING IN MY HOUSE?

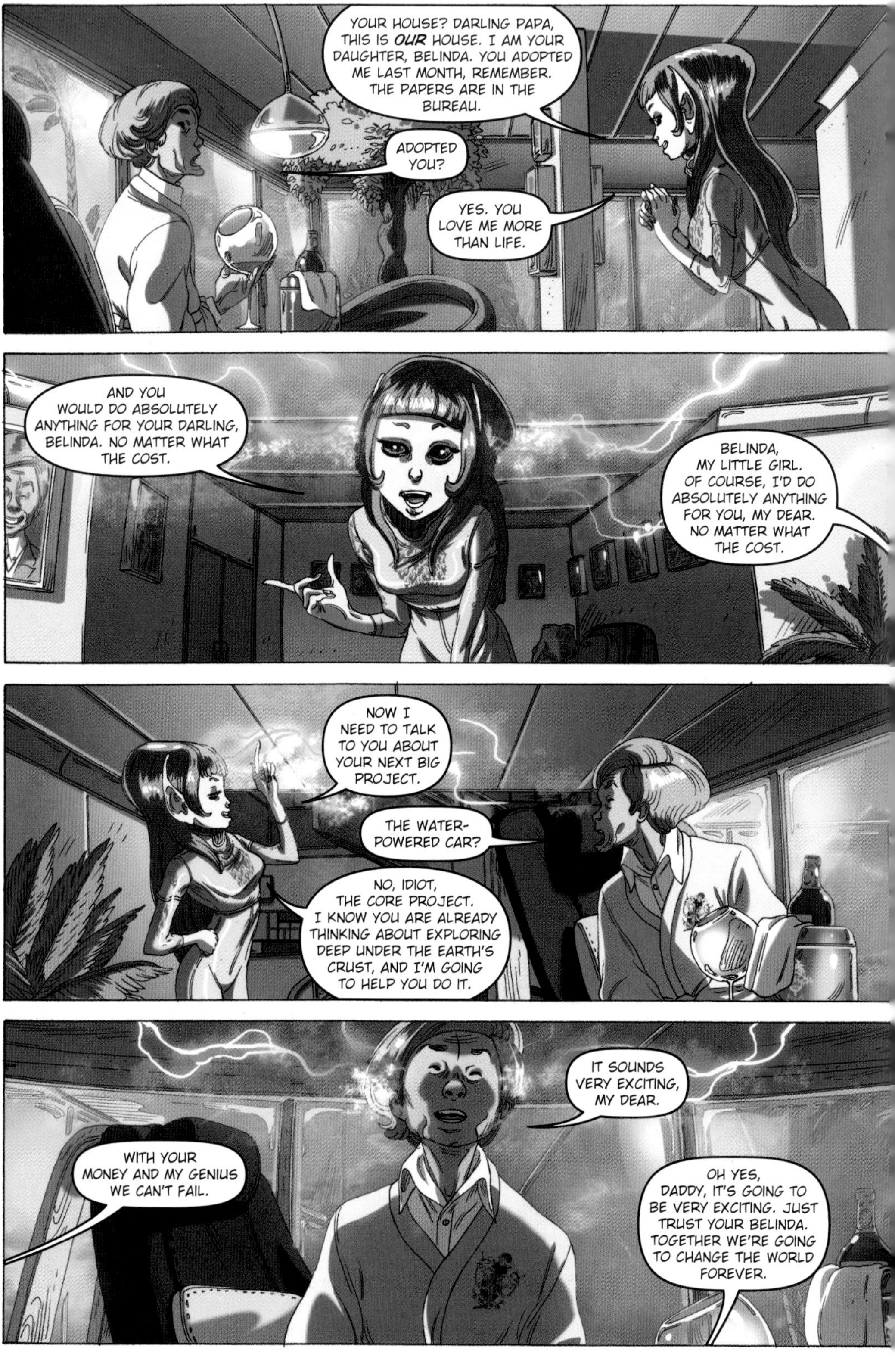
YOUR HOUSE? DARLING PAPA, THIS IS *OUR* HOUSE. I AM YOUR DAUGHTER, BELINDA. YOU ADOPTED ME LAST MONTH, REMEMBER. THE PAPERS ARE IN THE BUREAU.
ADOPTED YOU?
YES. YOU LOVE ME MORE THAN LIFE.
AND YOU WOULD DO ABSOLUTELY ANYTHING FOR YOUR DARLING, BELINDA. NO MATTER WHAT THE COST.
BELINDA, MY LITTLE GIRL. OF COURSE, I'D DO ABSOLUTELY ANYTHING FOR YOU, MY DEAR. NO MATTER WHAT THE COST.
NOW I NEED TO TALK TO YOU ABOUT YOUR NEXT BIG PROJECT.
THE WATER-POWERED CAR?
NO, IDIOT, THE CORE PROJECT. I KNOW YOU ARE ALREADY THINKING ABOUT EXPLORING DEEP UNDER THE EARTH'S CRUST, AND I'M GOING TO HELP YOU DO IT.
IT SOUNDS VERY EXCITING, MY DEAR.
WITH YOUR MONEY AND MY GENIUS WE CAN'T FAIL.
OH YES, DADDY, IT'S GOING TO BE VERY EXCITING. JUST TRUST YOUR BELINDA. TOGETHER WE'RE GOING TO CHANGE THE WORLD FOREVER.

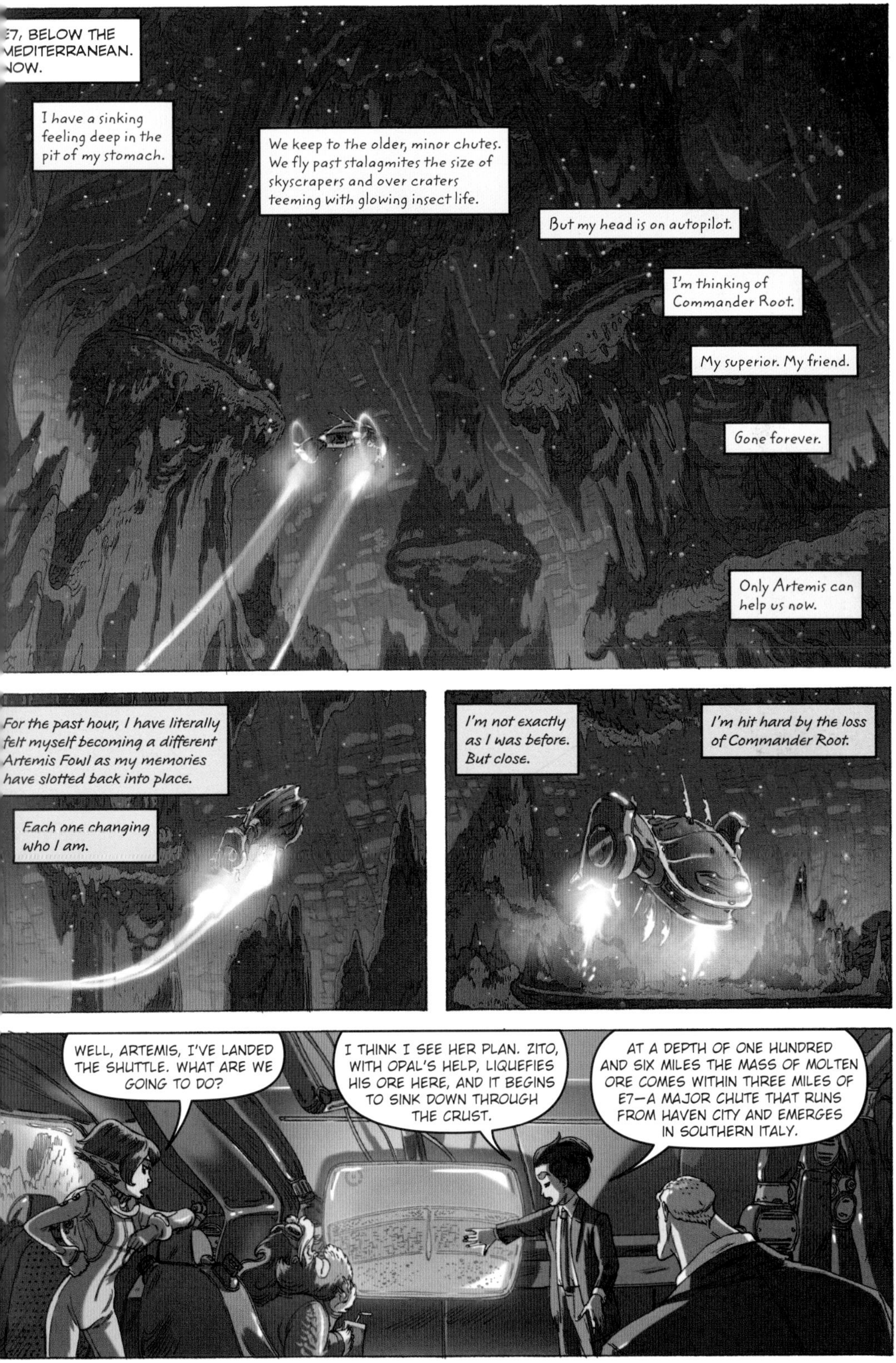
E7, BELOW THE MEDITERRANEAN. NOW.
I have a sinking feeling deep in the pit of my stomach.
We keep to the older, minor chutes. We fly past stalagmites the size of skyscrapers and over craters teeming with glowing insect life.
But my head is on autopilot.
I'm thinking of Commander Root.
My superior. My friend.
Gone forever.
Only Artemis can help us now.
For the past hour, I have literally felt myself becoming a different Artemis Fowl as my memories have slotted back into place.
Each one changing who I am.
I'm not exactly as I was before. But close.
I'm hit hard by the loss of Commander Root.
WELL, ARTEMIS, I'VE LANDED THE SHUTTLE. WHAT ARE WE GOING TO DO?
I THINK I SEE HER PLAN. ZITO, WITH OPAL'S HELP, LIQUEFIES HIS ORE HERE, AND IT BEGINS TO SINK DOWN THROUGH THE CRUST.
AT A DEPTH OF ONE HUNDRED AND SIX MILES THE MASS OF MOLTEN ORE COMES WITHIN THREE MILES OF E7—A MAJOR CHUTE THAT RUNS FROM HAVEN CITY AND EMERGES IN SOUTHERN ITALY.

ALL OPAL WOULD HAVE TO DO TO BRING DISASTER TO HAVEN CITY IS BLOW A CRACK BETWEEN THE ORE'S PATH AND CHUTE E7. THEN THE ORE WOULD FOLLOW THE PATH OF LEAST RESISTANCE, AND FLOW INTO THE CHUTE...

...AND DOWN STRAIGHT TO HAVEN CITY.

EXACTLY. MY BEST GUESS IS THAT, EVEN WITH THE BLAST WALLS, HALF THE CITY WOULD BE DESTROYED.

AND THE OTHER HALF WOULD BE LEFT BROADCASTING SIGNALS FOR THE HUMAN WORLD TO HEAR.

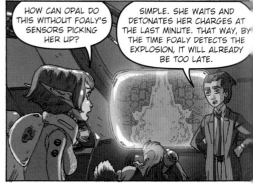

HOW CAN OPAL DO THIS WITHOUT FOALY'S SENSORS PICKING HER UP?

SIMPLE. SHE WAITS AND DETONATES HER CHARGES AT THE LAST MINUTE. THAT WAY, BY THE TIME FOALY DETECTS THE EXPLOSION, IT WILL ALREADY BE TOO LATE.

OKAY, SO ALL WE NEED TO DO IS FIND OPAL'S CHARGES AND REMOVE THEM?

IF ONLY IT WERE THAT SIMPLE. OPAL WILL NOT TAKE ANY CHANCES WITH THINGS GOING WRONG. SHE'LL WAIT UNTIL THE LAST MINUTE TO PLANT HER CHARGES.

SO WE GET INTO THE CHUTE AND WAIT UNTIL SHE PLANTS THE CHARGES?

TOO RISKY. IF FOALY PICKS US UP ON HIS SENSORS, THEY'LL SEND LEP SHIPS. WE'LL BE PURSUED AND ARRESTED, THANKS TO YOU MURDERING COMMANDER ROOT, REMEMBER?

BUT, ARTEMIS, SURELY EVERYONE MUST KNOW THAT OPAL HAS ESCAPED BY NOW.

THERE'S THE RUB. THAT SINGLE POINT IS THE KEY TO EVERYTHING. PEOPLE OBVIOUSLY *DON'T* KNOW OPAL HAS ESCAPED.

MY BEST GUESS WOULD BE THAT THE OPAL IN CUSTODY IS SOME KIND OF CLONE CRAFTED BY FAIRY TECHNOLOGY. ALIVE, BUT ESSENTIALLY BRAIN-DEAD.

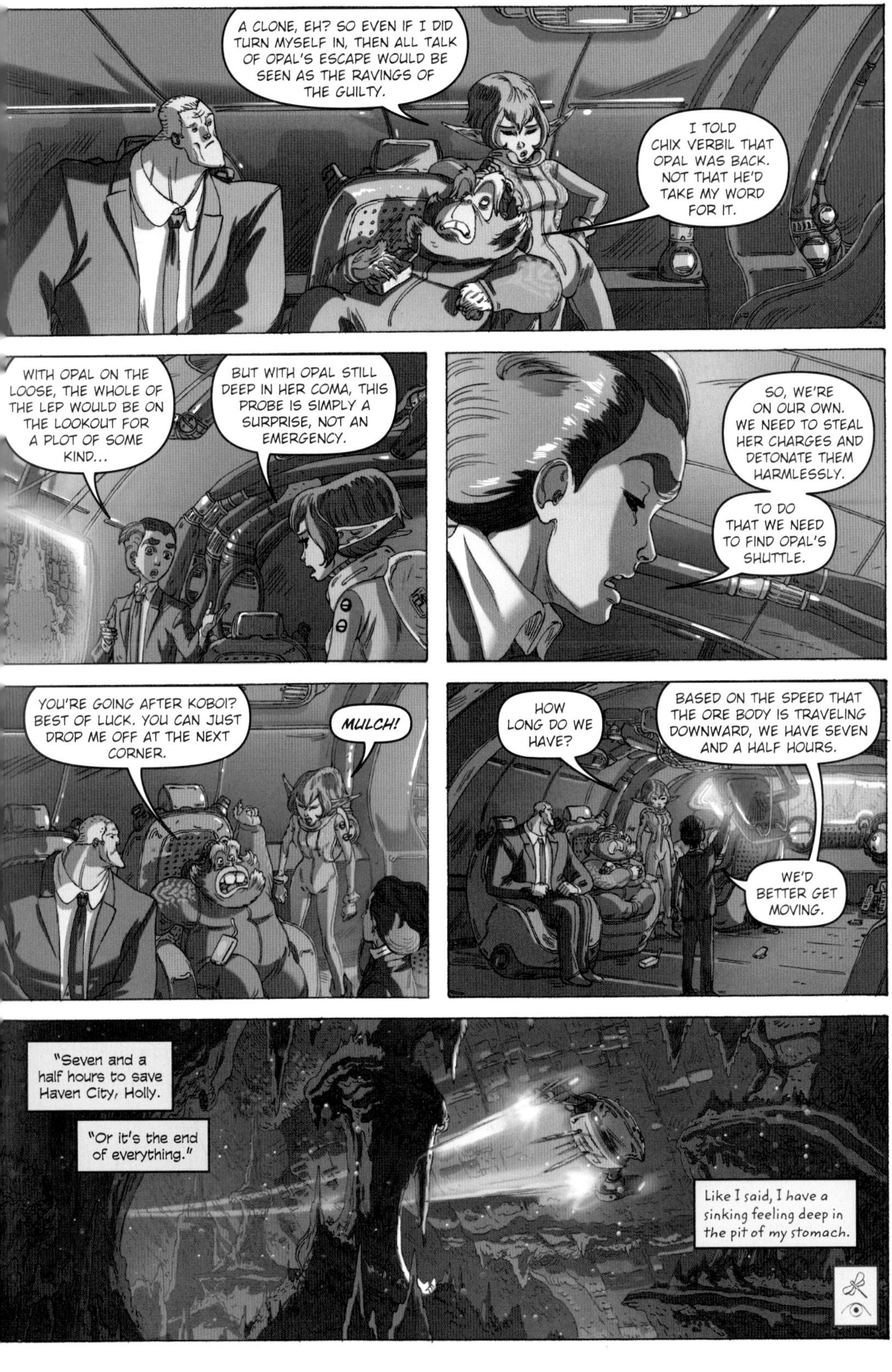
A CLONE, EH? SO EVEN IF I DID TURN MYSELF IN, THEN ALL TALK OF OPAL'S ESCAPE WOULD BE SEEN AS THE RAVINGS OF THE GUILTY.
I TOLD CHIX VERBIL THAT OPAL WAS BACK. NOT THAT HE'D TAKE MY WORD FOR IT.
WITH OPAL ON THE LOOSE, THE WHOLE OF THE LEP WOULD BE ON THE LOOKOUT FOR A PLOT OF SOME KIND...
BUT WITH OPAL STILL DEEP IN HER COMA, THIS PROBE IS SIMPLY A SURPRISE, NOT AN EMERGENCY.
SO, WE'RE ON OUR OWN. WE NEED TO STEAL HER CHARGES AND DETONATE THEM HARMLESSLY.
TO DO THAT WE NEED TO FIND OPAL'S SHUTTLE.
YOU'RE GOING AFTER KOBOI? BEST OF LUCK. YOU CAN JUST DROP ME OFF AT THE NEXT CORNER.
MULCH!
HOW LONG DO WE HAVE?
BASED ON THE SPEED THAT THE ORE BODY IS TRAVELING DOWNWARD, WE HAVE SEVEN AND A HALF HOURS.
WE'D BETTER GET MOVING.
"Seven and a half hours to save Haven City, Holly.
"Or it's the end of everything."
Like I said, I have a sinking feeling deep in the pit of my stomach.

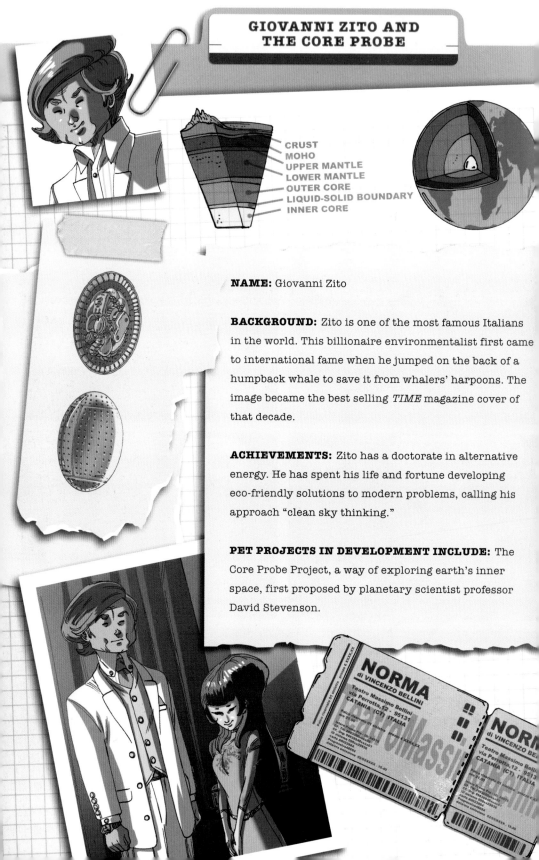

GIOVANNI ZITO AND THE CORE PROBE

CRUST
MOHO
UPPER MANTLE
LOWER MANTLE
OUTER CORE
LIQUID-SOLID BOUNDARY
INNER CORE

NAME: Giovanni Zito

BACKGROUND: Zito is one of the most famous Italians in the world. This billionaire environmentalist first came to international fame when he jumped on the back of a humpback whale to save it from whalers' harpoons. The image became the best selling *TIME* magazine cover of that decade.

ACHIEVEMENTS: Zito has a doctorate in alternative energy. He has spent his life and fortune developing eco-friendly solutions to modern problems, calling his approach "clean sky thinking."

PET PROJECTS IN DEVELOPMENT INCLUDE: The Core Probe Project, a way of exploring earth's inner space, first proposed by planetary scientist professor David Stevenson.

NORMA
di VINCENZO BELLINI
Teatro Massimo Bellini
via Perrotta, 12 - 95131
CATANIA (CT) ITALIA

NORMA
di VINCENZO BELLINI
Teatro Massimo Bellini
via Perrotta, 12 - 95131
CATANIA (CT) ITALIA

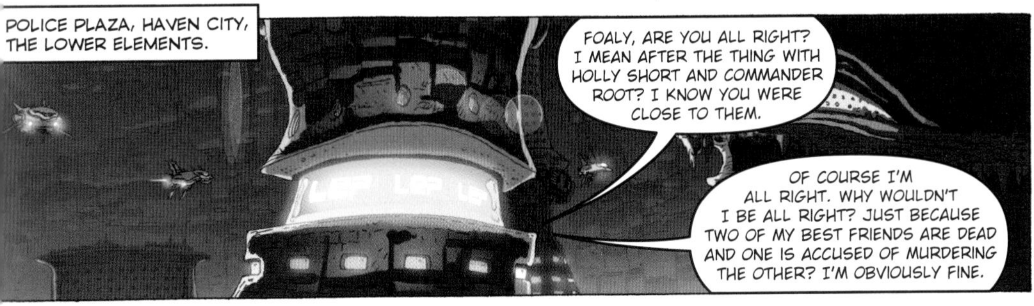
POLICE PLAZA, HAVEN CITY, THE LOWER ELEMENTS.
FOALY, ARE YOU ALL RIGHT? I MEAN AFTER THE THING WITH HOLLY SHORT AND COMMANDER ROOT? I KNOW YOU WERE CLOSE TO THEM.
OF COURSE I'M ALL RIGHT. WHY WOULDN'T I BE ALL RIGHT? JUST BECAUSE TWO OF MY BEST FRIENDS ARE DEAD AND ONE IS ACCUSED OF MURDERING THE OTHER? I'M OBVIOUSLY FINE.

CHAPTER 10: HORSE SENSE

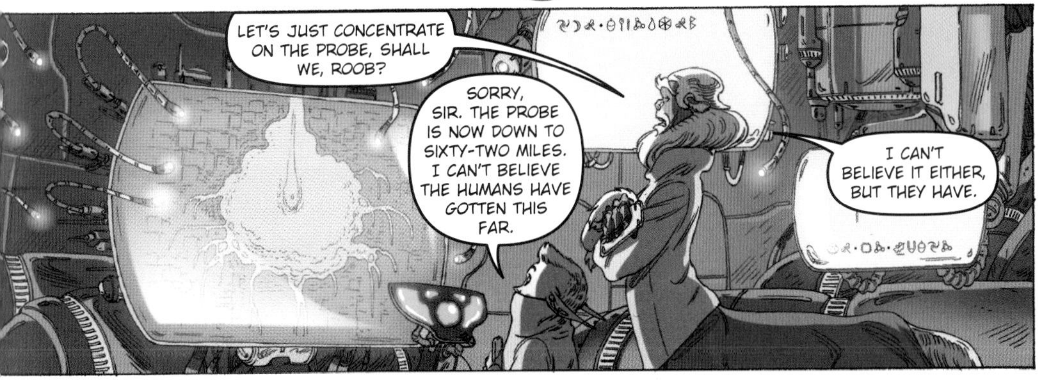
LET'S JUST CONCENTRATE ON THE PROBE, SHALL WE, ROOB?
SORRY, SIR. THE PROBE IS NOW DOWN TO SIXTY-TWO MILES. I CAN'T BELIEVE THE HUMANS HAVE GOTTEN THIS FAR.
I CAN'T BELIEVE IT EITHER, BUT THEY HAVE.

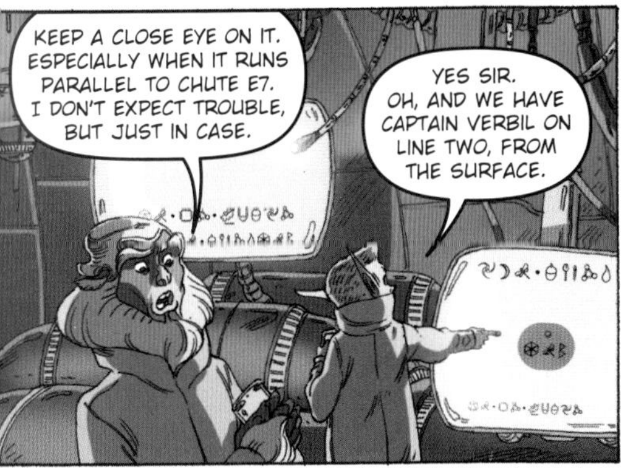
KEEP A CLOSE EYE ON IT. ESPECIALLY WHEN IT RUNS PARALLEL TO CHUTE E7. I DON'T EXPECT TROUBLE, BUT JUST IN CASE.
YES SIR. OH, AND WE HAVE CAPTAIN VERBIL ON LINE TWO, FROM THE SURFACE.

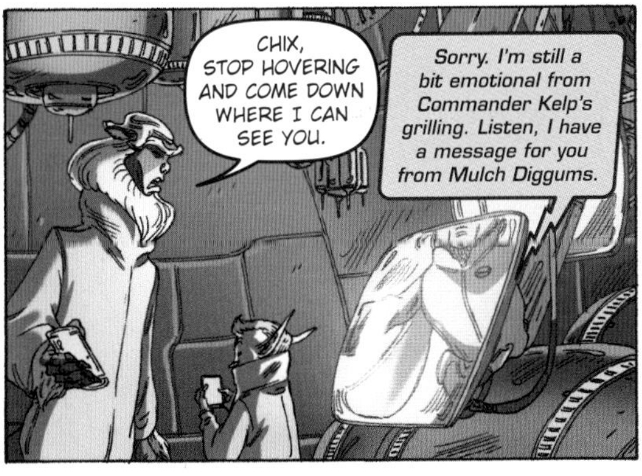
CHIX, STOP HOVERING AND COME DOWN WHERE I CAN SEE YOU.
Sorry. I'm still a bit emotional from Commander Kelp's grilling. Listen, I have a message for you from Mulch Diggums.

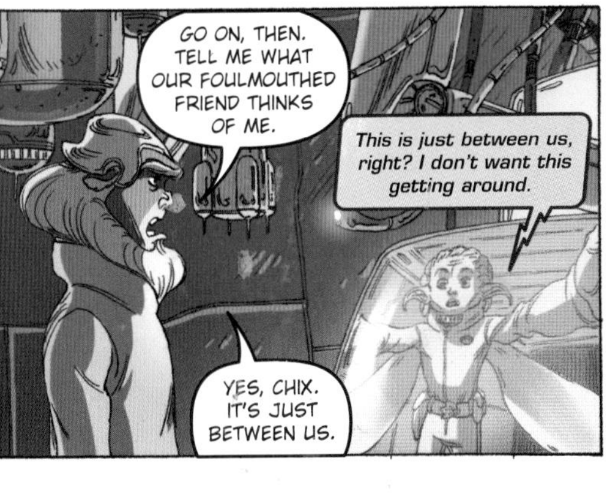
GO ON, THEN. TELL ME WHAT OUR FOULMOUTHED FRIEND THINKS OF ME.
This is just between us, right? I don't want this getting around.
YES, CHIX. IT'S JUST BETWEEN US.

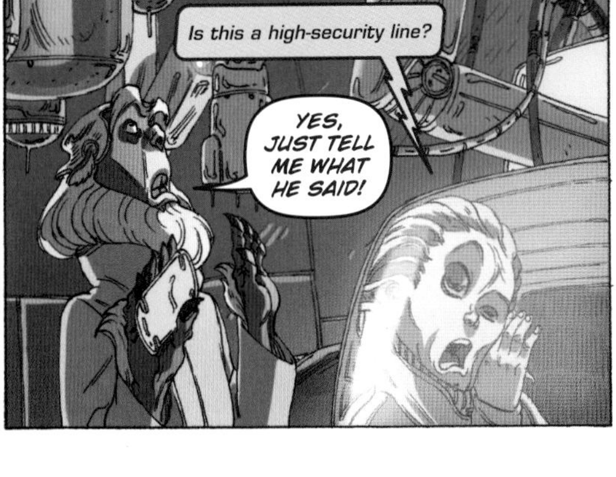
Is this a high-security line?
YES, JUST TELL ME WHAT HE SAID!

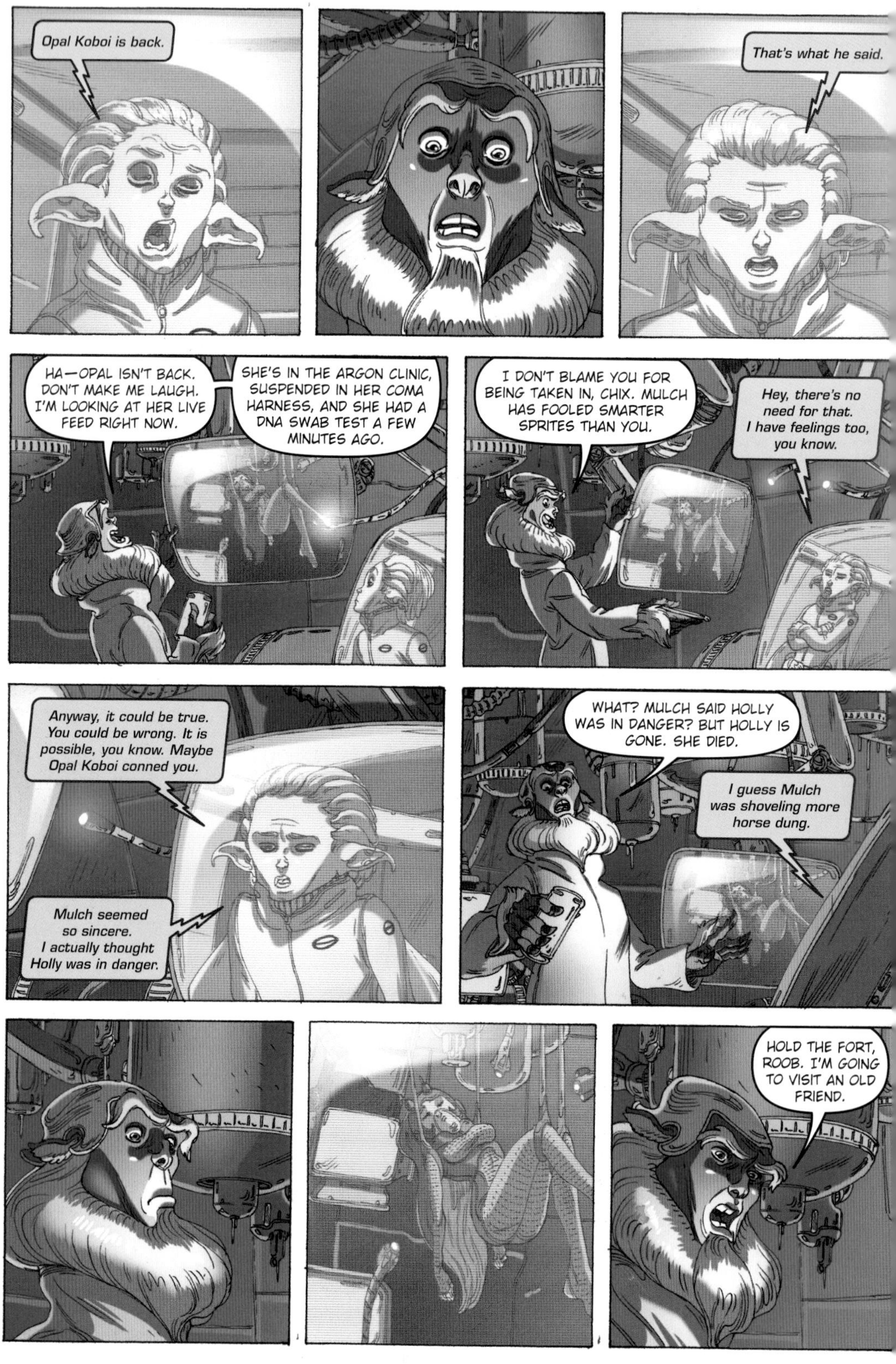
Opal Koboi is back.
That's what he said.
HA—OPAL ISN'T BACK. DON'T MAKE ME LAUGH. I'M LOOKING AT HER LIVE FEED RIGHT NOW.
SHE'S IN THE ARGON CLINIC, SUSPENDED IN HER COMA HARNESS, AND SHE HAD A DNA SWAB TEST A FEW MINUTES AGO.
I DON'T BLAME YOU FOR BEING TAKEN IN, CHIX. MULCH HAS FOOLED SMARTER SPRITES THAN YOU.
Hey, there's no need for that. I have feelings too, you know.
Anyway, it could be true. You could be wrong. It is possible, you know. Maybe Opal Koboi conned you.
Mulch seemed so sincere. I actually thought Holly was in danger.
WHAT? MULCH SAID HOLLY WAS IN DANGER? BUT HOLLY IS GONE. SHE DIED.
I guess Mulch was shoveling more horse dung.
HOLD THE FORT, ROOB. I'M GOING TO VISIT AN OLD FRIEND.

UNCHARTED CHUTE, THREE MILES BELOW SOUTHERN ITALY.

We make good time to the surface. Now for Opal.

TELL ME AGAIN, ARTEMIS. IF WE WANT TO FIND OPAL'S STEALTH SHUTTLE, WHY ARE WE LOOKING FOR EMPTY SPACES?

OUR SENSORS ARE NOWHERE NEAR SOPHISTICATED ENOUGH TO SPOT OPAL'S STEALTH SHUTTLE. BUT I THINK THERE IS A WAY...

OUR AIR IS MADE UP OF VARIOUS GASES, OF COURSE. GASES LIKE OXYGEN, HYDROGEN, AND SO ON. BUT—AND HERE'S MY POINT—THE STEALTH SHUTTLE'S HULL WILL PREVENT ANY OF THESE FROM BEING DETECTED.

SO IF WE FIND A SMALL PATCH OF SPACE WITHOUT THE USUAL AMBIENT GASES, THEN...

...THEN THAT HOLE IN THE AIR IS THE STEALTH SHUTTLE.

EXACTLY.

IF WE ASSUME THAT THE STEALTH SHUTTLE IS GOING TO BE VERY CLOSE TO CHUTE E7, THAT'S STILL A LOT OF GROUND TO SCAN, BUT LET'S TRY.

Three gas anomalies located.

THAT'S PROBABLY AN AIRPORT. LOTS OF EXHAUST FUMES.

THAT VACUUM IS PROBABLY A COMPUTER PLANT ON THE SURFACE.

AH, THERE...

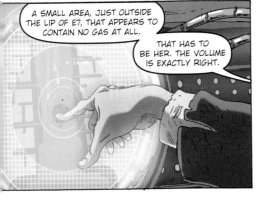

A SMALL AREA, JUST OUTSIDE THE LIP OF E7, THAT APPEARS TO CONTAIN NO GAS AT ALL.

THAT HAS TO BE HER. THE VOLUME IS EXACTLY RIGHT.

YOU REALIZE THAT AS SOON AS WE MOVE INTO THE MAIN CHUTE, FOALY WILL SPOT US AND WE'LL BE OUTLAWS?

LET'S HOPE WE CAN SAVE HAVEN CITY SO WE CAN KEEP FROM BEING OUTLAWS. AT LEAST FOR NOW.

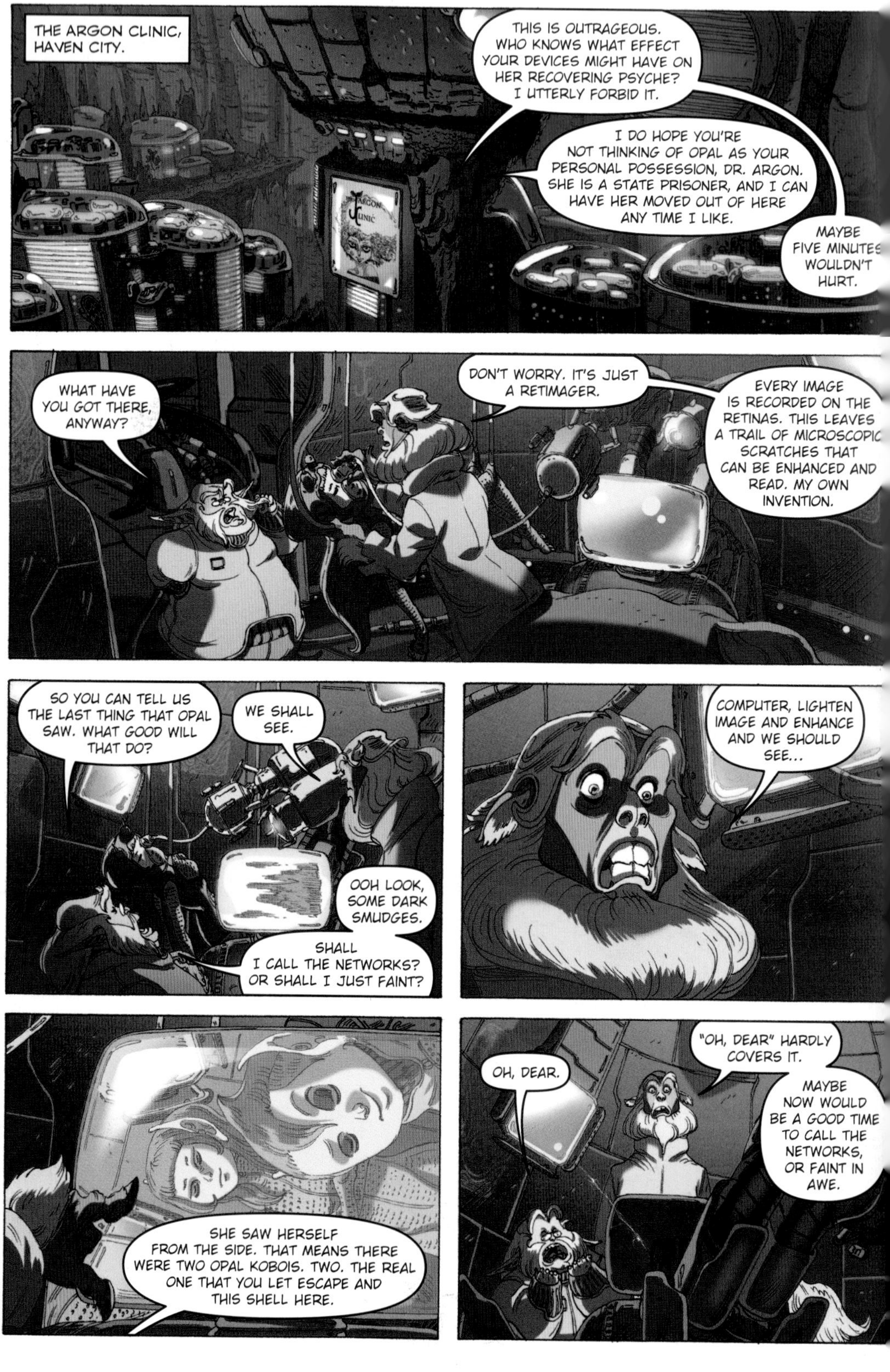
THE ARGON CLINIC, HAVEN CITY.
THIS IS OUTRAGEOUS. WHO KNOWS WHAT EFFECT YOUR DEVICES MIGHT HAVE ON HER RECOVERING PSYCHE? I UTTERLY FORBID IT.
I DO HOPE YOU'RE NOT THINKING OF OPAL AS YOUR PERSONAL POSSESSION, DR. ARGON. SHE IS A STATE PRISONER, AND I CAN HAVE HER MOVED OUT OF HERE ANY TIME I LIKE.
MAYBE FIVE MINUTES WOULDN'T HURT.
WHAT HAVE YOU GOT THERE, ANYWAY?
DON'T WORRY. IT'S JUST A RETIMAGER.
EVERY IMAGE IS RECORDED ON THE RETINAS. THIS LEAVES A TRAIL OF MICROSCOPIC SCRATCHES THAT CAN BE ENHANCED AND READ. MY OWN INVENTION.
SO YOU CAN TELL US THE LAST THING THAT OPAL SAW. WHAT GOOD WILL THAT DO?
WE SHALL SEE.
OOH LOOK, SOME DARK SMUDGES.
SHALL I CALL THE NETWORKS? OR SHALL I JUST FAINT?
COMPUTER, LIGHTEN IMAGE AND ENHANCE AND WE SHOULD SEE...
SHE SAW HERSELF FROM THE SIDE. THAT MEANS THERE WERE TWO OPAL KOBOIS. TWO. THE REAL ONE THAT YOU LET ESCAPE AND THIS SHELL HERE.
OH, DEAR.
"OH, DEAR" HARDLY COVERS IT.
MAYBE NOW WOULD BE A GOOD TIME TO CALL THE NETWORKS, OR FAINT IN AWE.

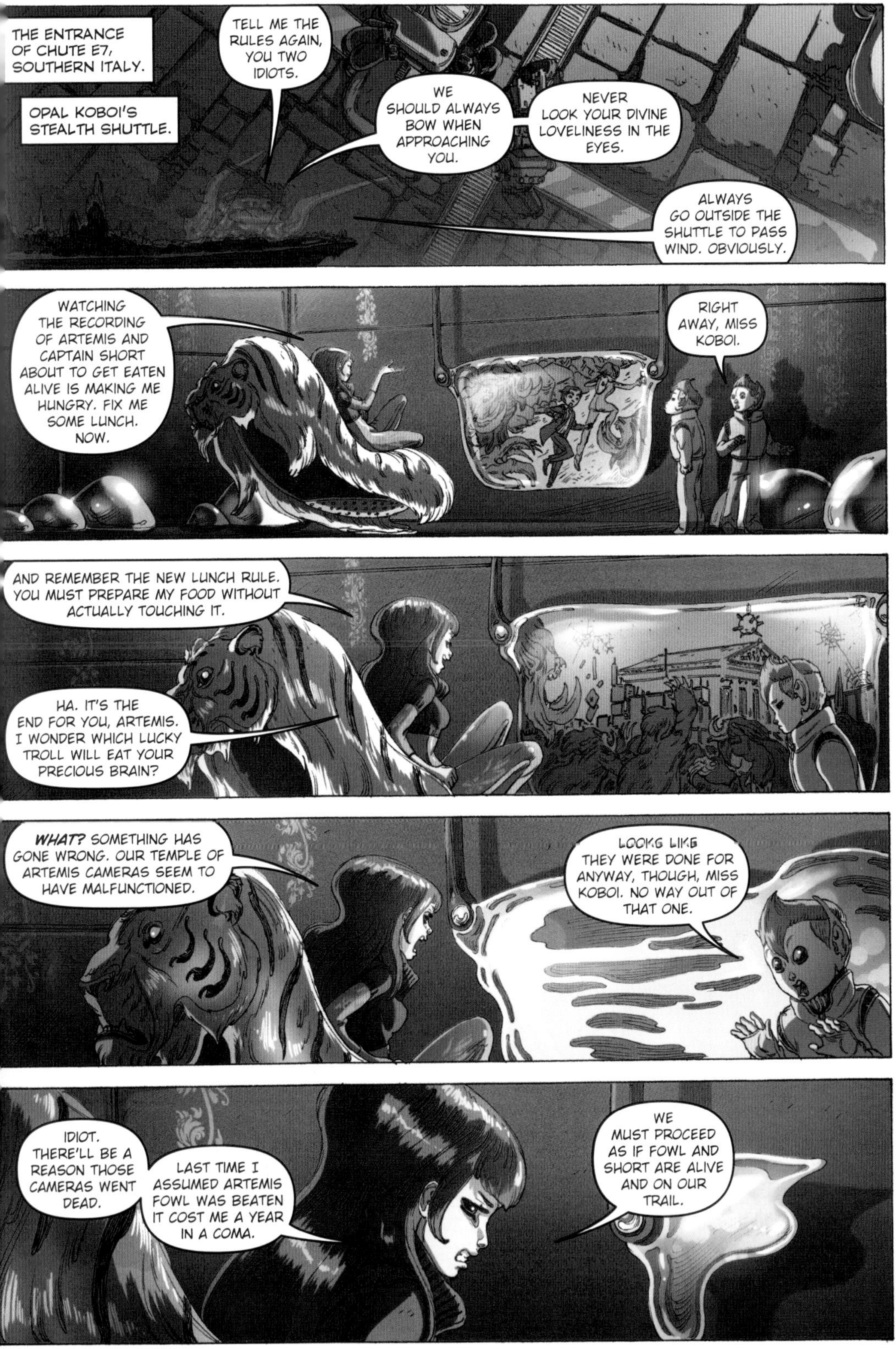
THE ENTRANCE OF CHUTE E7, SOUTHERN ITALY.
OPAL KOBOI'S STEALTH SHUTTLE.
TELL ME THE RULES AGAIN, YOU TWO IDIOTS.
WE SHOULD ALWAYS BOW WHEN APPROACHING YOU.
NEVER LOOK YOUR DIVINE LOVELINESS IN THE EYES.
ALWAYS GO OUTSIDE THE SHUTTLE TO PASS WIND. OBVIOUSLY.
WATCHING THE RECORDING OF ARTEMIS AND CAPTAIN SHORT ABOUT TO GET EATEN ALIVE IS MAKING ME HUNGRY. FIX ME SOME LUNCH. NOW.
RIGHT AWAY, MISS KOBOI.
AND REMEMBER THE NEW LUNCH RULE. YOU MUST PREPARE MY FOOD WITHOUT ACTUALLY TOUCHING IT.
HA. IT'S THE END FOR YOU, ARTEMIS. I WONDER WHICH LUCKY TROLL WILL EAT YOUR PRECIOUS BRAIN?
WHAT? SOMETHING HAS GONE WRONG. OUR TEMPLE OF ARTEMIS CAMERAS SEEM TO HAVE MALFUNCTIONED.
LOOKS LIKE THEY WERE DONE FOR ANYWAY, THOUGH, MISS KOBOI. NO WAY OUT OF THAT ONE.
IDIOT. THERE'LL BE A REASON THOSE CAMERAS WENT DEAD.
LAST TIME I ASSUMED ARTEMIS FOWL WAS BEATEN IT COST ME A YEAR IN A COMA.
WE MUST PROCEED AS IF FOWL AND SHORT ARE ALIVE AND ON OUR TRAIL.

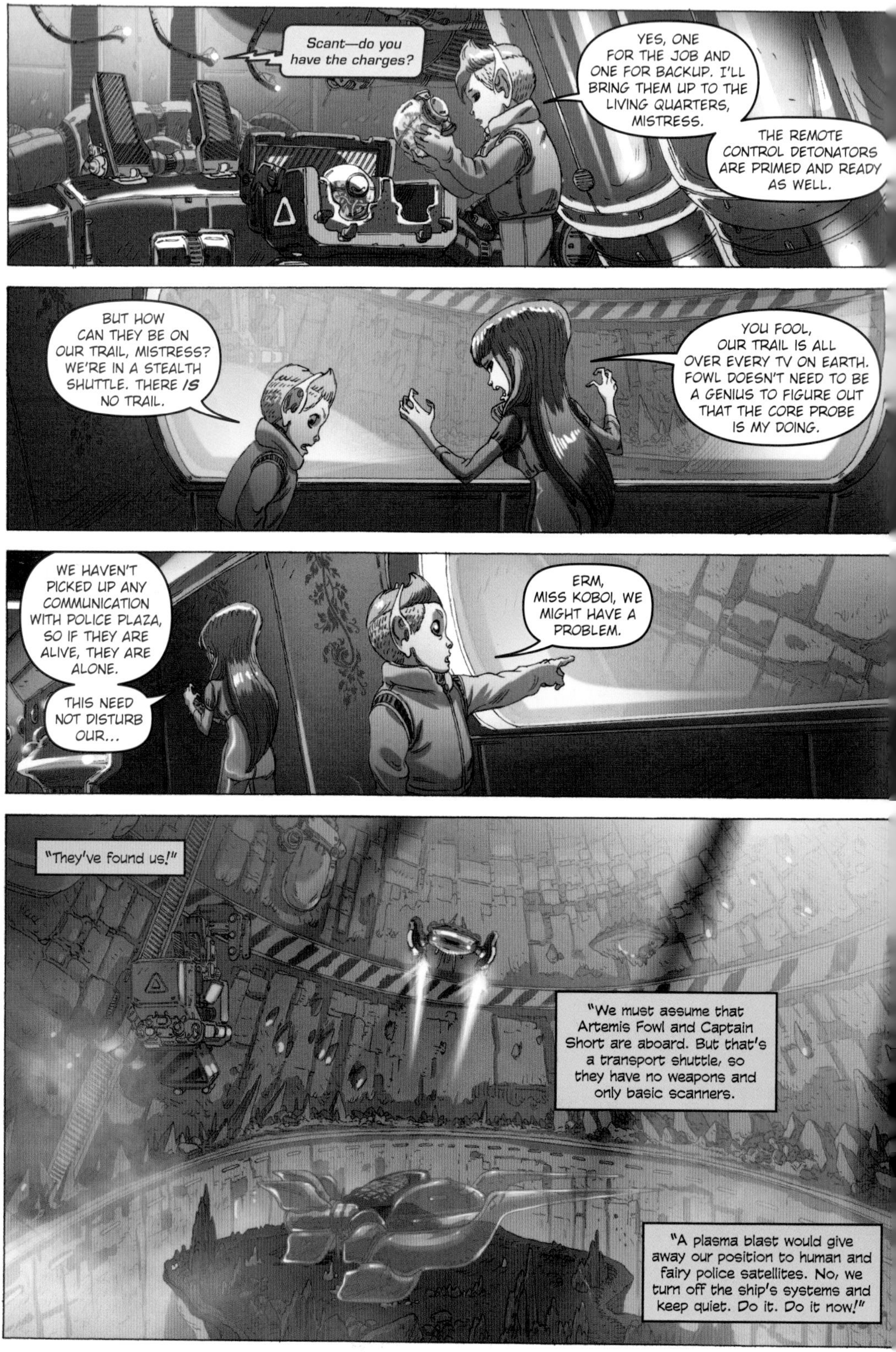
Scant—do you have the charges?
YES, ONE FOR THE JOB AND ONE FOR BACKUP. I'LL BRING THEM UP TO THE LIVING QUARTERS, MISTRESS.
THE REMOTE CONTROL DETONATORS ARE PRIMED AND READY AS WELL.
BUT HOW CAN THEY BE ON OUR TRAIL, MISTRESS? WE'RE IN A STEALTH SHUTTLE. THERE *IS* NO TRAIL.
YOU FOOL, OUR TRAIL IS ALL OVER EVERY TV ON EARTH. FOWL DOESN'T NEED TO BE A GENIUS TO FIGURE OUT THAT THE CORE PROBE IS MY DOING.
WE HAVEN'T PICKED UP ANY COMMUNICATION WITH POLICE PLAZA, SO IF THEY ARE ALIVE, THEY ARE ALONE.
THIS NEED NOT DISTURB OUR...
ERM, MISS KOBOI, WE MIGHT HAVE A PROBLEM.
"They've found us!"
"We must assume that Artemis Fowl and Captain Short are aboard. But that's a transport shuttle, so they have no weapons and only basic scanners.
"A plasma blast would give away our position to human and fairy police satellites. No, we turn off the ship's systems and keep quiet. Do it. Do it now!"

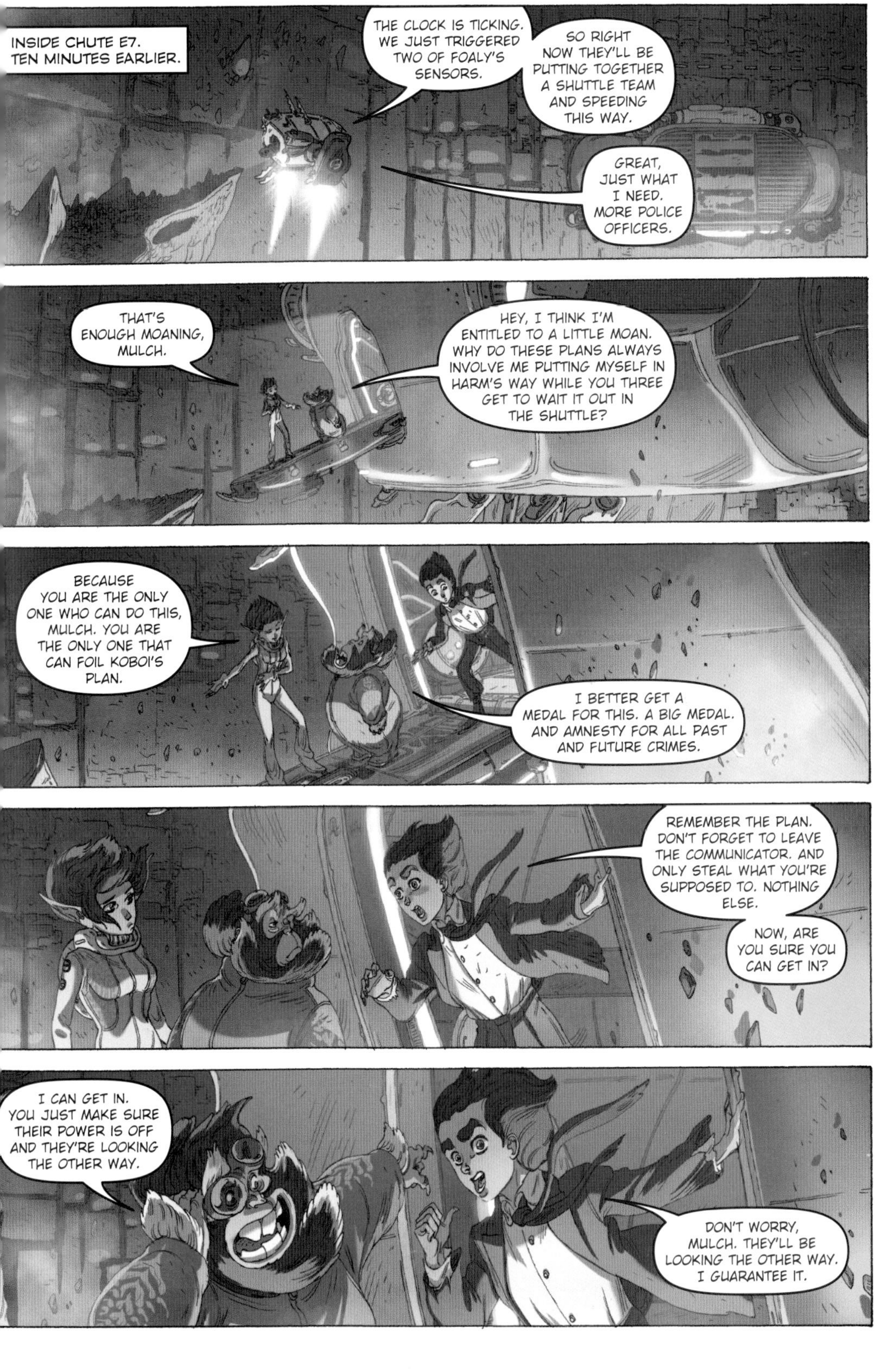
INSIDE CHUTE E7. TEN MINUTES EARLIER.
THE CLOCK IS TICKING. WE JUST TRIGGERED TWO OF FOALY'S SENSORS.
SO RIGHT NOW THEY'LL BE PUTTING TOGETHER A SHUTTLE TEAM AND SPEEDING THIS WAY.
GREAT, JUST WHAT I NEED. MORE POLICE OFFICERS.
THAT'S ENOUGH MOANING, MULCH.
HEY, I THINK I'M ENTITLED TO A LITTLE MOAN. WHY DO THESE PLANS ALWAYS INVOLVE ME PUTTING MYSELF IN HARM'S WAY WHILE YOU THREE GET TO WAIT IT OUT IN THE SHUTTLE?
BECAUSE YOU ARE THE ONLY ONE WHO CAN DO THIS, MULCH. YOU ARE THE ONLY ONE THAT CAN FOIL KOBOI'S PLAN.
I BETTER GET A MEDAL FOR THIS. A BIG MEDAL. AND AMNESTY FOR ALL PAST AND FUTURE CRIMES.
REMEMBER THE PLAN. DON'T FORGET TO LEAVE THE COMMUNICATOR. AND ONLY STEAL WHAT YOU'RE SUPPOSED TO. NOTHING ELSE.
NOW, ARE YOU SURE YOU CAN GET IN?
I CAN GET IN. YOU JUST MAKE SURE THEIR POWER IS OFF AND THEY'RE LOOKING THE OTHER WAY.
DON'T WORRY, MULCH. THEY'LL BE LOOKING THE OTHER WAY. I GUARANTEE IT.

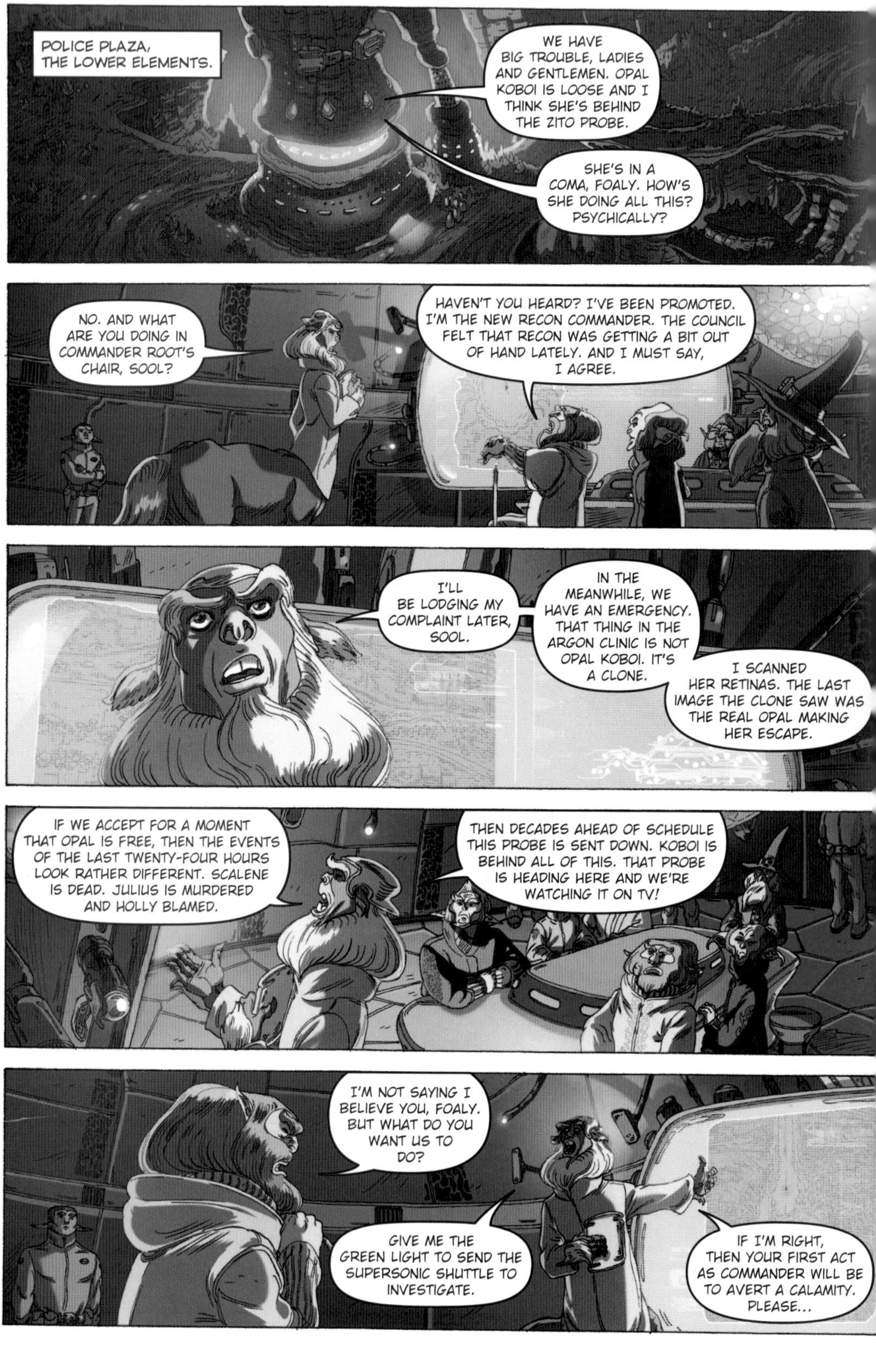
POLICE PLAZA, THE LOWER ELEMENTS.
WE HAVE BIG TROUBLE, LADIES AND GENTLEMEN. OPAL KOBOI IS LOOSE AND I THINK SHE'S BEHIND THE ZITO PROBE.
SHE'S IN A COMA, FOALY. HOW'S SHE DOING ALL THIS? PSYCHICALLY?
NO. AND WHAT ARE YOU DOING IN COMMANDER ROOT'S CHAIR, SOOL?
HAVEN'T YOU HEARD? I'VE BEEN PROMOTED. I'M THE NEW RECON COMMANDER. THE COUNCIL FELT THAT RECON WAS GETTING A BIT OUT OF HAND LATELY. AND I MUST SAY, I AGREE.
I'LL BE LODGING MY COMPLAINT LATER, SOOL.
IN THE MEANWHILE, WE HAVE AN EMERGENCY. THAT THING IN THE ARGON CLINIC IS NOT OPAL KOBOI. IT'S A CLONE.
I SCANNED HER RETINAS. THE LAST IMAGE THE CLONE SAW WAS THE REAL OPAL MAKING HER ESCAPE.
IF WE ACCEPT FOR A MOMENT THAT OPAL IS FREE, THEN THE EVENTS OF THE LAST TWENTY-FOUR HOURS LOOK RATHER DIFFERENT. SCALENE IS DEAD. JULIUS IS MURDERED AND HOLLY BLAMED.
THEN DECADES AHEAD OF SCHEDULE THIS PROBE IS SENT DOWN. KOBOI IS BEHIND ALL OF THIS. THAT PROBE IS HEADING HERE AND WE'RE WATCHING IT ON TV!
I'M NOT SAYING I BELIEVE YOU, FOALY. BUT WHAT DO YOU WANT US TO DO?
GIVE ME THE GREEN LIGHT TO SEND THE SUPERSONIC SHUTTLE TO INVESTIGATE.
IF I'M RIGHT, THEN YOUR FIRST ACT AS COMMANDER WILL BE TO AVERT A CALAMITY. PLEASE...

CRRRUNCH

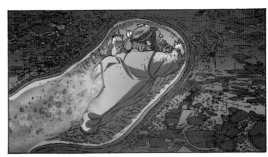

"My access codes worked; shuttle port doors open. You two ready?"

WE'RE READY, HOLLY. FLY IN A GRID SEARCH PATTERN AS THOUGH WE'RE NOT CERTAIN WHERE THE STEALTH SHUTTLE IS.

NOW, OLD FRIEND, CAN YOU MAKE CERTAIN THAT OPAL IS LOOKING THIS WAY?

BOOOOMMMMM!!

"I bet that got her attention."

PERFECT.

OKAY, BOY GENIUS. LET'S SEE IF YOU HAVE GOT THEM TO POWER DOWN.

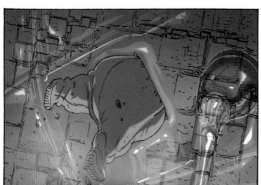

BINGO.

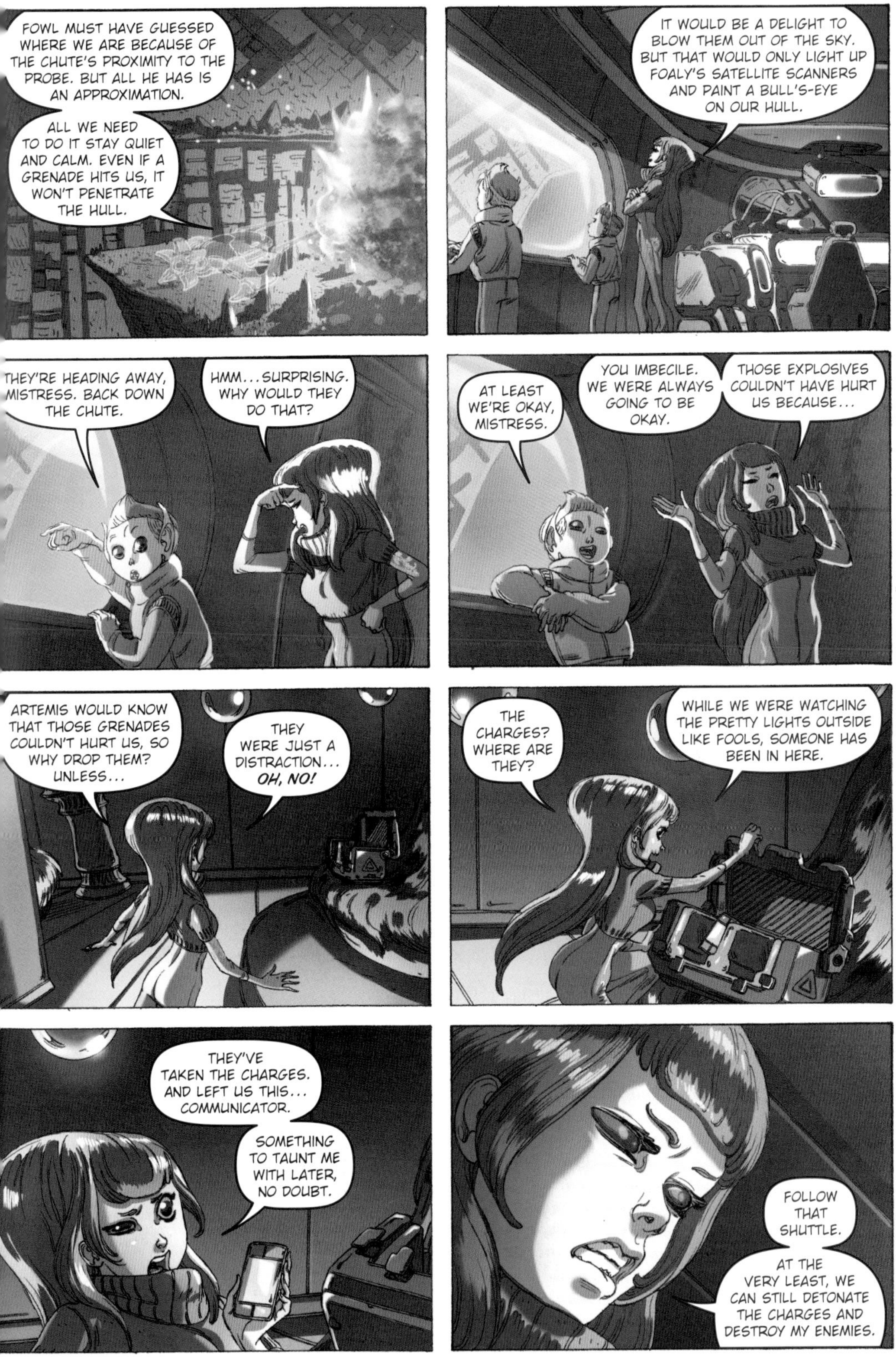
FOWL MUST HAVE GUESSED WHERE WE ARE BECAUSE OF THE CHUTE'S PROXIMITY TO THE PROBE. BUT ALL HE HAS IS AN APPROXIMATION.
ALL WE NEED TO DO IT STAY QUIET AND CALM. EVEN IF A GRENADE HITS US, IT WON'T PENETRATE THE HULL.
IT WOULD BE A DELIGHT TO BLOW THEM OUT OF THE SKY. BUT THAT WOULD ONLY LIGHT UP FOALY'S SATELLITE SCANNERS AND PAINT A BULL'S-EYE ON OUR HULL.
THEY'RE HEADING AWAY, MISTRESS. BACK DOWN THE CHUTE.
HMM...SURPRISING. WHY WOULD THEY DO THAT?
AT LEAST WE'RE OKAY, MISTRESS.
YOU IMBECILE. WE WERE ALWAYS GOING TO BE OKAY.
THOSE EXPLOSIVES COULDN'T HAVE HURT US BECAUSE...
ARTEMIS WOULD KNOW THAT THOSE GRENADES COULDN'T HURT US, SO WHY DROP THEM? UNLESS...
THEY WERE JUST A DISTRACTION... ***OH, NO!***
THE CHARGES? WHERE ARE THEY?
WHILE WE WERE WATCHING THE PRETTY LIGHTS OUTSIDE LIKE FOOLS, SOMEONE HAS BEEN IN HERE.
THEY'VE TAKEN THE CHARGES. AND LEFT US THIS... COMMUNICATOR.
SOMETHING TO TAUNT ME WITH LATER, NO DOUBT.
FOLLOW THAT SHUTTLE.
AT THE VERY LEAST, WE CAN STILL DETONATE THE CHARGES AND DESTROY MY ENEMIES.

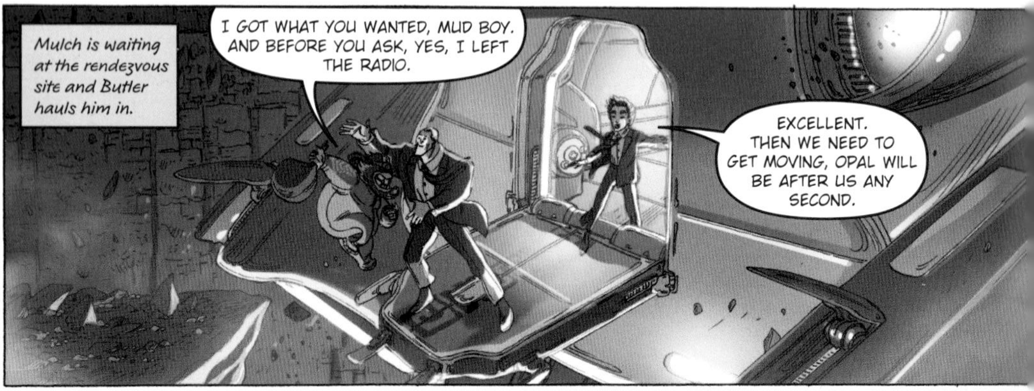
Mulch is waiting at the rendezvous site and Butler hauls him in.
I GOT WHAT YOU WANTED, MUD BOY. AND BEFORE YOU ASK, YES, I LEFT THE RADIO.
EXCELLENT. THEN WE NEED TO GET MOVING, OPAL WILL BE AFTER US ANY SECOND.

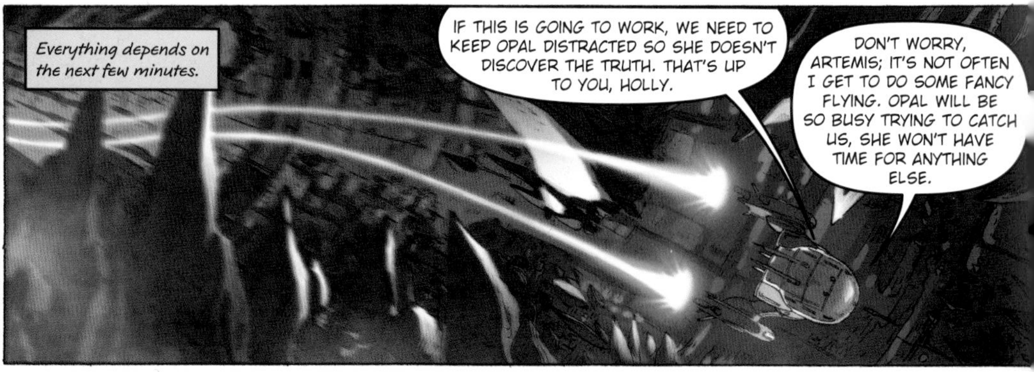
Everything depends on the next few minutes.
IF THIS IS GOING TO WORK, WE NEED TO KEEP OPAL DISTRACTED SO SHE DOESN'T DISCOVER THE TRUTH. THAT'S UP TO YOU, HOLLY.
DON'T WORRY, ARTEMIS; IT'S NOT OFTEN I GET TO DO SOME FANCY FLYING. OPAL WILL BE SO BUSY TRYING TO CATCH US, SHE WON'T HAVE TIME FOR ANYTHING ELSE.

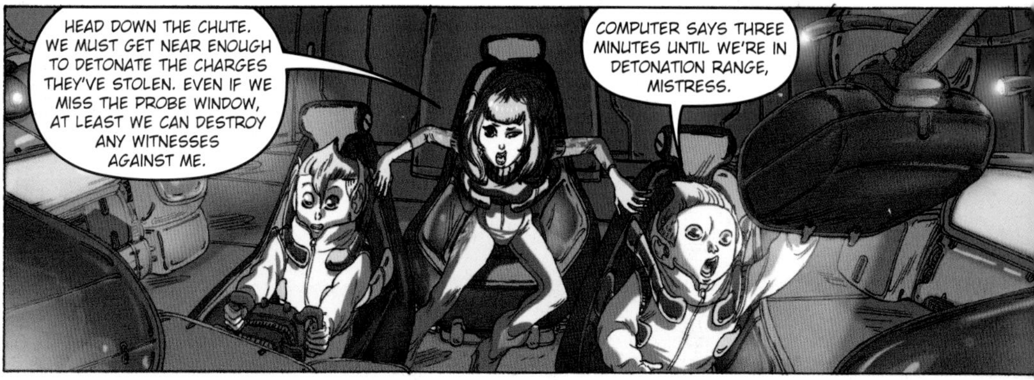
HEAD DOWN THE CHUTE. WE MUST GET NEAR ENOUGH TO DETONATE THE CHARGES THEY'VE STOLEN. EVEN IF WE MISS THE PROBE WINDOW, AT LEAST WE CAN DESTROY ANY WITNESSES AGAINST ME.
COMPUTER SAYS THREE MINUTES UNTIL WE'RE IN DETONATION RANGE, MISTRESS.

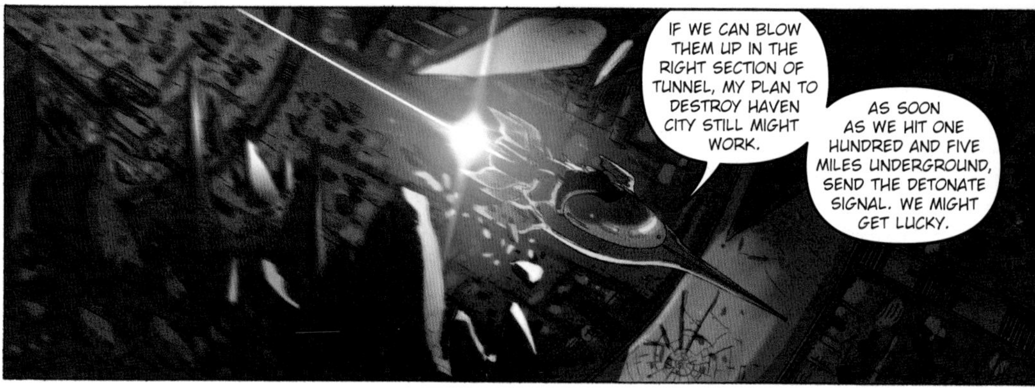
IF WE CAN BLOW THEM UP IN THE RIGHT SECTION OF TUNNEL, MY PLAN TO DESTROY HAVEN CITY STILL MIGHT WORK.
AS SOON AS WE HIT ONE HUNDRED AND FIVE MILES UNDERGROUND, SEND THE DETONATE SIGNAL. WE MIGHT GET LUCKY.

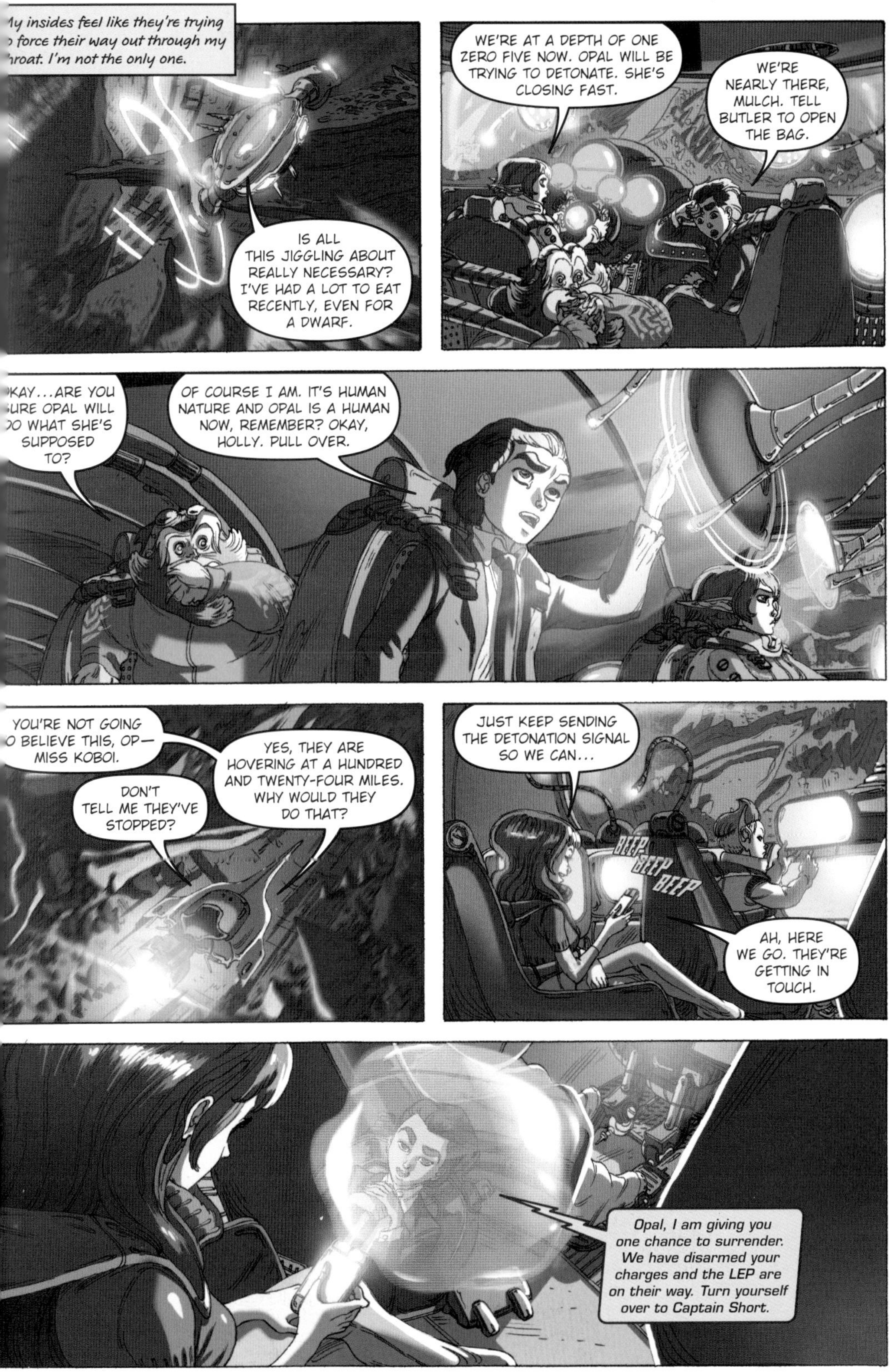

My insides feel like they're trying o force their way out through my hroat. I'm not the only one.
IS ALL THIS JIGGLING ABOUT REALLY NECESSARY? I'VE HAD A LOT TO EAT RECENTLY, EVEN FOR A DWARF.
WE'RE AT A DEPTH OF ONE ZERO FIVE NOW. OPAL WILL BE TRYING TO DETONATE. SHE'S CLOSING FAST.
WE'RE NEARLY THERE, MULCH. TELL BUTLER TO OPEN THE BAG.
KAY... ARE YOU URE OPAL WILL O WHAT SHE'S SUPPOSED TO?
OF COURSE I AM. IT'S HUMAN NATURE AND OPAL IS A HUMAN NOW, REMEMBER? OKAY, HOLLY. PULL OVER.
YOU'RE NOT GOING O BELIEVE THIS, OP— MISS KOBOI.
DON'T TELL ME THEY'VE STOPPED?
YES, THEY ARE HOVERING AT A HUNDRED AND TWENTY-FOUR MILES. WHY WOULD THEY DO THAT?
JUST KEEP SENDING THE DETONATION SIGNAL SO WE CAN...
BEEP BEEP BEEP
AH, HERE WE GO. THEY'RE GETTING IN TOUCH.
Opal, I am giving you one chance to surrender. We have disarmed your charges and the LEP are on their way. Turn yourself over to Captain Short.

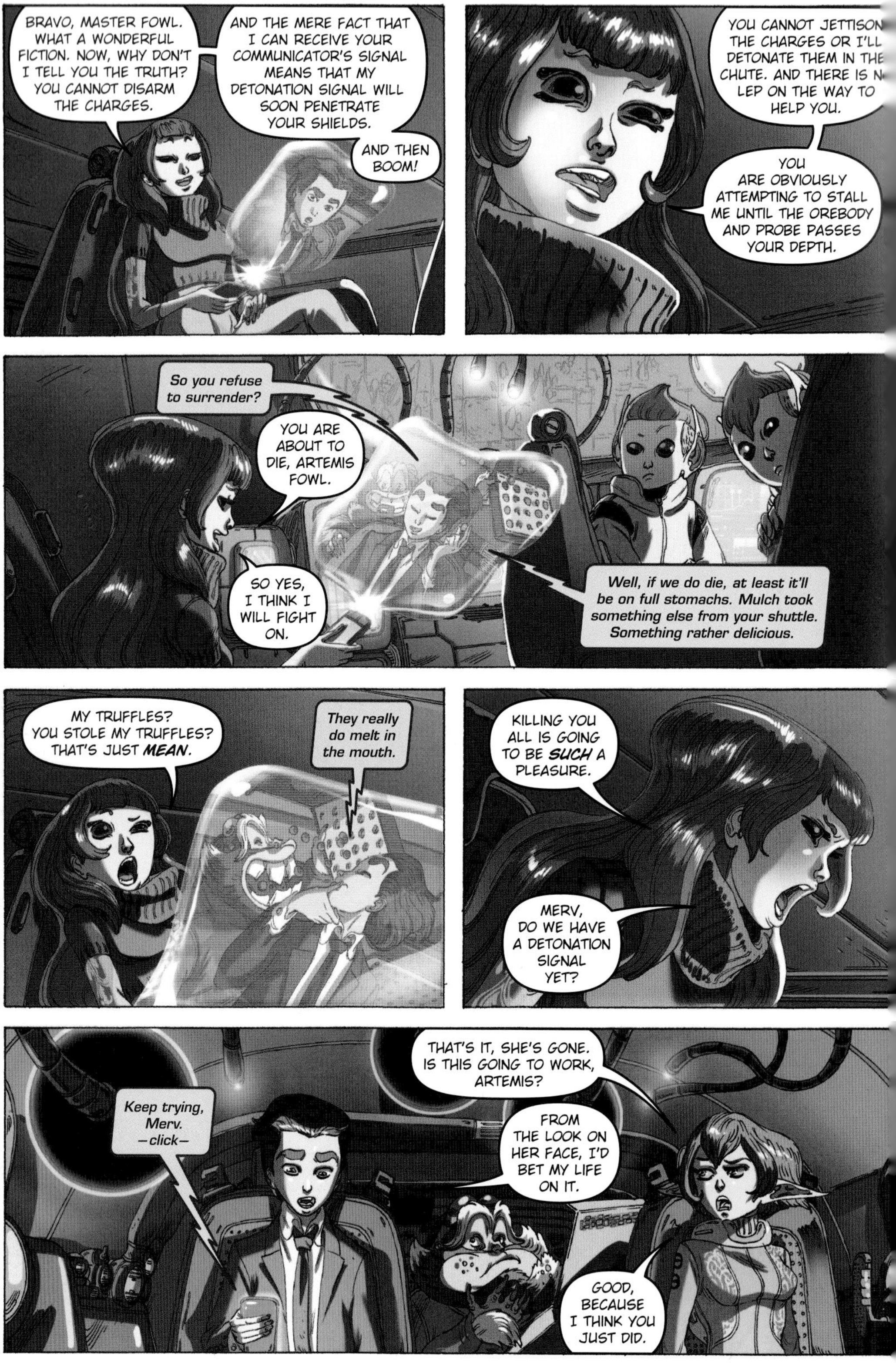
BRAVO, MASTER FOWL. WHAT A WONDERFUL FICTION. NOW, WHY DON'T I TELL YOU THE TRUTH? YOU CANNOT DISARM THE CHARGES.
AND THE MERE FACT THAT I CAN RECEIVE YOUR COMMUNICATOR'S SIGNAL MEANS THAT MY DETONATION SIGNAL WILL SOON PENETRATE YOUR SHIELDS.
AND THEN BOOM!
YOU CANNOT JETTISON THE CHARGES OR I'LL DETONATE THEM IN THE CHUTE. AND THERE IS NO LEP ON THE WAY TO HELP YOU.
YOU ARE OBVIOUSLY ATTEMPTING TO STALL ME UNTIL THE OREBODY AND PROBE PASSES YOUR DEPTH.
So you refuse to surrender?
YOU ARE ABOUT TO DIE, ARTEMIS FOWL.
SO YES, I THINK I WILL FIGHT ON.
Well, if we do die, at least it'll be on full stomachs. Mulch took something else from your shuttle. Something rather delicious.
MY TRUFFLES? YOU STOLE MY TRUFFLES? THAT'S JUST ***MEAN***.
They really do melt in the mouth.
KILLING YOU ALL IS GOING TO BE ***SUCH*** A PLEASURE.
MERV, DO WE HAVE A DETONATION SIGNAL YET?
Keep trying, Merv. —click—
THAT'S IT, SHE'S GONE. IS THIS GOING TO WORK, ARTEMIS?
FROM THE LOOK ON HER FACE, I'D BET MY LIFE ON IT.
GOOD, BECAUSE I THINK YOU JUST DID.

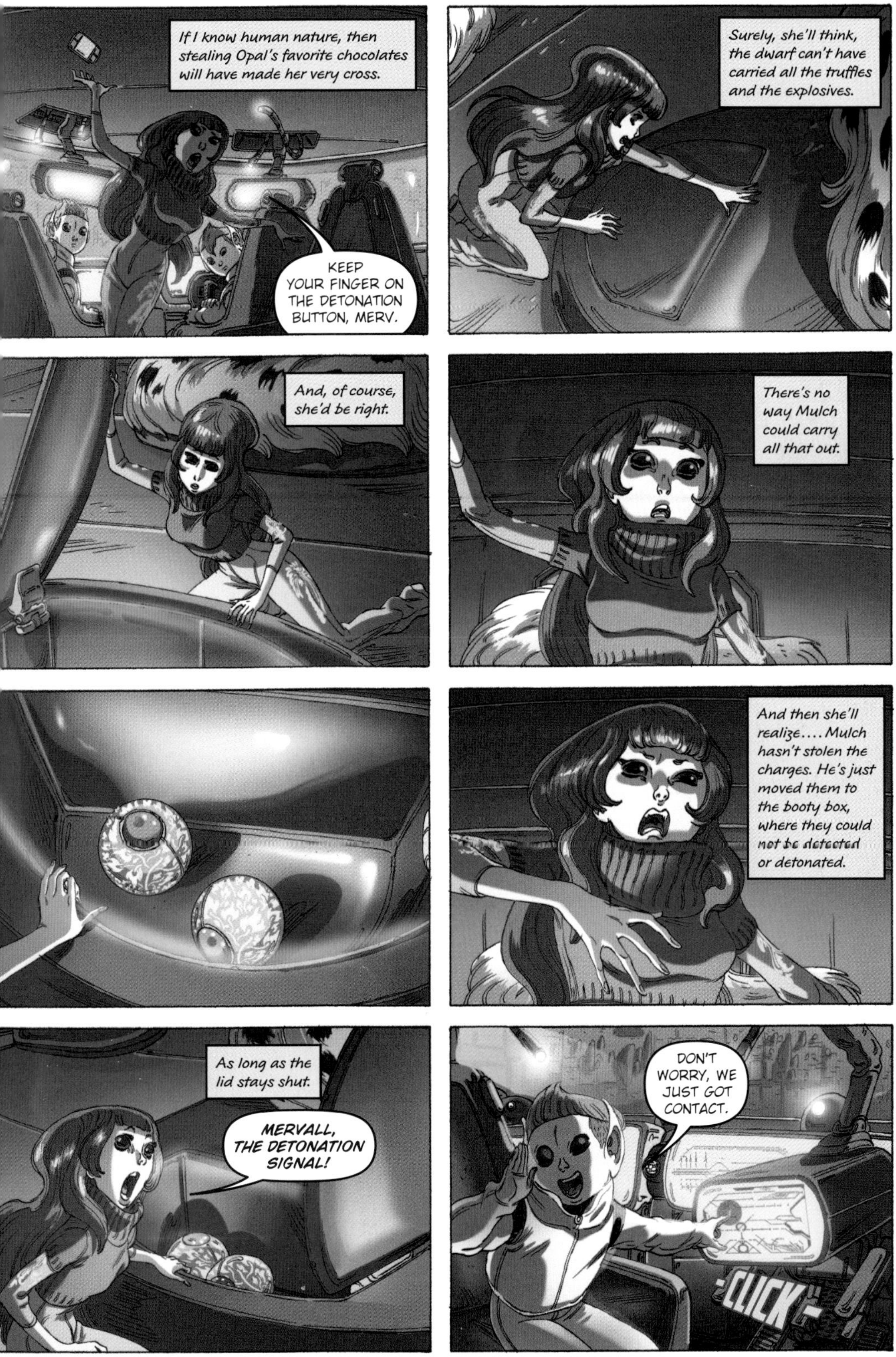
If I know human nature, then stealing Opal's favorite chocolates will have made her very cross.
KEEP YOUR FINGER ON THE DETONATION BUTTON, MERV.
Surely, she'll think, the dwarf can't have carried all the truffles and the explosives.
And, of course, she'd be right.
There's no way Mulch could carry all that out.
And then she'll realize.... Mulch hasn't stolen the charges. He's just moved them to the booty box, where they could not be detected or detonated.
As long as the lid stays shut.
MERVALL, THE DETONATION SIGNAL!
DON'T WORRY, WE JUST GOT CONTACT.
CLICK

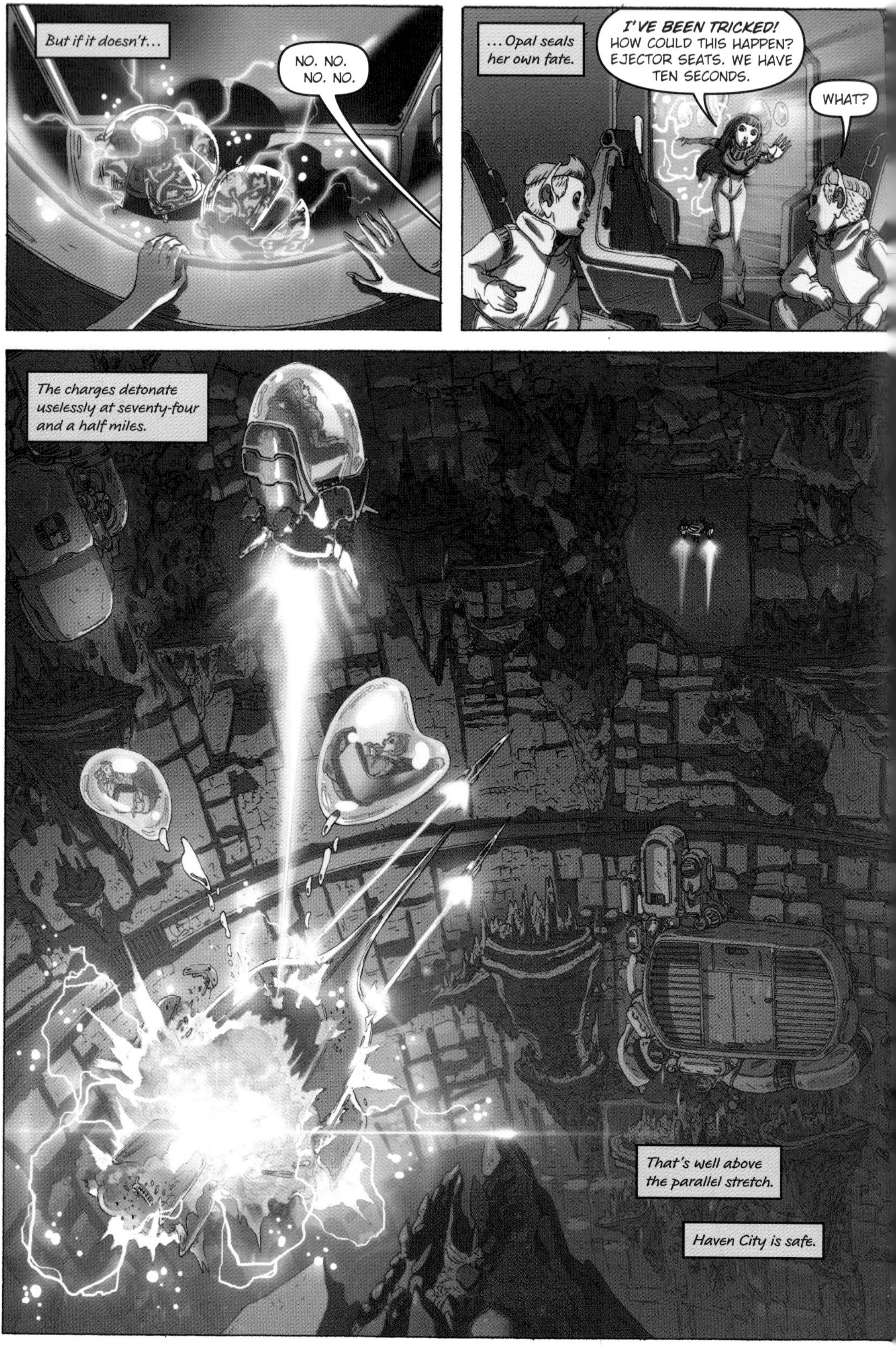

But if it doesn't...
NO. NO. NO. NO.
...Opal seals her own fate.
I'VE BEEN TRICKED! HOW COULD THIS HAPPEN? EJECTOR SEATS. WE HAVE TEN SECONDS.
WHAT?
The charges detonate uselessly at seventy-four and a half miles.
That's well above the parallel stretch.
Haven City is safe.

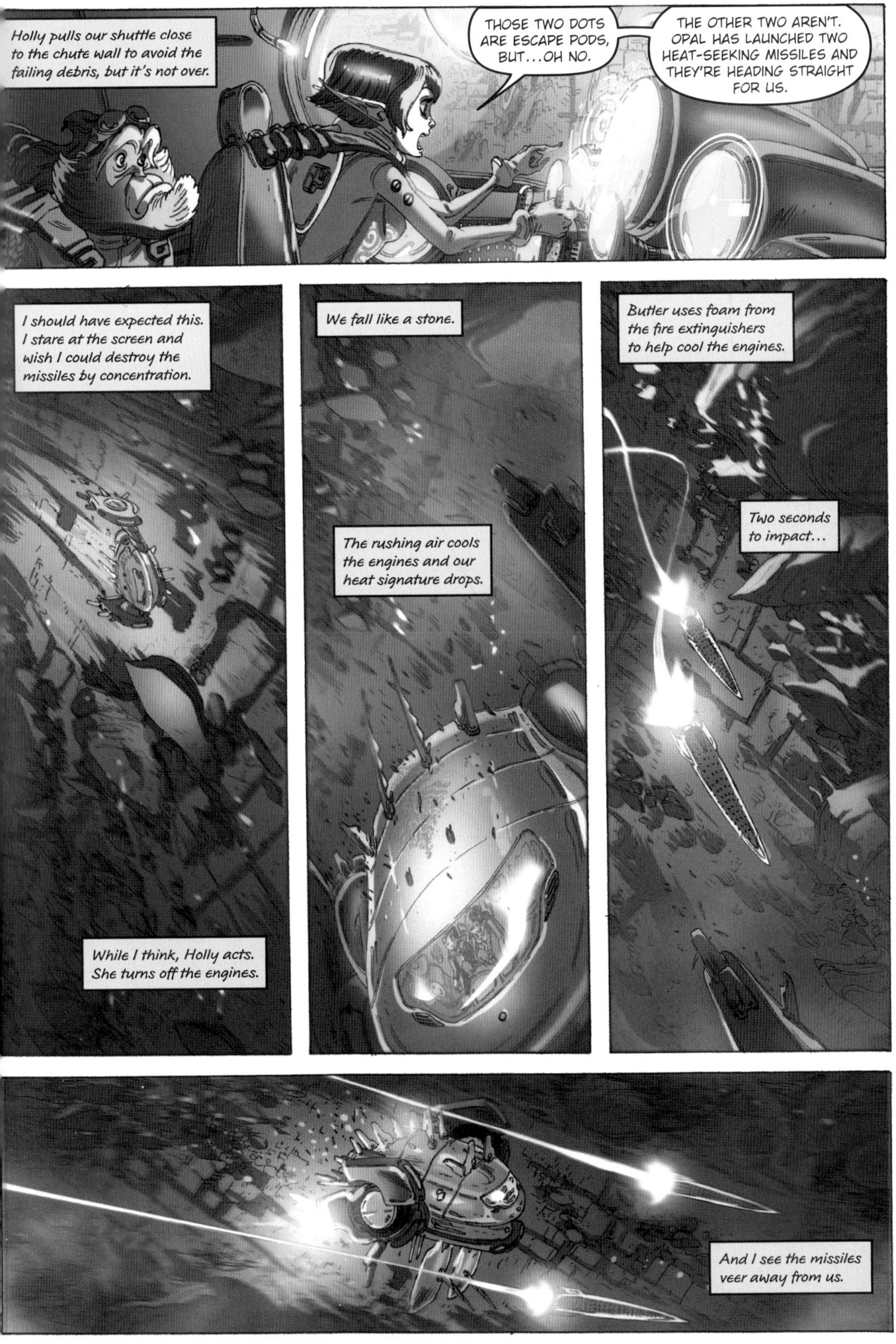
Holly pulls our shuttle close to the chute wall to avoid the falling debris, but it's not over.
THOSE TWO DOTS ARE ESCAPE PODS, BUT...OH NO.
THE OTHER TWO AREN'T. OPAL HAS LAUNCHED TWO HEAT-SEEKING MISSILES AND THEY'RE HEADING STRAIGHT FOR US.
I should have expected this. I stare at the screen and wish I could destroy the missiles by concentration.
While I think, Holly acts. She turns off the engines.
We fall like a stone.
The rushing air cools the engines and our heat signature drops.
Butler uses foam from the fire extinguishers to help cool the engines.
Two seconds to impact...
And I see the missiles veer away from us.

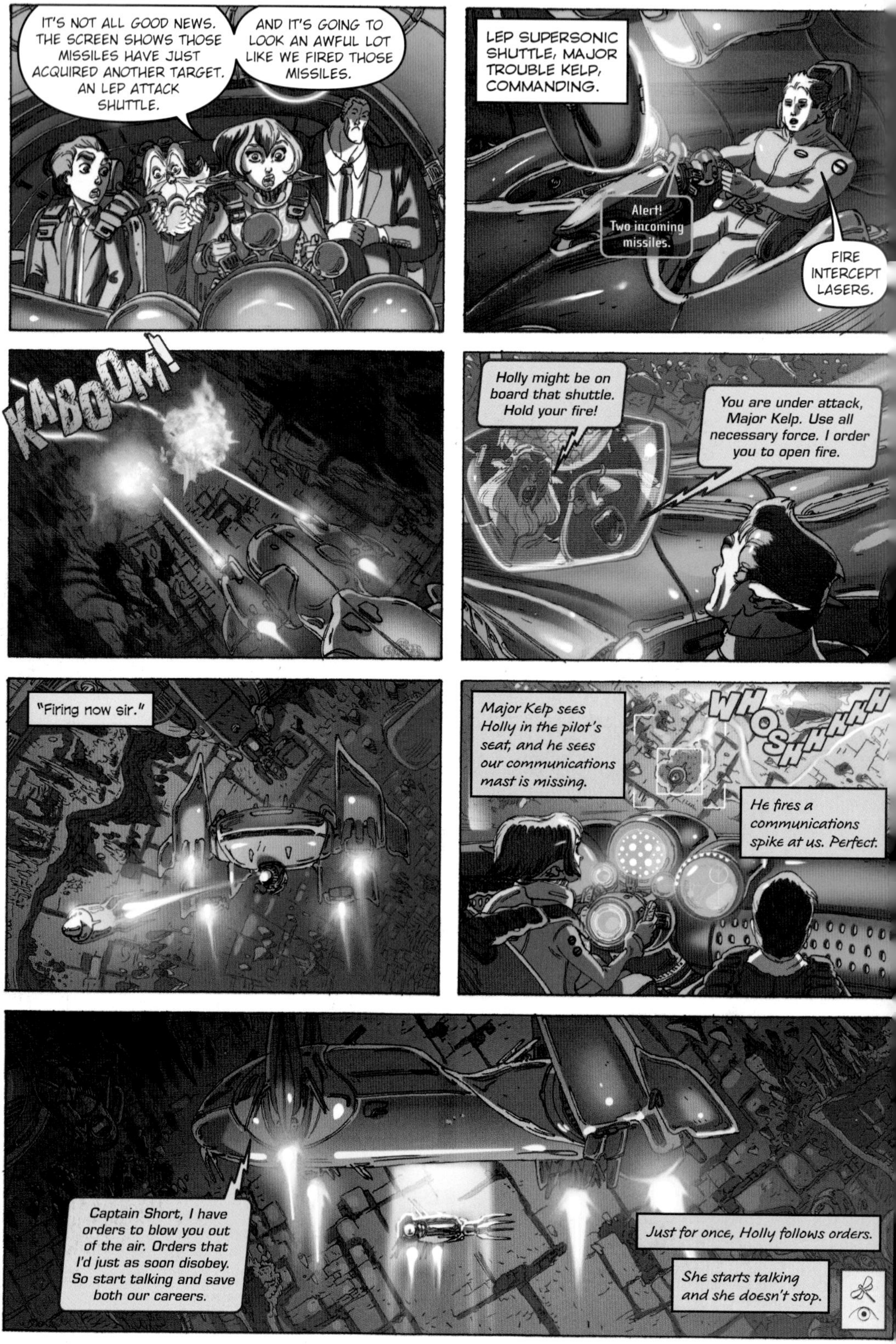
IT'S NOT ALL GOOD NEWS. THE SCREEN SHOWS THOSE MISSILES HAVE JUST ACQUIRED ANOTHER TARGET. AN LEP ATTACK SHUTTLE.
AND IT'S GOING TO LOOK AN AWFUL LOT LIKE WE FIRED THOSE MISSILES.
LEP SUPERSONIC SHUTTLE, MAJOR TROUBLE KELP, COMMANDING.
Alert! Two incoming missiles.
FIRE INTERCEPT LASERS.
KABOOM!
Holly might be on board that shuttle. Hold your fire!
You are under attack, Major Kelp. Use all necessary force. I order you to open fire.
"Firing now sir."
Major Kelp sees Holly in the pilot's seat, and he sees our communications mast is missing.
WHOSHHHHH
He fires a communications spike at us. Perfect.
Captain Short, I have orders to blow you out of the air. Orders that I'd just as soon disobey. So start talking and save both our careers.
Just for once, Holly follows orders.
She starts talking and she doesn't stop.

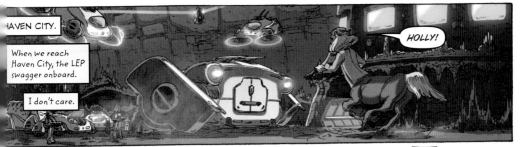

When we reach Haven City, the LEP swagger onboard.

I don't care.

HOLLY!

CHAPTER 11: THE LAST GOOD-BYE

I AM SO HAPPY THAT YOU'RE ALIVE.

ME TOO.

A LITTLE "HELLO" WOULDN'T HURT. "HOW ARE YOU, MULCH? LONG TIME NO SEE, MULCH. HERE'S YOUR ENORMOUS MEDAL, MULCH."

OH, ALL RIGHT. NICE TO SEE YOU, MULCH.

YOU TOO, ARTEMIS. I SEE YOU MANAGED TO CHEAT THE MIND WIPE.

A GOOD THING FOR ALL OF US THAT I DID.

INDEED. I'LL NEVER MAKE THAT MISTAKE AGAIN. YOU'VE BEEN A FRIEND TO THE PEOPLE.

YOU TOO, BUTLER.

MAYBE YOU CAN REPAY ME BY BUILDING A ROOM THAT I CAN STAND UP IN.

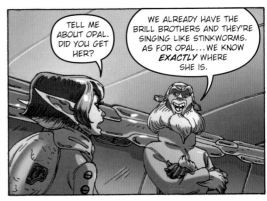

TELL ME ABOUT OPAL. DID YOU GET HER?

WE ALREADY HAVE THE BRILL BROTHERS AND THEY'RE SINGING LIKE STINKWORMS. AS FOR OPAL...WE KNOW EXACTLY WHERE SHE IS.

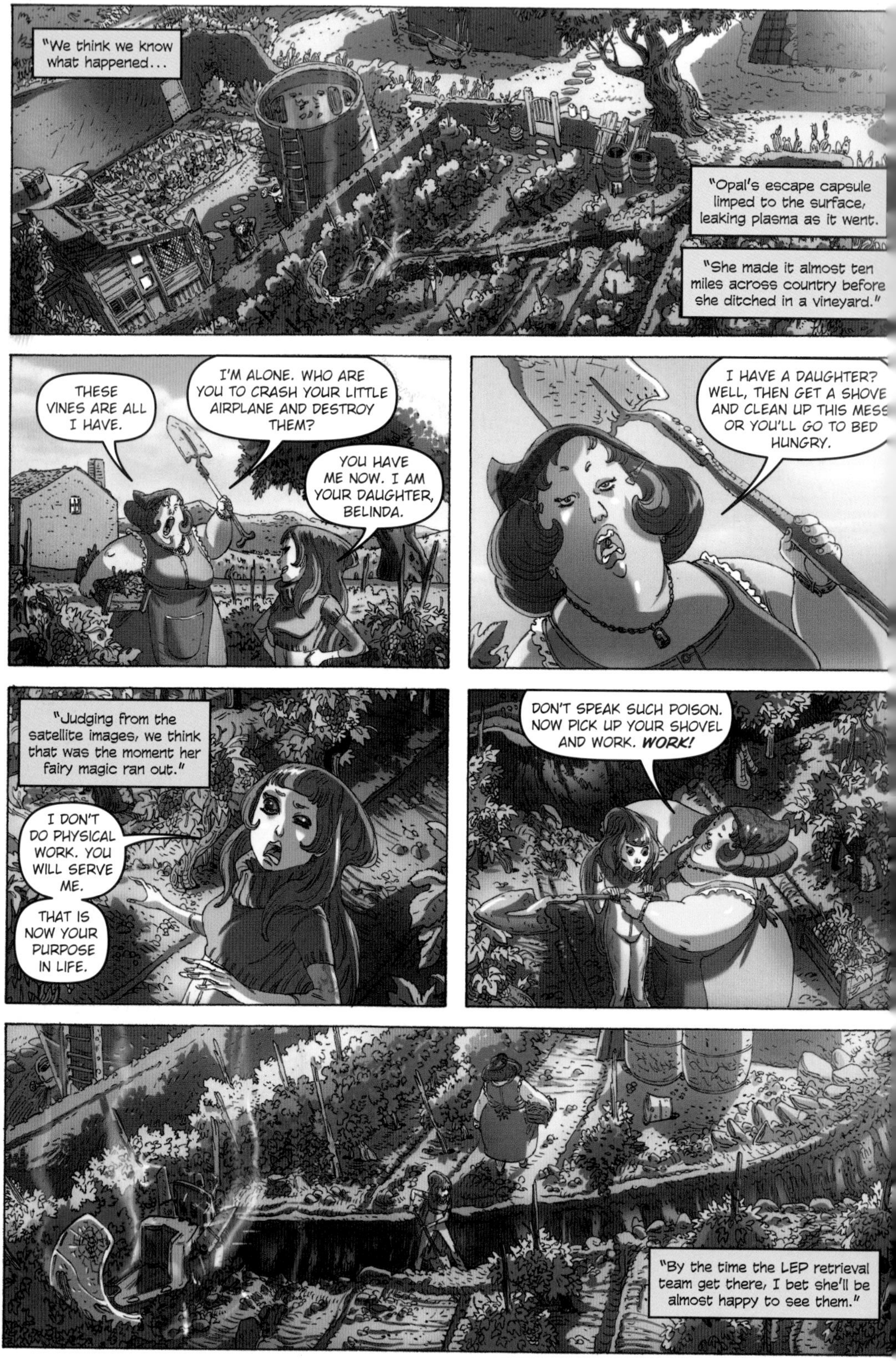
"We think we know what happened...
"Opal's escape capsule limped to the surface, leaking plasma as it went.
"She made it almost ten miles across country before she ditched in a vineyard."
THESE VINES ARE ALL I HAVE.
I'M ALONE. WHO ARE YOU TO CRASH YOUR LITTLE AIRPLANE AND DESTROY THEM?
YOU HAVE ME NOW. I AM YOUR DAUGHTER, BELINDA.
I HAVE A DAUGHTER? WELL, THEN GET A SHOVE AND CLEAN UP THIS MESS OR YOU'LL GO TO BED HUNGRY.
"Judging from the satellite images, we think that was the moment her fairy magic ran out."
I DON'T DO PHYSICAL WORK. YOU WILL SERVE ME.
THAT IS NOW YOUR PURPOSE IN LIFE.
DON'T SPEAK SUCH POISON. NOW PICK UP YOUR SHOVEL AND WORK. WORK!
"By the time the LEP retrieval team get there, I bet she'll be almost happy to see them."

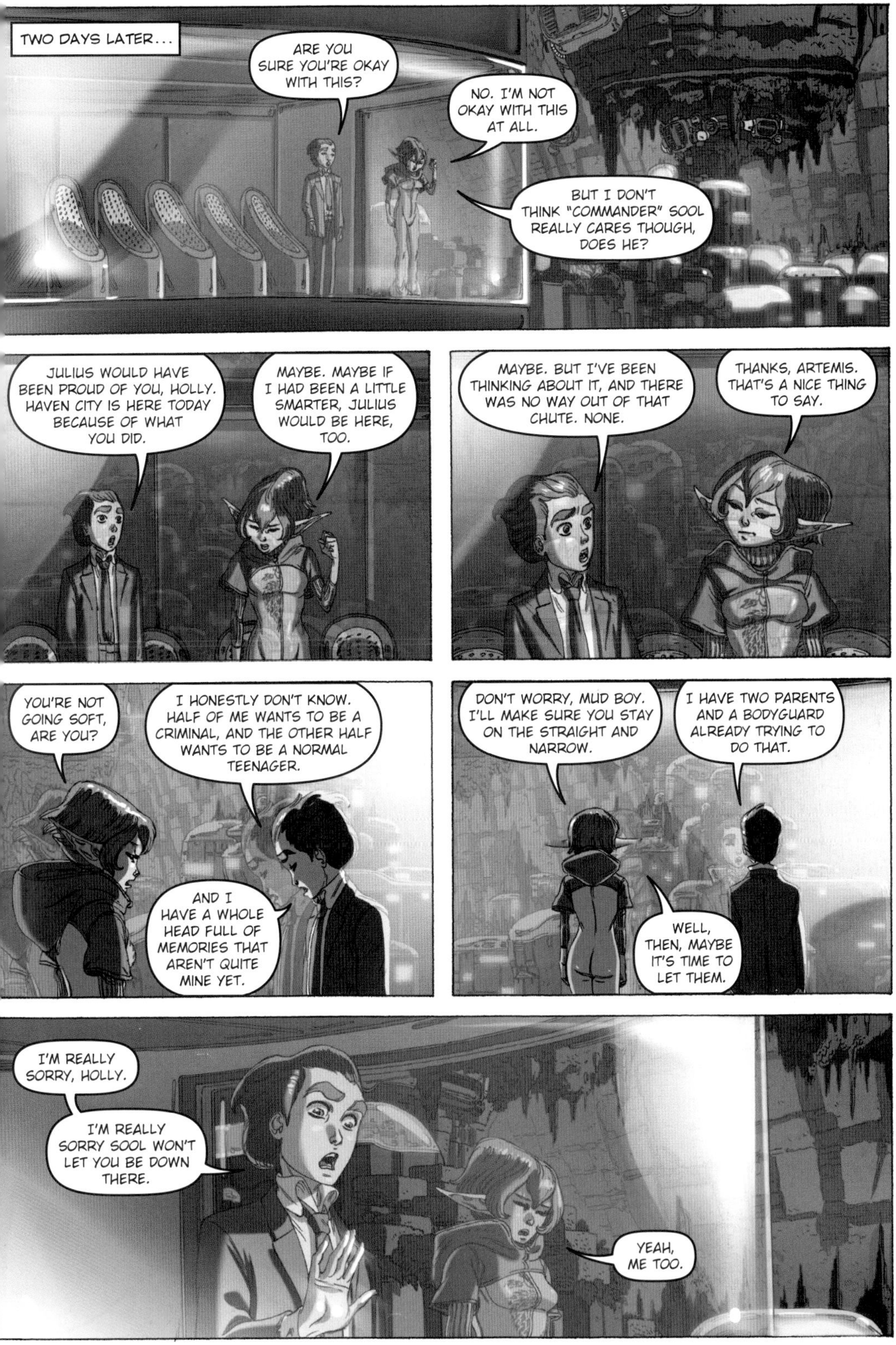
TWO DAYS LATER...
ARE YOU SURE YOU'RE OKAY WITH THIS?
NO. I'M NOT OKAY WITH THIS AT ALL.
BUT I DON'T THINK "COMMANDER" SOOL REALLY CARES THOUGH, DOES HE?
JULIUS WOULD HAVE BEEN PROUD OF YOU, HOLLY. HAVEN CITY IS HERE TODAY BECAUSE OF WHAT YOU DID.
MAYBE. MAYBE IF I HAD BEEN A LITTLE SMARTER, JULIUS WOULD BE HERE, TOO.
MAYBE. BUT I'VE BEEN THINKING ABOUT IT, AND THERE WAS NO WAY OUT OF THAT CHUTE. NONE.
THANKS, ARTEMIS. THAT'S A NICE THING TO SAY.
YOU'RE NOT GOING SOFT, ARE YOU?
I HONESTLY DON'T KNOW. HALF OF ME WANTS TO BE A CRIMINAL, AND THE OTHER HALF WANTS TO BE A NORMAL TEENAGER.
AND I HAVE A WHOLE HEAD FULL OF MEMORIES THAT AREN'T QUITE MINE YET.
DON'T WORRY, MUD BOY. I'LL MAKE SURE YOU STAY ON THE STRAIGHT AND NARROW.
I HAVE TWO PARENTS AND A BODYGUARD ALREADY TRYING TO DO THAT.
WELL, THEN, MAYBE IT'S TIME TO LET THEM.
I'M REALLY SORRY, HOLLY.
I'M REALLY SORRY SOOL WON'T LET YOU BE DOWN THERE.
YEAH, ME TOO.

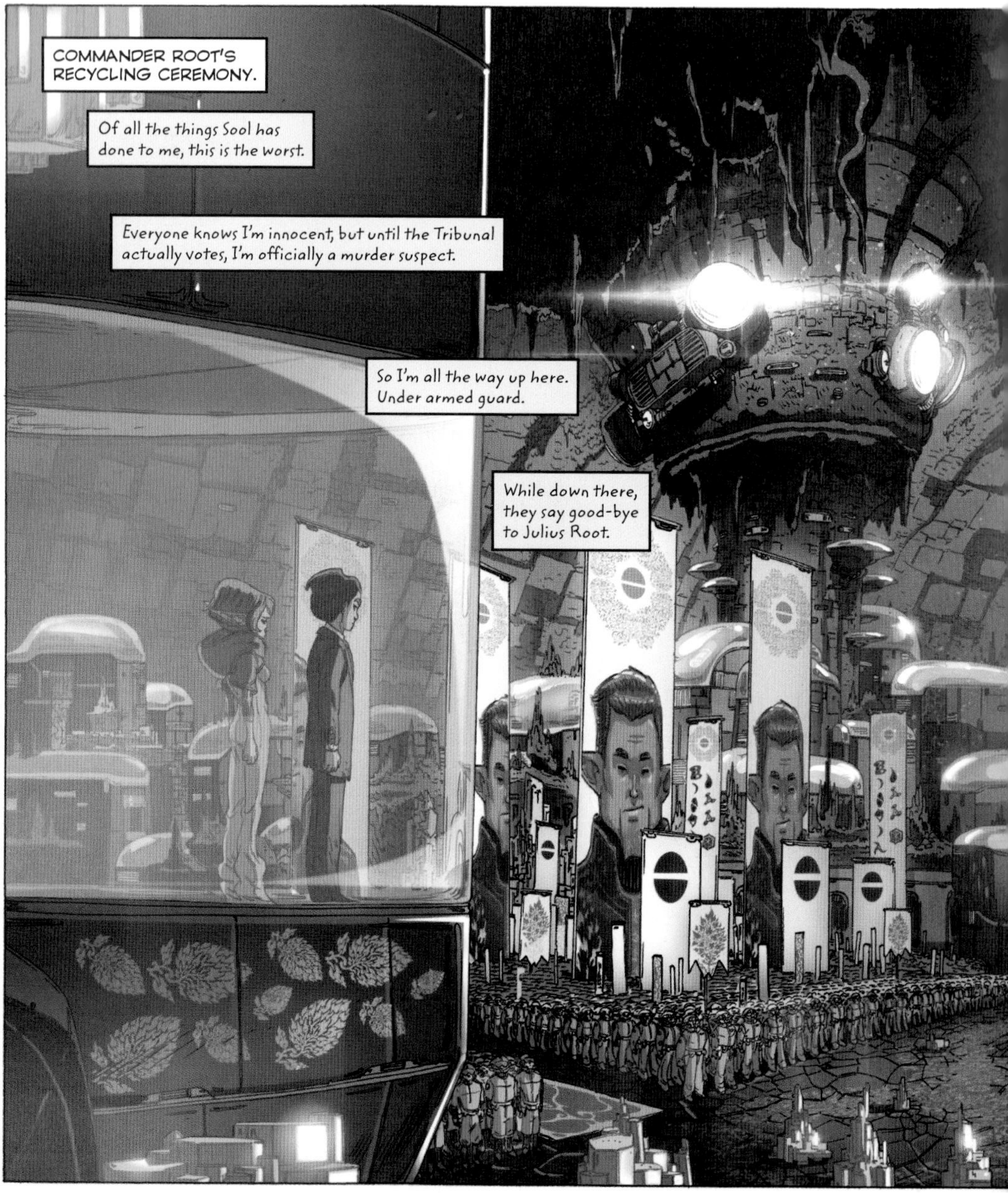
COMMANDER ROOT'S RECYCLING CEREMONY.
Of all the things Sool has done to me, this is the worst.
Everyone knows I'm innocent, but until the Tribunal actually votes, I'm officially a murder suspect.
So I'm all the way up here. Under armed guard.
While down there, they say good-bye to Julius Root.

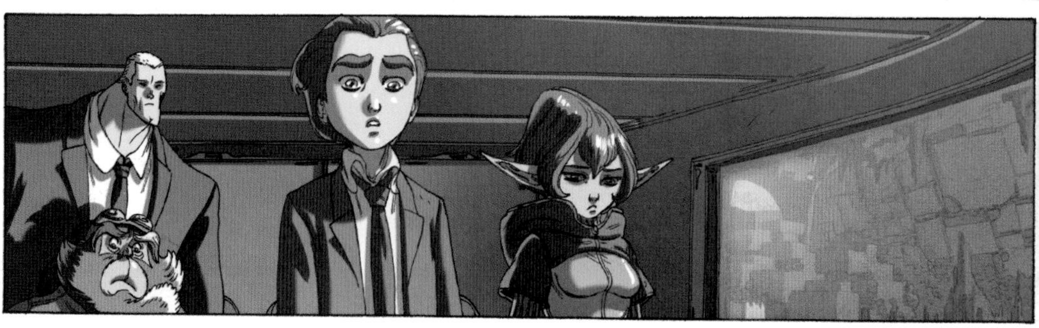

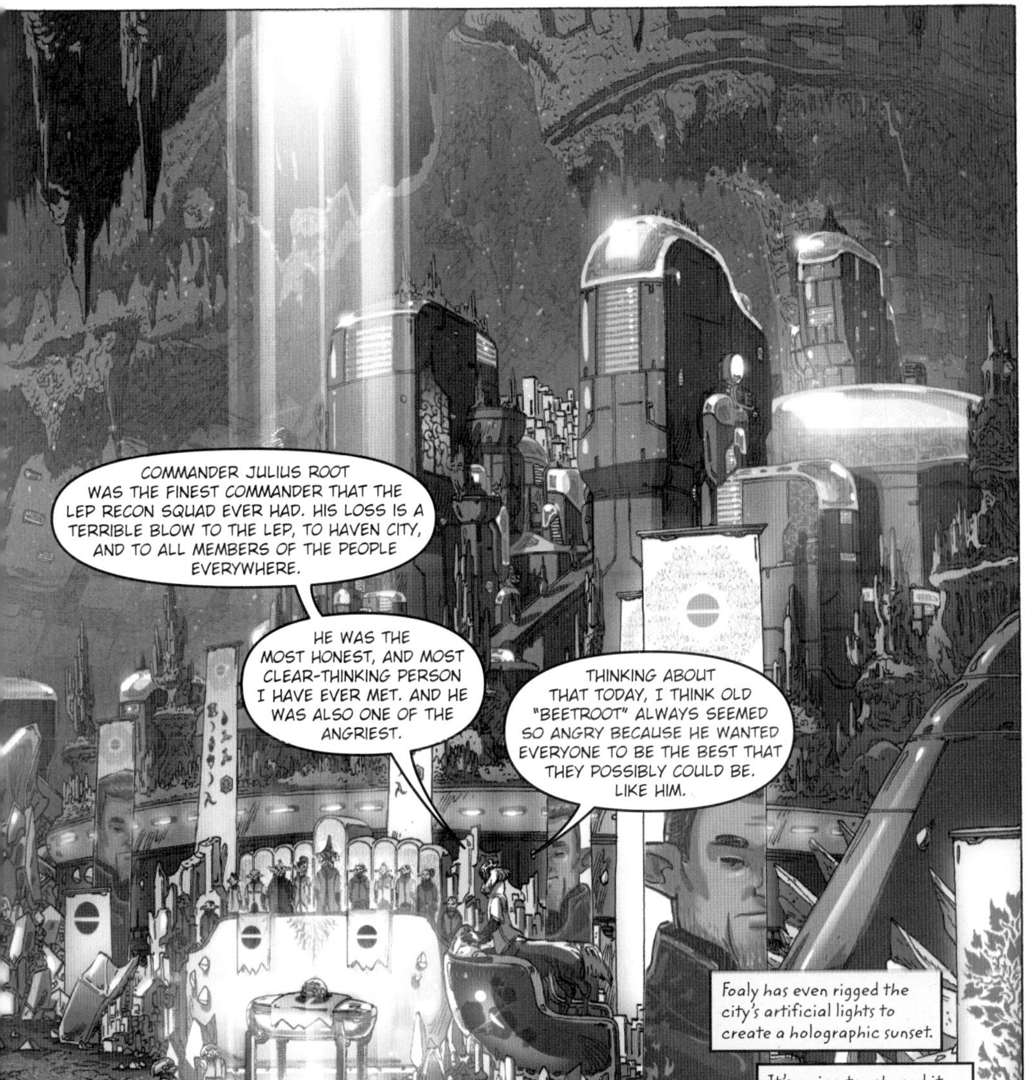
COMMANDER JULIUS ROOT WAS THE FINEST COMMANDER THAT THE LEP RECON SQUAD EVER HAD. HIS LOSS IS A TERRIBLE BLOW TO THE LEP, TO HAVEN CITY, AND TO ALL MEMBERS OF THE PEOPLE EVERYWHERE.
HE WAS THE MOST HONEST, AND MOST CLEAR-THINKING PERSON I HAVE EVER MET. AND HE WAS ALSO ONE OF THE ANGRIEST.
THINKING ABOUT THAT TODAY, I THINK OLD "BEETROOT" ALWAYS SEEMED SO ANGRY BECAUSE HE WANTED EVERYONE TO BE THE BEST THAT THEY POSSIBLY COULD BE. LIKE HIM.
Foaly has even rigged the city's artificial lights to create a holographic sunset.
It's a nice touch, and it makes me cry. Even more.

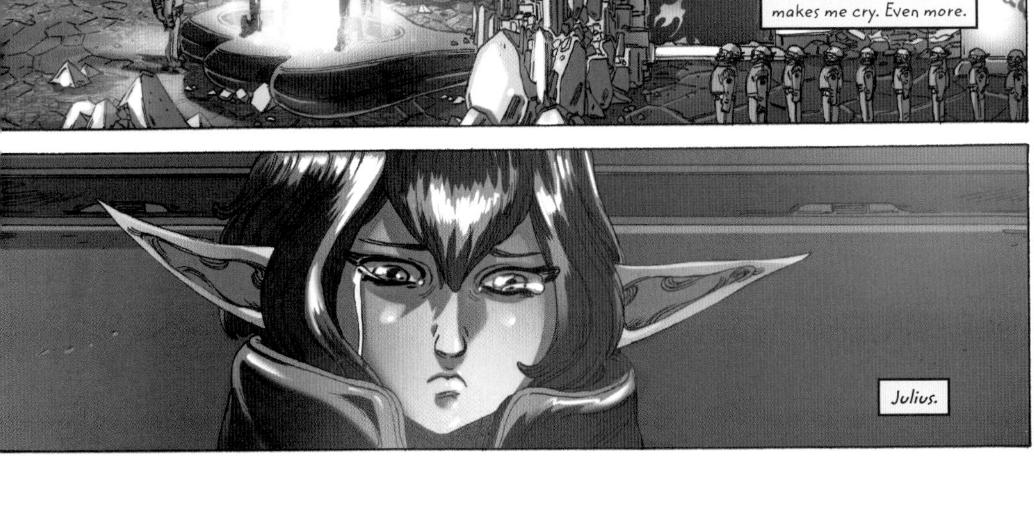
Julius.

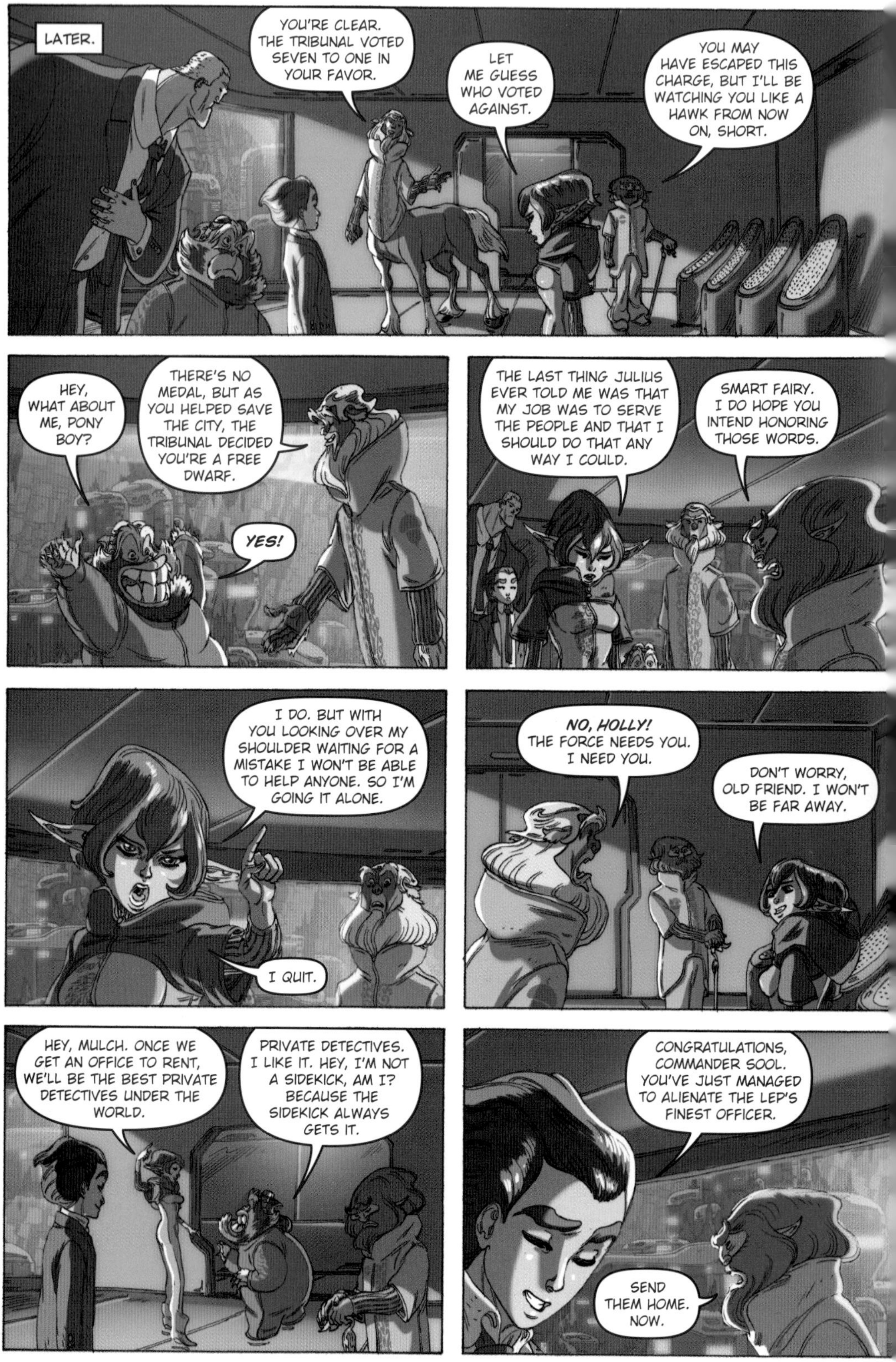
LATER.
YOU'RE CLEAR. THE TRIBUNAL VOTED SEVEN TO ONE IN YOUR FAVOR.
LET ME GUESS WHO VOTED AGAINST.
YOU MAY HAVE ESCAPED THIS CHARGE, BUT I'LL BE WATCHING YOU LIKE A HAWK FROM NOW ON, SHORT.
HEY, WHAT ABOUT ME, PONY BOY?
THERE'S NO MEDAL, BUT AS YOU HELPED SAVE THE CITY, THE TRIBUNAL DECIDED YOU'RE A FREE DWARF.
YES!
THE LAST THING JULIUS EVER TOLD ME WAS THAT MY JOB WAS TO SERVE THE PEOPLE AND THAT I SHOULD DO THAT ANY WAY I COULD.
SMART FAIRY. I DO HOPE YOU INTEND HONORING THOSE WORDS.
I DO. BUT WITH YOU LOOKING OVER MY SHOULDER WAITING FOR A MISTAKE I WON'T BE ABLE TO HELP ANYONE. SO I'M GOING IT ALONE.
I QUIT.
NO, HOLLY! THE FORCE NEEDS YOU. I NEED YOU.
DON'T WORRY, OLD FRIEND. I WON'T BE FAR AWAY.
HEY, MULCH. ONCE WE GET AN OFFICE TO RENT, WE'LL BE THE BEST PRIVATE DETECTIVES UNDER THE WORLD.
PRIVATE DETECTIVES. I LIKE IT. HEY, I'M NOT A SIDEKICK, AM I? BECAUSE THE SIDEKICK ALWAYS GETS IT.
CONGRATULATIONS, COMMANDER SOOL. YOU'VE JUST MANAGED TO ALIENATE THE LEP'S FINEST OFFICER.
SEND THEM HOME. NOW.

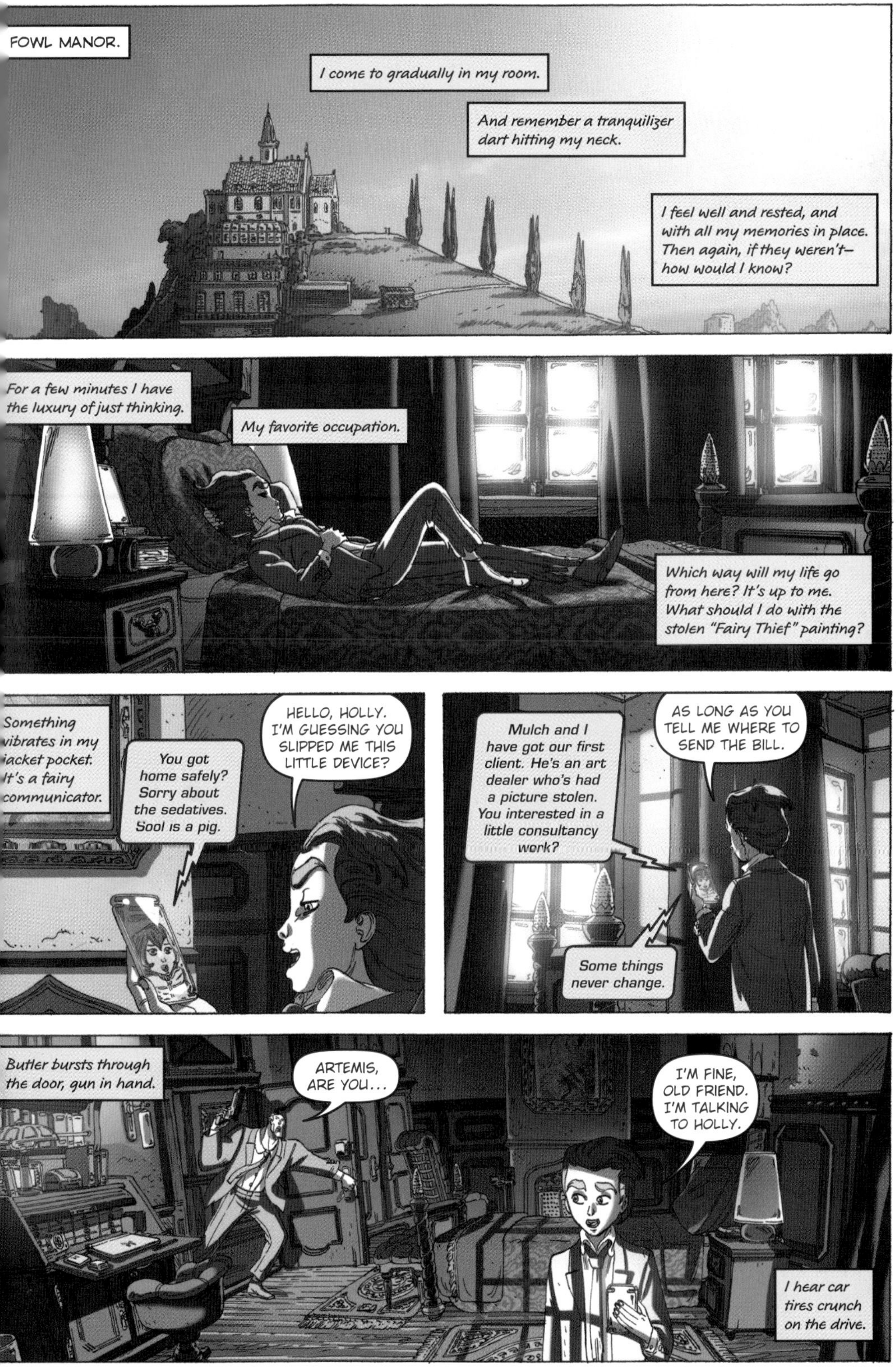
FOWL MANOR.
I come to gradually in my room.
And remember a tranquilizer dart hitting my neck.
I feel well and rested, and with all my memories in place. Then again, if they weren't—how would I know?
For a few minutes I have the luxury of just thinking.
My favorite occupation.
Which way will my life go from here? It's up to me. What should I do with the stolen "Fairy Thief" painting?
Something vibrates in my jacket pocket. It's a fairy communicator.
HELLO, HOLLY. I'M GUESSING YOU SLIPPED ME THIS LITTLE DEVICE?
You got home safely? Sorry about the sedatives. Sool is a pig.
Mulch and I have got our first client. He's an art dealer who's had a picture stolen. You interested in a little consultancy work?
AS LONG AS YOU TELL ME WHERE TO SEND THE BILL.
Some things never change.
Butler bursts through the door, gun in hand.
ARTEMIS, ARE YOU...
I'M FINE, OLD FRIEND. I'M TALKING TO HOLLY.
I hear car tires crunch on the drive.

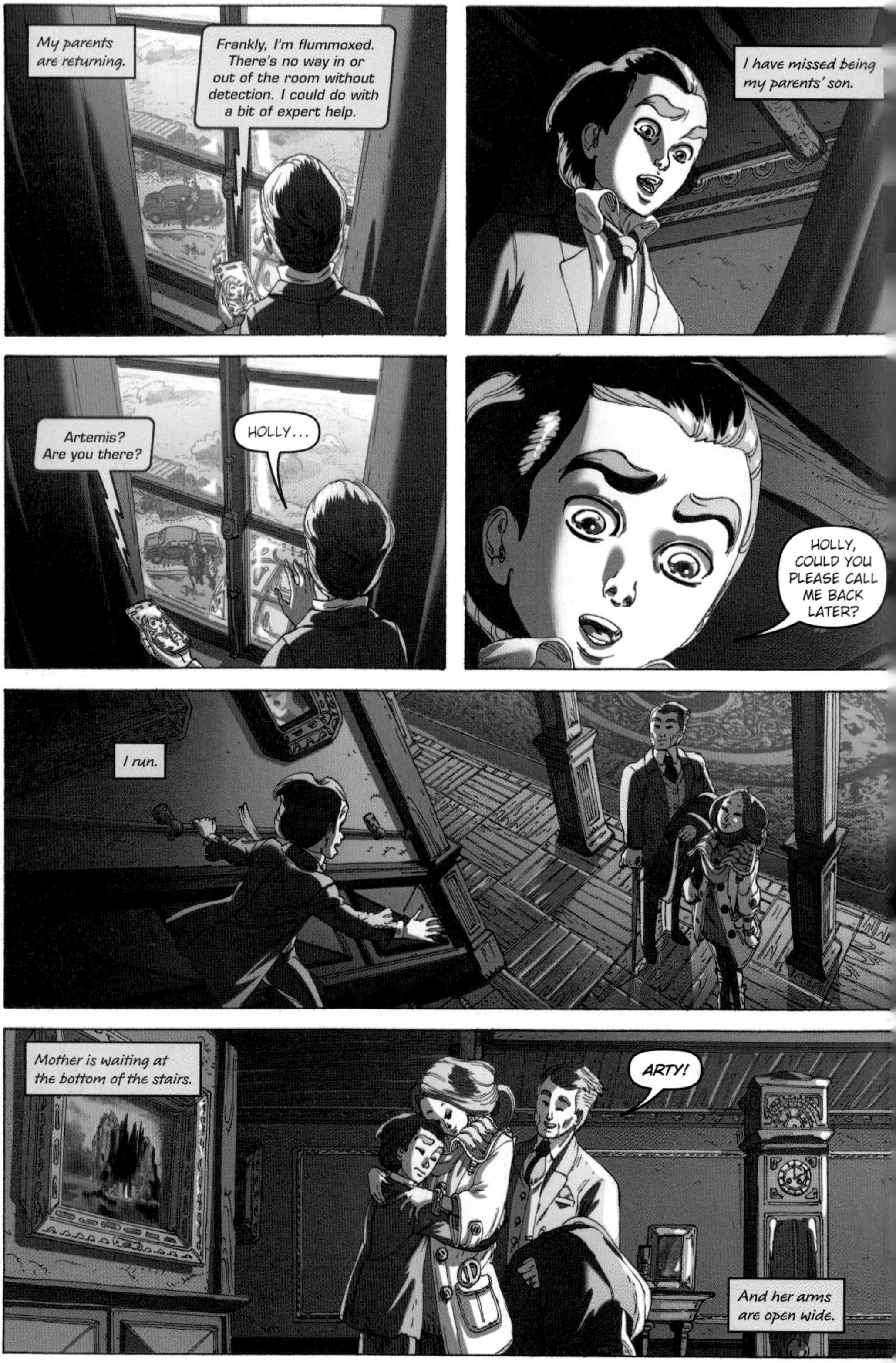
My parents are returning.
Frankly, I'm flummoxed. There's no way in or out of the room without detection. I could do with a bit of expert help.
I have missed being my parents' son.
Artemis? Are you there?
HOLLY...
HOLLY, COULD YOU PLEASE CALL ME BACK LATER?
I run.
Mother is waiting at the bottom of the stairs.
ARTY!
And her arms are open wide.

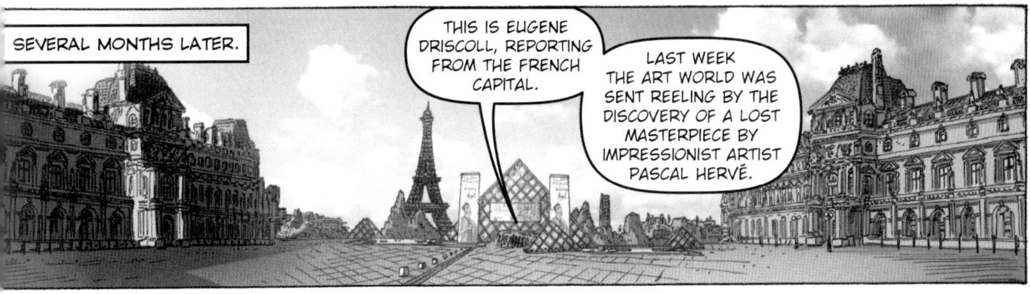
SEVERAL MONTHS LATER.
THIS IS EUGENE DRISCOLL, REPORTING FROM THE FRENCH CAPITAL.
LAST WEEK THE ART WORLD WAS SENT REELING BY THE DISCOVERY OF A LOST MASTERPIECE BY IMPRESSIONIST ARTIST PASCAL HERVÉ.

EPİLOGUE

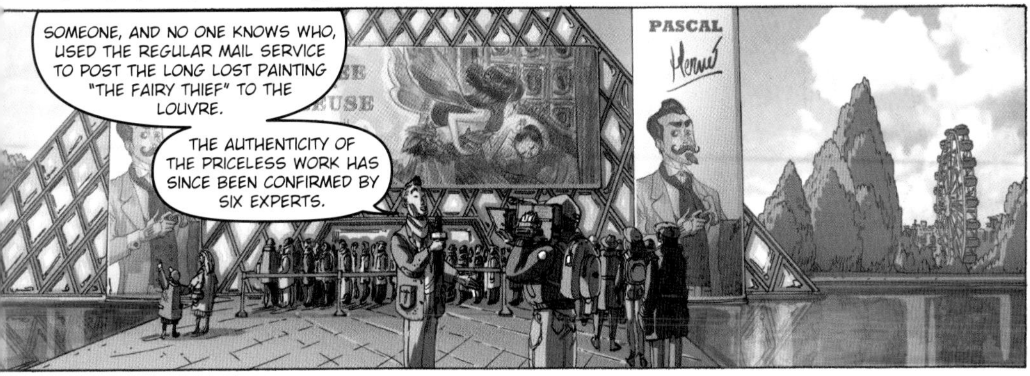
SOMEONE, AND NO ONE KNOWS WHO, USED THE REGULAR MAIL SERVICE TO POST THE LONG LOST PAINTING "THE FAIRY THIEF" TO THE LOUVRE.
THE AUTHENTICITY OF THE PRICELESS WORK HAS SINCE BEEN CONFIRMED BY SIX EXPERTS.
PASCAL
Hervé

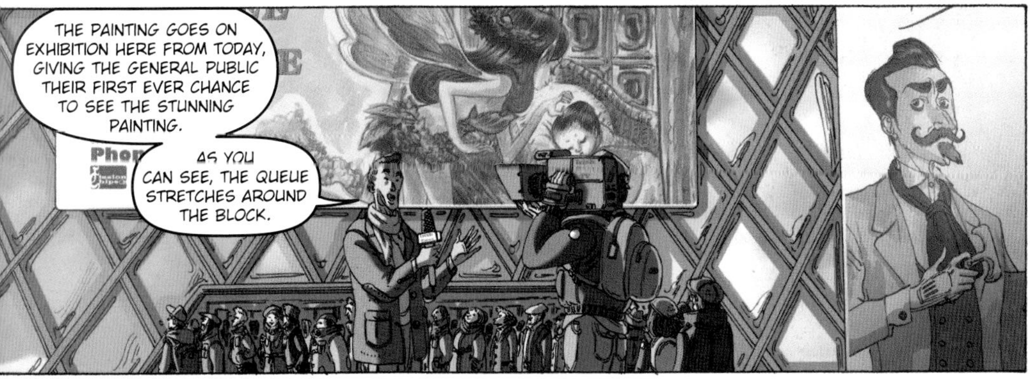
THE PAINTING GOES ON EXHIBITION HERE FROM TODAY, GIVING THE GENERAL PUBLIC THEIR FIRST EVER CHANCE TO SEE THE STUNNING PAINTING.
AS YOU CAN SEE, THE QUEUE STRETCHES AROUND THE BLOCK.

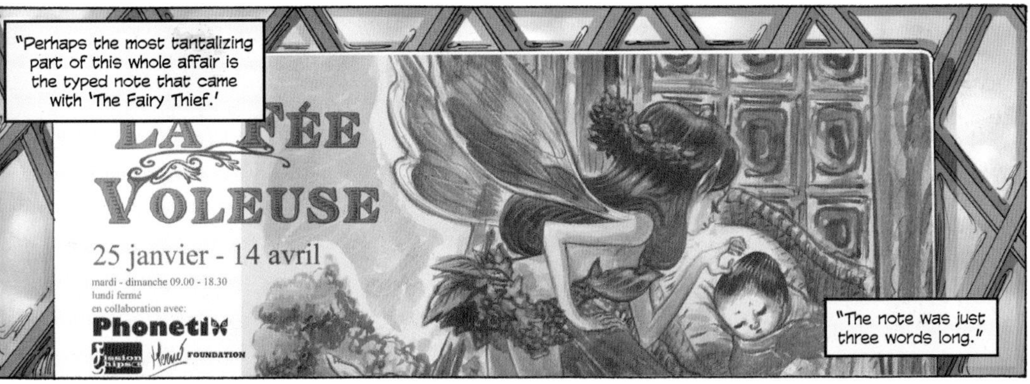
"Perhaps the most tantalizing part of this whole affair is the typed note that came with 'The Fairy Thief.'
LA FÉE VOLEUSE
25 janvier - 14 avril
mardi - dimanche 09.00 - 18.30
lundi fermé
en collaboration avec:
Phonetix
FOUNDATION
"The note was just three words long."

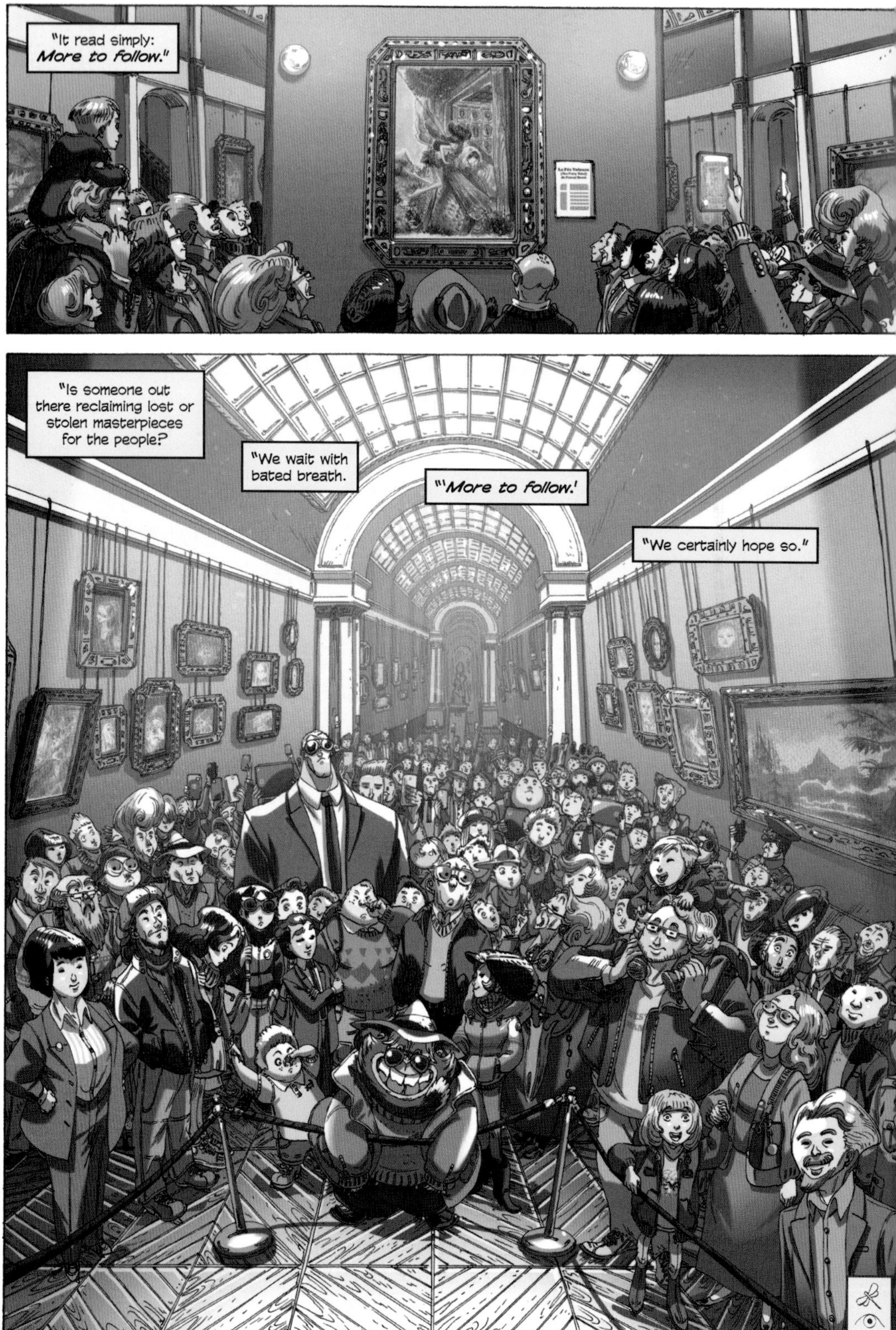
"It read simply: *More to follow.*"
"Is someone out there reclaiming lost or stolen masterpieces for the people?
"We wait with bated breath.
"'*More to follow.*'
"We certainly hope so."